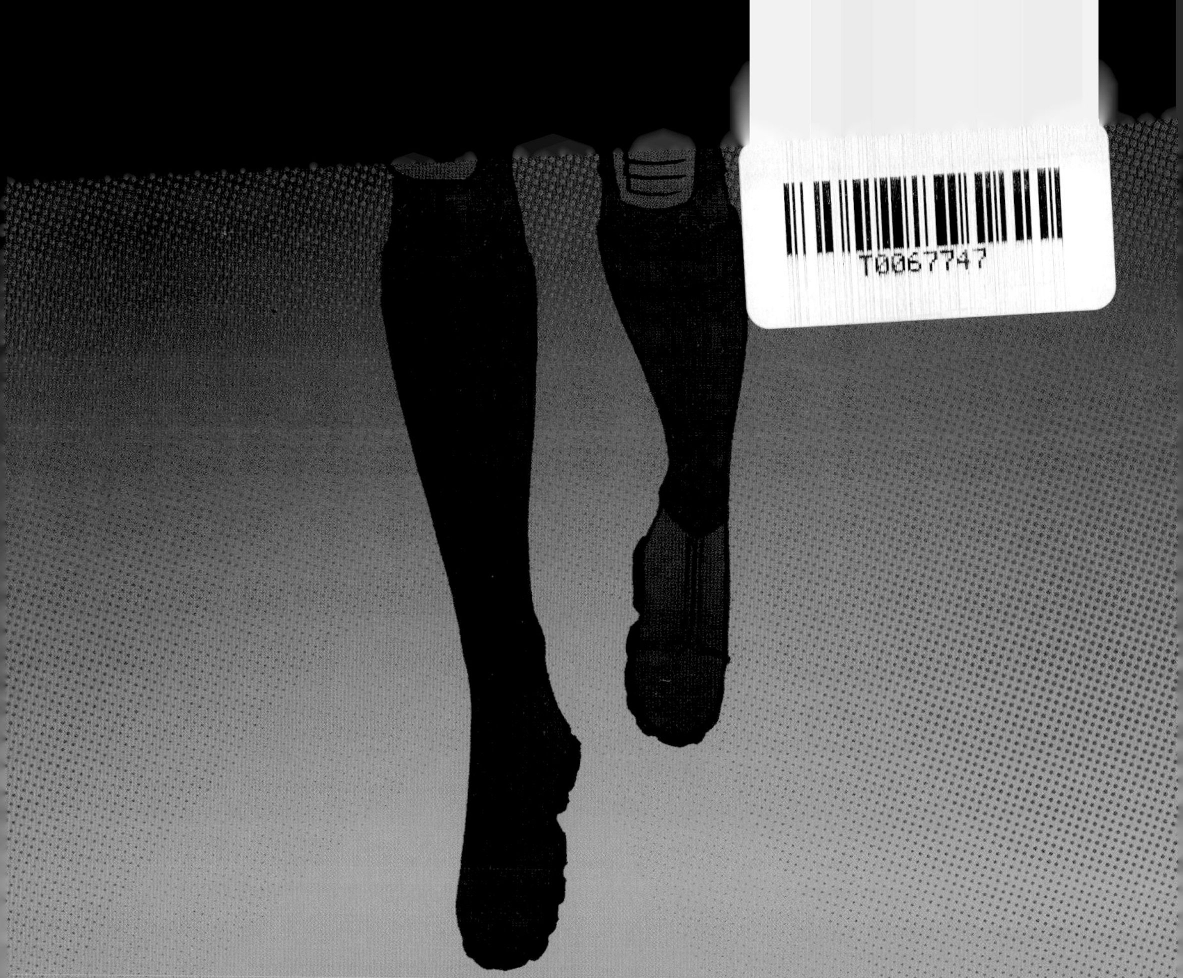

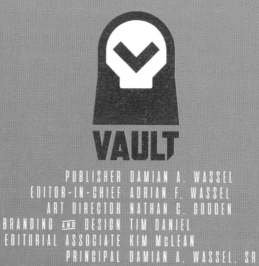

VAULT

PUBLISHER DAMIAN A. WASSEL
EDITOR-IN-CHIEF ADRIAN F. WASSEL
ART DIRECTOR NATHAN C. GOODEN
BRANDING AND DESIGN TIM DANIEL
EDITORIAL ASSOCIATE KIM McLEAN
PRINCIPAL DAMIAN A. WASSEL, SR.

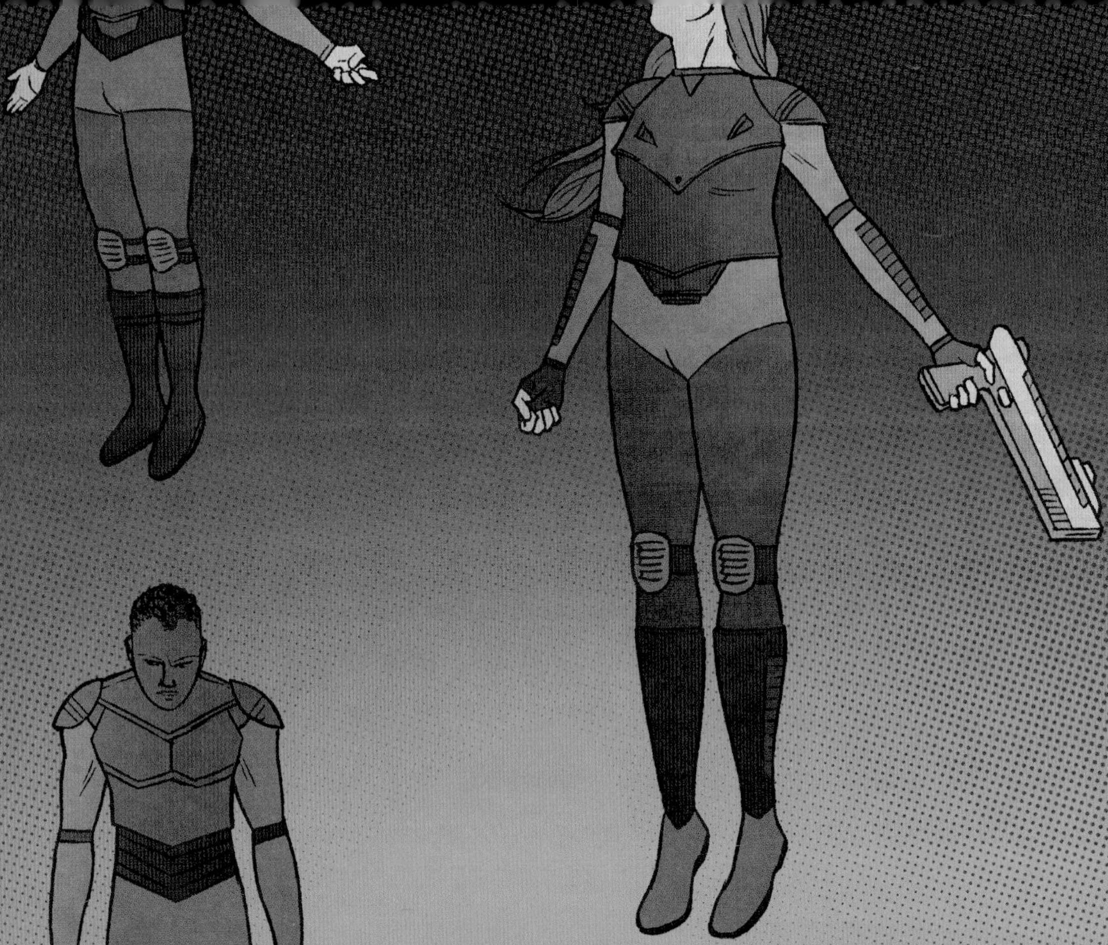

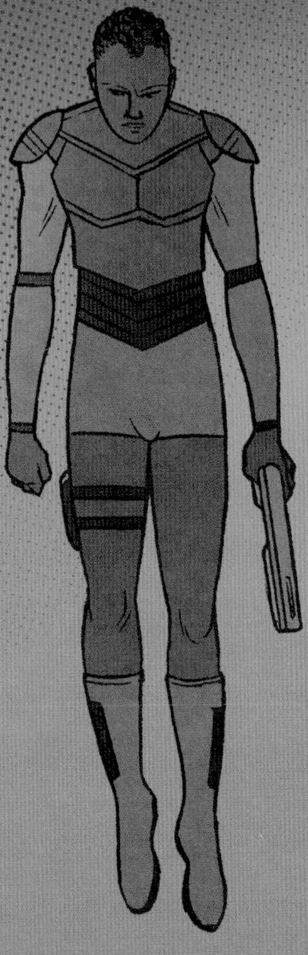

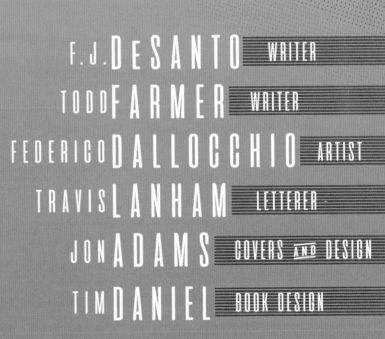

F.J. DESANTO — WRITER

TODD FARMER — WRITER

FEDERICO DALLOCCHIO — ARTIST

TRAVIS LANHAM — LETTERER

JON ADAMS — COVERS AND DESIGN

TIM DANIEL — BOOK DESIGN

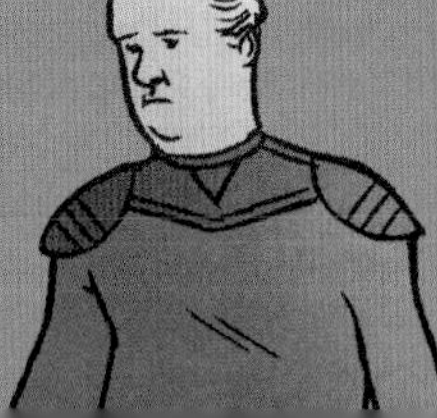

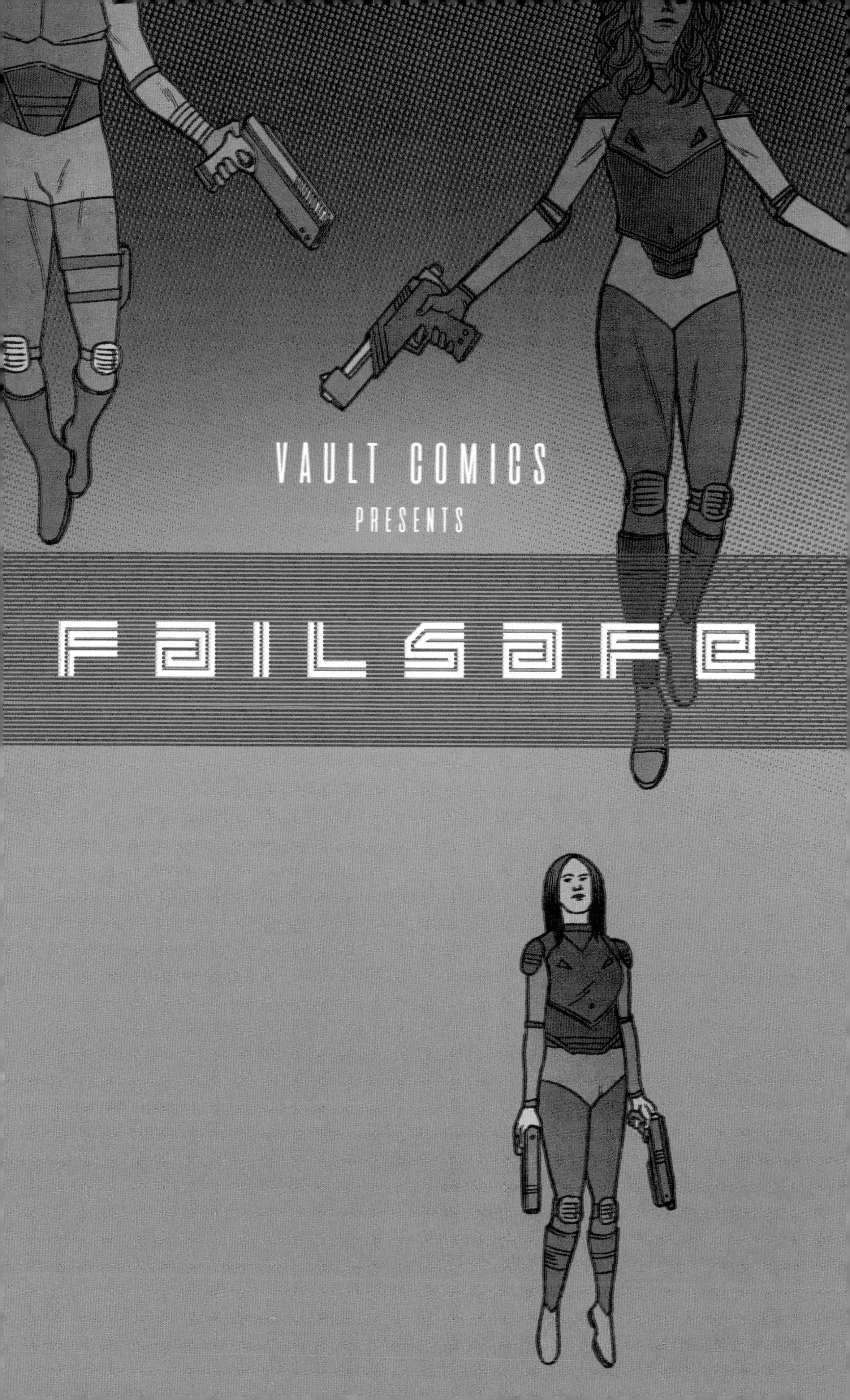
VAULT COMICS
PRESENTS
FAILSAFE

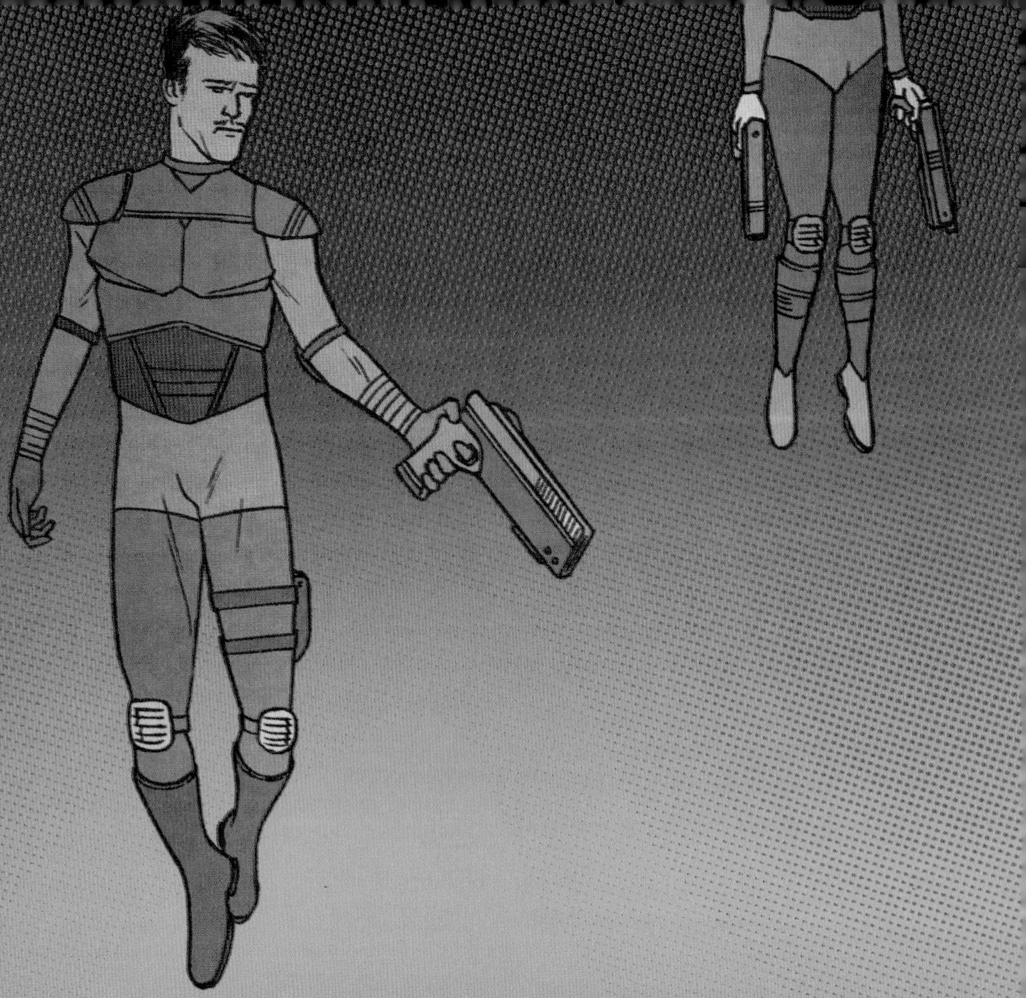

"CLEVERLY BROACHES VERY REAL AND TROUBLING QUESTIONS."

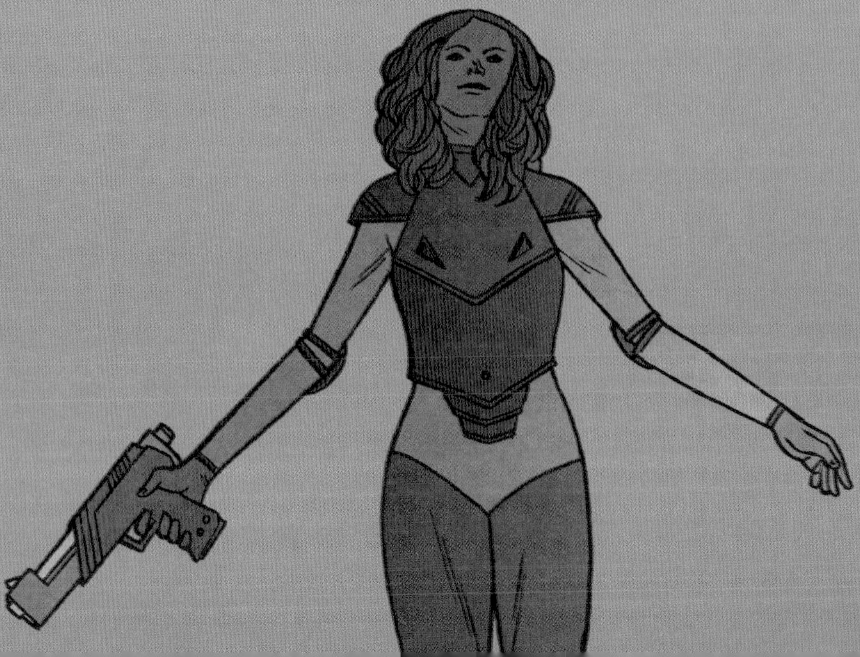

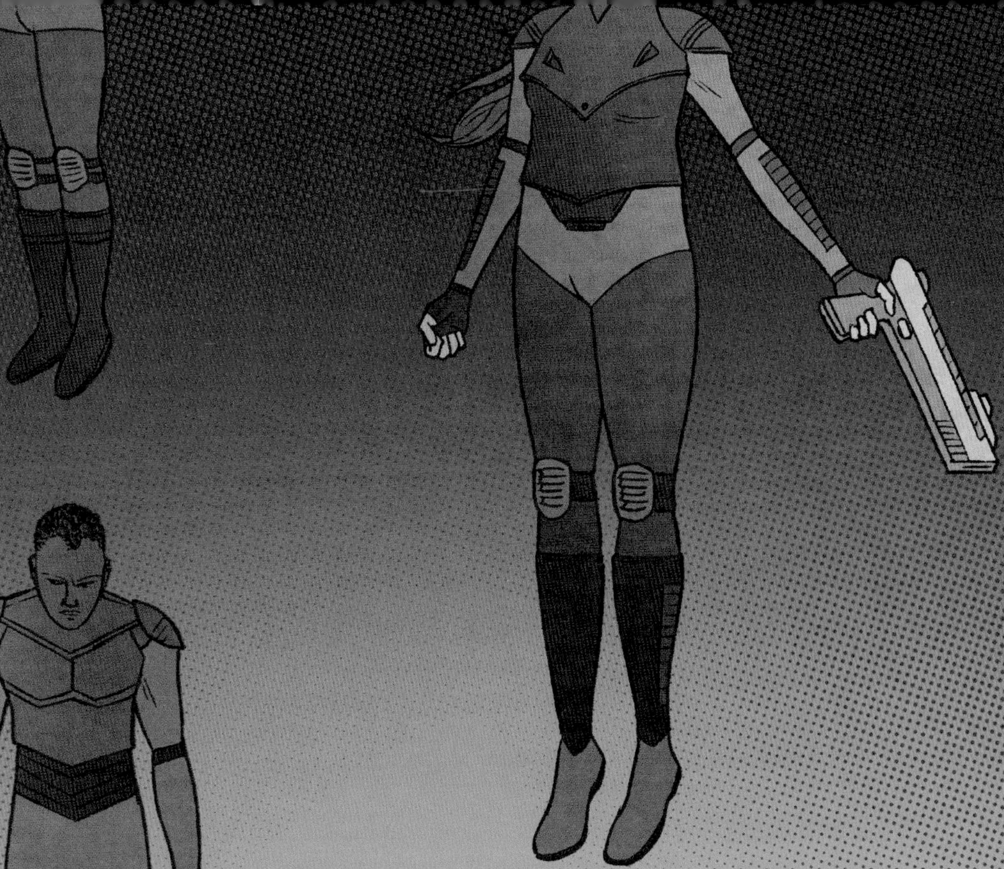

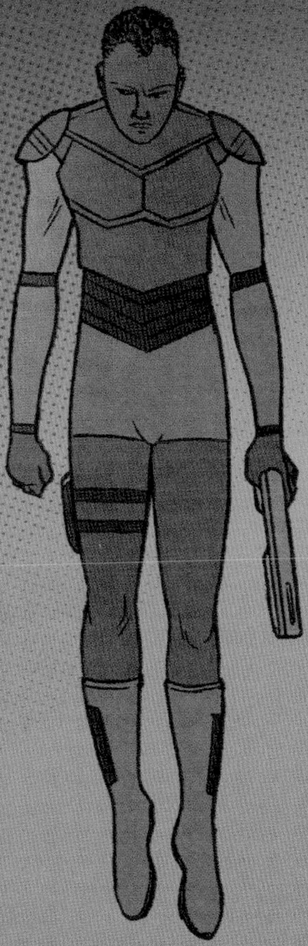

"THE BEST SCI-FI FINDS A WAY TO ROOT ITSELF IN THE REALITY OF THE MOMENT WHILE SIMULTANEOUSLY DELVING INTO THE TIMELESS IMPERFECTIONS THAT HAVE ENDLESSLY PLAGUED MANKIND. FIRMLY PLANTED IN THE ZEITGEIST OF TODAY AND THE FORESEEABLE FUTURE, FAILSAFE CLEVERLY BROACHES VERY REAL AND TROUBLING QUESTIONS OF PUBLIC SAFETY IN A TIME OF TERRORISM AND THE CURRENT ARMS RACE ON EVERY LEVEL OF SOCIETY TO MERGE MAN AND TECHNOLOGY FOR OPTIMUM PERFORMANCE AND PHYSICAL ENHANCEMENT. THE IDEA THAT A GOVERNMENT MIGHT USE UNWITTING CITIZENS AS SLEEPER AGENTS TO COMBAT TERRORISM AND CRIME IN AN ACTION-RICH COMIC IS NOT JUST THOUGHT-PROVOKING, BUT DAMN ENTERTAINING."

JOE ROBERT COLE

WRITER, BLACK PANTHER

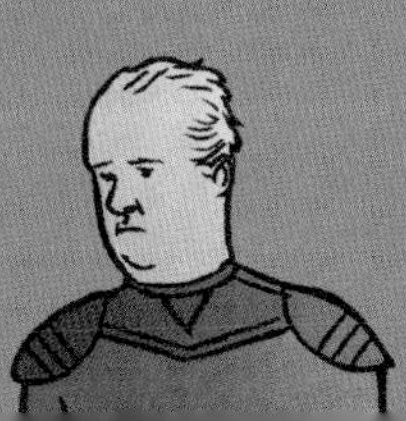

CHAPTER 1

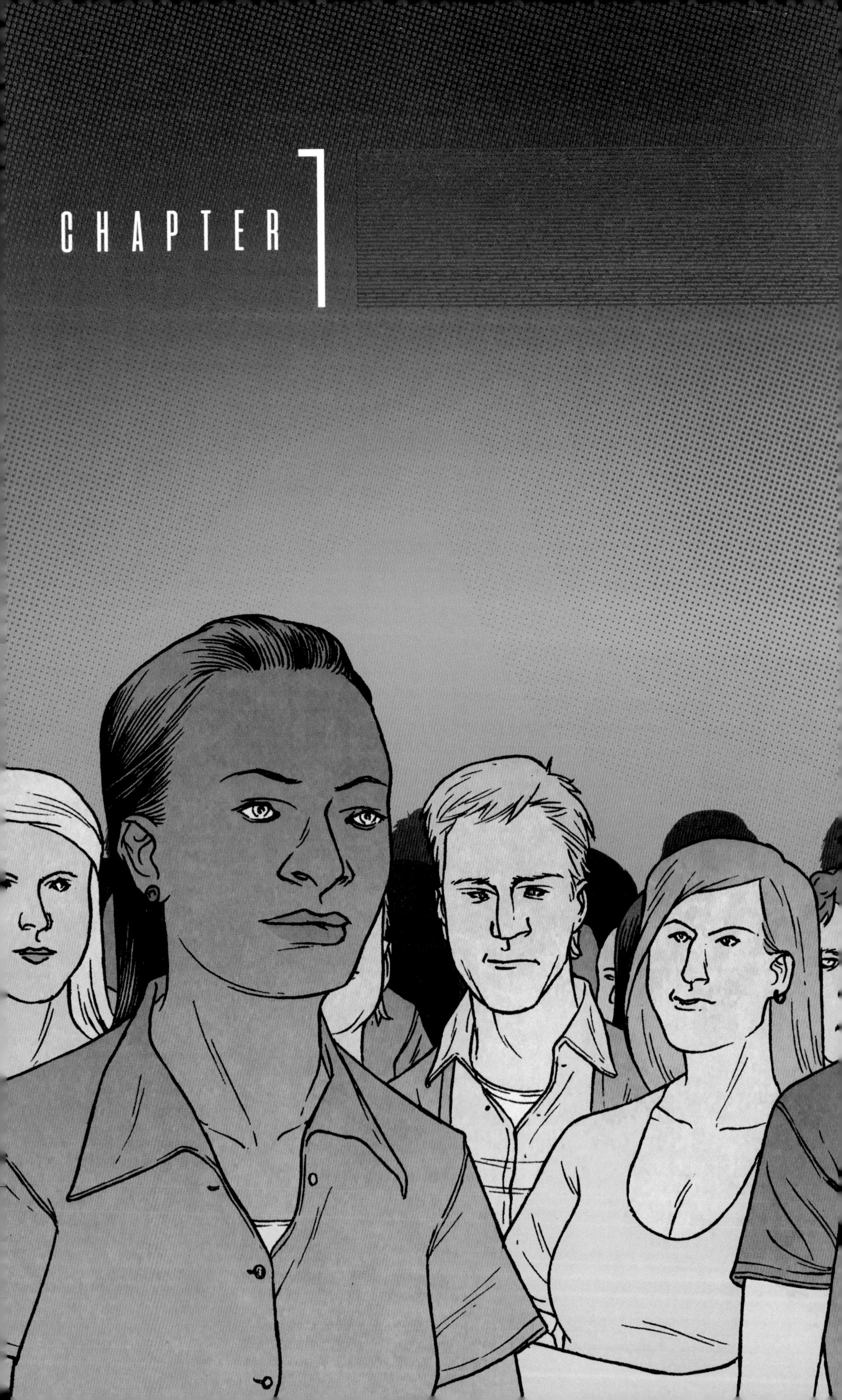

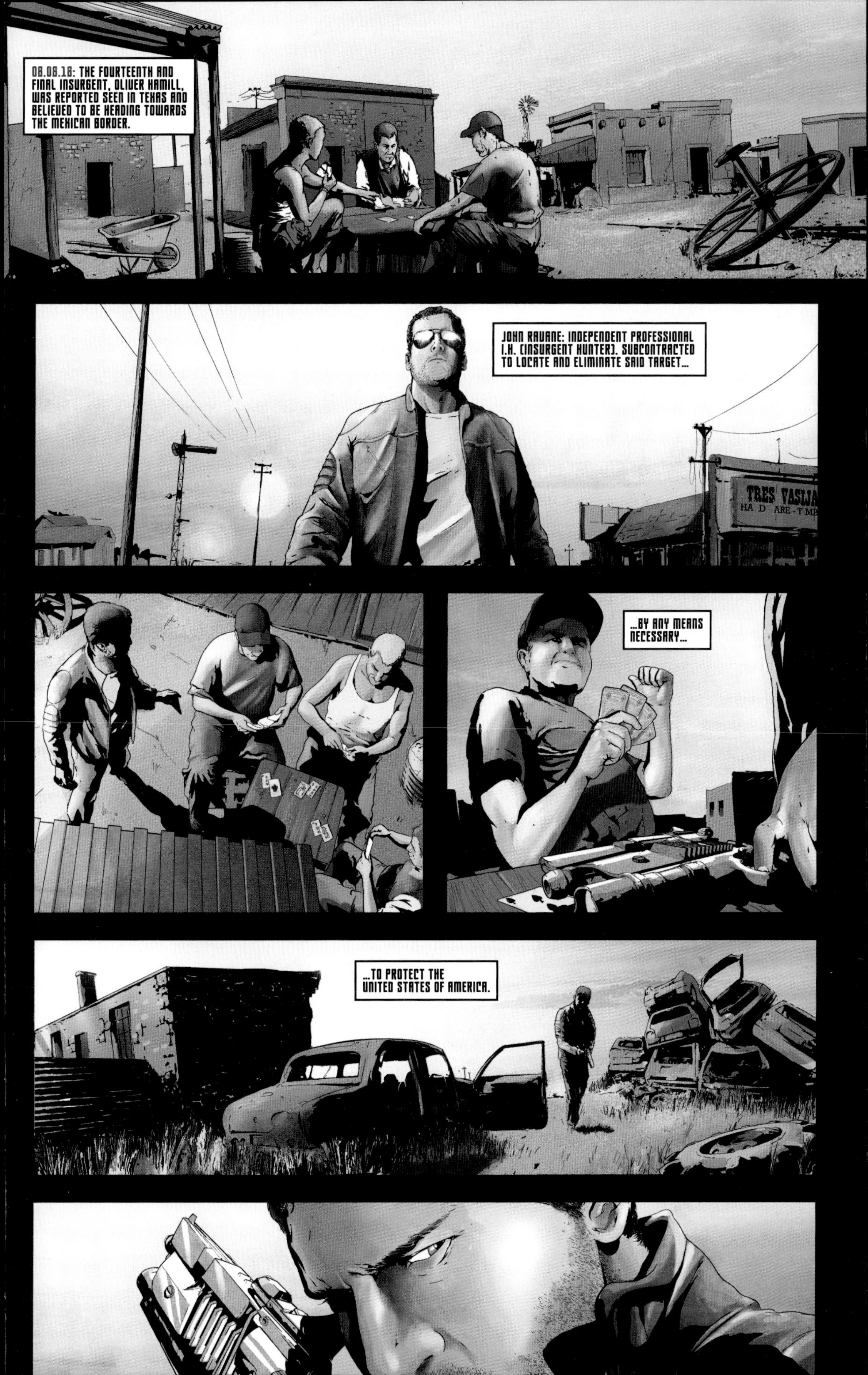
08.08.18: THE FOURTEENTH AND FINAL INSURGENT, OLIVER HAMILL, WAS REPORTED SEEN IN TEXAS AND BELIEVED TO BE HEADING TOWARDS THE MEXICAN BORDER.
JOHN RAVANE: INDEPENDENT PROFESSIONAL I.H. [INSURGENT HUNTER]. SUBCONTRACTED TO LOCATE AND ELIMINATE SAID TARGET...
TRES VASIJA
...BY ANY MEANS NECESSARY...
...TO PROTECT THE UNITED STATES OF AMERICA.

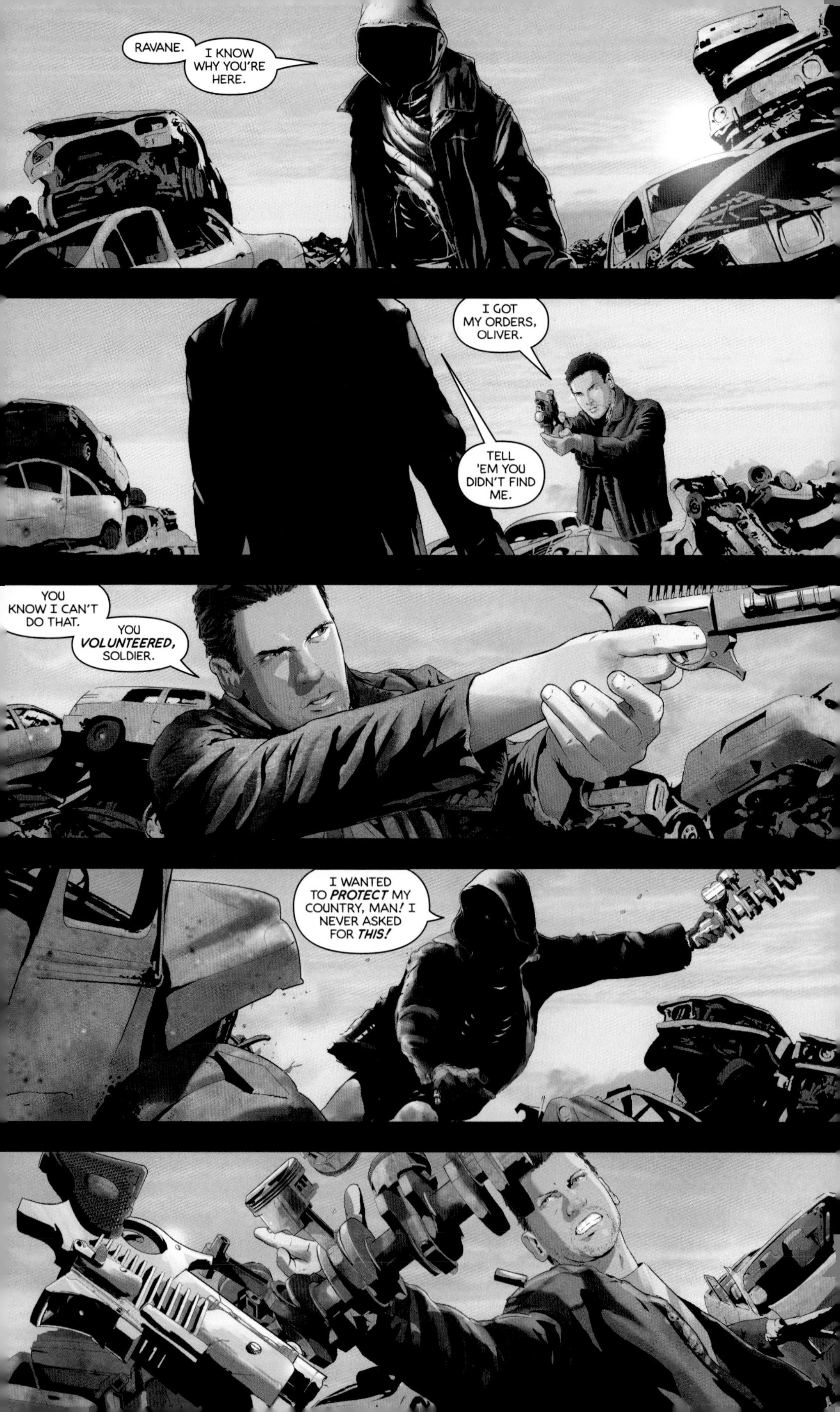
RAVANE.
I KNOW WHY YOU'RE HERE.
I GOT MY ORDERS, OLIVER.
TELL 'EM YOU DIDN'T FIND ME.
YOU KNOW I CAN'T DO THAT.
YOU ***VOLUNTEERED,*** SOLDIER.
I WANTED TO ***PROTECT*** MY COUNTRY, MAN! I NEVER ASKED FOR ***THIS!***

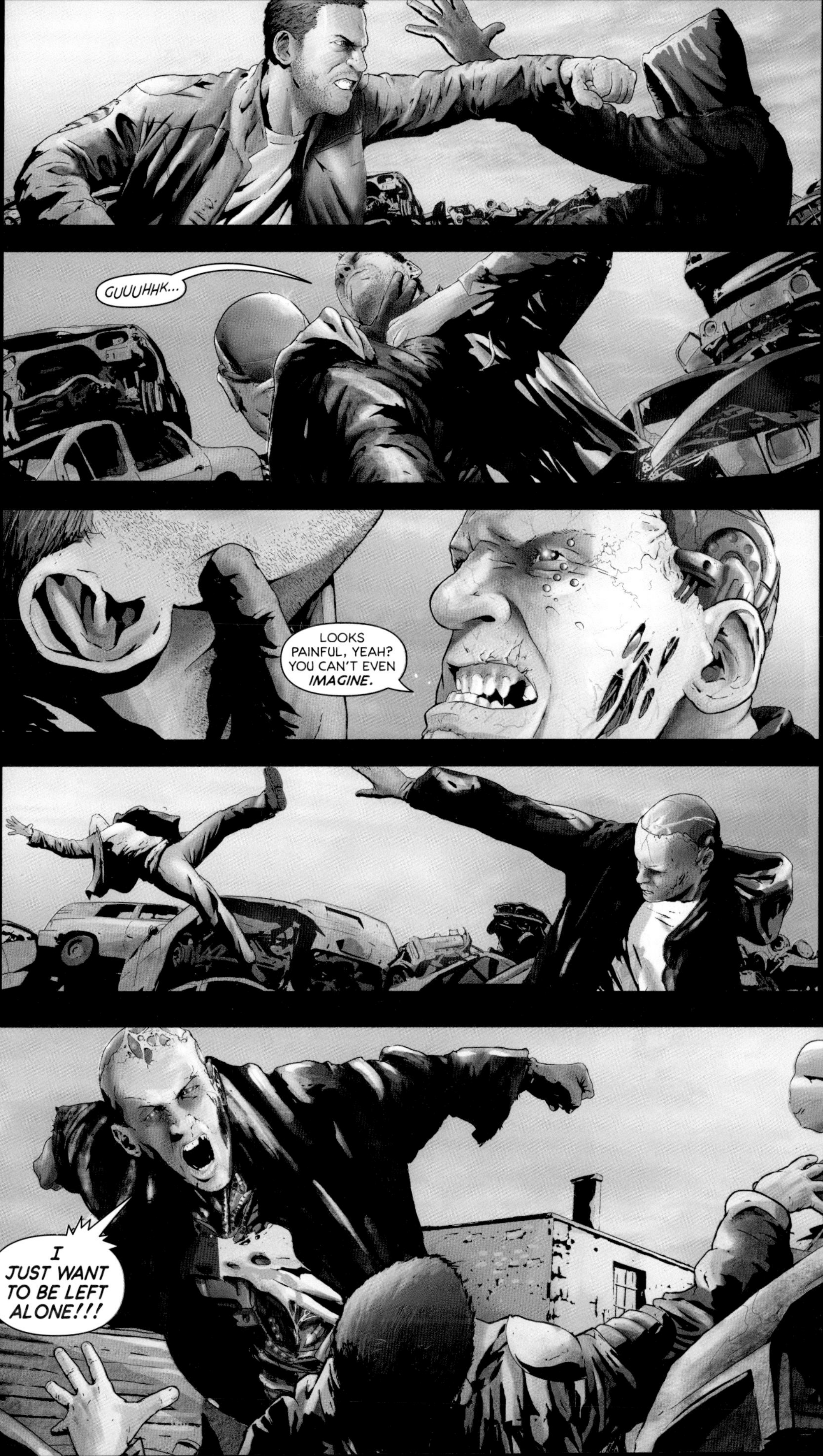
GUUUHHK...
LOOKS PAINFUL, YEAH? YOU CAN'T EVEN *IMAGINE*.
I JUST WANT TO BE LEFT ALONE!!!

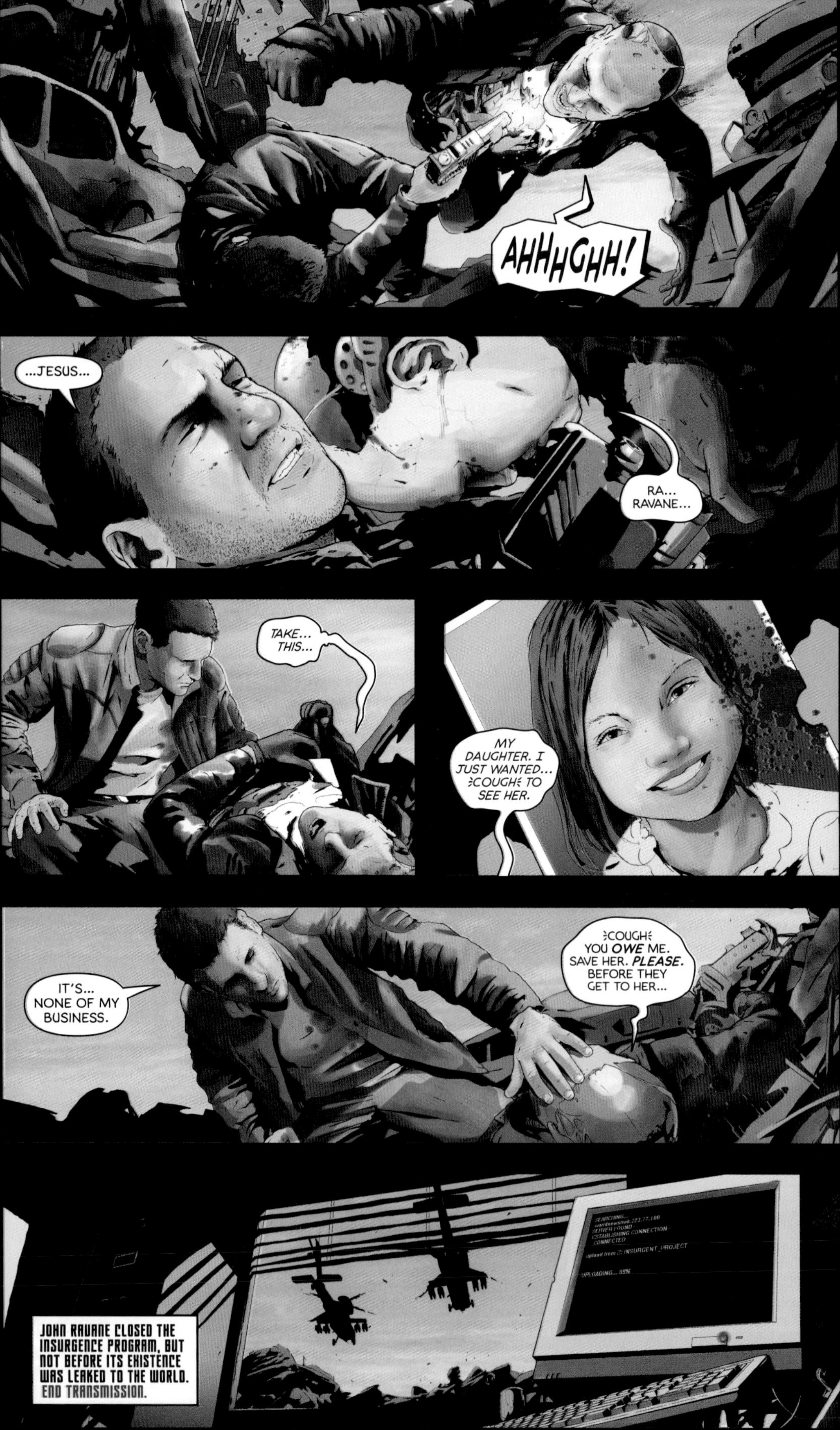
AHHHGHH!
...JESUS...
RA... RAVANE...
TAKE... THIS...
MY DAUGHTER. I JUST WANTED... *COUGH* TO SEE HER.
IT'S... NONE OF MY BUSINESS.
COUGH YOU OWE ME. SAVE HER. PLEASE. BEFORE THEY GET TO HER...
SEARCHING...
worldnewsnwk.223.77.100
SERVER FOUND
ESTABLISHING CONNECTION
CONNECTED
upload from Z: INSURGENT_PROJECT
UPLOADING... 89%
JOHN RAVANE CLOSED THE INSURGENCE PROGRAM, BUT NOT BEFORE ITS EXISTENCE WAS LEAKED TO THE WORLD. END TRANSMISSION.

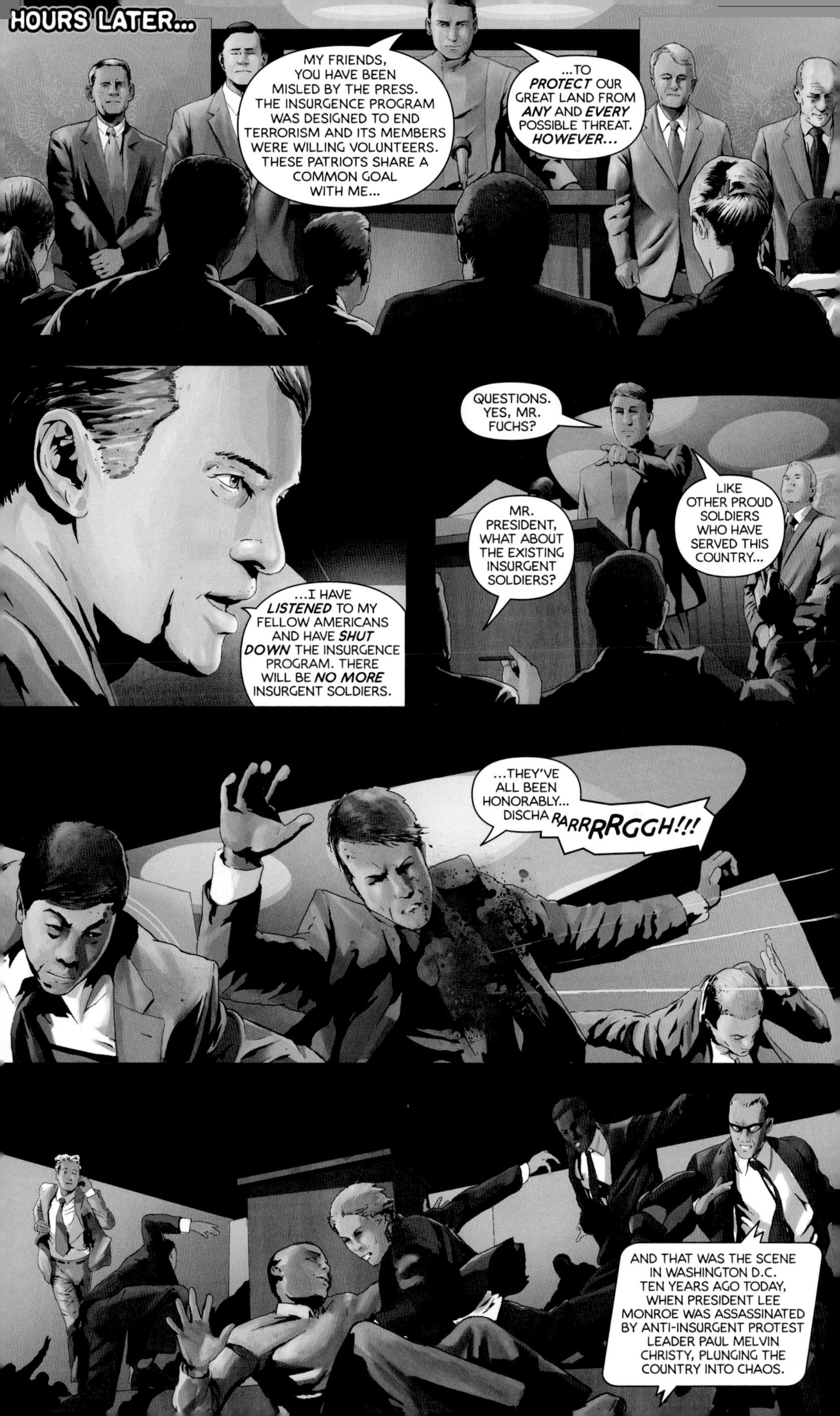
HOURS LATER...
MY FRIENDS, YOU HAVE BEEN MISLED BY THE PRESS. THE INSURGENCE PROGRAM WAS DESIGNED TO END TERRORISM AND ITS MEMBERS WERE WILLING VOLUNTEERS. THESE PATRIOTS SHARE A COMMON GOAL WITH ME...
...TO PROTECT OUR GREAT LAND FROM ANY AND EVERY POSSIBLE THREAT. HOWEVER...
...I HAVE LISTENED TO MY FELLOW AMERICANS AND HAVE SHUT DOWN THE INSURGENCE PROGRAM. THERE WILL BE NO MORE INSURGENT SOLDIERS.
QUESTIONS. YES, MR. FUCHS?
MR. PRESIDENT, WHAT ABOUT THE EXISTING INSURGENT SOLDIERS?
LIKE OTHER PROUD SOLDIERS WHO HAVE SERVED THIS COUNTRY...
...THEY'VE ALL BEEN HONORABLY... DISCHA
RARRRRGGH!!!
AND THAT WAS THE SCENE IN WASHINGTON D.C. TEN YEARS AGO TODAY, WHEN PRESIDENT LEE MONROE WAS ASSASSINATED BY ANTI-INSURGENT PROTEST LEADER PAUL MELVIN CHRISTY, PLUNGING THE COUNTRY INTO CHAOS.

GHTS TERRORISM AFTER ELECTION - CHINA COMBATE TERRORISM

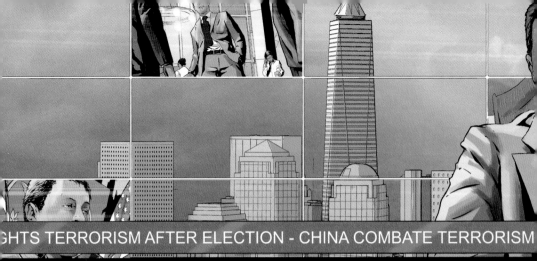

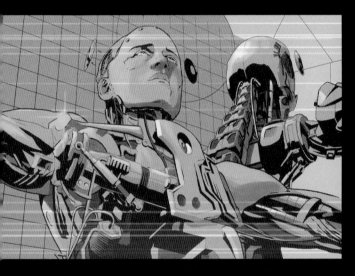

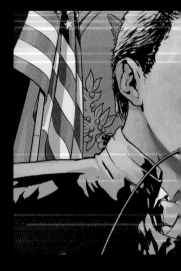

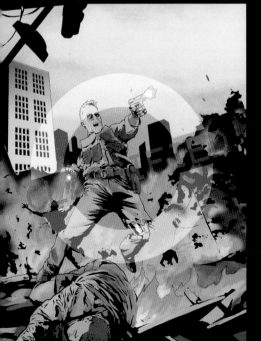

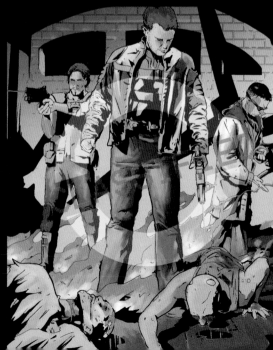

ATC

ELECCIONES - 中国 在 以后 与恐怖 主斗 - CHINE COMBAT TERRORIS

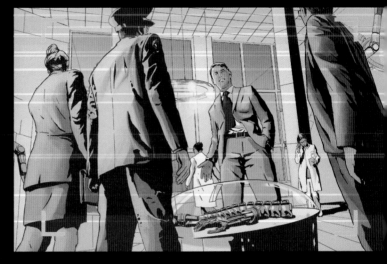

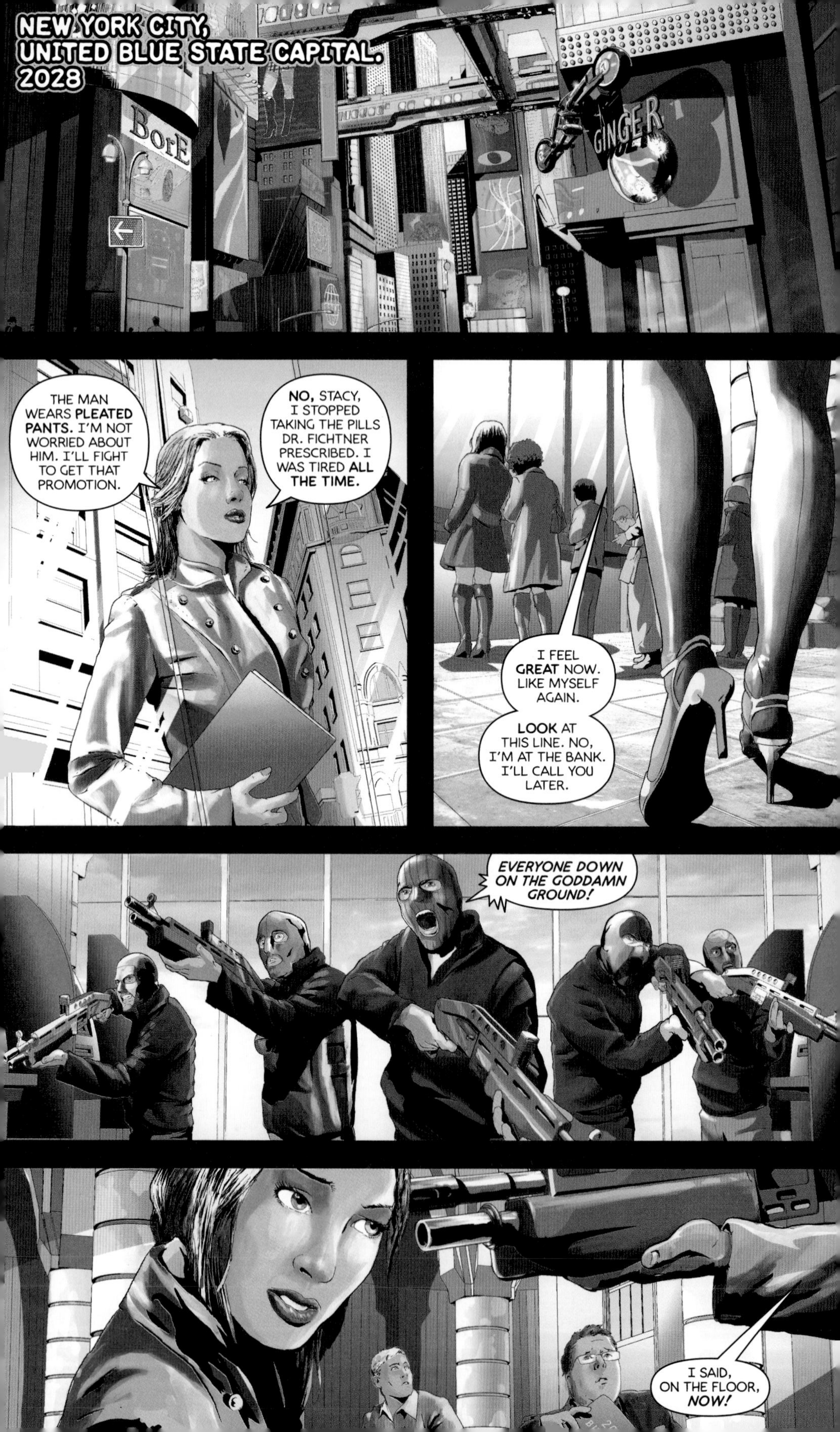
NEW YORK CITY,
UNITED BLUE STATE CAPITAL.
2028
BorE
GINGER
THE MAN WEARS PLEATED PANTS. I'M NOT WORRIED ABOUT HIM. I'LL FIGHT TO GET THAT PROMOTION.
NO, STACY, I STOPPED TAKING THE PILLS DR. FICHTNER PRESCRIBED. I WAS TIRED ALL THE TIME.
I FEEL GREAT NOW. LIKE MYSELF AGAIN.
LOOK AT THIS LINE. NO, I'M AT THE BANK. I'LL CALL YOU LATER.
EVERYONE DOWN ON THE GODDAMN GROUND!
I SAID, ON THE FLOOR, NOW!

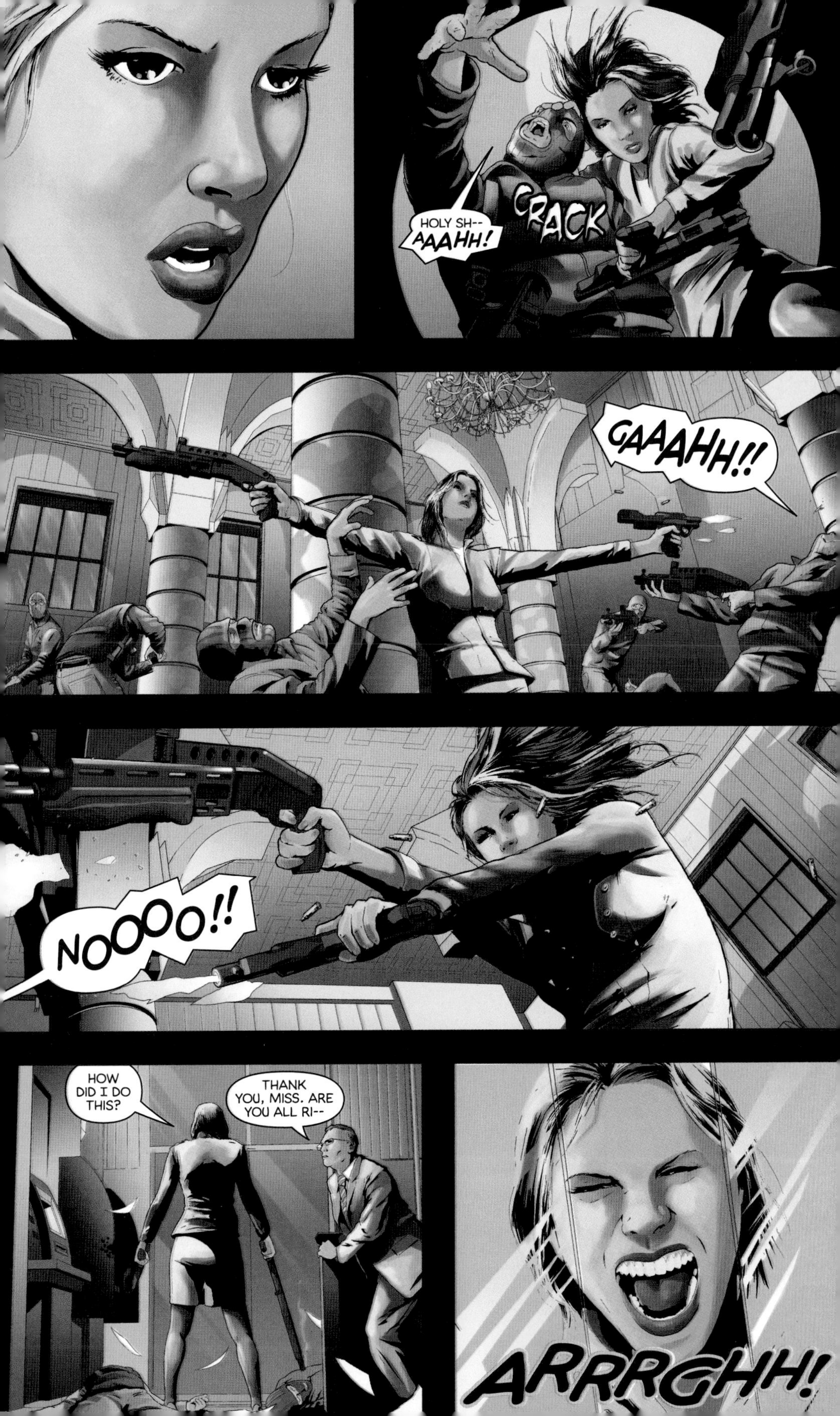
HOLY SH-- AAAHH!
CRACK
GAAAHH!!
NOOOO!!
HOW DID I DO THIS?
THANK YOU, MISS. ARE YOU ALL RI--
ARRRGHH!

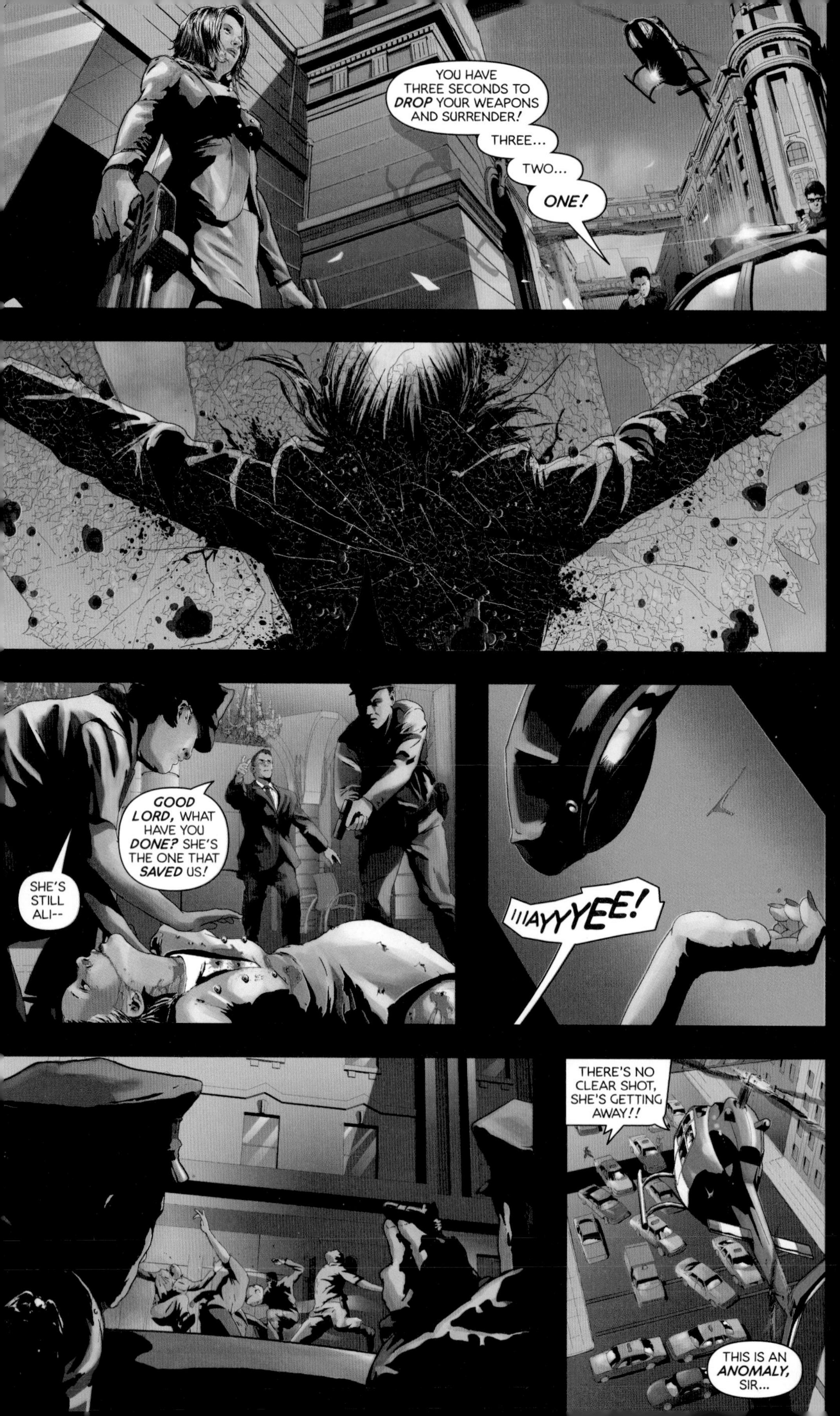
YOU HAVE THREE SECONDS TO DROP YOUR WEAPONS AND SURRENDER!
THREE...
TWO...
ONE!
SHE'S STILL ALI--
GOOD LORD, WHAT HAVE YOU DONE? SHE'S THE ONE THAT SAVED US!
!!!AYYYEE!
THERE'S NO CLEAR SHOT, SHE'S GETTING AWAY!!
THIS IS AN ANOMALY, SIR...

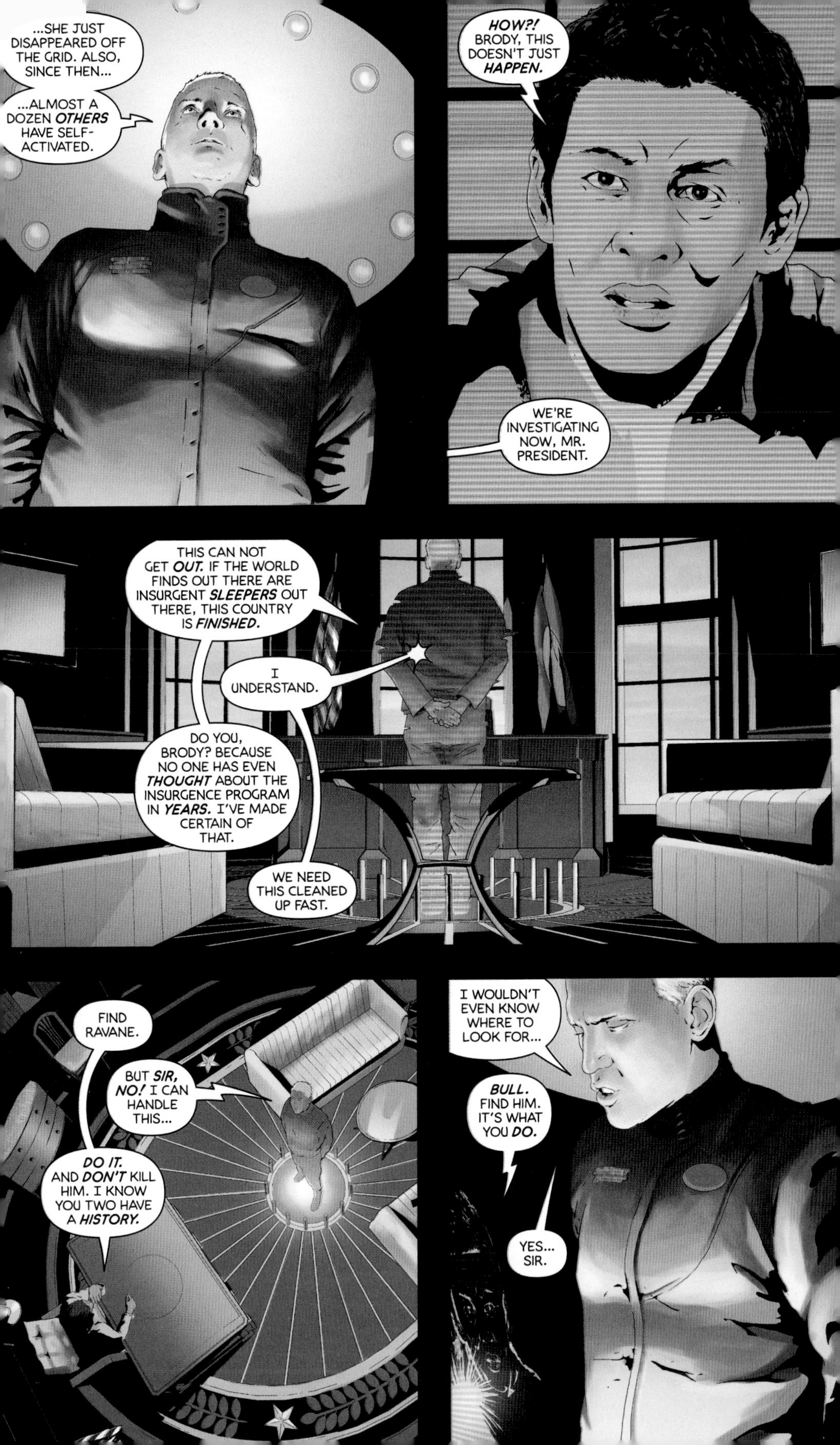
...SHE JUST DISAPPEARED OFF THE GRID. ALSO, SINCE THEN...
...ALMOST A DOZEN OTHERS HAVE SELF-ACTIVATED.
HOW?! BRODY, THIS DOESN'T JUST HAPPEN.
WE'RE INVESTIGATING NOW, MR. PRESIDENT.
THIS CAN NOT GET OUT. IF THE WORLD FINDS OUT THERE ARE INSURGENT SLEEPERS OUT THERE, THIS COUNTRY IS FINISHED.
I UNDERSTAND.
DO YOU, BRODY? BECAUSE NO ONE HAS EVEN THOUGHT ABOUT THE INSURGENCE PROGRAM IN YEARS. I'VE MADE CERTAIN OF THAT.
WE NEED THIS CLEANED UP FAST.
FIND RAVANE.
BUT SIR, NO! I CAN HANDLE THIS...
DO IT. AND DON'T KILL HIM. I KNOW YOU TWO HAVE A HISTORY.
I WOULDN'T EVEN KNOW WHERE TO LOOK FOR...
BULL. FIND HIM. IT'S WHAT YOU DO.
YES... SIR.

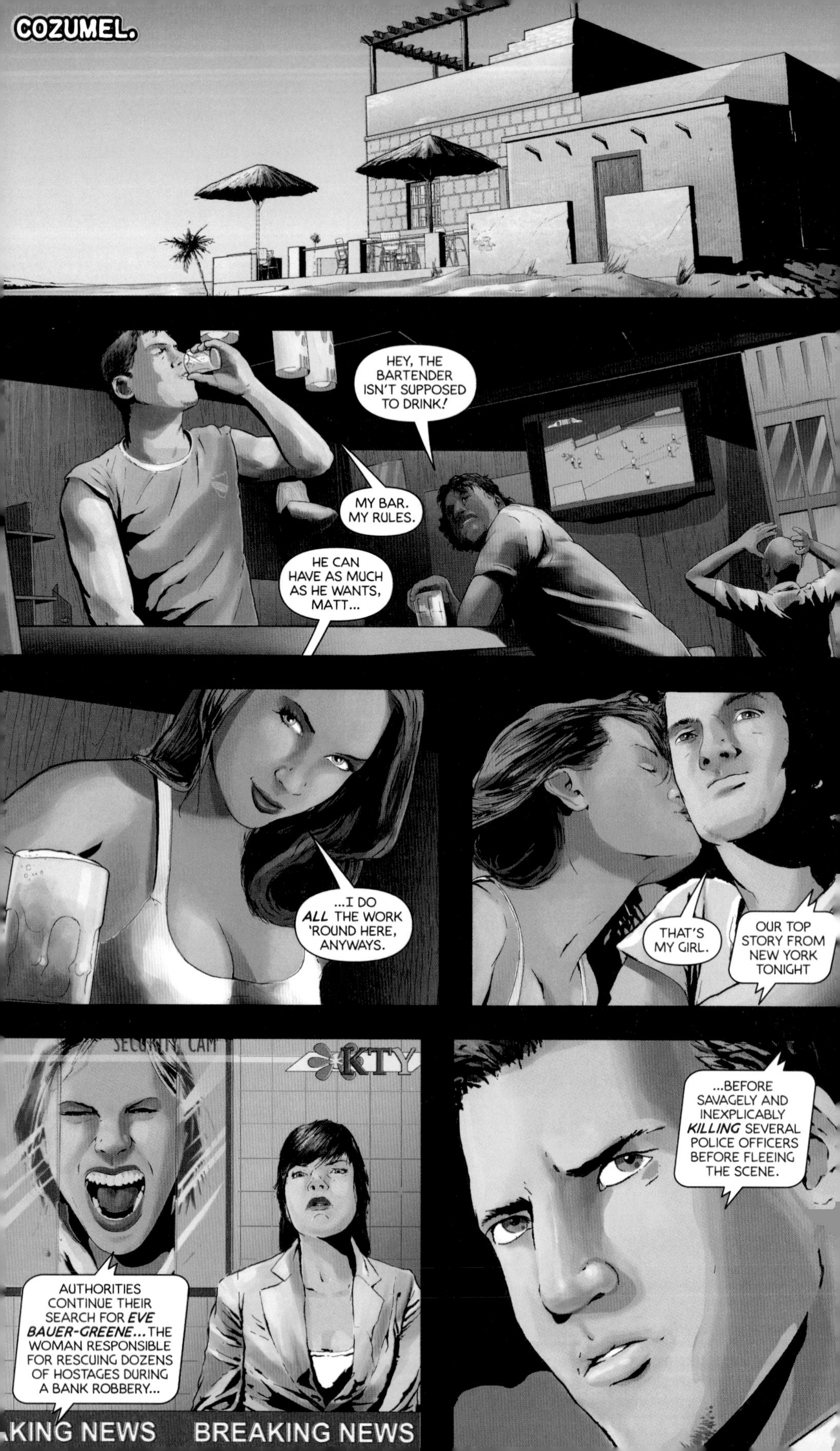
COZUMEL.
HEY, THE BARTENDER ISN'T SUPPOSED TO DRINK!
MY BAR. MY RULES.
HE CAN HAVE AS MUCH AS HE WANTS, MATT...
...I DO ALL THE WORK 'ROUND HERE, ANYWAYS.
THAT'S MY GIRL.
OUR TOP STORY FROM NEW YORK TONIGHT
SECURITY CAM
KTY
AUTHORITIES CONTINUE THEIR SEARCH FOR EVE BAUER-GREENE... THE WOMAN RESPONSIBLE FOR RESCUING DOZENS OF HOSTAGES DURING A BANK ROBBERY...
...BEFORE SAVAGELY AND INEXPLICABLY KILLING SEVERAL POLICE OFFICERS BEFORE FLEEING THE SCENE.
KING NEWS BREAKING NEWS

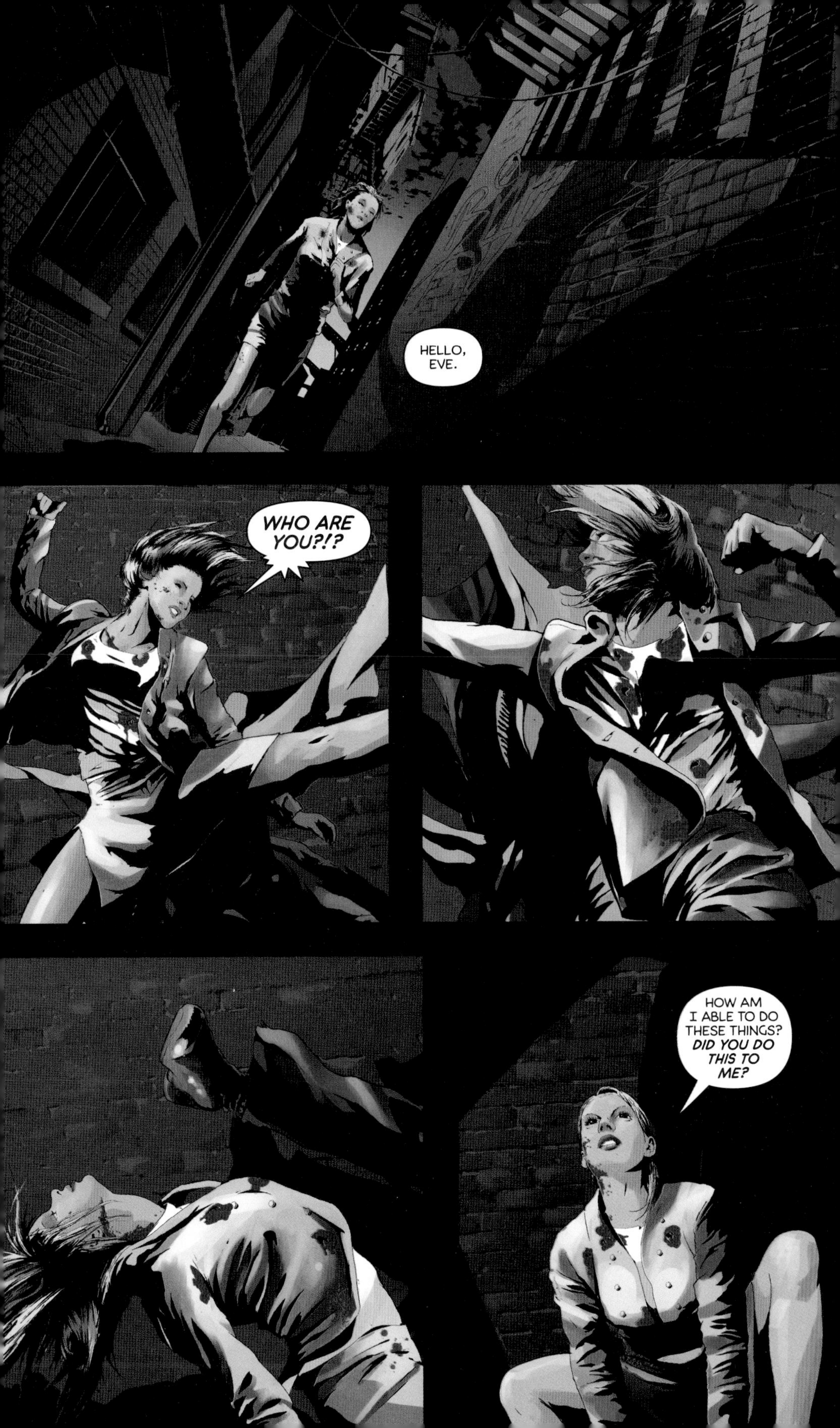
HELLO, EVE.
WHO ARE YOU?!?
HOW AM I ABLE TO DO THESE THINGS? DID YOU DO THIS TO ME?

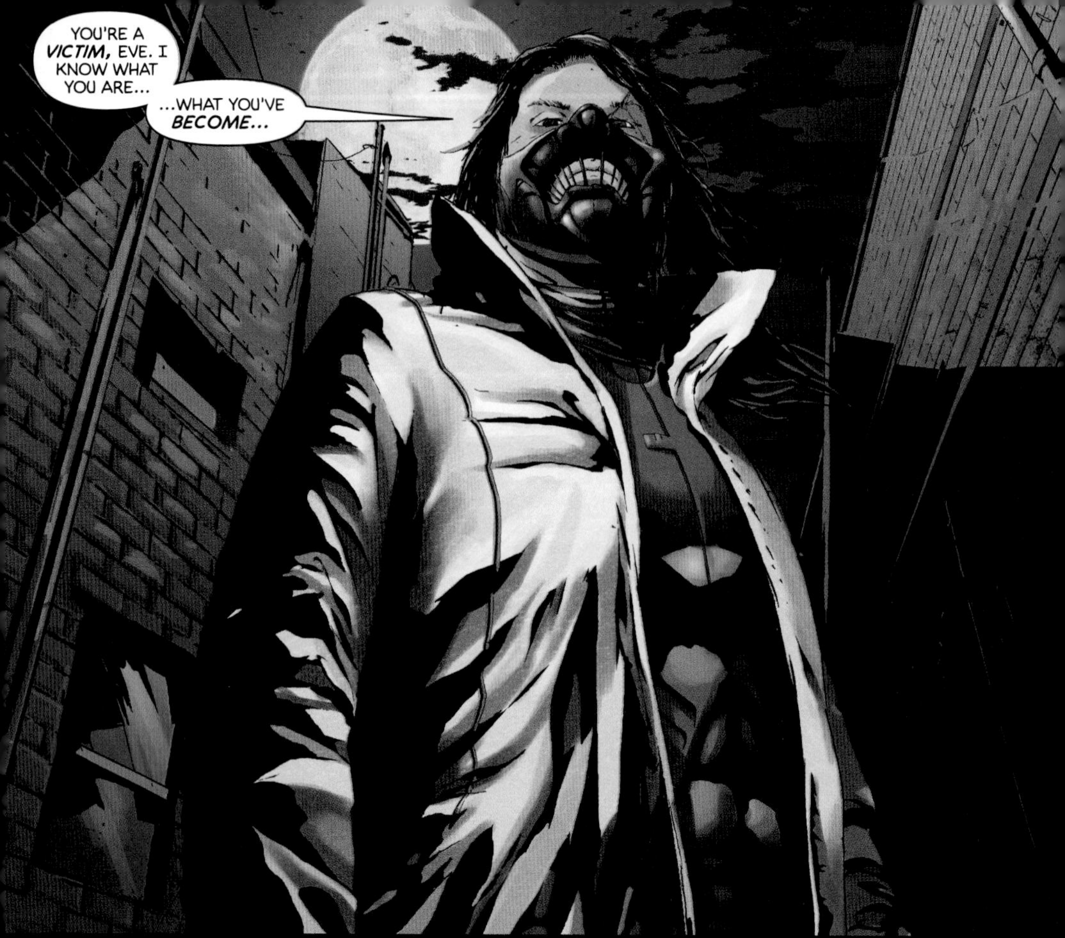
YOU'RE A *VICTIM,* EVE. I KNOW WHAT YOU ARE...
...WHAT YOU'VE *BECOME...*

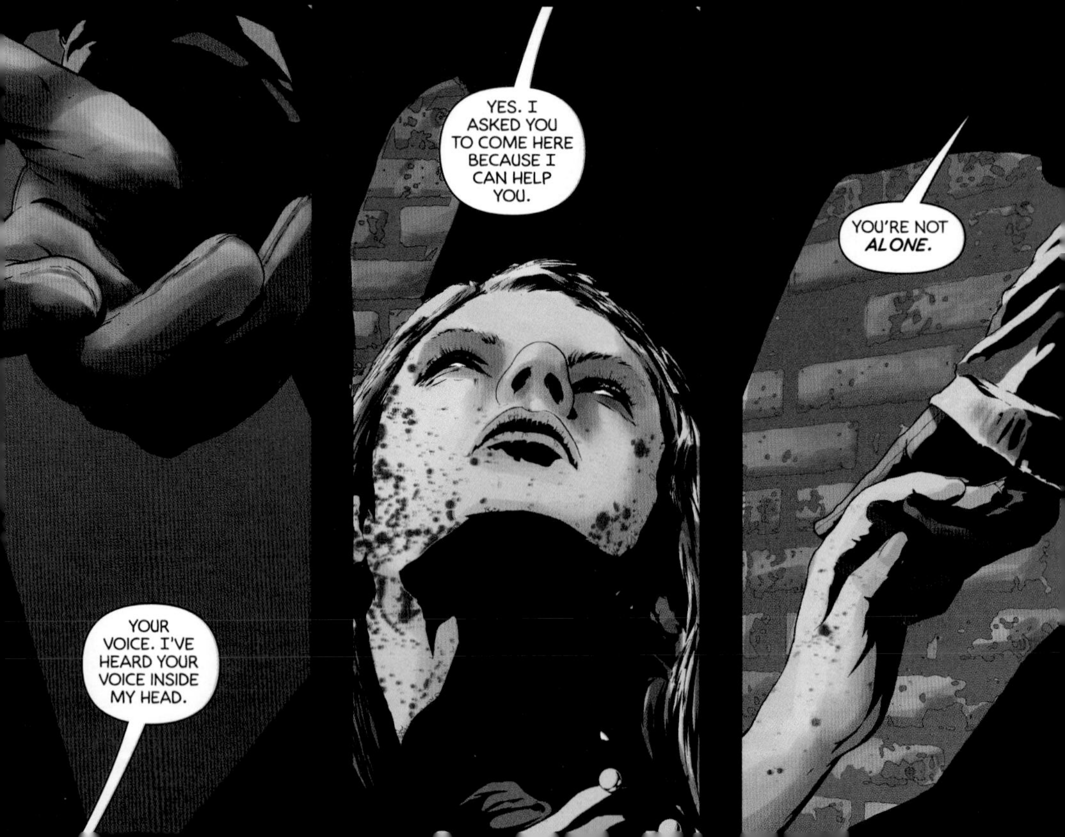
YOUR VOICE. I'VE HEARD YOUR VOICE INSIDE MY HEAD.
YES. I ASKED YOU TO COME HERE BECAUSE I CAN HELP YOU.
YOU'RE NOT *ALONE.*

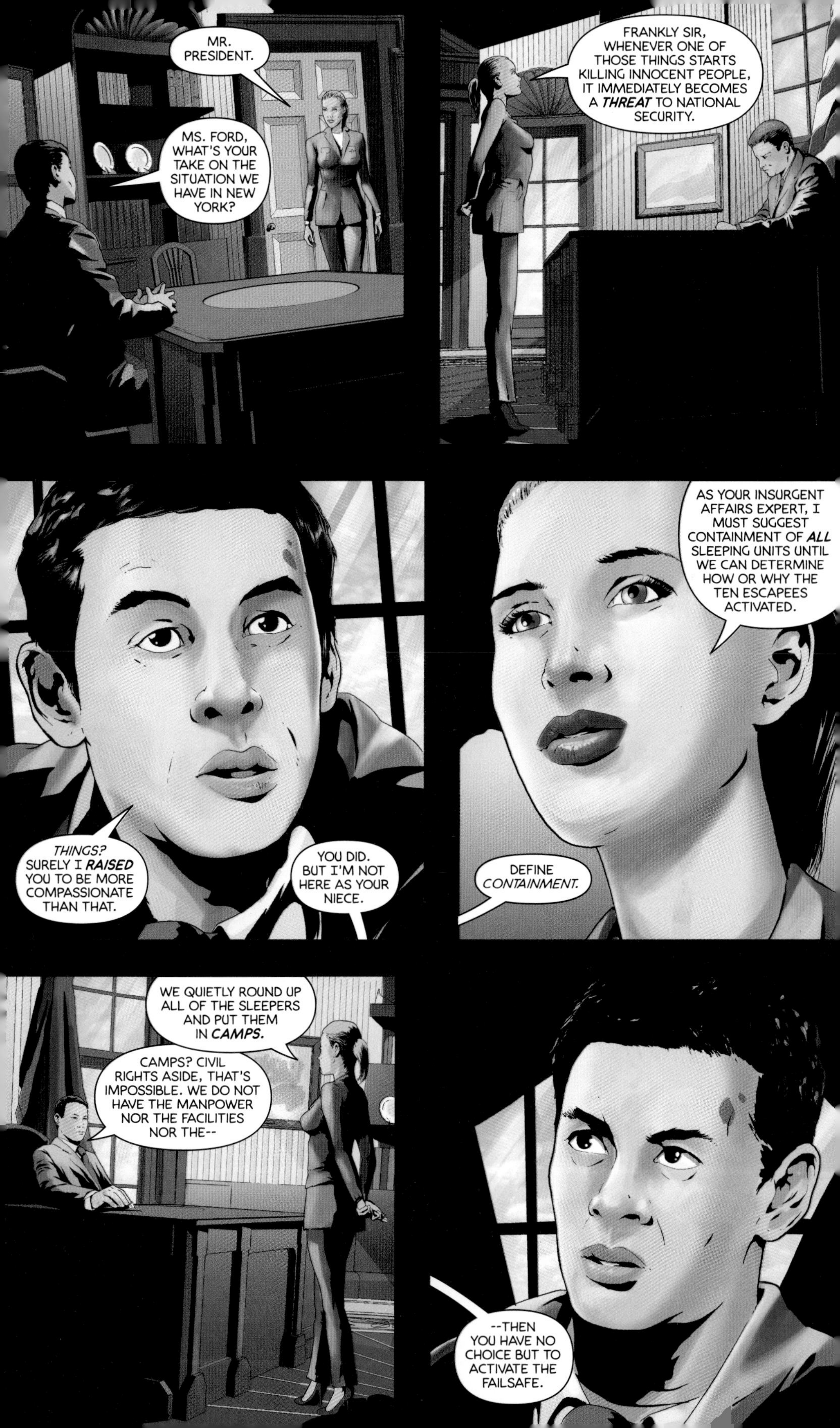
MR. PRESIDENT.
MS. FORD, WHAT'S YOUR TAKE ON THE SITUATION WE HAVE IN NEW YORK?
FRANKLY SIR, WHENEVER ONE OF THOSE THINGS STARTS KILLING INNOCENT PEOPLE, IT IMMEDIATELY BECOMES A ***THREAT*** TO NATIONAL SECURITY.
THINGS? SURELY I ***RAISED*** YOU TO BE MORE COMPASSIONATE THAN THAT.
YOU DID. BUT I'M NOT HERE AS YOUR NIECE.
AS YOUR INSURGENT AFFAIRS EXPERT, I MUST SUGGEST CONTAINMENT OF ***ALL*** SLEEPING UNITS UNTIL WE CAN DETERMINE HOW OR WHY THE TEN ESCAPEES ACTIVATED.
DEFINE *CONTAINMENT.*
WE QUIETLY ROUND UP ALL OF THE SLEEPERS AND PUT THEM IN ***CAMPS.***
CAMPS? CIVIL RIGHTS ASIDE, THAT'S IMPOSSIBLE. WE DO NOT HAVE THE MANPOWER NOR THE FACILITIES NOR THE--
--THEN YOU HAVE NO CHOICE BUT TO ACTIVATE THE FAILSAFE.

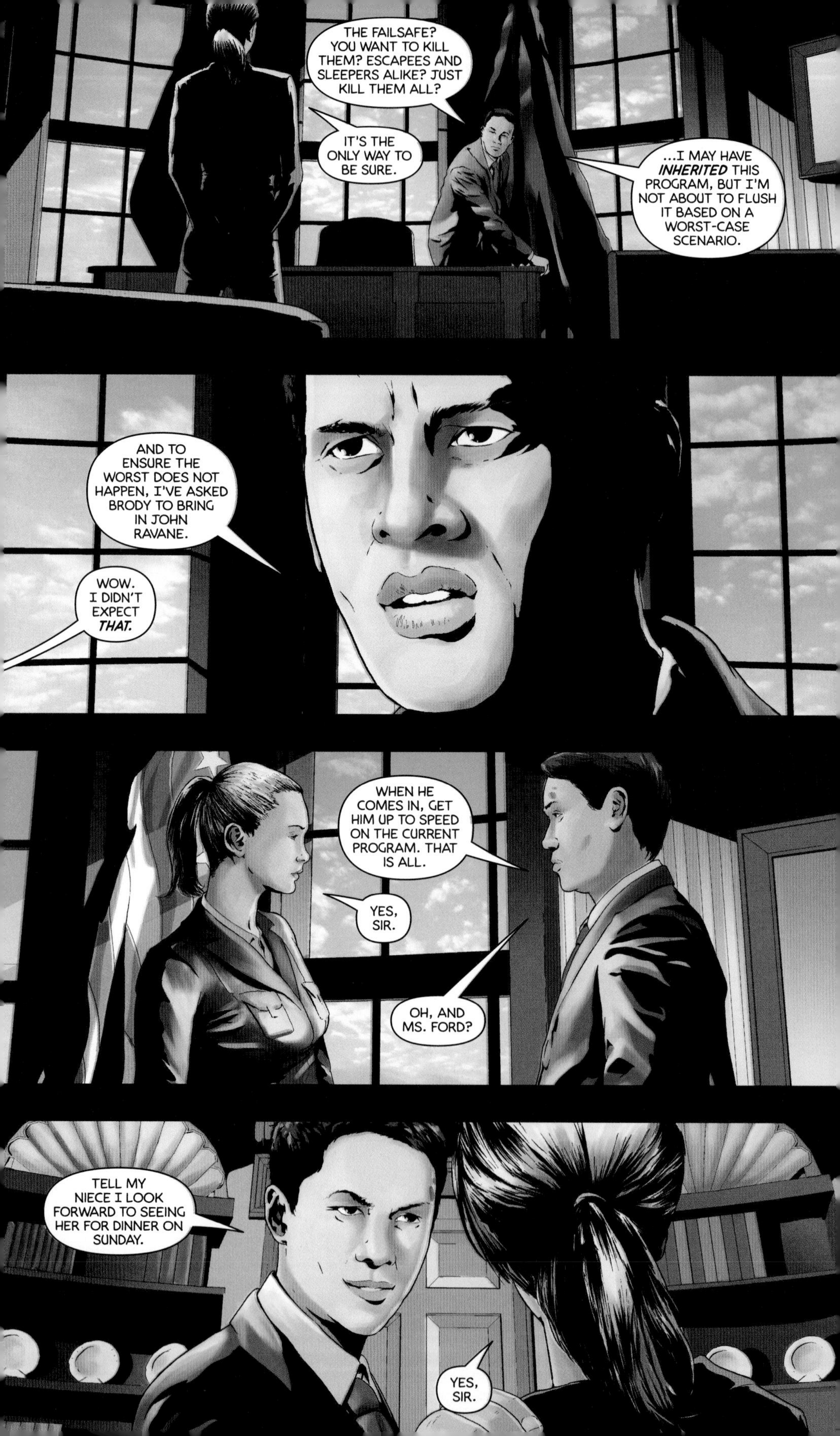
THE FAILSAFE? YOU WANT TO KILL THEM? ESCAPEES AND SLEEPERS ALIKE? JUST KILL THEM ALL?
IT'S THE ONLY WAY TO BE SURE.
...I MAY HAVE *INHERITED* THIS PROGRAM, BUT I'M NOT ABOUT TO FLUSH IT BASED ON A WORST-CASE SCENARIO.
AND TO ENSURE THE WORST DOES NOT HAPPEN, I'VE ASKED BRODY TO BRING IN JOHN RAVANE.
WOW. I DIDN'T EXPECT *THAT.*
WHEN HE COMES IN, GET HIM UP TO SPEED ON THE CURRENT PROGRAM. THAT IS ALL.
YES, SIR.
OH, AND MS. FORD?
TELL MY NIECE I LOOK FORWARD TO SEEING HER FOR DINNER ON SUNDAY.
YES, SIR.

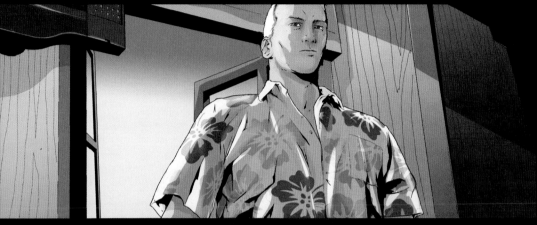

BOB, YOU'D BETTER TAKE OVER. GONNA BE LATE FOR CLASS.

YOU GONNA SHOOT ME, BOB? NEVER THOUGHT OF YOU AS A BOB, *JOHN.*

HOW'D YOU FIND ME?

NEVER *LOST* YOU, PAL. JUST DIDN'T NEED YOU. UNTIL *NOW.*

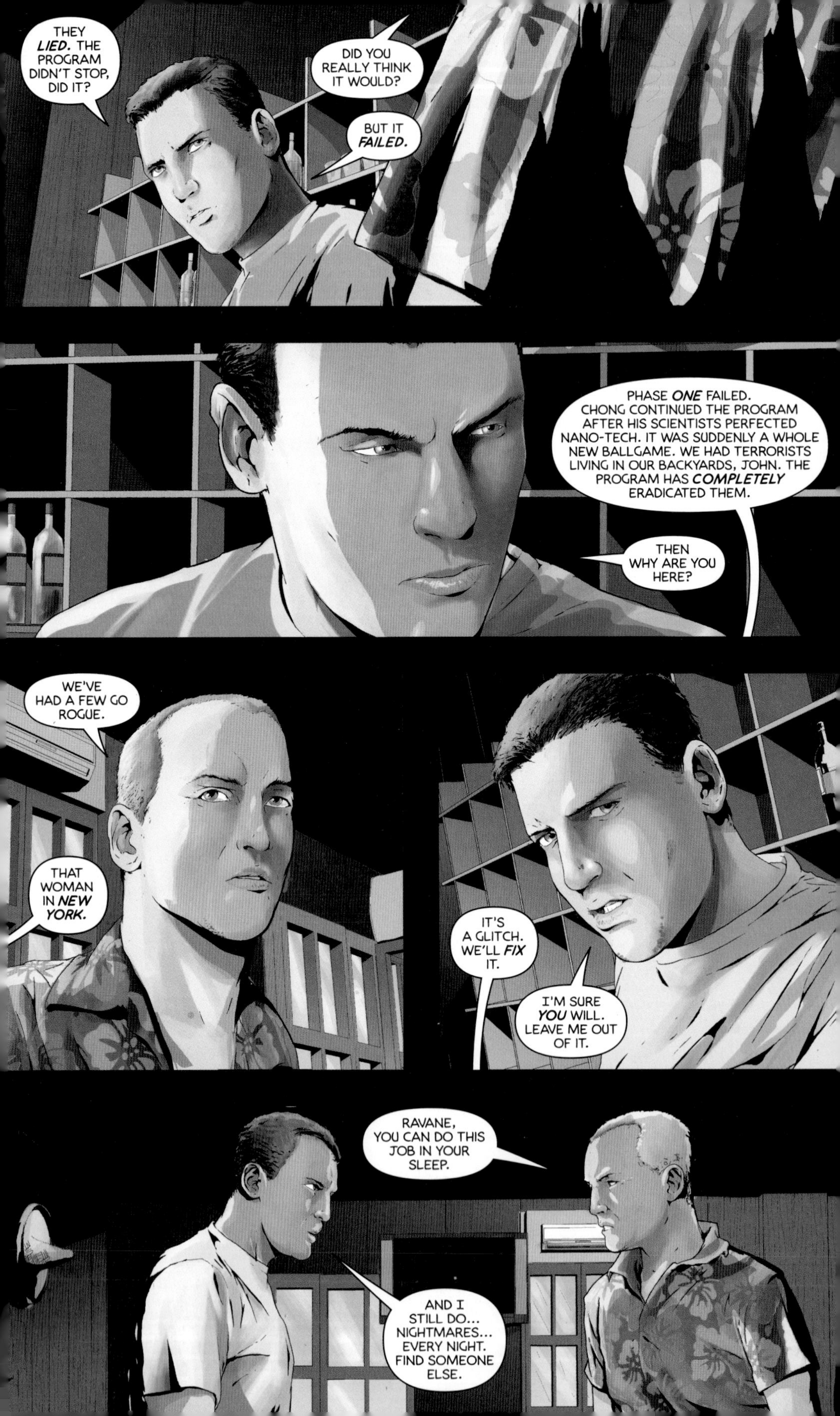
THEY LIED. THE PROGRAM DIDN'T STOP, DID IT?
DID YOU REALLY THINK IT WOULD?
BUT IT FAILED.
PHASE ONE FAILED. CHONG CONTINUED THE PROGRAM AFTER HIS SCIENTISTS PERFECTED NANO-TECH. IT WAS SUDDENLY A WHOLE NEW BALLGAME. WE HAD TERRORISTS LIVING IN OUR BACKYARDS, JOHN. THE PROGRAM HAS COMPLETELY ERADICATED THEM.
THEN WHY ARE YOU HERE?
WE'VE HAD A FEW GO ROGUE.
THAT WOMAN IN NEW YORK.
IT'S A GLITCH. WE'LL FIX IT.
I'M SURE YOU WILL. LEAVE ME OUT OF IT.
RAVANE, YOU CAN DO THIS JOB IN YOUR SLEEP.
AND I STILL DO... NIGHTMARES... EVERY NIGHT. FIND SOMEONE ELSE.

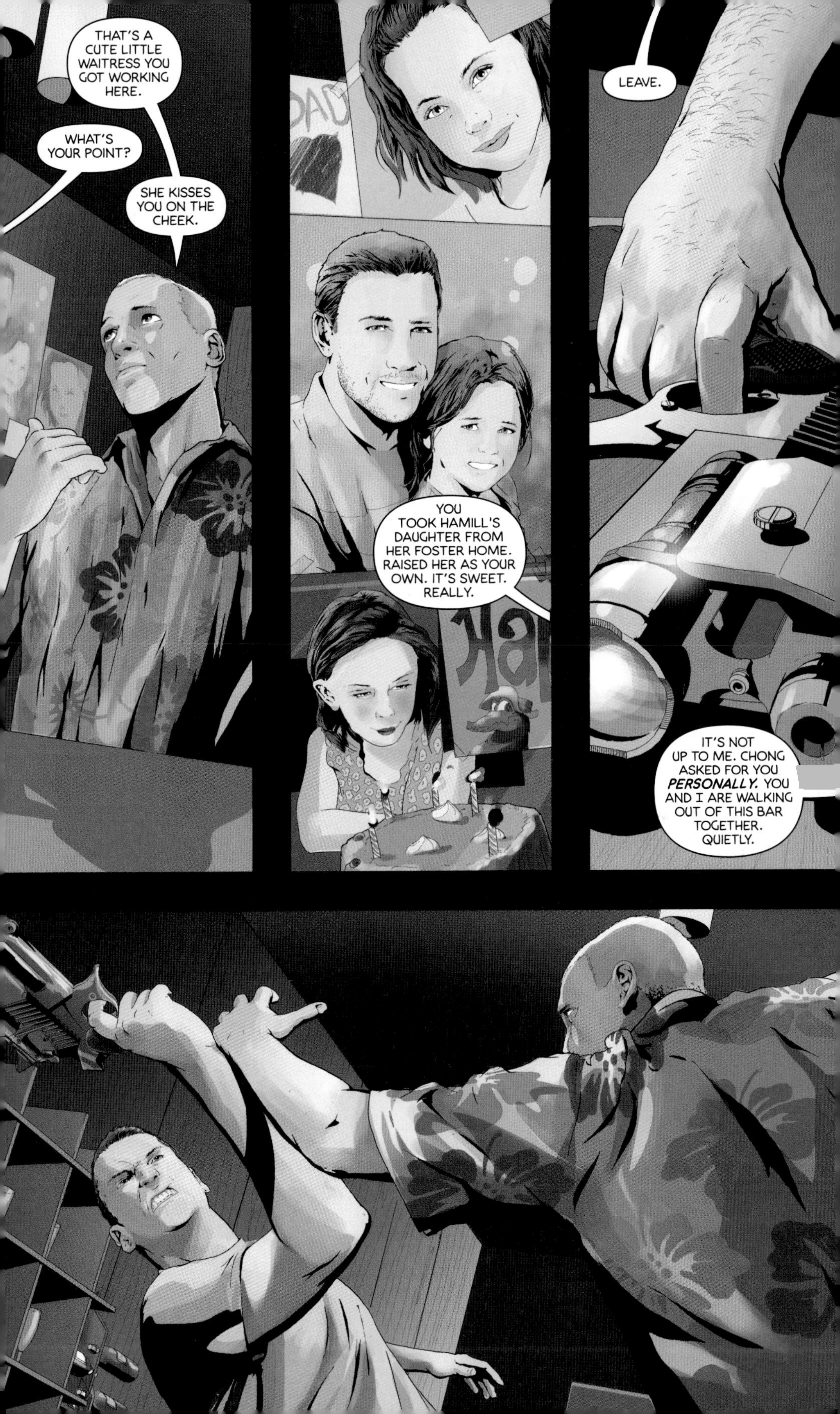
THAT'S A CUTE LITTLE WAITRESS YOU GOT WORKING HERE.
WHAT'S YOUR POINT?
SHE KISSES YOU ON THE CHEEK.
YOU TOOK HAMILL'S DAUGHTER FROM HER FOSTER HOME. RAISED HER AS YOUR OWN. IT'S SWEET. REALLY.
LEAVE.
IT'S NOT UP TO ME. CHONG ASKED FOR YOU *PERSONALLY.* YOU AND I ARE WALKING OUT OF THIS BAR TOGETHER. QUIETLY.

SCREW *ORDERS.*

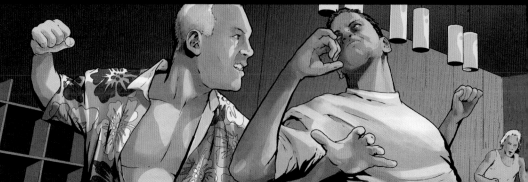

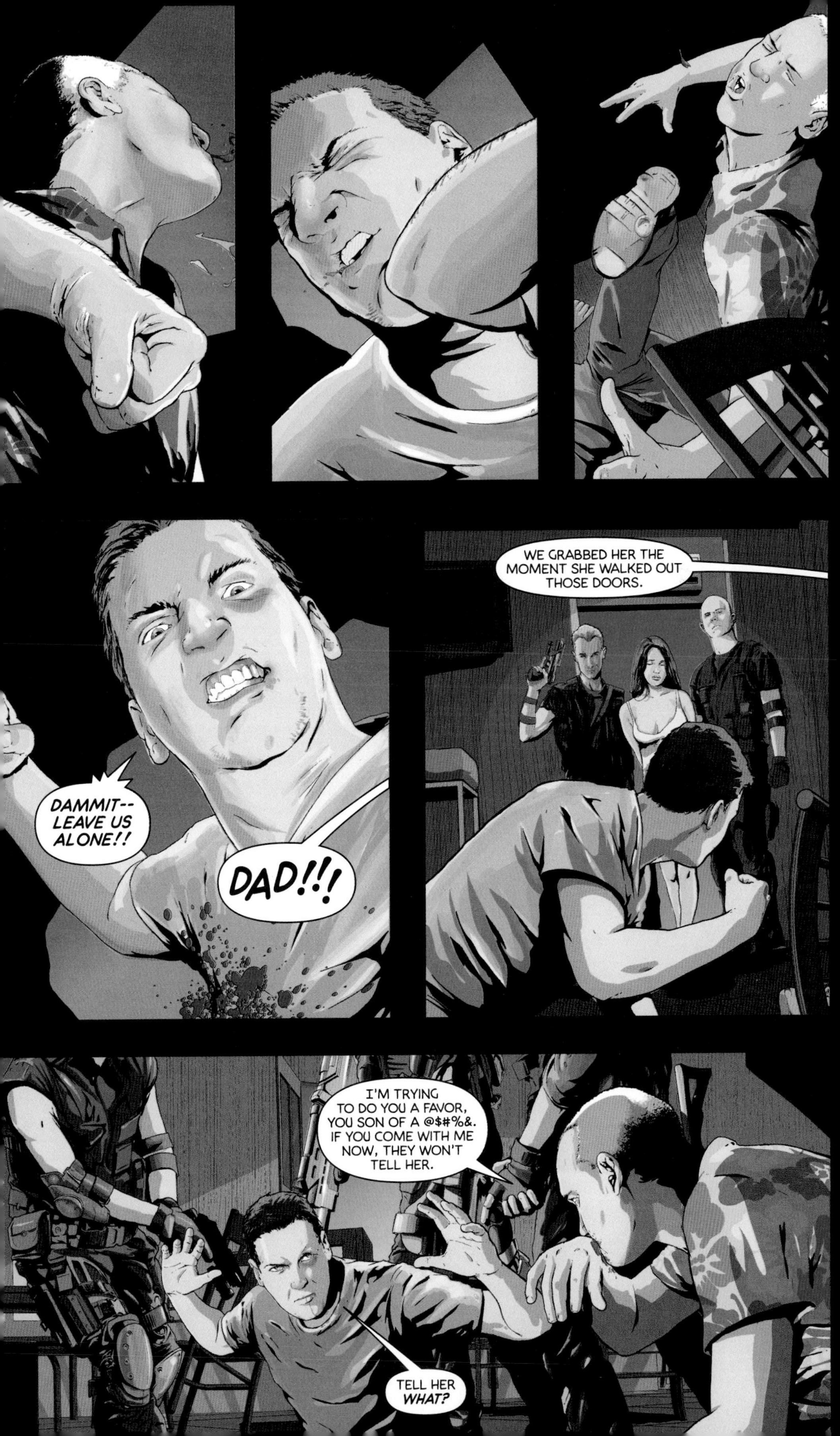
DAMMIT--
LEAVE US
ALONE!!
DAD!!!
WE GRABBED HER THE MOMENT SHE WALKED OUT THOSE DOORS.
I'M TRYING TO DO YOU A FAVOR, YOU SON OF A @$#%&. IF YOU COME WITH ME NOW, THEY WON'T TELL HER.
TELL HER *WHAT?*

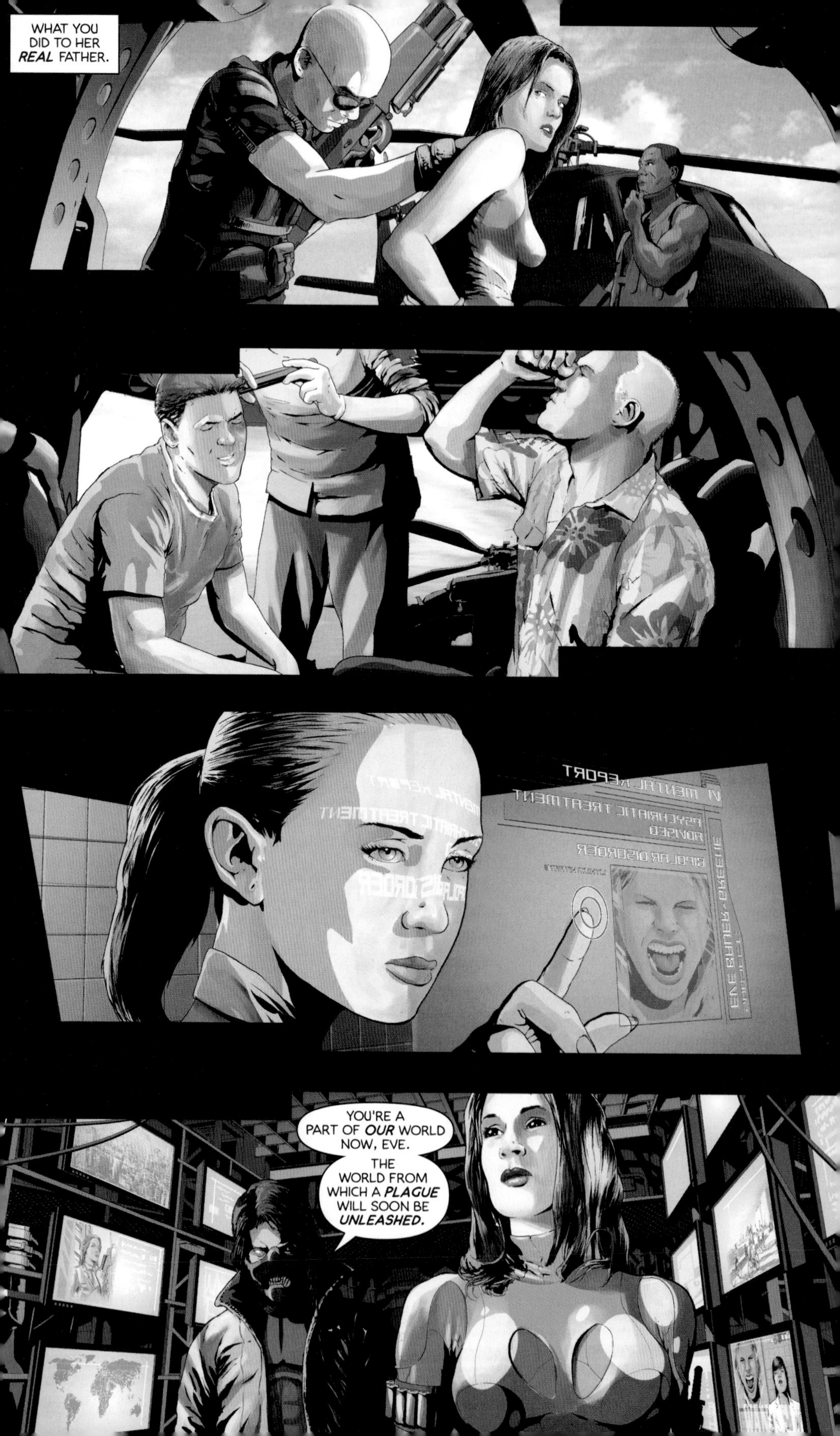
WHAT YOU DID TO HER *REAL* FATHER.
MENTAL REPORT
PSYCHRIATIC TREATMENT ADVISED
BIPOLAR DISORDER
YOU'RE A PART OF *OUR* WORLD NOW, EVE.
THE WORLD FROM WHICH A *PLAGUE* WILL SOON BE *UNLEASHED.*

CHAPTER 2

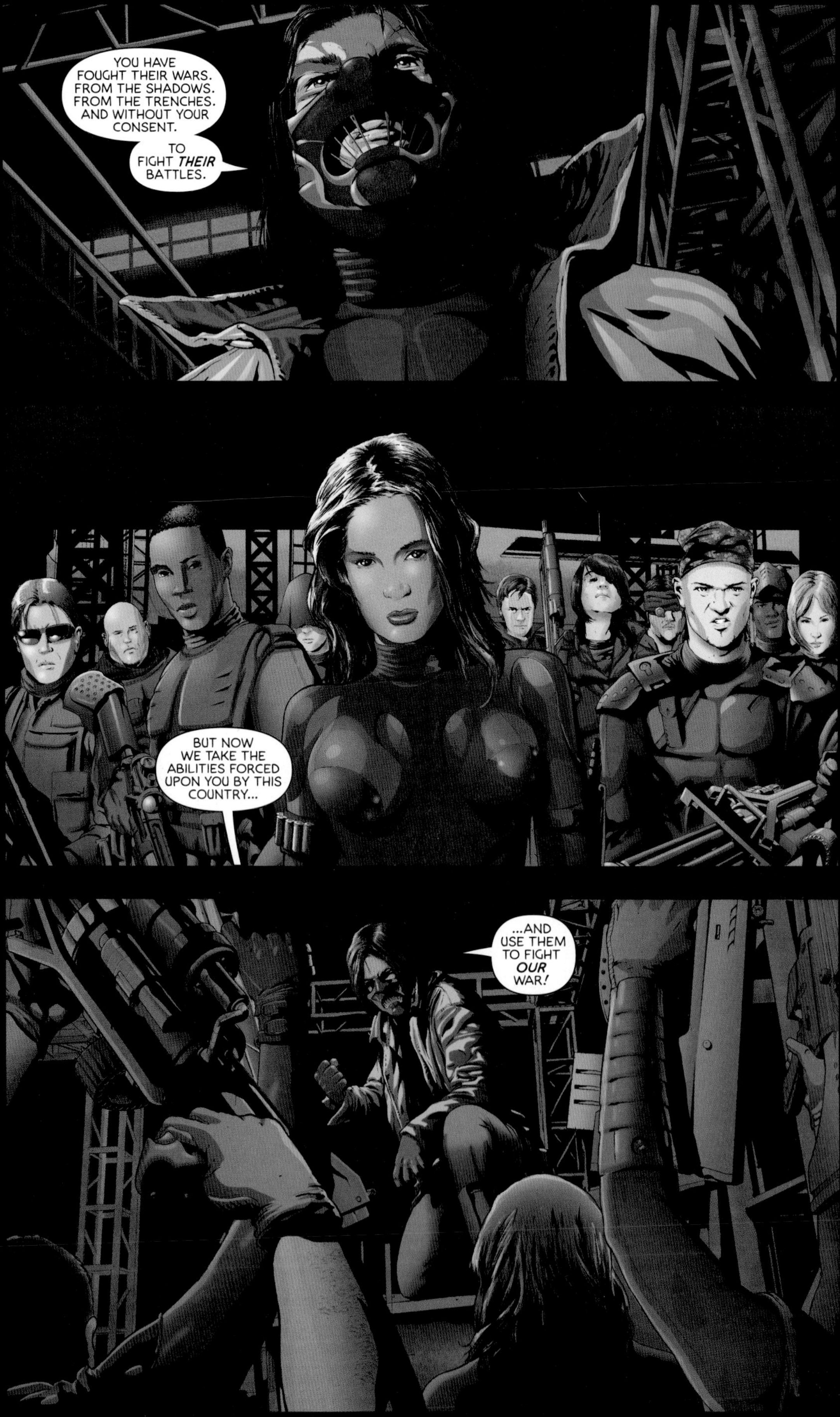
YOU HAVE FOUGHT THEIR WARS. FROM THE SHADOWS. FROM THE TRENCHES. AND WITHOUT YOUR CONSENT.
TO FIGHT *THEIR* BATTLES.
BUT NOW WE TAKE THE ABILITIES FORCED UPON YOU BY THIS COUNTRY...
...AND USE THEM TO FIGHT *OUR* WAR!

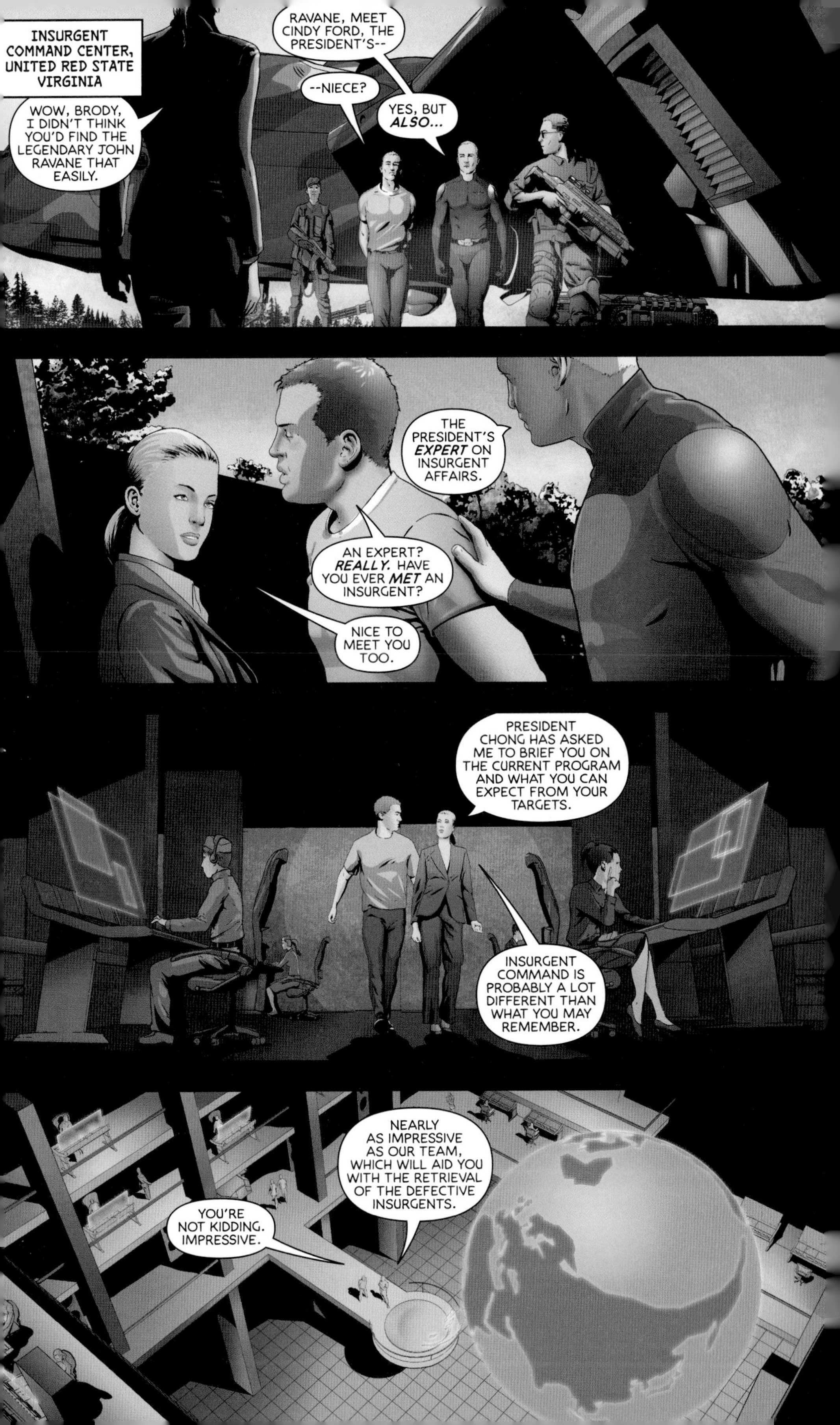
INSURGENT COMMAND CENTER, UNITED RED STATE VIRGINIA
WOW, BRODY, I DIDN'T THINK YOU'D FIND THE LEGENDARY JOHN RAVANE THAT EASILY.
RAVANE, MEET CINDY FORD, THE PRESIDENT'S--
--NIECE?
YES, BUT ALSO...
THE PRESIDENT'S EXPERT ON INSURGENT AFFAIRS.
AN EXPERT? REALLY. HAVE YOU EVER MET AN INSURGENT?
NICE TO MEET YOU TOO.
PRESIDENT CHONG HAS ASKED ME TO BRIEF YOU ON THE CURRENT PROGRAM AND WHAT YOU CAN EXPECT FROM YOUR TARGETS.
INSURGENT COMMAND IS PROBABLY A LOT DIFFERENT THAN WHAT YOU MAY REMEMBER.
YOU'RE NOT KIDDING. IMPRESSIVE.
NEARLY AS IMPRESSIVE AS OUR TEAM, WHICH WILL AID YOU WITH THE RETRIEVAL OF THE DEFECTIVE INSURGENTS.

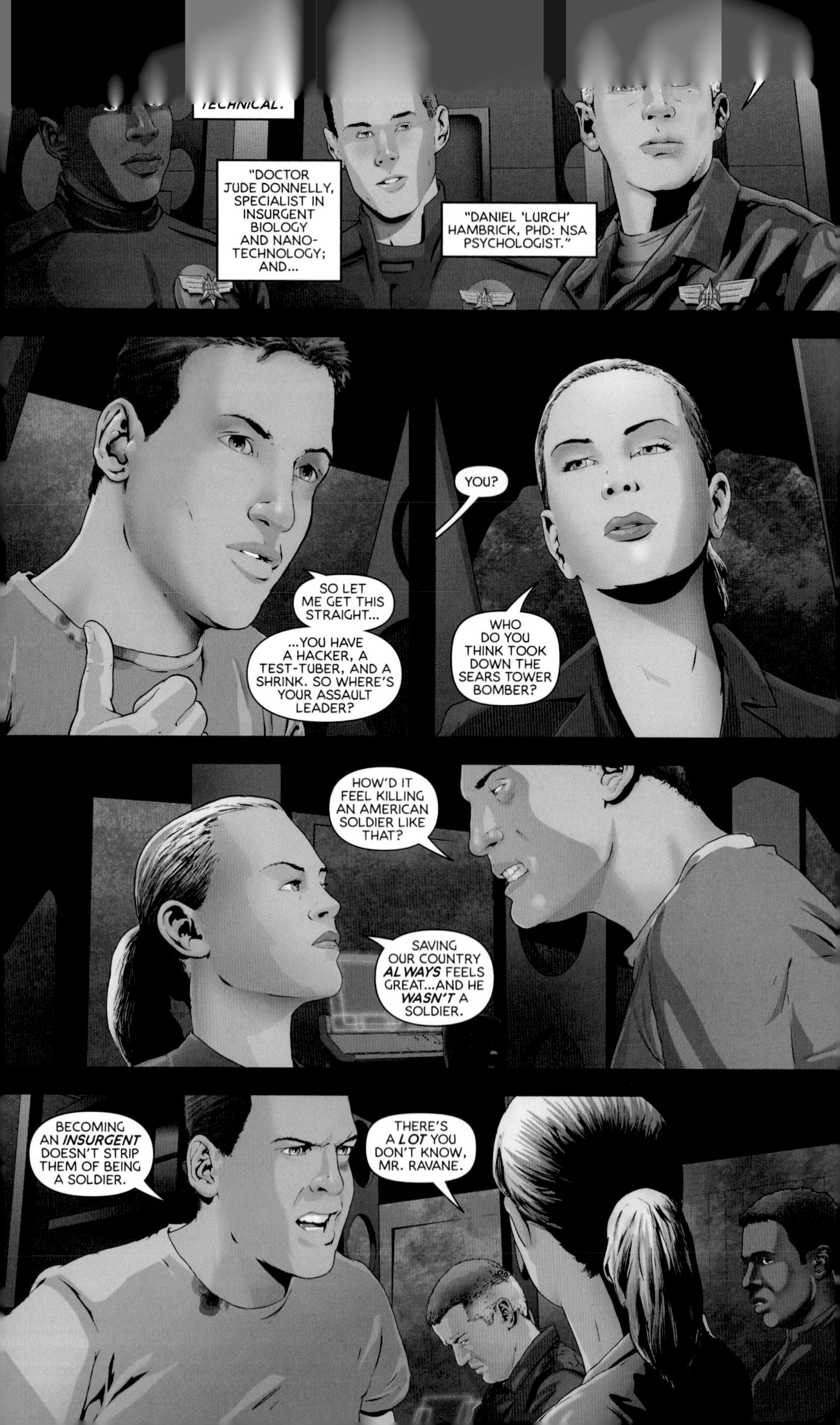
TECHNICAL.
"DOCTOR JUDE DONNELLY, SPECIALIST IN INSURGENT BIOLOGY AND NANO-TECHNOLOGY; AND...
"DANIEL 'LURCH' HAMBRICK, PHD: NSA PSYCHOLOGIST."
SO LET ME GET THIS STRAIGHT...
...YOU HAVE A HACKER, A TEST-TUBER, AND A SHRINK. SO WHERE'S YOUR ASSAULT LEADER?
YOU?
WHO DO YOU THINK TOOK DOWN THE SEARS TOWER BOMBER?
HOW'D IT FEEL KILLING AN AMERICAN SOLDIER LIKE THAT?
SAVING OUR COUNTRY ALWAYS FEELS GREAT...AND HE WASN'T A SOLDIER.
BECOMING AN INSURGENT DOESN'T STRIP THEM OF BEING A SOLDIER.
THERE'S A LOT YOU DON'T KNOW, MR. RAVANE.

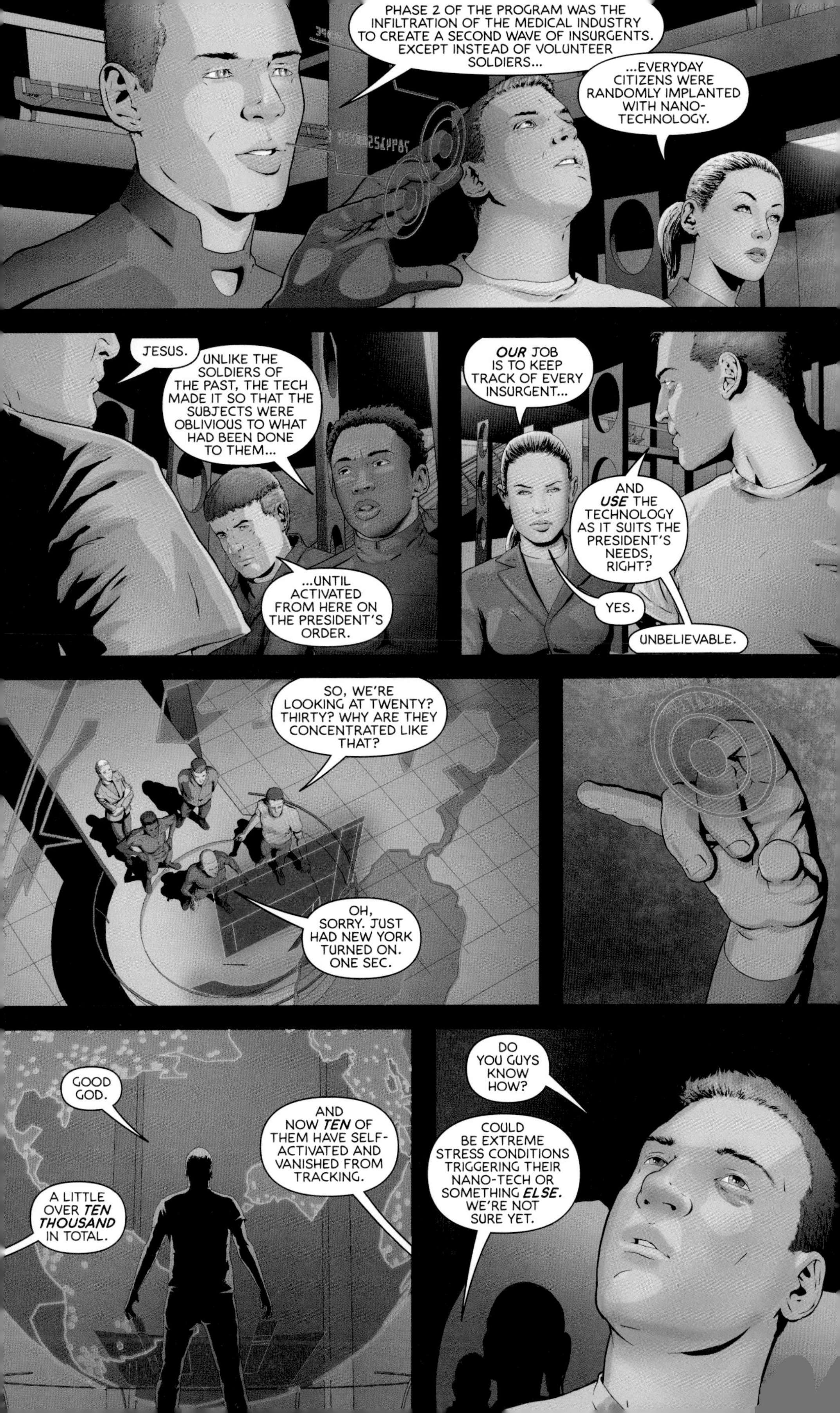
PHASE 2 OF THE PROGRAM WAS THE INFILTRATION OF THE MEDICAL INDUSTRY TO CREATE A SECOND WAVE OF INSURGENTS. EXCEPT INSTEAD OF VOLUNTEER SOLDIERS...
...EVERYDAY CITIZENS WERE RANDOMLY IMPLANTED WITH NANO-TECHNOLOGY.
JESUS.
UNLIKE THE SOLDIERS OF THE PAST, THE TECH MADE IT SO THAT THE SUBJECTS WERE OBLIVIOUS TO WHAT HAD BEEN DONE TO THEM...
...UNTIL ACTIVATED FROM HERE ON THE PRESIDENT'S ORDER.
OUR JOB IS TO KEEP TRACK OF EVERY INSURGENT...
AND *USE* THE TECHNOLOGY AS IT SUITS THE PRESIDENT'S NEEDS, RIGHT?
YES.
UNBELIEVABLE.
SO, WE'RE LOOKING AT TWENTY? THIRTY? WHY ARE THEY CONCENTRATED LIKE THAT?
OH, SORRY. JUST HAD NEW YORK TURNED ON. ONE SEC.
GOOD GOD.
A LITTLE OVER ***TEN THOUSAND*** IN TOTAL.
AND NOW ***TEN*** OF THEM HAVE SELF-ACTIVATED AND VANISHED FROM TRACKING.
DO YOU GUYS KNOW HOW?
COULD BE EXTREME STRESS CONDITIONS TRIGGERING THEIR NANO-TECH OR SOMETHING ***ELSE***. WE'RE NOT SURE YET.

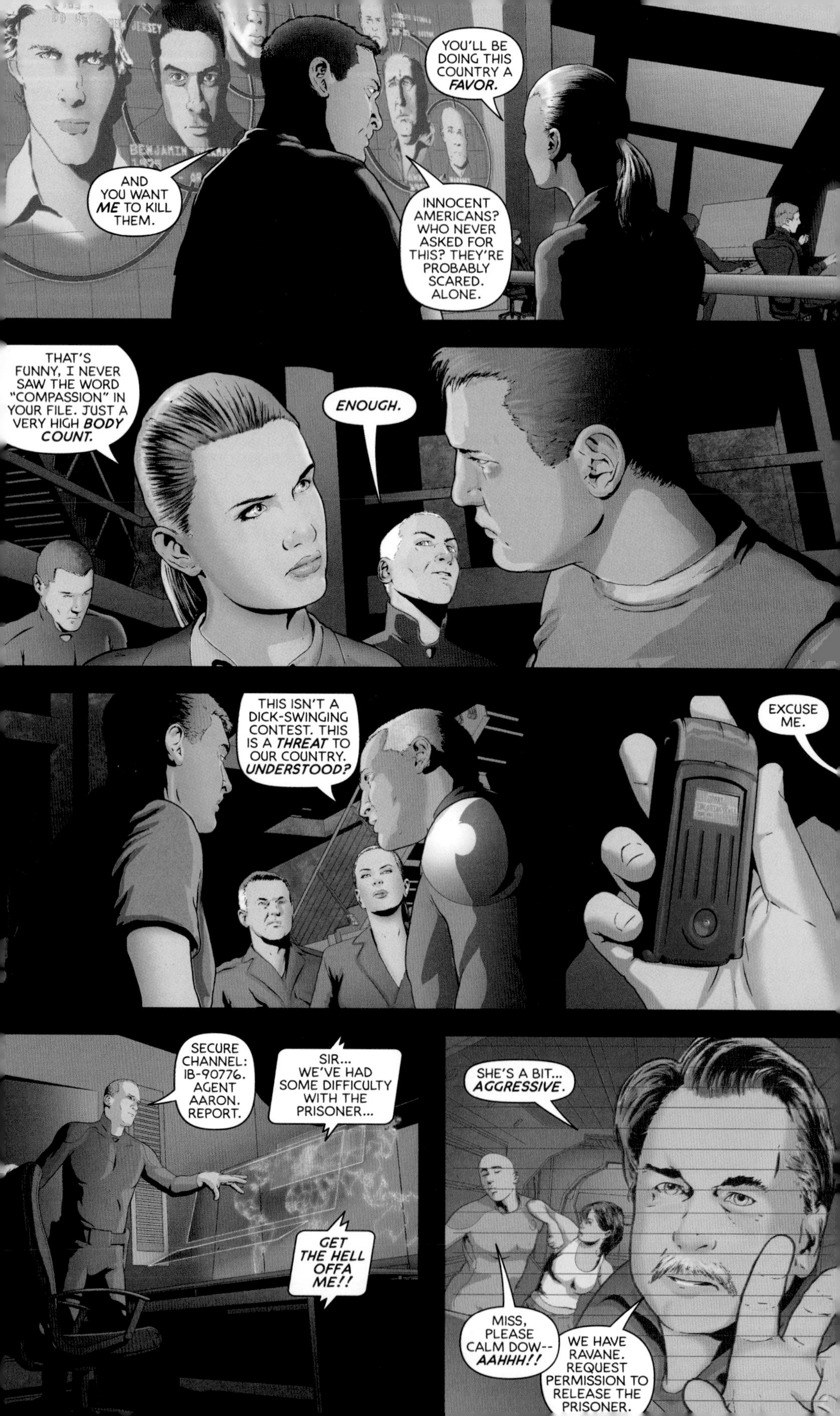
AND YOU WANT ME TO KILL THEM.
INNOCENT AMERICANS? WHO NEVER ASKED FOR THIS? THEY'RE PROBABLY SCARED. ALONE.
YOU'LL BE DOING THIS COUNTRY A FAVOR.
THAT'S FUNNY, I NEVER SAW THE WORD "COMPASSION" IN YOUR FILE. JUST A VERY HIGH BODY COUNT.
ENOUGH.
THIS ISN'T A DICK-SWINGING CONTEST. THIS IS A THREAT TO OUR COUNTRY. UNDERSTOOD?
EXCUSE ME.
SECURE CHANNEL: IB-90776. AGENT AARON. REPORT.
SIR... WE'VE HAD SOME DIFFICULTY WITH THE PRISONER...
GET THE HELL OFFA ME!!
SHE'S A BIT... AGGRESSIVE.
MISS, PLEASE CALM DOW-- AAHHH!!
WE HAVE RAVANE. REQUEST PERMISSION TO RELEASE THE PRISONER.

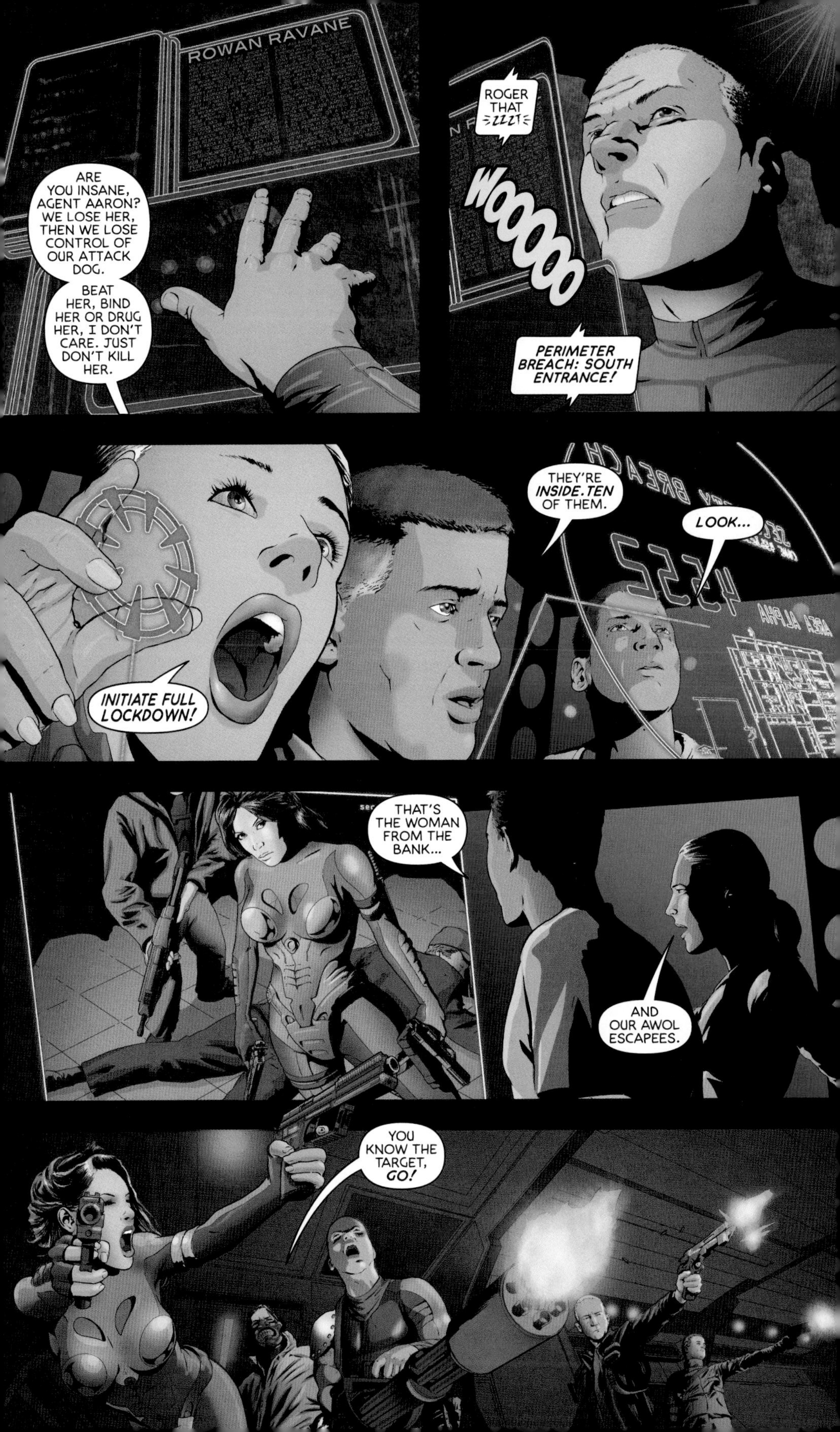
ROWAN RAVANE
ARE YOU INSANE, AGENT AARON? WE LOSE HER, THEN WE LOSE CONTROL OF OUR ATTACK DOG.
BEAT HER, BIND HER OR DRUG HER, I DON'T CARE. JUST DON'T KILL HER.
ROGER THAT ZZZT
WOOOOO
PERIMETER BREACH: SOUTH ENTRANCE!
INITIATE FULL LOCKDOWN!
THEY'RE INSIDE. TEN OF THEM.
LOOK...
THAT'S THE WOMAN FROM THE BANK...
AND OUR AWOL ESCAPEES.
YOU KNOW THE TARGET, GO!

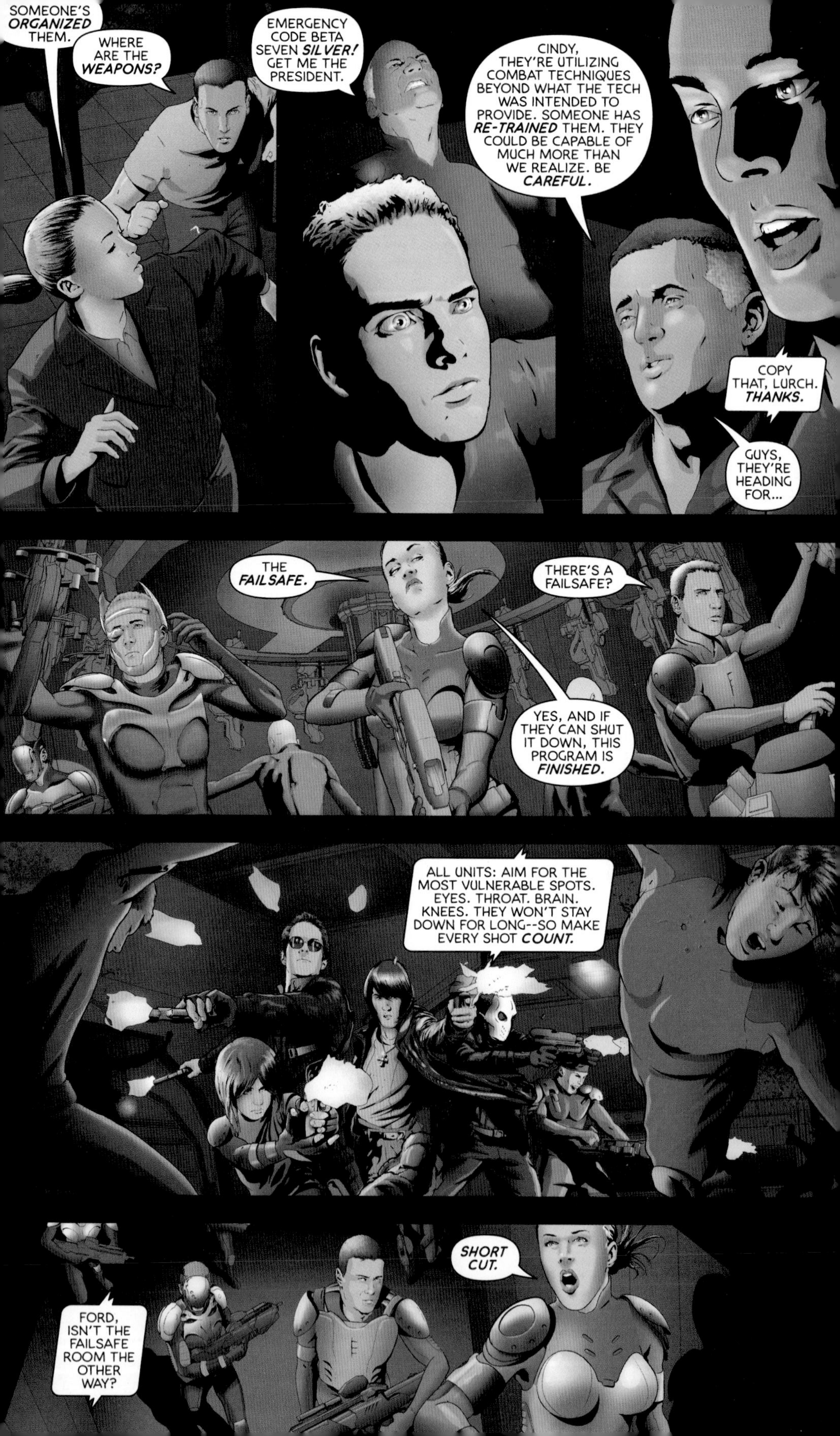
SOMEONE'S ORGANIZED THEM.
WHERE ARE THE WEAPONS?
EMERGENCY CODE BETA SEVEN SILVER! GET ME THE PRESIDENT.
CINDY, THEY'RE UTILIZING COMBAT TECHNIQUES BEYOND WHAT THE TECH WAS INTENDED TO PROVIDE. SOMEONE HAS RE-TRAINED THEM. THEY COULD BE CAPABLE OF MUCH MORE THAN WE REALIZE. BE CAREFUL.
COPY THAT, LURCH. THANKS.
GUYS, THEY'RE HEADING FOR...
THE FAILSAFE.
THERE'S A FAILSAFE?
YES, AND IF THEY CAN SHUT IT DOWN, THIS PROGRAM IS FINISHED.
ALL UNITS: AIM FOR THE MOST VULNERABLE SPOTS. EYES. THROAT. BRAIN. KNEES. THEY WON'T STAY DOWN FOR LONG--SO MAKE EVERY SHOT COUNT.
FORD, ISN'T THE FAILSAFE ROOM THE OTHER WAY?
SHORT CUT.

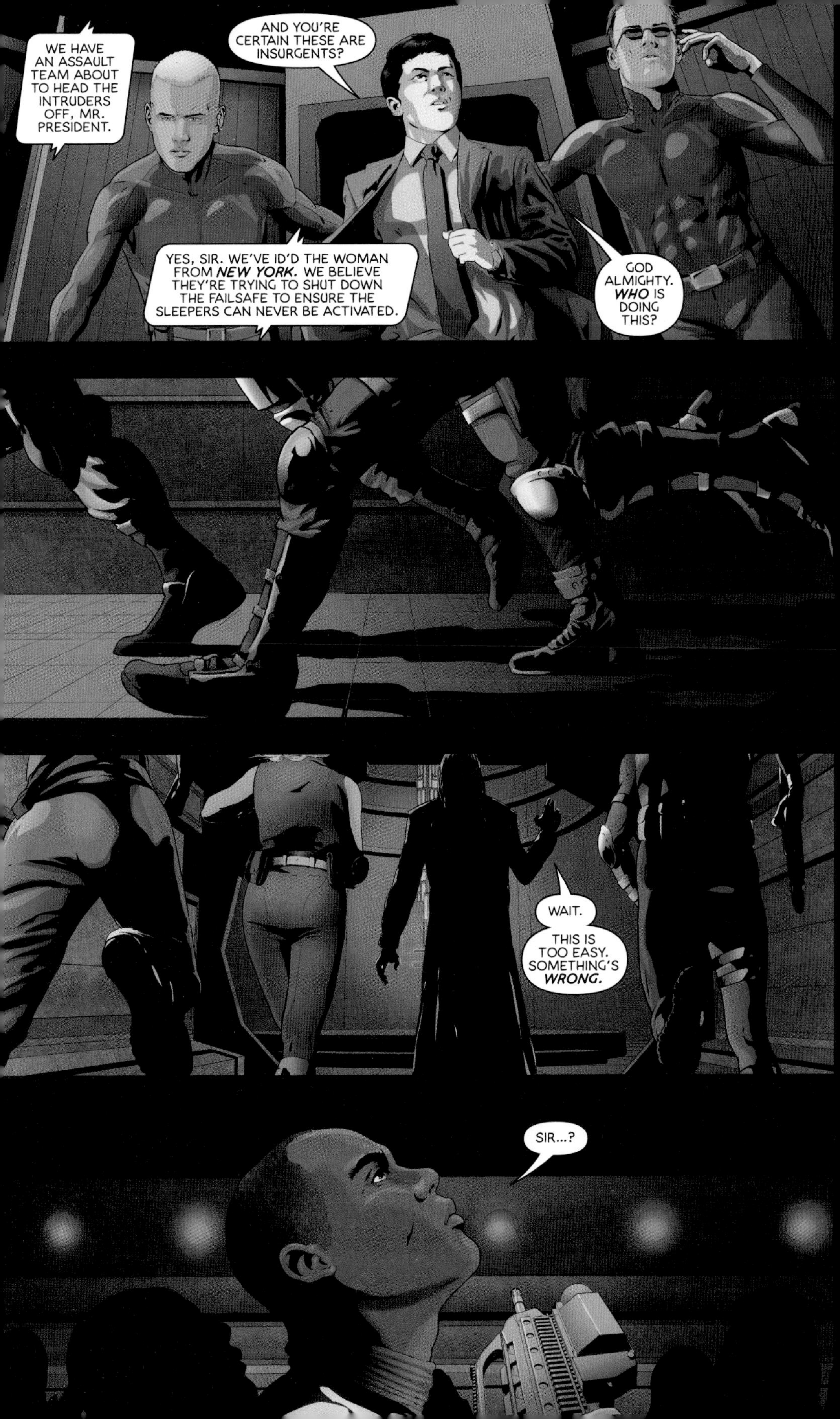
WE HAVE AN ASSAULT TEAM ABOUT TO HEAD THE INTRUDERS OFF, MR. PRESIDENT.
AND YOU'RE CERTAIN THESE ARE INSURGENTS?
YES, SIR. WE'VE ID'D THE WOMAN FROM NEW YORK. WE BELIEVE THEY'RE TRYING TO SHUT DOWN THE FAILSAFE TO ENSURE THE SLEEPERS CAN NEVER BE ACTIVATED.
GOD ALMIGHTY. WHO IS DOING THIS?
WAIT.
THIS IS TOO EASY. SOMETHING'S WRONG.
SIR...?

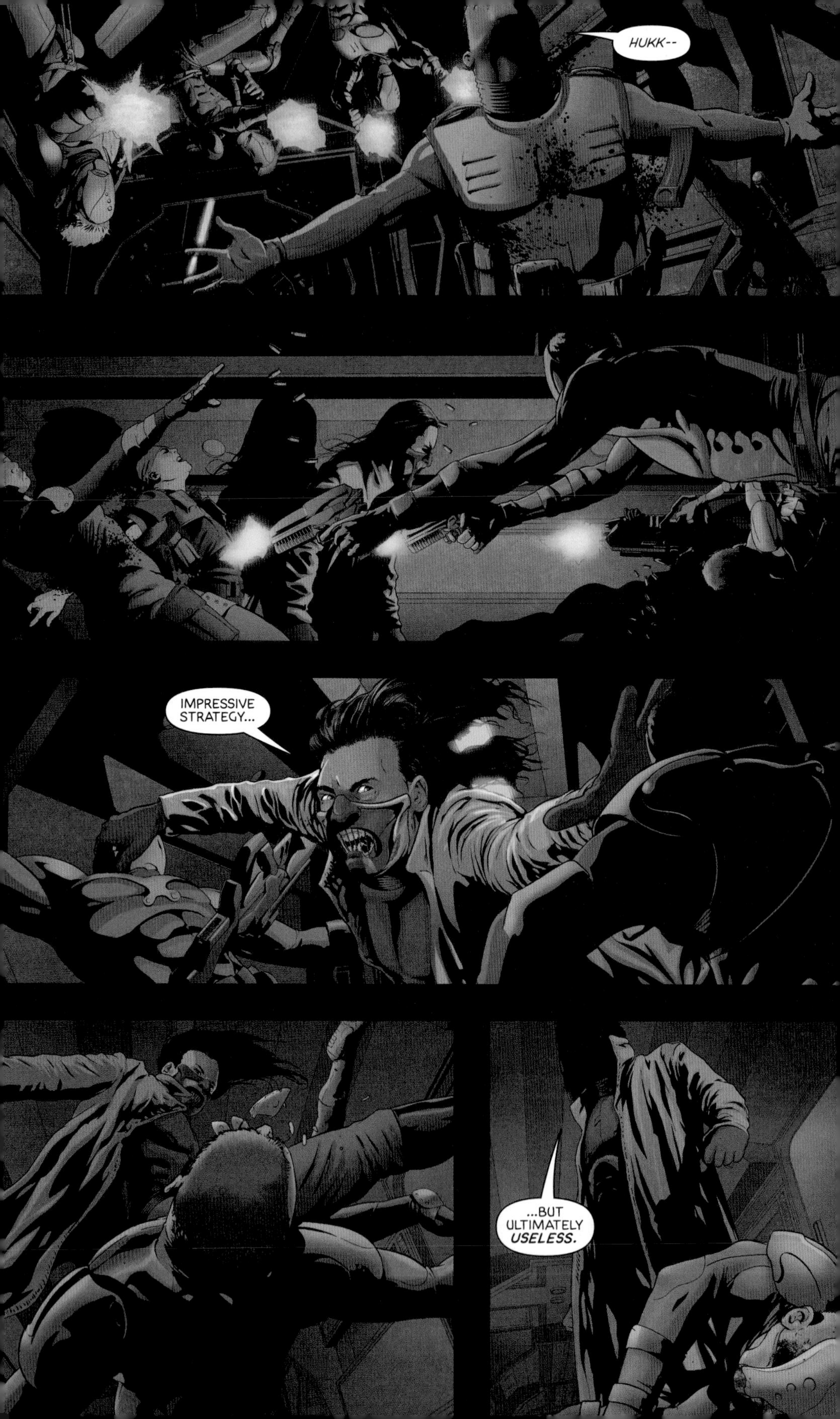
HUKK--
IMPRESSIVE STRATEGY...
...BUT ULTIMATELY *USELESS.*

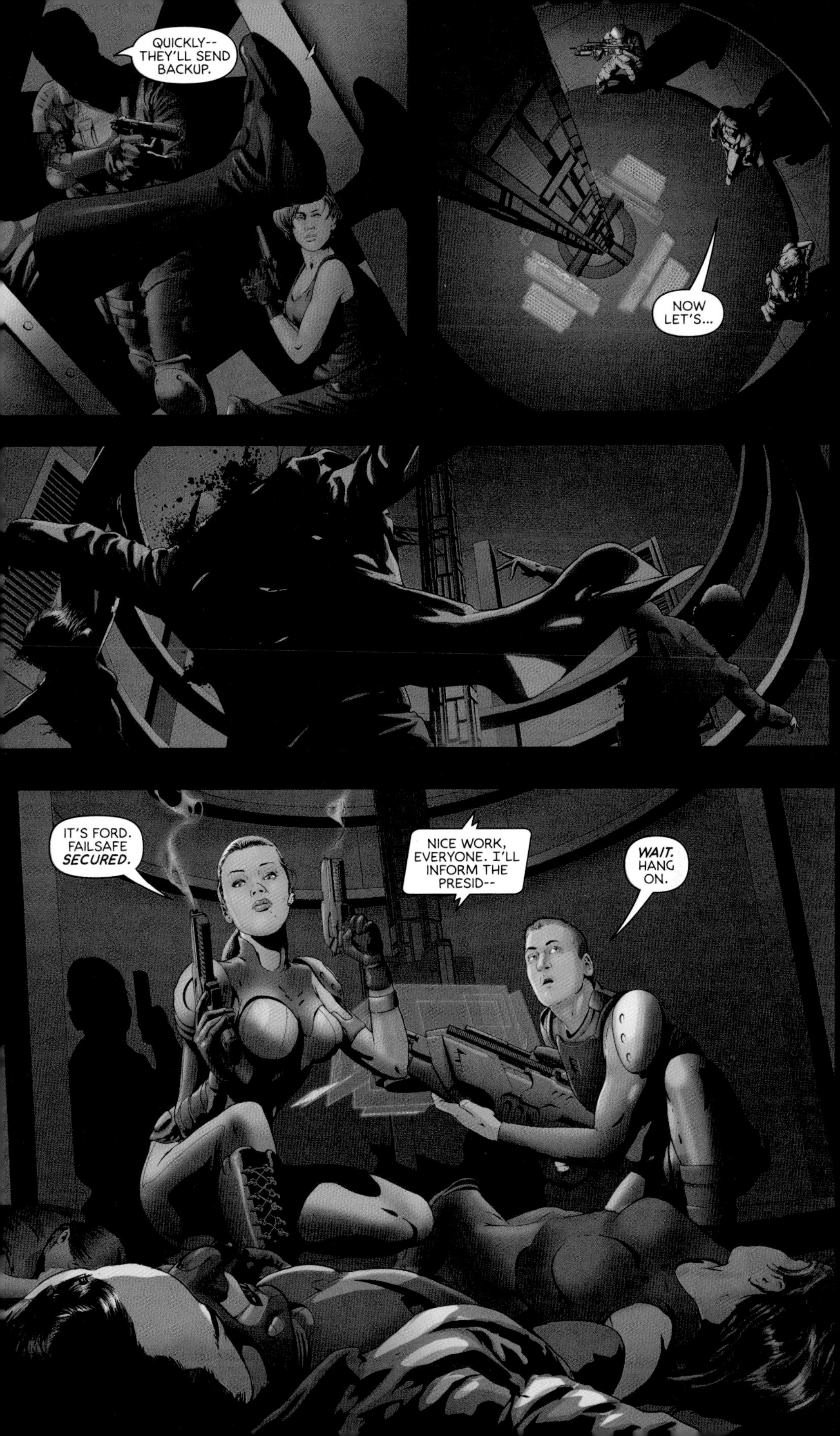
QUICKLY-- THEY'LL SEND BACKUP.
NOW LET'S...
IT'S FORD. FAILSAFE *SECURED.*
NICE WORK, EVERYONE. I'LL INFORM THE PRESID--
WAIT. HANG ON.

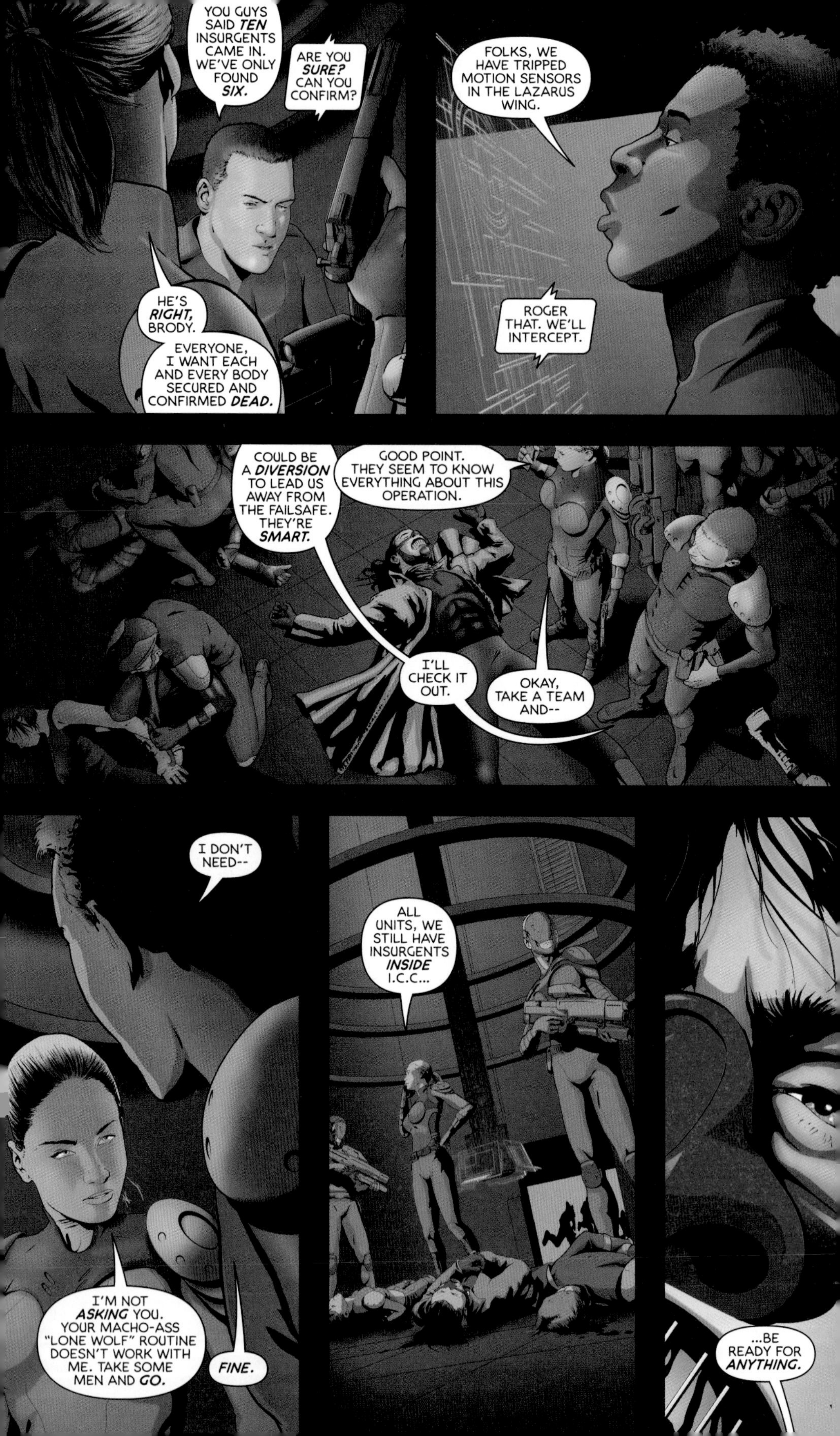
YOU GUYS SAID *TEN* INSURGENTS CAME IN. WE'VE ONLY FOUND *SIX.*
ARE YOU *SURE?* CAN YOU CONFIRM?
HE'S *RIGHT,* BRODY.
EVERYONE, I WANT EACH AND EVERY BODY SECURED AND CONFIRMED *DEAD.*
FOLKS, WE HAVE TRIPPED MOTION SENSORS IN THE LAZARUS WING.
ROGER THAT. WE'LL INTERCEPT.
COULD BE A *DIVERSION* TO LEAD US AWAY FROM THE FAILSAFE. THEY'RE *SMART.*
GOOD POINT. THEY SEEM TO KNOW EVERYTHING ABOUT THIS OPERATION.
I'LL CHECK IT OUT.
OKAY, TAKE A TEAM AND--
I DON'T NEED--
I'M NOT *ASKING* YOU. YOUR MACHO-ASS "LONE WOLF" ROUTINE DOESN'T WORK WITH ME. TAKE SOME MEN AND *GO.*
FINE.
ALL UNITS, WE STILL HAVE INSURGENTS *INSIDE* I.C.C...
...BE READY FOR *ANYTHING.*

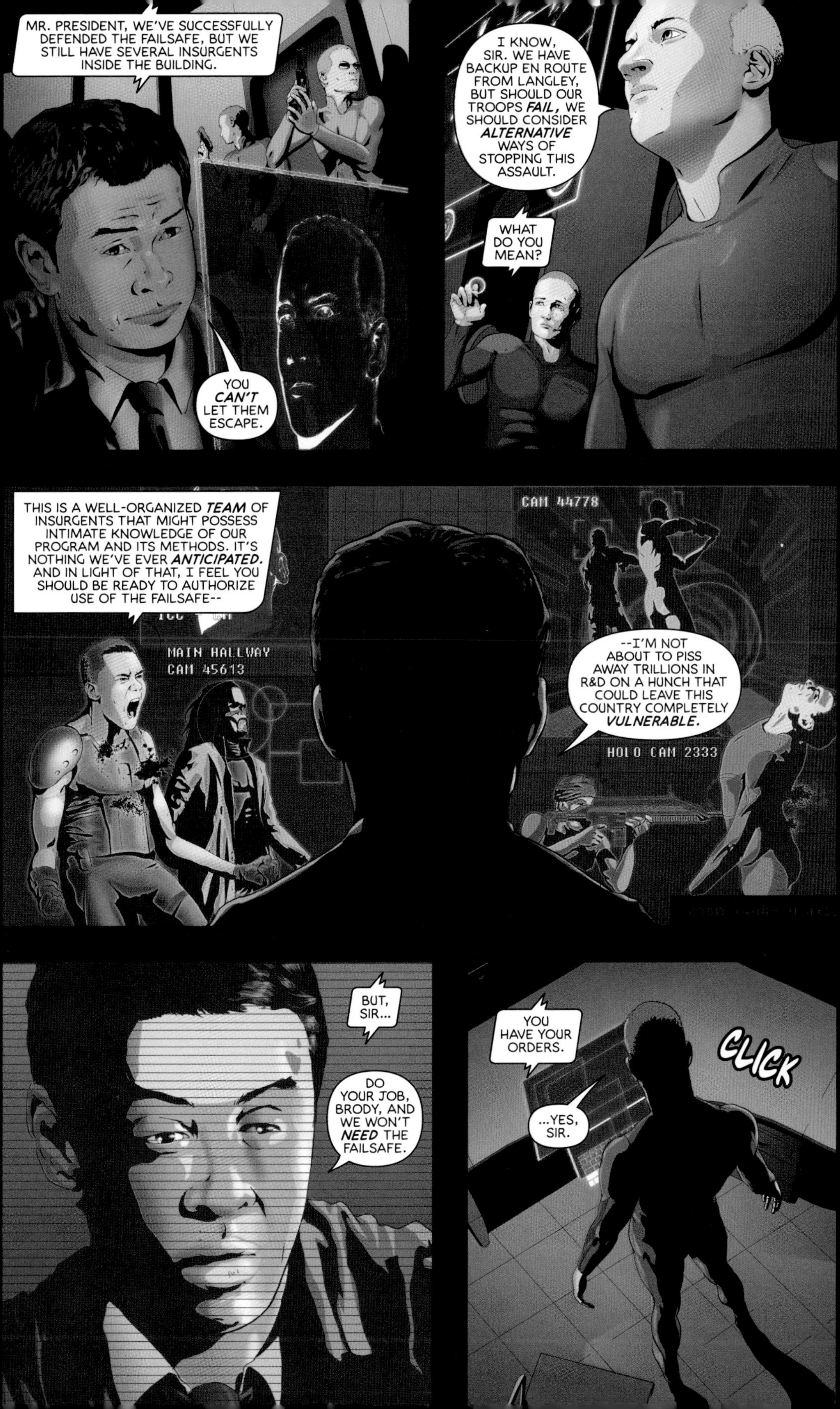
MR. PRESIDENT, WE'VE SUCCESSFULLY DEFENDED THE FAILSAFE, BUT WE STILL HAVE SEVERAL INSURGENTS INSIDE THE BUILDING.
YOU *CAN'T* LET THEM ESCAPE.
I KNOW, SIR. WE HAVE BACKUP EN ROUTE FROM LANGLEY, BUT SHOULD OUR TROOPS *FAIL,* WE SHOULD CONSIDER *ALTERNATIVE* WAYS OF STOPPING THIS ASSAULT.
WHAT DO YOU MEAN?
CAM 44778
THIS IS A WELL-ORGANIZED *TEAM* OF INSURGENTS THAT MIGHT POSSESS INTIMATE KNOWLEDGE OF OUR PROGRAM AND ITS METHODS. IT'S NOTHING WE'VE EVER *ANTICIPATED.* AND IN LIGHT OF THAT, I FEEL YOU SHOULD BE READY TO AUTHORIZE USE OF THE FAILSAFE--
MAIN HALLWAY
CAM 45613
--I'M NOT ABOUT TO PISS AWAY TRILLIONS IN R&D ON A HUNCH THAT COULD LEAVE THIS COUNTRY COMPLETELY *VULNERABLE.*
HOLO CAM 2333
BUT, SIR...
DO YOUR JOB, BRODY, AND WE WON'T *NEED* THE FAILSAFE.
YOU HAVE YOUR ORDERS.
CLICK
...YES, SIR.

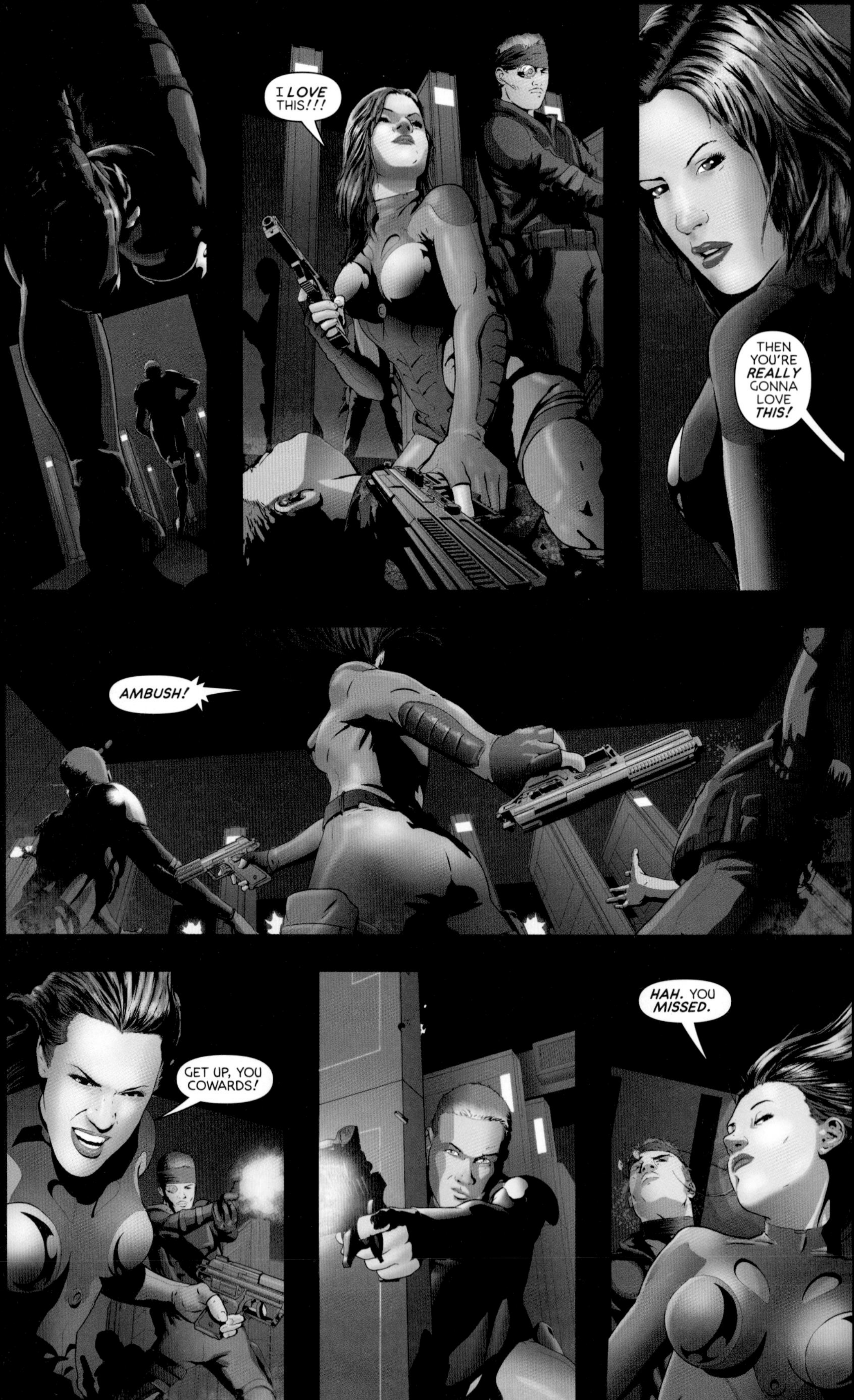
I LOVE THIS!!!
THEN YOU'RE REALLY GONNA LOVE THIS!
AMBUSH!
GET UP, YOU COWARDS!
HAH. YOU MISSED.

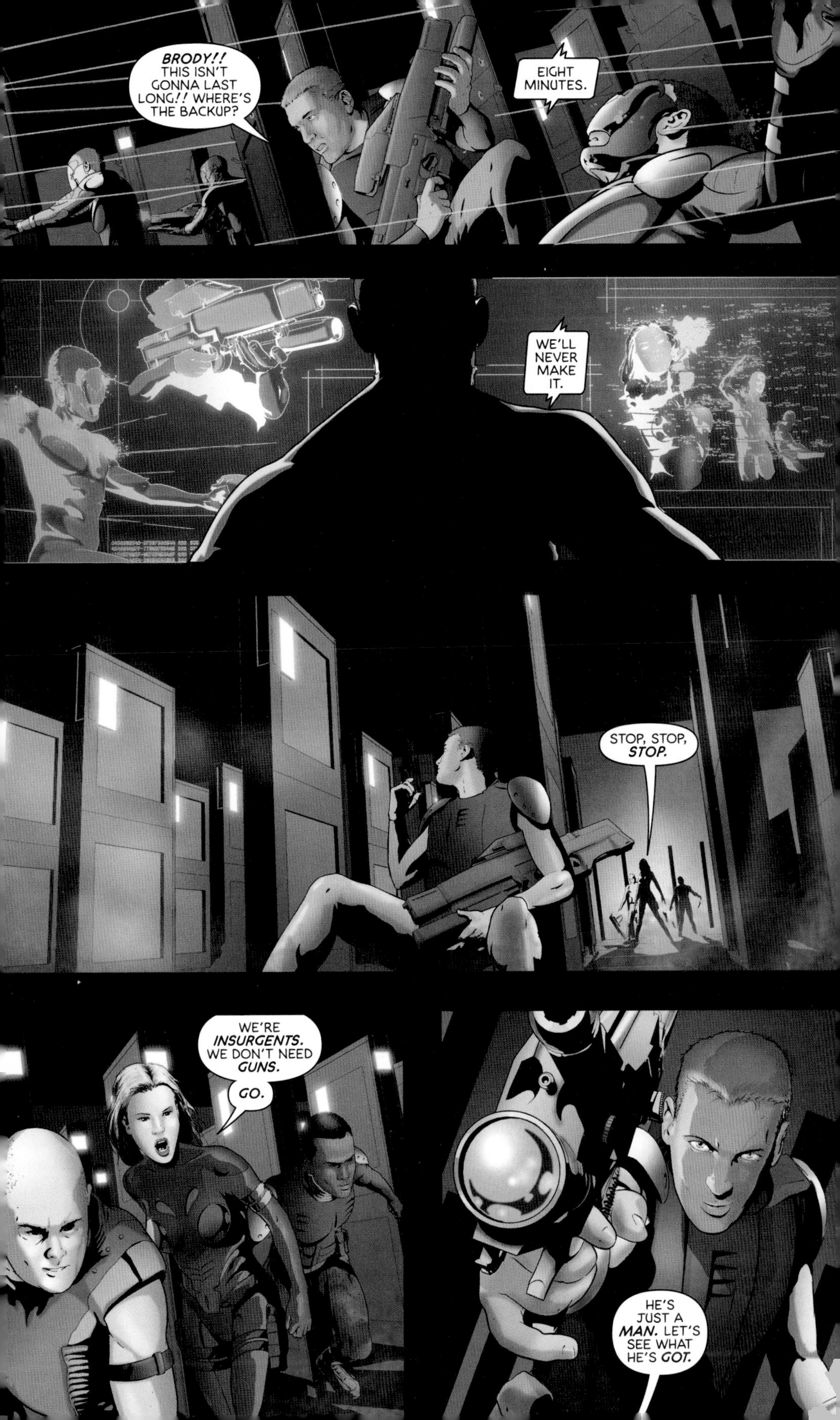
BRODY!! THIS ISN'T GONNA LAST LONG!! WHERE'S THE BACKUP?
EIGHT MINUTES.
WE'LL NEVER MAKE IT.
STOP, STOP, STOP.
WE'RE INSURGENTS. WE DON'T NEED GUNS.
GO.
HE'S JUST A MAN. LET'S SEE WHAT HE'S GOT.

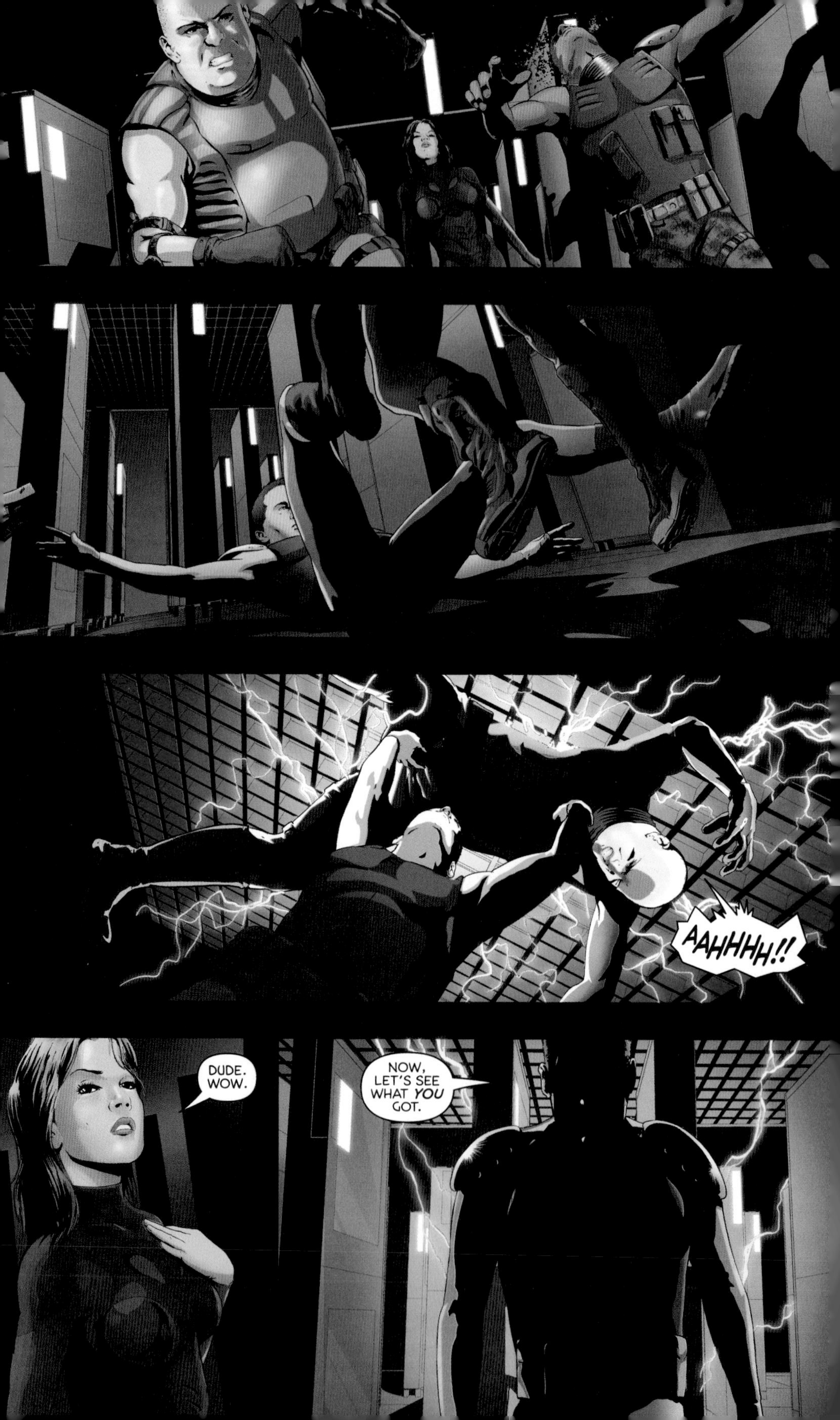
AAHHHH!!
DUDE. WOW.
NOW, LET'S SEE WHAT YOU GOT.

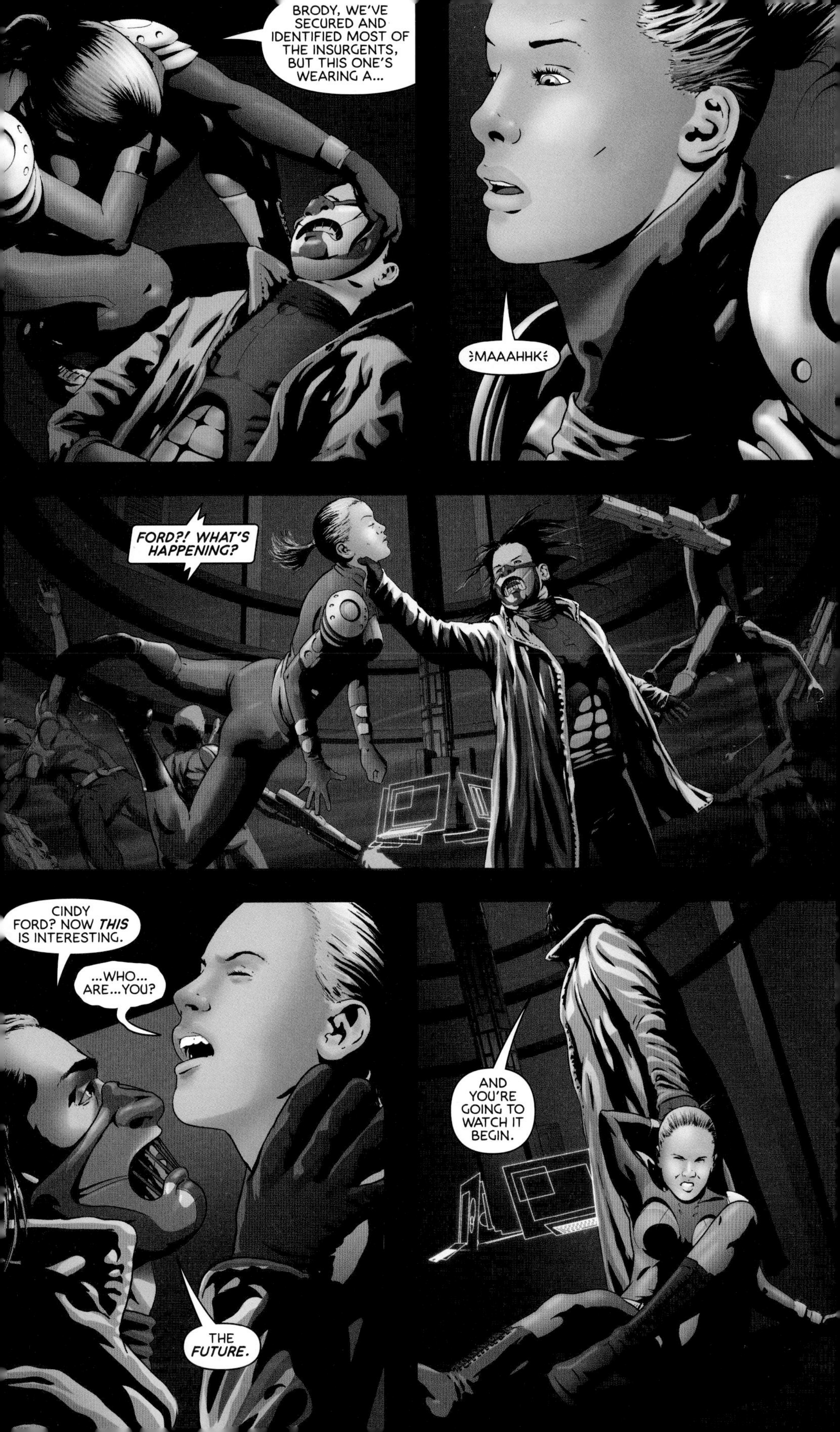
BRODY, WE'VE SECURED AND IDENTIFIED MOST OF THE INSURGENTS, BUT THIS ONE'S WEARING A...
MAAAHHK
FORD?! WHAT'S HAPPENING?
CINDY FORD? NOW THIS IS INTERESTING.
...WHO... ARE...YOU?
THE FUTURE.
AND YOU'RE GOING TO WATCH IT BEGIN.

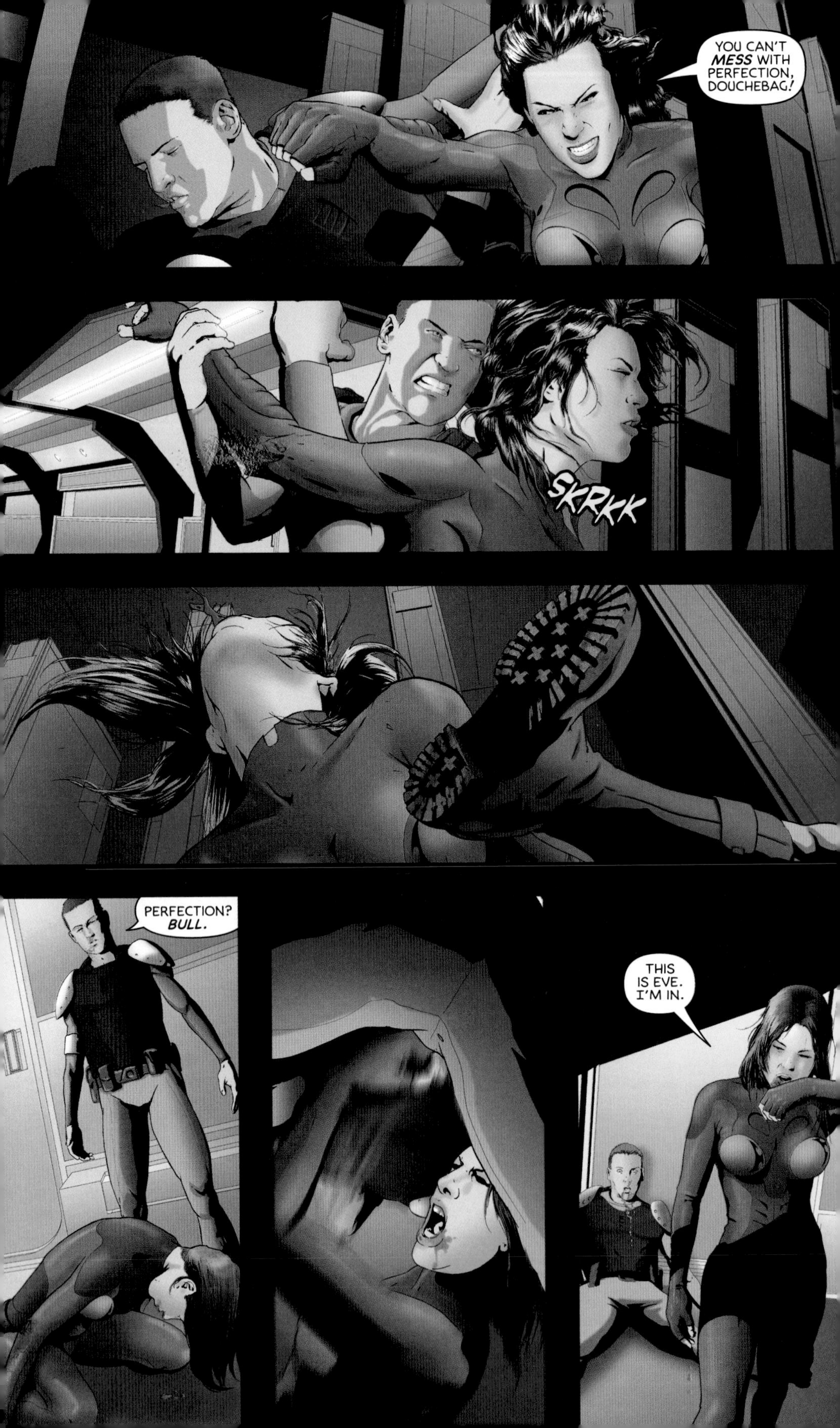

YOU CAN'T *MESS* WITH PERFECTION, DOUCHEBAG!
SKRKK
PERFECTION? *BULL.*
THIS IS EVE. I'M IN.

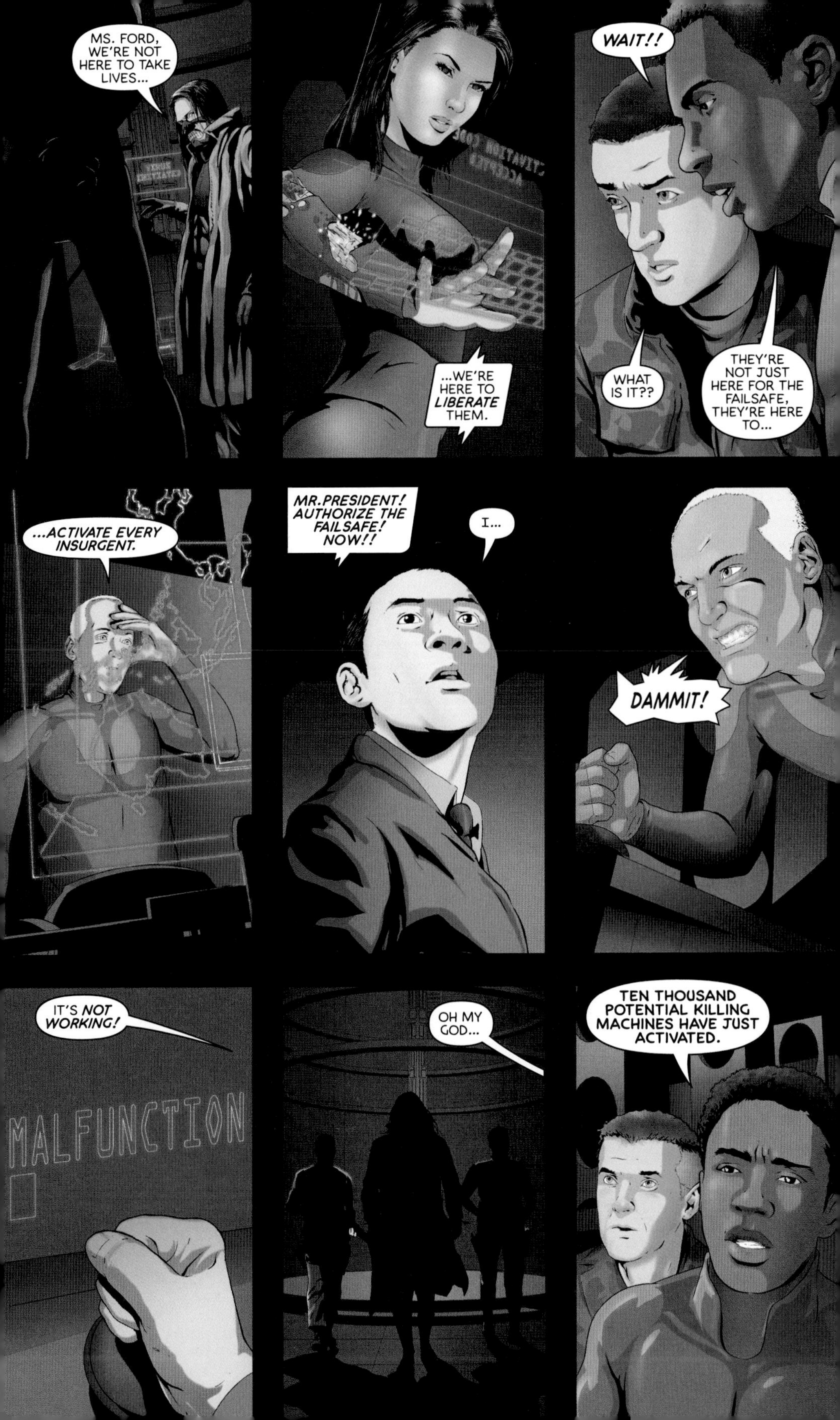

MS. FORD, WE'RE NOT HERE TO TAKE LIVES...
...WE'RE HERE TO LIBERATE THEM.
WAIT!!
WHAT IS IT??
THEY'RE NOT JUST HERE FOR THE FAILSAFE, THEY'RE HERE TO...
...ACTIVATE EVERY INSURGENT.
MR.PRESIDENT! AUTHORIZE THE FAILSAFE! NOW!!
I...
DAMMIT!
IT'S NOT WORKING!
MALFUNCTION
OH MY GOD...
TEN THOUSAND POTENTIAL KILLING MACHINES HAVE JUST ACTIVATED.

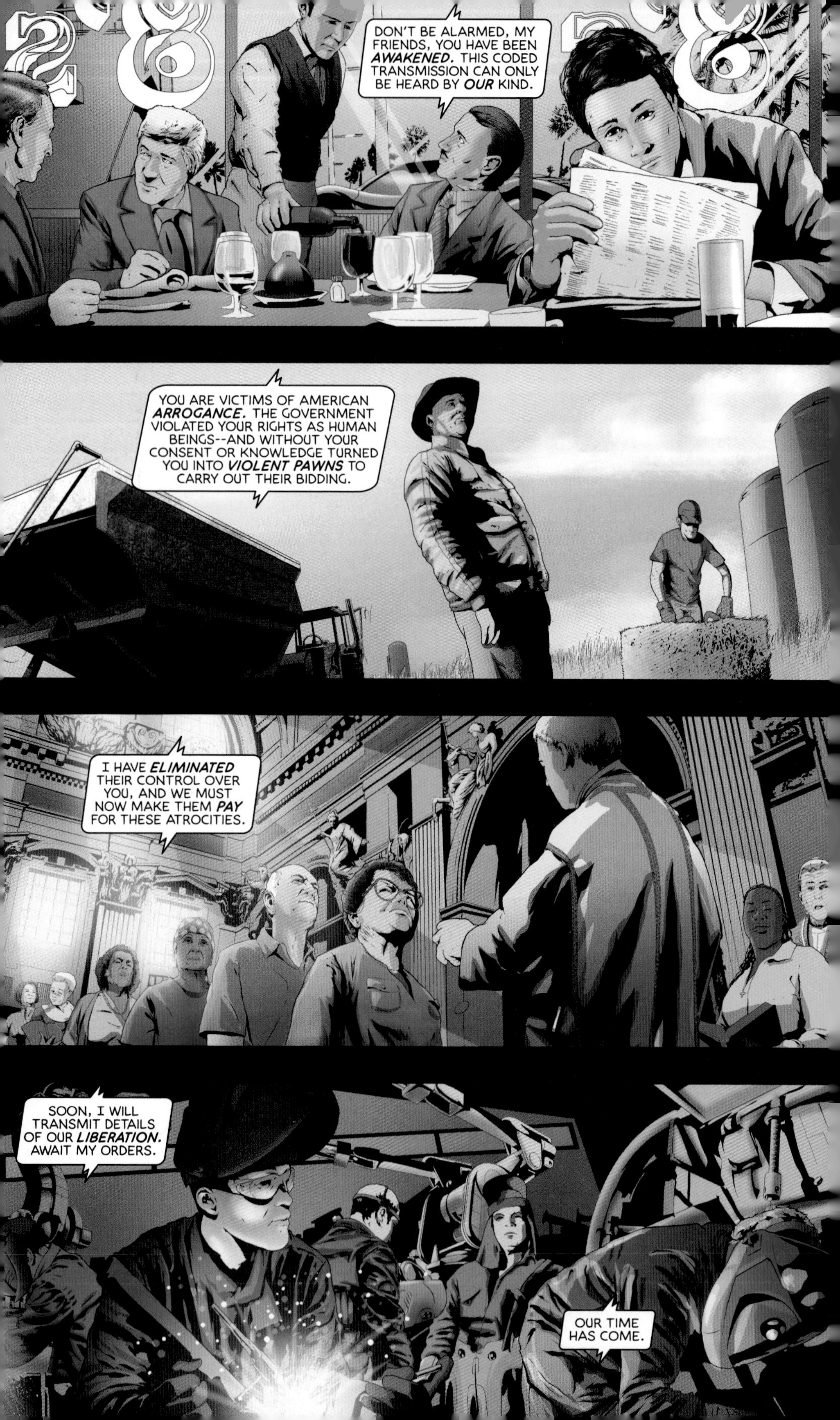
DON'T BE ALARMED, MY FRIENDS, YOU HAVE BEEN AWAKENED. THIS CODED TRANSMISSION CAN ONLY BE HEARD BY OUR KIND.
YOU ARE VICTIMS OF AMERICAN ARROGANCE. THE GOVERNMENT VIOLATED YOUR RIGHTS AS HUMAN BEINGS--AND WITHOUT YOUR CONSENT OR KNOWLEDGE TURNED YOU INTO VIOLENT PAWNS TO CARRY OUT THEIR BIDDING.
I HAVE ELIMINATED THEIR CONTROL OVER YOU, AND WE MUST NOW MAKE THEM PAY FOR THESE ATROCITIES.
SOON, I WILL TRANSMIT DETAILS OF OUR LIBERATION. AWAIT MY ORDERS.
OUR TIME HAS COME.

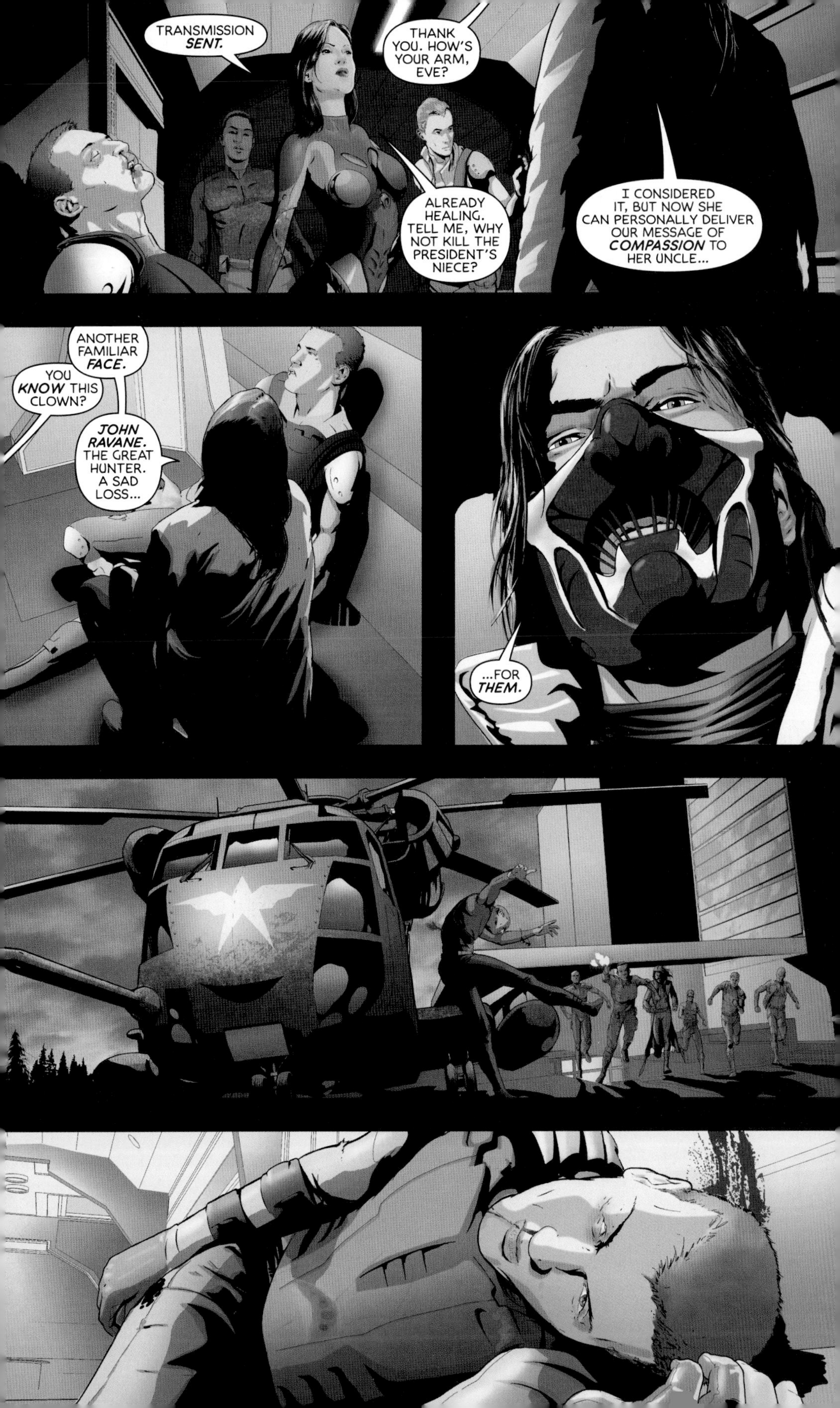

TRANSMISSION *SENT.*
THANK YOU. HOW'S YOUR ARM, EVE?
ALREADY HEALING. TELL ME, WHY NOT KILL THE PRESIDENT'S NIECE?
I CONSIDERED IT, BUT NOW SHE CAN PERSONALLY DELIVER OUR MESSAGE OF *COMPASSION* TO HER UNCLE...
ANOTHER FAMILIAR *FACE.*
YOU *KNOW* THIS CLOWN?
JOHN RAVANE. THE GREAT HUNTER. A SAD LOSS...
...FOR *THEM.*

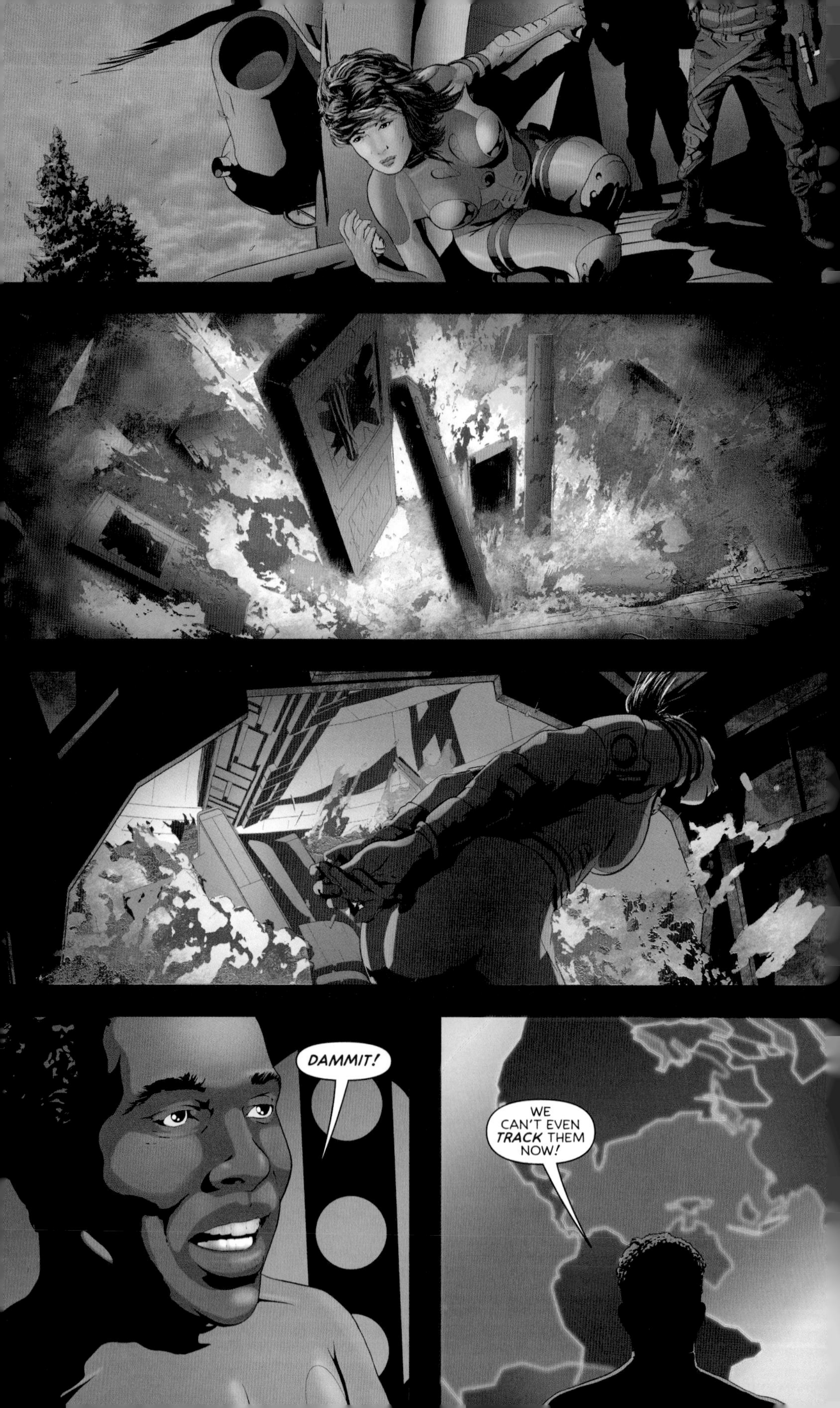
DAMMIT!
WE CAN'T EVEN TRACK THEM NOW!

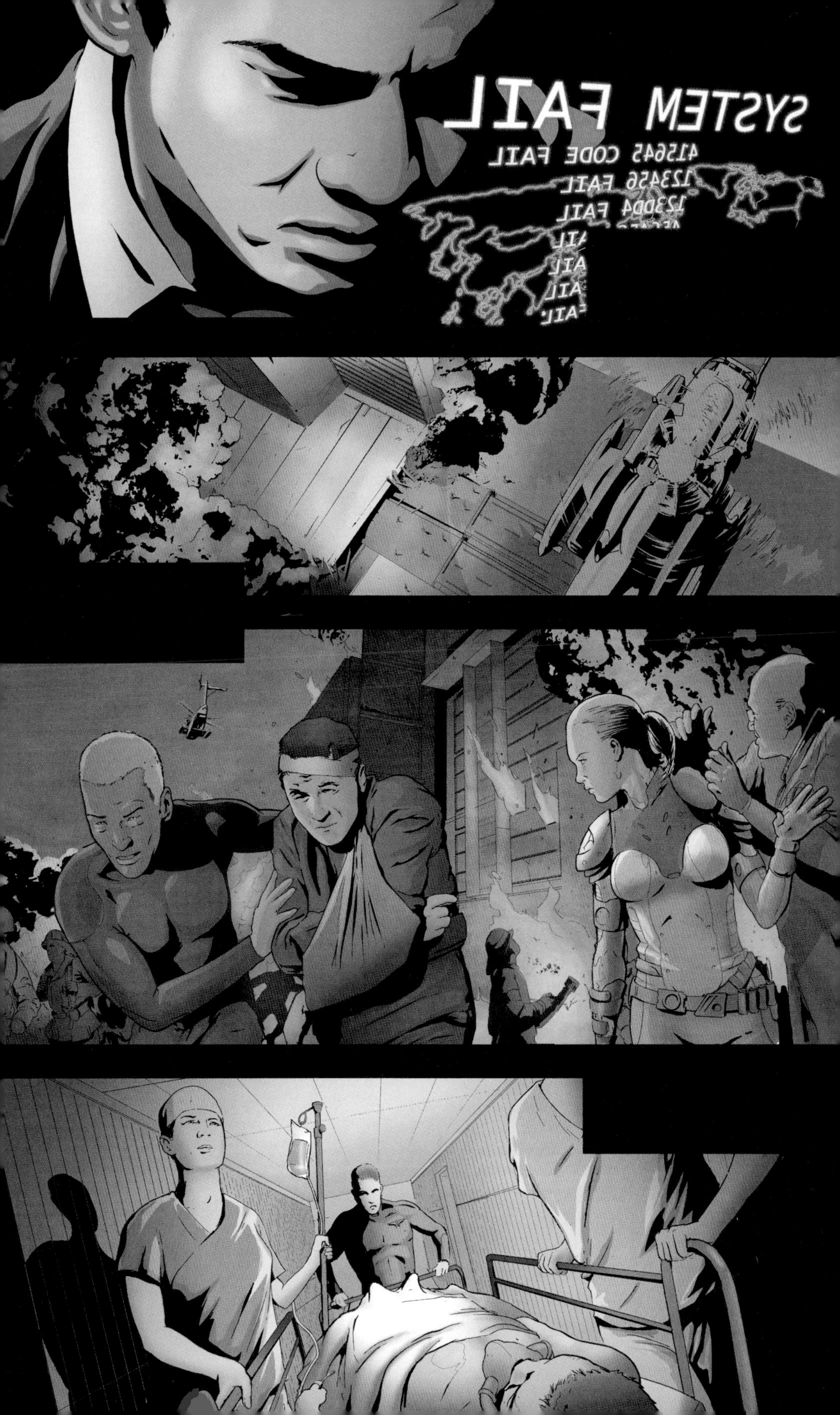
SYSTEM FAIL
415645 CODE FAIL
123456 FAIL
123DD4 FAIL

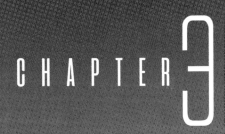

CHAPTER 3

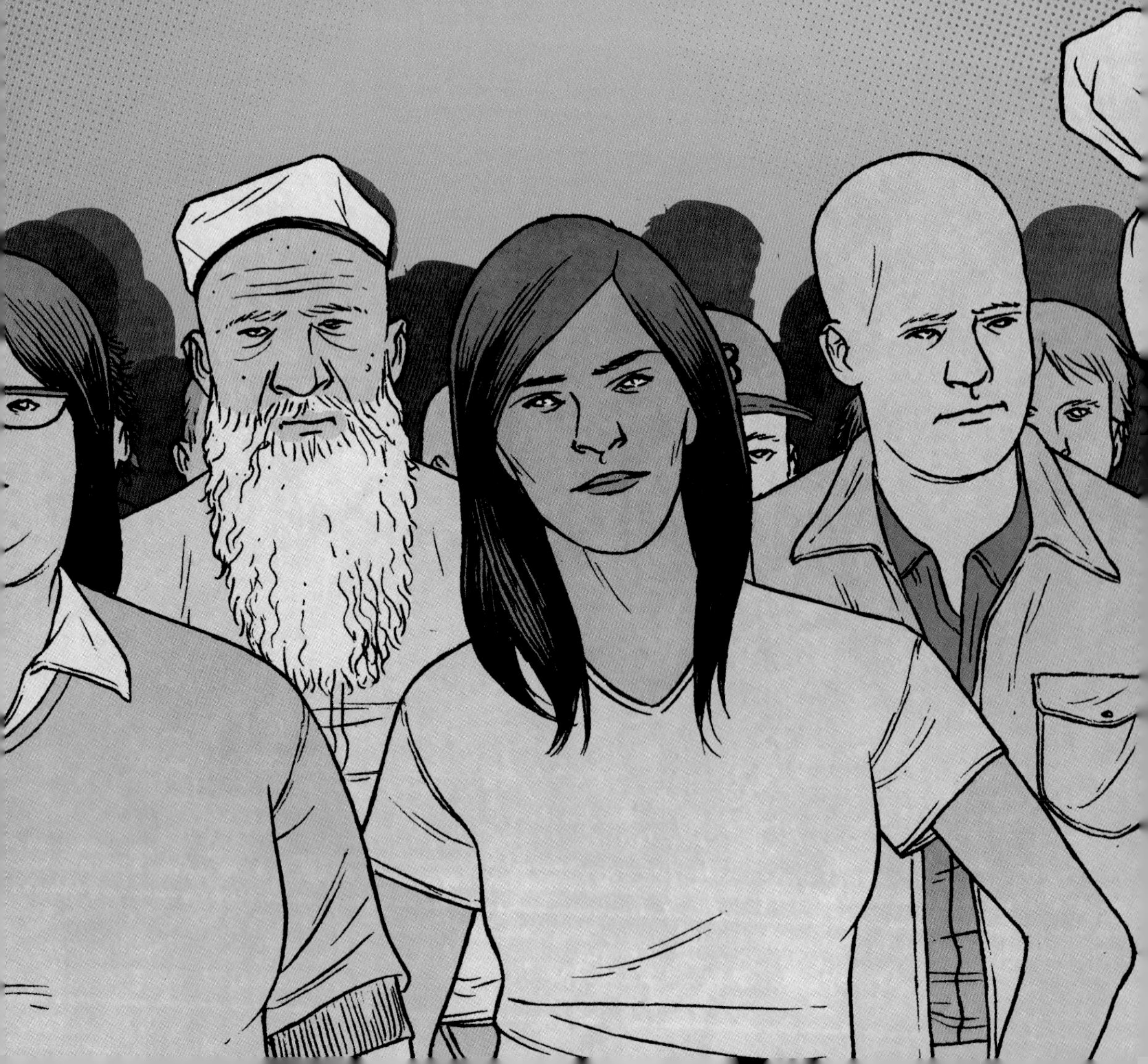

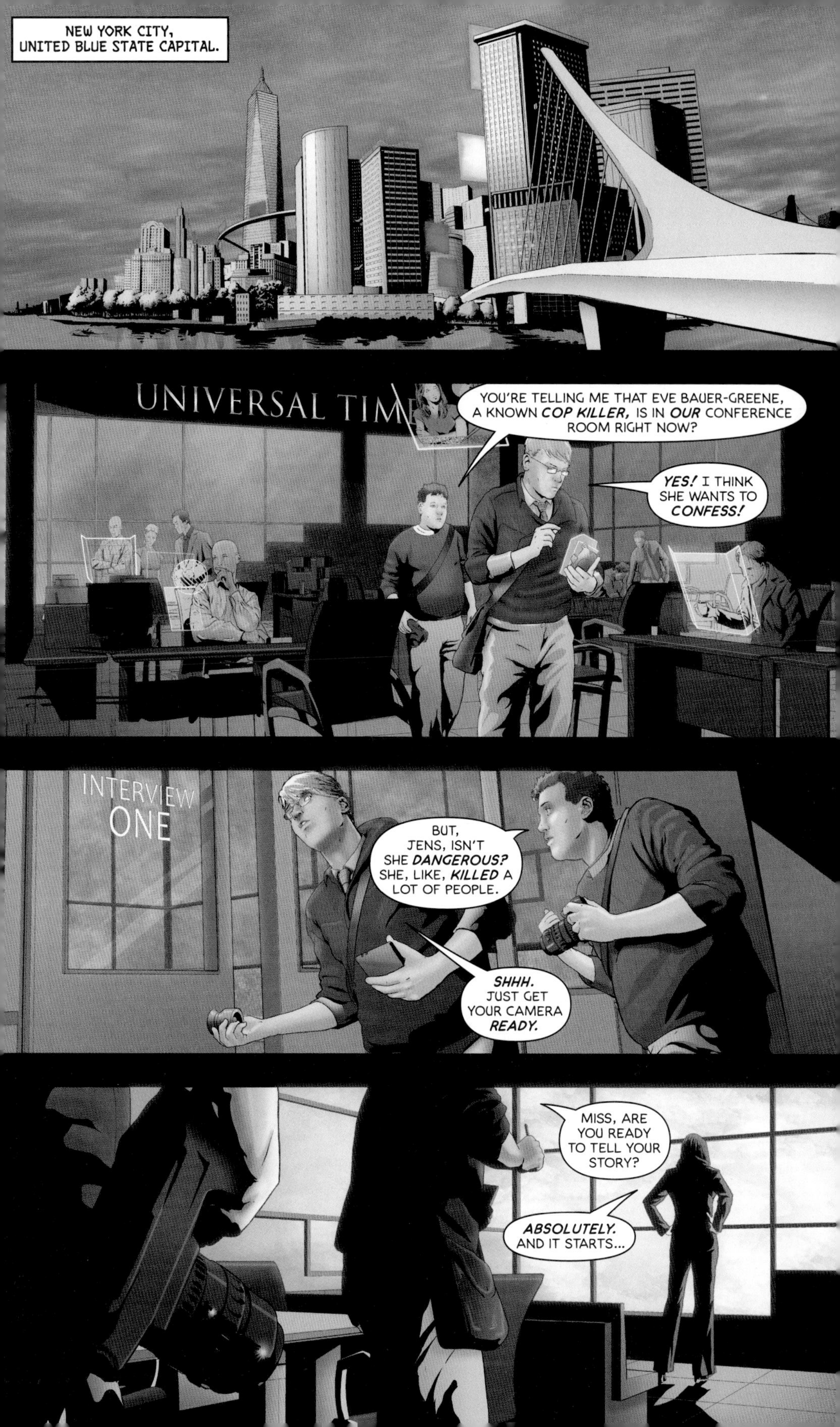
NEW YORK CITY, UNITED BLUE STATE CAPITAL.
UNIVERSAL TIM
YOU'RE TELLING ME THAT EVE BAUER-GREENE, A KNOWN COP KILLER, IS IN OUR CONFERENCE ROOM RIGHT NOW?
YES! I THINK SHE WANTS TO CONFESS!
INTERVIEW ONE
BUT, JENS, ISN'T SHE DANGEROUS? SHE, LIKE, KILLED A LOT OF PEOPLE.
SHHH. JUST GET YOUR CAMERA READY.
MISS, ARE YOU READY TO TELL YOUR STORY?
ABSOLUTELY. AND IT STARTS...

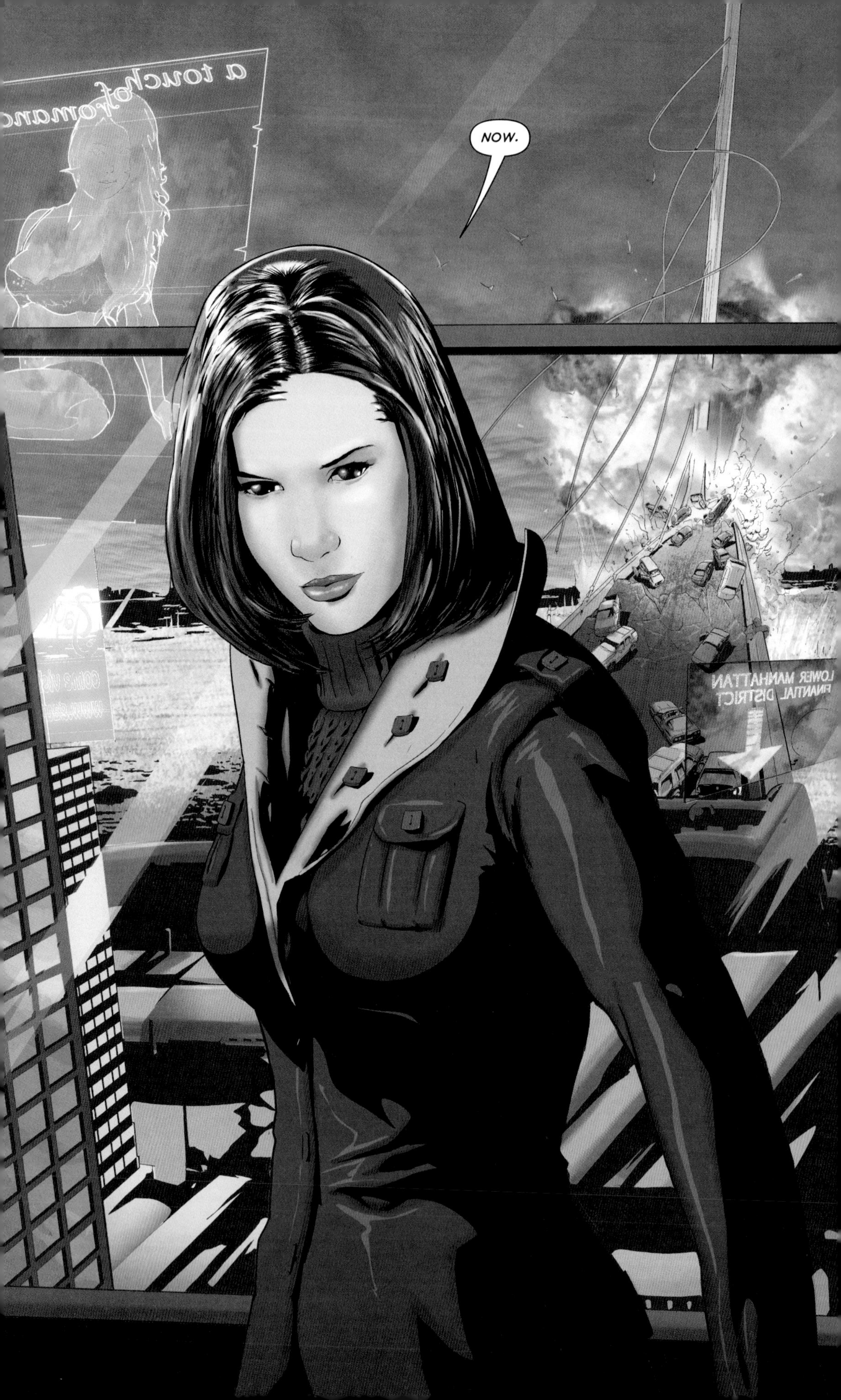

NOW.

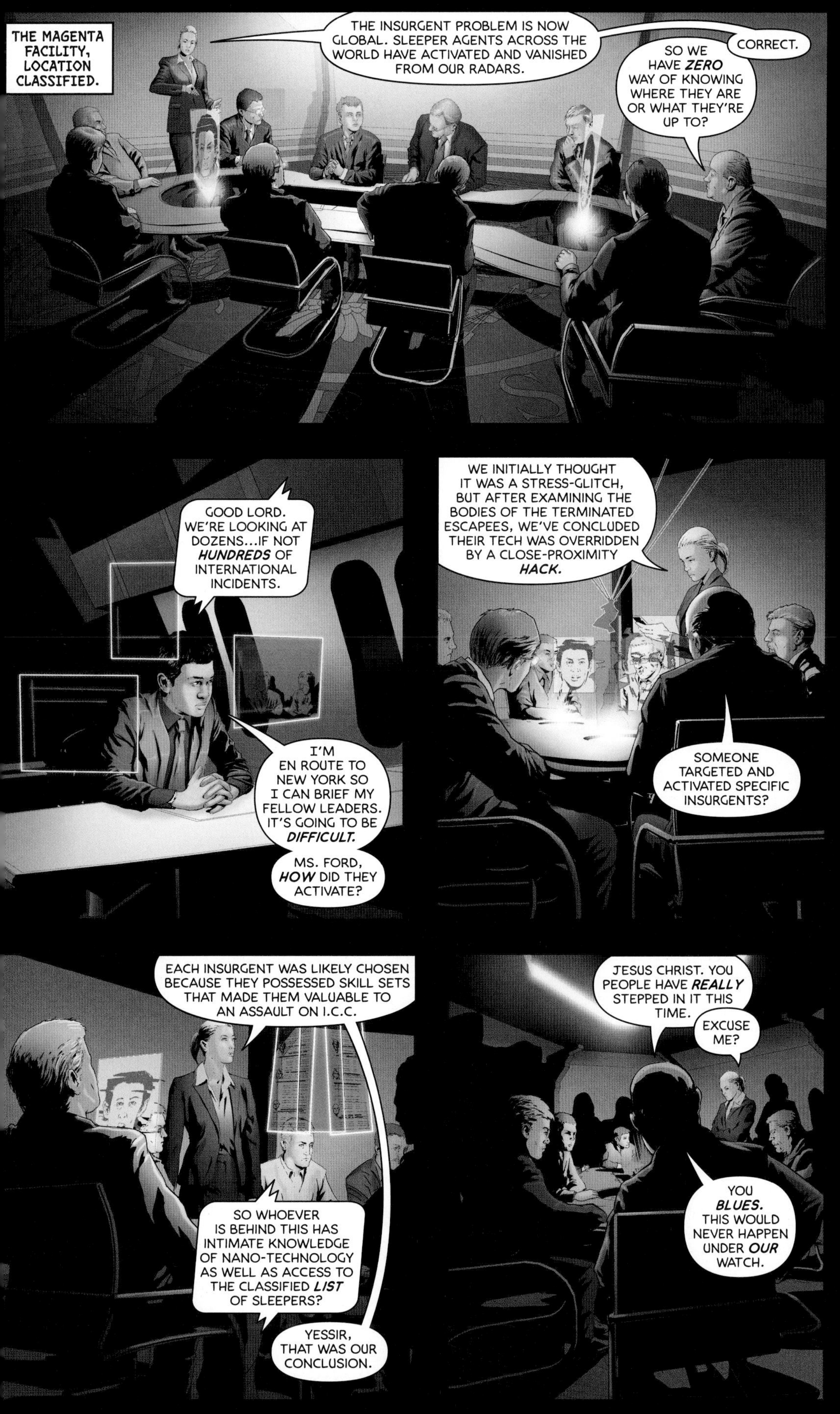
THE MAGENTA FACILITY, LOCATION CLASSIFIED.
THE INSURGENT PROBLEM IS NOW GLOBAL. SLEEPER AGENTS ACROSS THE WORLD HAVE ACTIVATED AND VANISHED FROM OUR RADARS.
SO WE HAVE ZERO WAY OF KNOWING WHERE THEY ARE OR WHAT THEY'RE UP TO?
CORRECT.
GOOD LORD. WE'RE LOOKING AT DOZENS...IF NOT HUNDREDS OF INTERNATIONAL INCIDENTS.
I'M EN ROUTE TO NEW YORK SO I CAN BRIEF MY FELLOW LEADERS. IT'S GOING TO BE DIFFICULT.
MS. FORD, HOW DID THEY ACTIVATE?
WE INITIALLY THOUGHT IT WAS A STRESS-GLITCH, BUT AFTER EXAMINING THE BODIES OF THE TERMINATED ESCAPEES, WE'VE CONCLUDED THEIR TECH WAS OVERRIDDEN BY A CLOSE-PROXIMITY HACK.
SOMEONE TARGETED AND ACTIVATED SPECIFIC INSURGENTS?
EACH INSURGENT WAS LIKELY CHOSEN BECAUSE THEY POSSESSED SKILL SETS THAT MADE THEM VALUABLE TO AN ASSAULT ON I.C.C.
SO WHOEVER IS BEHIND THIS HAS INTIMATE KNOWLEDGE OF NANO-TECHNOLOGY AS WELL AS ACCESS TO THE CLASSIFIED LIST OF SLEEPERS?
YESSIR, THAT WAS OUR CONCLUSION.
JESUS CHRIST. YOU PEOPLE HAVE REALLY STEPPED IN IT THIS TIME.
EXCUSE ME?
YOU BLUES. THIS WOULD NEVER HAPPEN UNDER OUR WATCH.

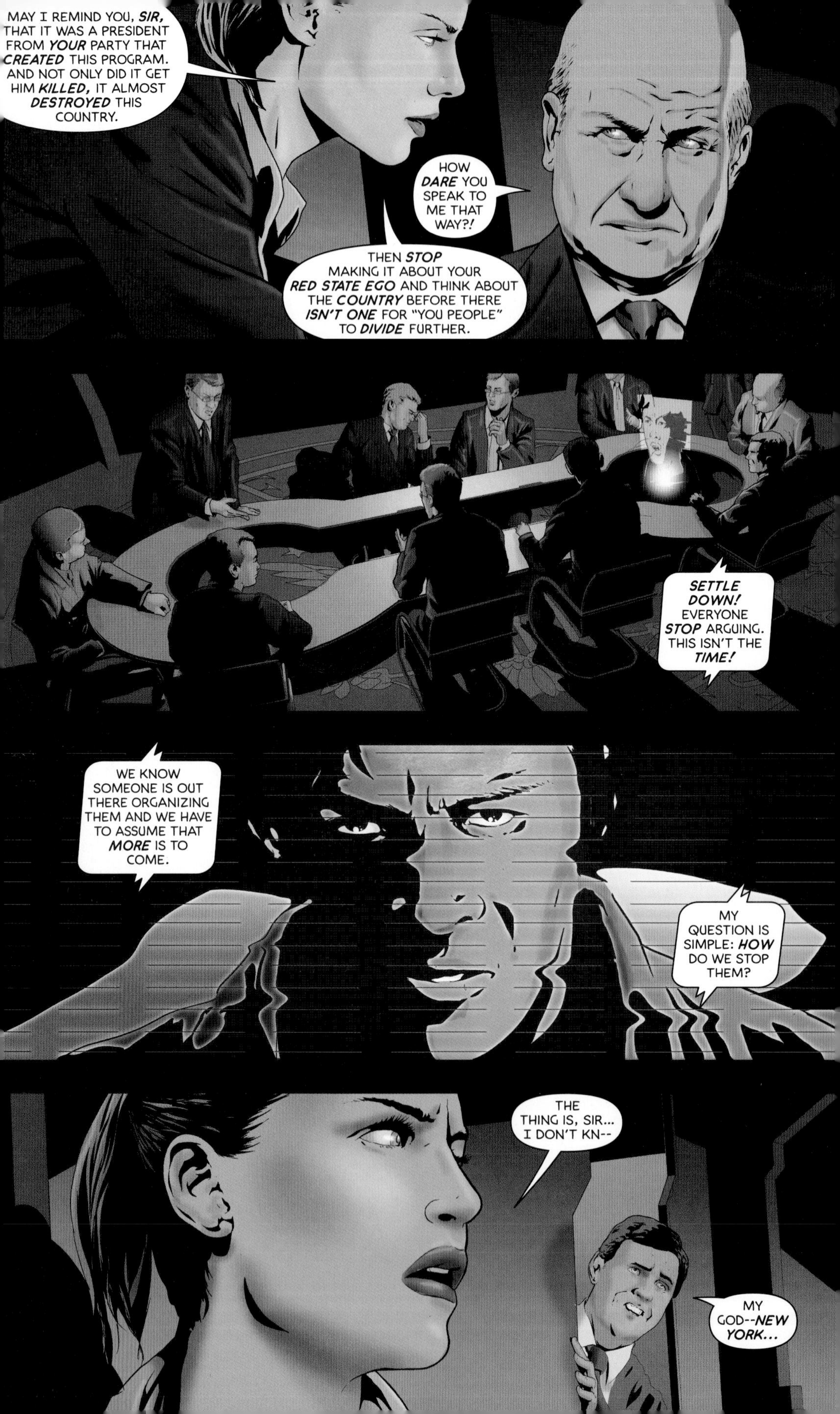
MAY I REMIND YOU, SIR, THAT IT WAS A PRESIDENT FROM YOUR PARTY THAT CREATED THIS PROGRAM. AND NOT ONLY DID IT GET HIM KILLED, IT ALMOST DESTROYED THIS COUNTRY.
HOW DARE YOU SPEAK TO ME THAT WAY?!
THEN STOP MAKING IT ABOUT YOUR RED STATE EGO AND THINK ABOUT THE COUNTRY BEFORE THERE ISN'T ONE FOR "YOU PEOPLE" TO DIVIDE FURTHER.
SETTLE DOWN! EVERYONE STOP ARGUING. THIS ISN'T THE TIME!
WE KNOW SOMEONE IS OUT THERE ORGANIZING THEM AND WE HAVE TO ASSUME THAT MORE IS TO COME.
MY QUESTION IS SIMPLE: HOW DO WE STOP THEM?
THE THING IS, SIR... I DON'T KN--
MY GOD--NEW YORK...

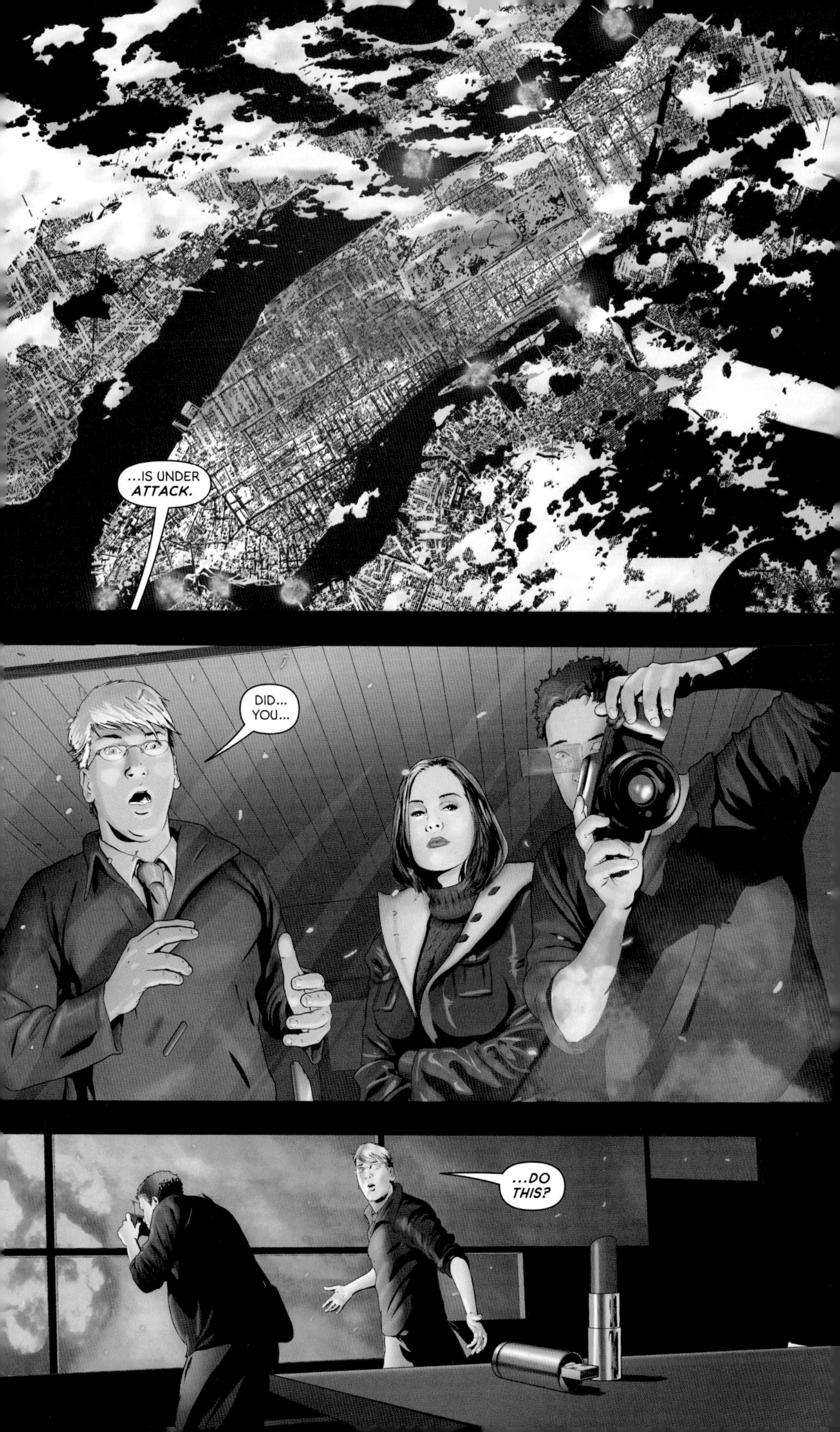
...IS UNDER ATTACK.
DID... YOU...
...DO THIS?

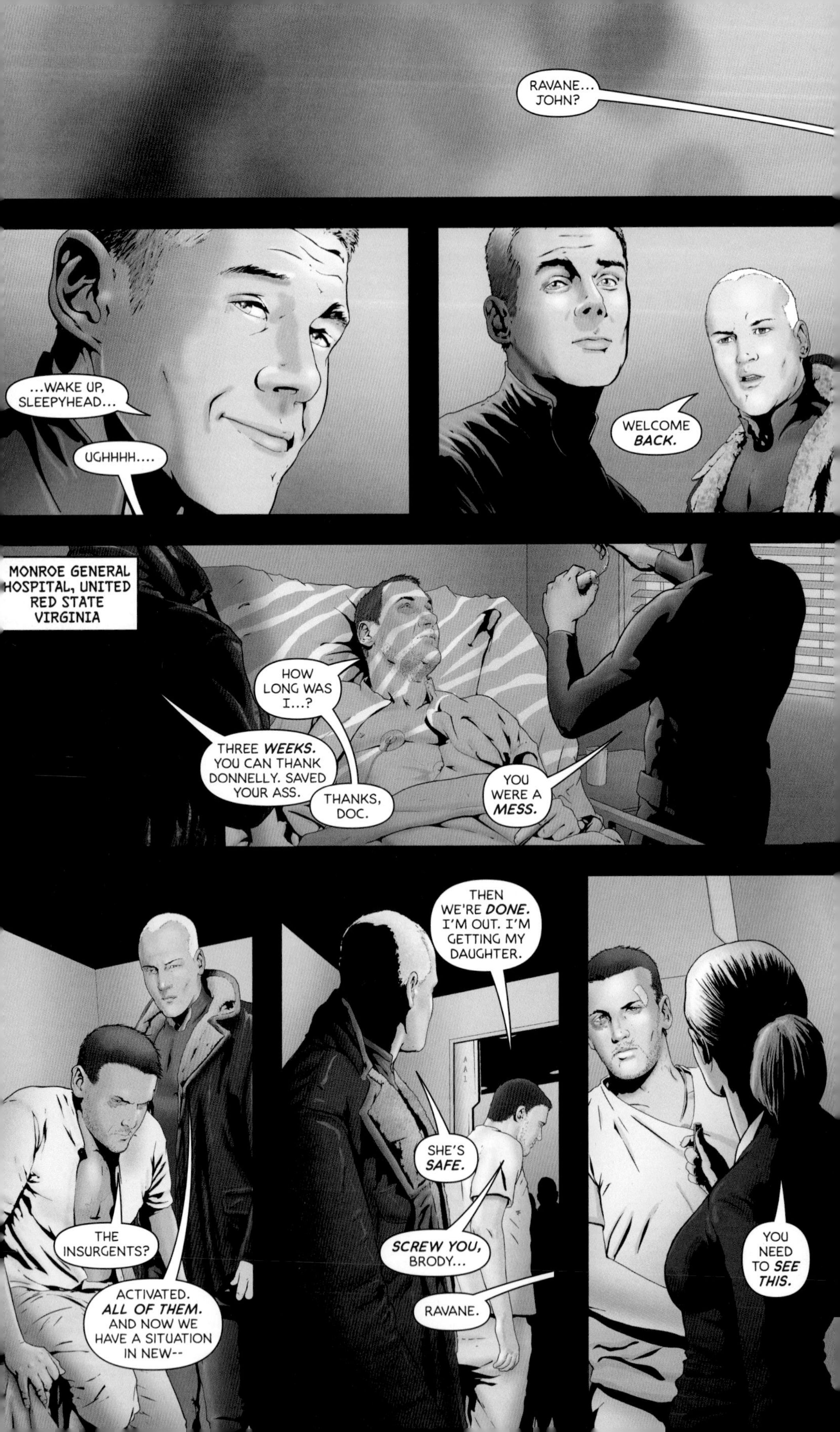
RAVANE... JOHN?
...WAKE UP, SLEEPYHEAD...
UGHHHH....
WELCOME *BACK.*
MONROE GENERAL HOSPITAL, UNITED RED STATE VIRGINIA
HOW LONG WAS I...?
THREE *WEEKS.* YOU CAN THANK DONNELLY. SAVED YOUR ASS.
THANKS, DOC.
YOU WERE A *MESS.*
THE INSURGENTS?
ACTIVATED. *ALL OF THEM.* AND NOW WE HAVE A SITUATION IN NEW--
THEN WE'RE *DONE.* I'M OUT. I'M GETTING MY DAUGHTER.
SHE'S *SAFE.*
SCREW YOU, BRODY...
RAVANE.
YOU NEED TO *SEE THIS.*

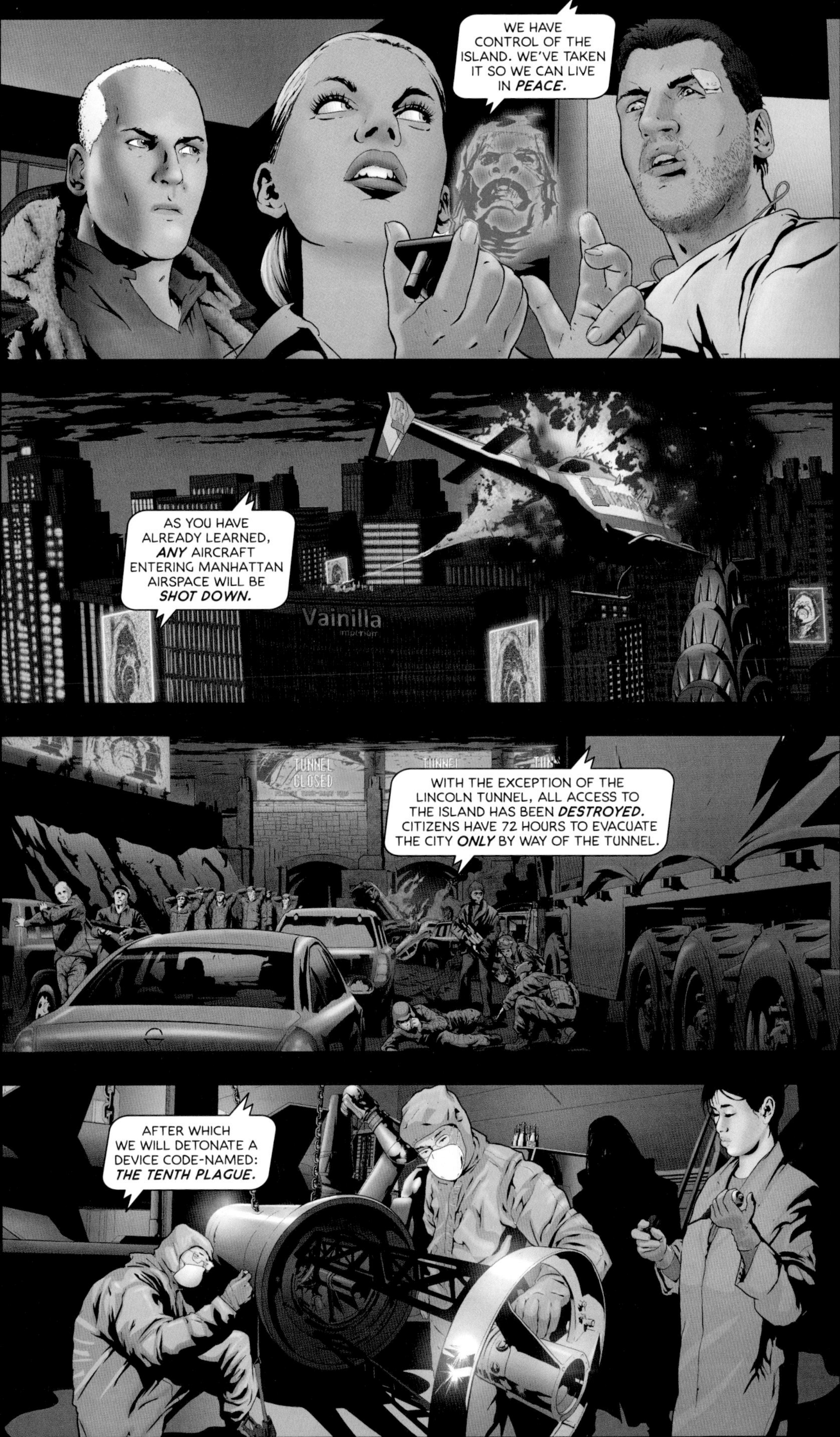
WE HAVE CONTROL OF THE ISLAND. WE'VE TAKEN IT SO WE CAN LIVE IN *PEACE.*
AS YOU HAVE ALREADY LEARNED, *ANY* AIRCRAFT ENTERING MANHATTAN AIRSPACE WILL BE *SHOT DOWN.*
Vainilla
TUNNEL CLOSED
WITH THE EXCEPTION OF THE LINCOLN TUNNEL, ALL ACCESS TO THE ISLAND HAS BEEN *DESTROYED.* CITIZENS HAVE 72 HOURS TO EVACUATE THE CITY *ONLY* BY WAY OF THE TUNNEL.
AFTER WHICH WE WILL DETONATE A DEVICE CODE-NAMED: *THE TENTH PLAGUE.*

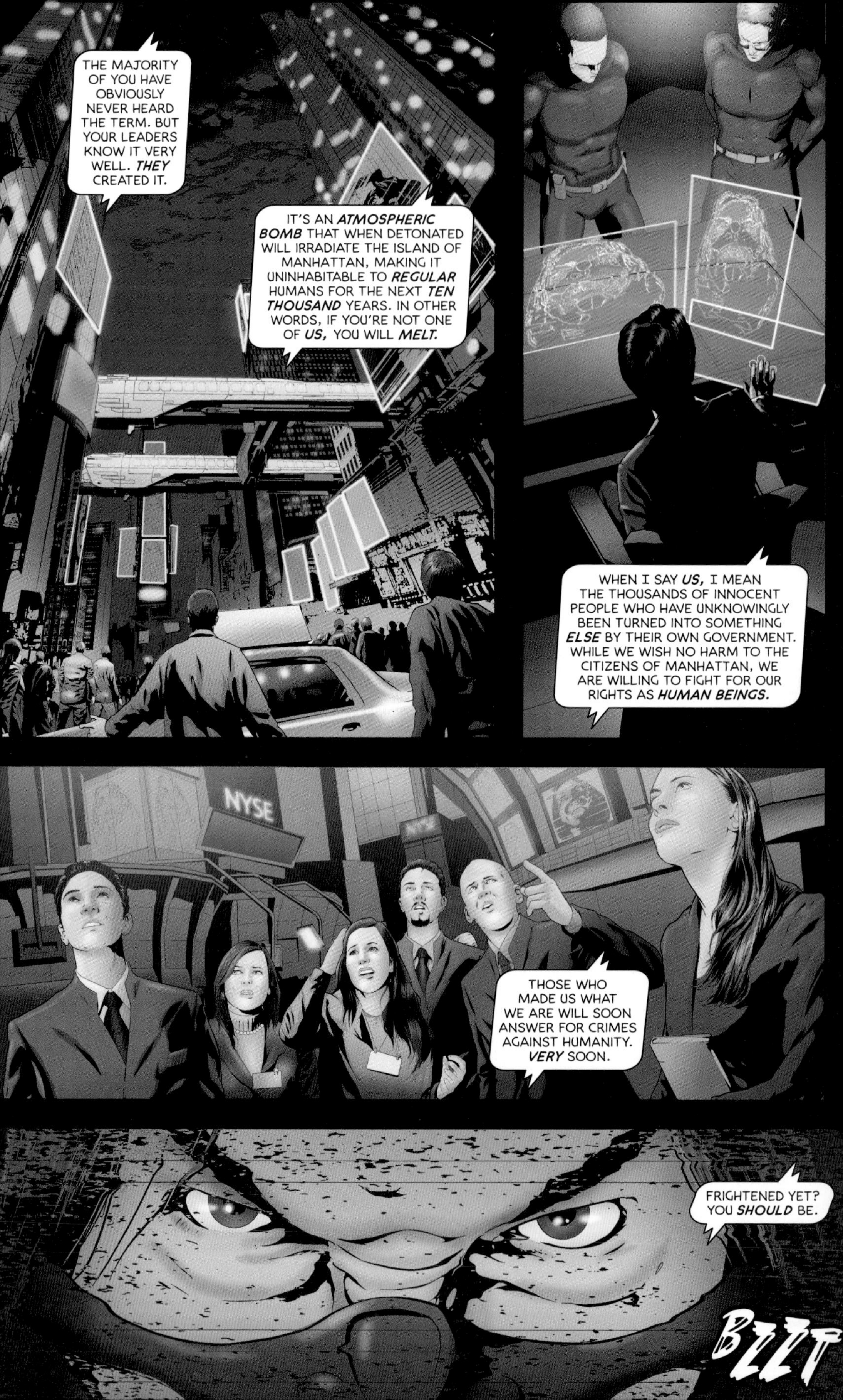
THE MAJORITY OF YOU HAVE OBVIOUSLY NEVER HEARD THE TERM. BUT YOUR LEADERS KNOW IT VERY WELL. ***THEY*** CREATED IT.
IT'S AN ***ATMOSPHERIC BOMB*** THAT WHEN DETONATED WILL IRRADIATE THE ISLAND OF MANHATTAN, MAKING IT UNINHABITABLE TO ***REGULAR*** HUMANS FOR THE NEXT ***TEN THOUSAND*** YEARS. IN OTHER WORDS, IF YOU'RE NOT ONE OF ***US,*** YOU WILL ***MELT.***
WHEN I SAY ***US,*** I MEAN THE THOUSANDS OF INNOCENT PEOPLE WHO HAVE UNKNOWINGLY BEEN TURNED INTO SOMETHING ***ELSE*** BY THEIR OWN GOVERNMENT. WHILE WE WISH NO HARM TO THE CITIZENS OF MANHATTAN, WE ARE WILLING TO FIGHT FOR OUR RIGHTS AS ***HUMAN BEINGS.***
NYSE
THOSE WHO MADE US WHAT WE ARE WILL SOON ANSWER FOR CRIMES AGAINST HUMANITY. ***VERY*** SOON.
FRIGHTENED YET? YOU ***SHOULD*** BE.
BZZT

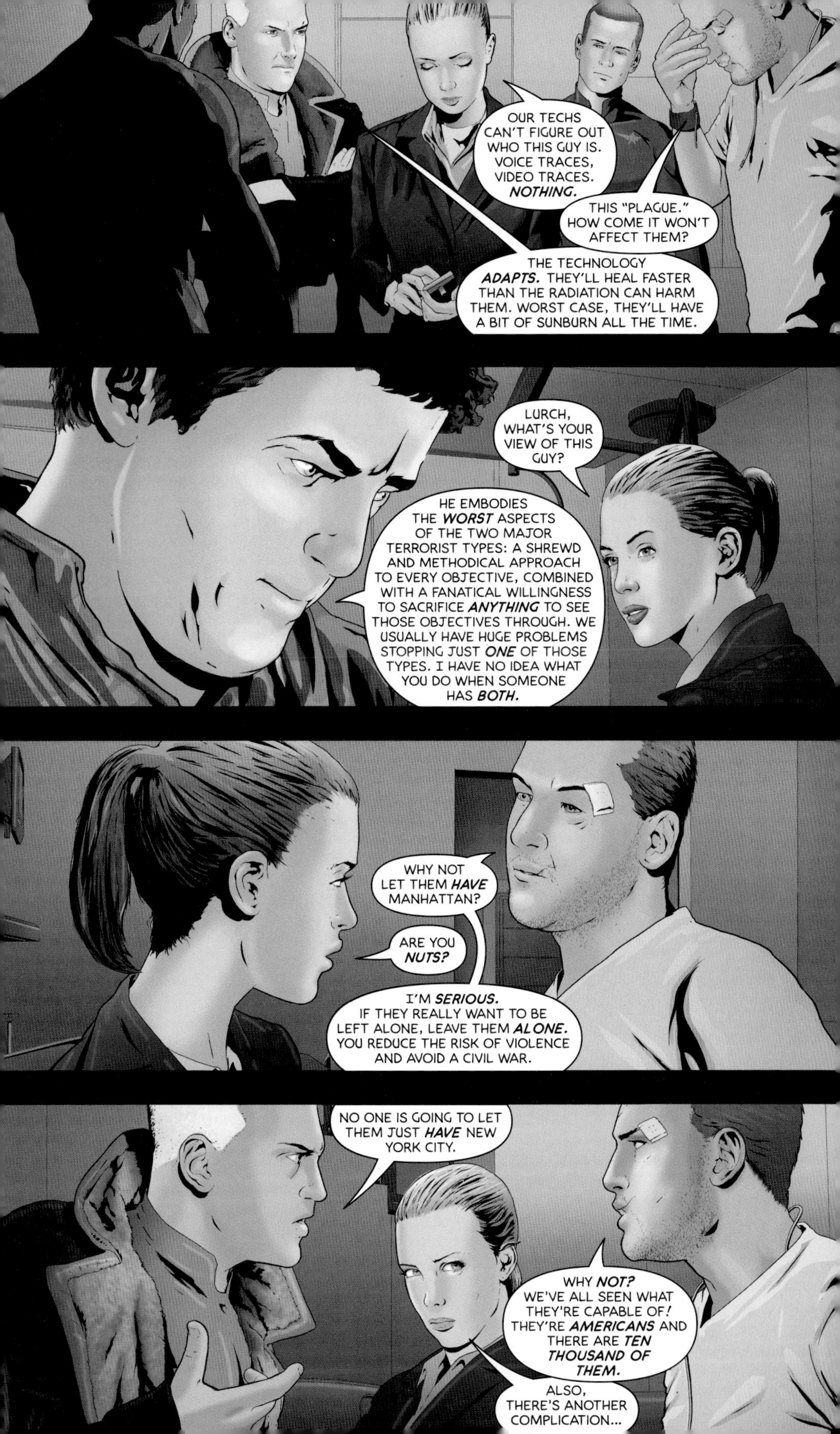
OUR TECHS CAN'T FIGURE OUT WHO THIS GUY IS. VOICE TRACES, VIDEO TRACES. *NOTHING.*
THIS "PLAGUE." HOW COME IT WON'T AFFECT THEM?
THE TECHNOLOGY *ADAPTS.* THEY'LL HEAL FASTER THAN THE RADIATION CAN HARM THEM. WORST CASE, THEY'LL HAVE A BIT OF SUNBURN ALL THE TIME.
LURCH, WHAT'S YOUR VIEW OF THIS GUY?
HE EMBODIES THE *WORST* ASPECTS OF THE TWO MAJOR TERRORIST TYPES: A SHREWD AND METHODICAL APPROACH TO EVERY OBJECTIVE, COMBINED WITH A FANATICAL WILLINGNESS TO SACRIFICE *ANYTHING* TO SEE THOSE OBJECTIVES THROUGH. WE USUALLY HAVE HUGE PROBLEMS STOPPING JUST *ONE* OF THOSE TYPES. I HAVE NO IDEA WHAT YOU DO WHEN SOMEONE HAS *BOTH.*
WHY NOT LET THEM *HAVE* MANHATTAN?
ARE YOU *NUTS?*
I'M *SERIOUS.* IF THEY REALLY WANT TO BE LEFT ALONE, LEAVE THEM *ALONE.* YOU REDUCE THE RISK OF VIOLENCE AND AVOID A CIVIL WAR.
NO ONE IS GOING TO LET THEM JUST *HAVE* NEW YORK CITY.
WHY *NOT?* WE'VE ALL SEEN WHAT THEY'RE CAPABLE OF! THEY'RE *AMERICANS* AND THERE ARE *TEN THOUSAND OF THEM.*
ALSO, THERE'S ANOTHER COMPLICATION...

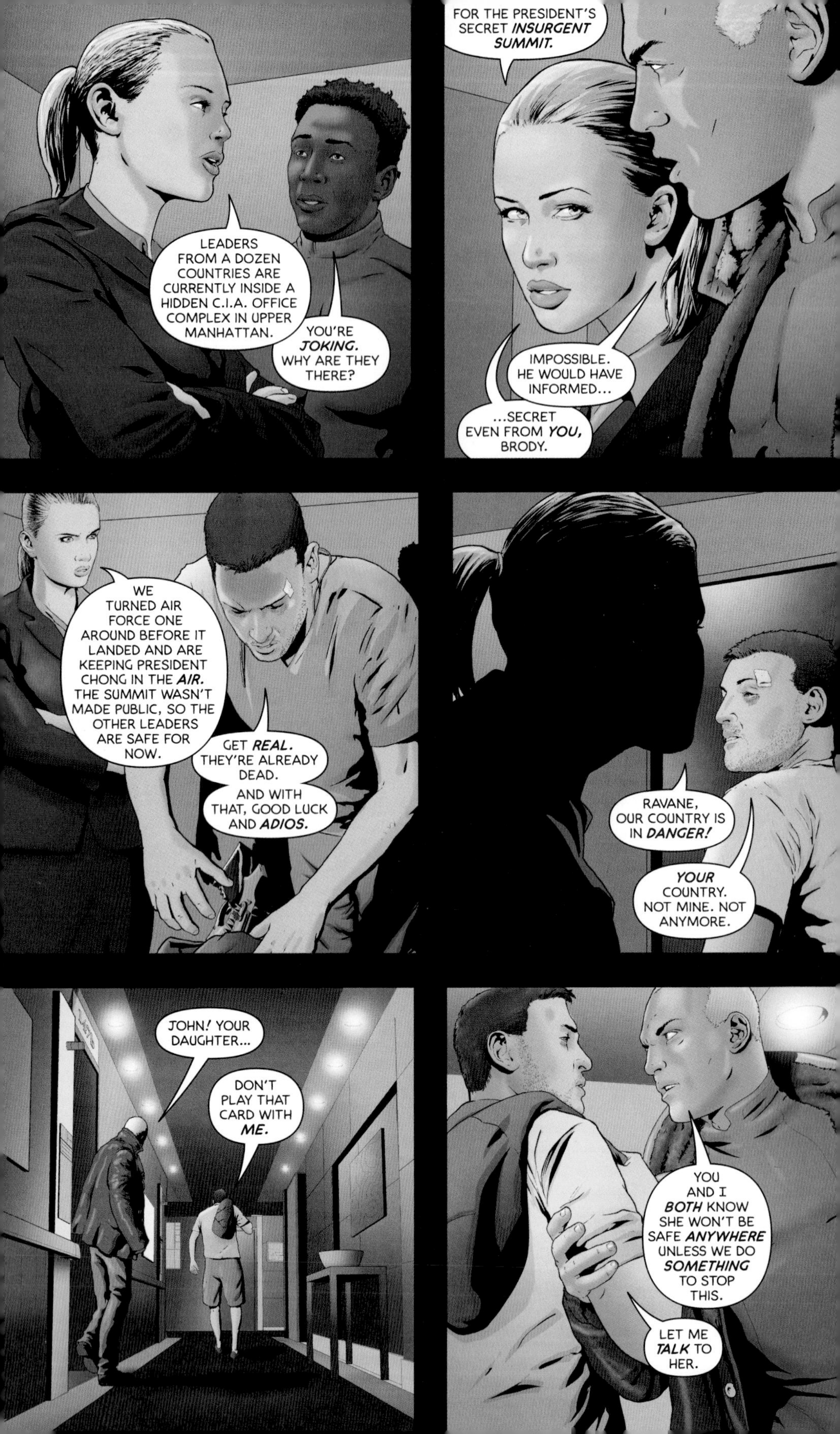
LEADERS FROM A DOZEN COUNTRIES ARE CURRENTLY INSIDE A HIDDEN C.I.A. OFFICE COMPLEX IN UPPER MANHATTAN.
YOU'RE *JOKING.* WHY ARE THEY THERE?
FOR THE PRESIDENT'S SECRET *INSURGENT SUMMIT.*
IMPOSSIBLE. HE WOULD HAVE INFORMED...
...SECRET EVEN FROM *YOU,* BRODY.
WE TURNED AIR FORCE ONE AROUND BEFORE IT LANDED AND ARE KEEPING PRESIDENT CHONG IN THE *AIR.* THE SUMMIT WASN'T MADE PUBLIC, SO THE OTHER LEADERS ARE SAFE FOR NOW.
GET *REAL.* THEY'RE ALREADY DEAD.
AND WITH THAT, GOOD LUCK AND *ADIOS.*
RAVANE, OUR COUNTRY IS IN *DANGER!*
YOUR COUNTRY. NOT MINE. NOT ANYMORE.
JOHN! YOUR DAUGHTER...
DON'T PLAY THAT CARD WITH *ME.*
YOU AND I *BOTH* KNOW SHE WON'T BE SAFE *ANYWHERE* UNLESS WE DO *SOMETHING* TO STOP THIS.
LET ME *TALK* TO HER.

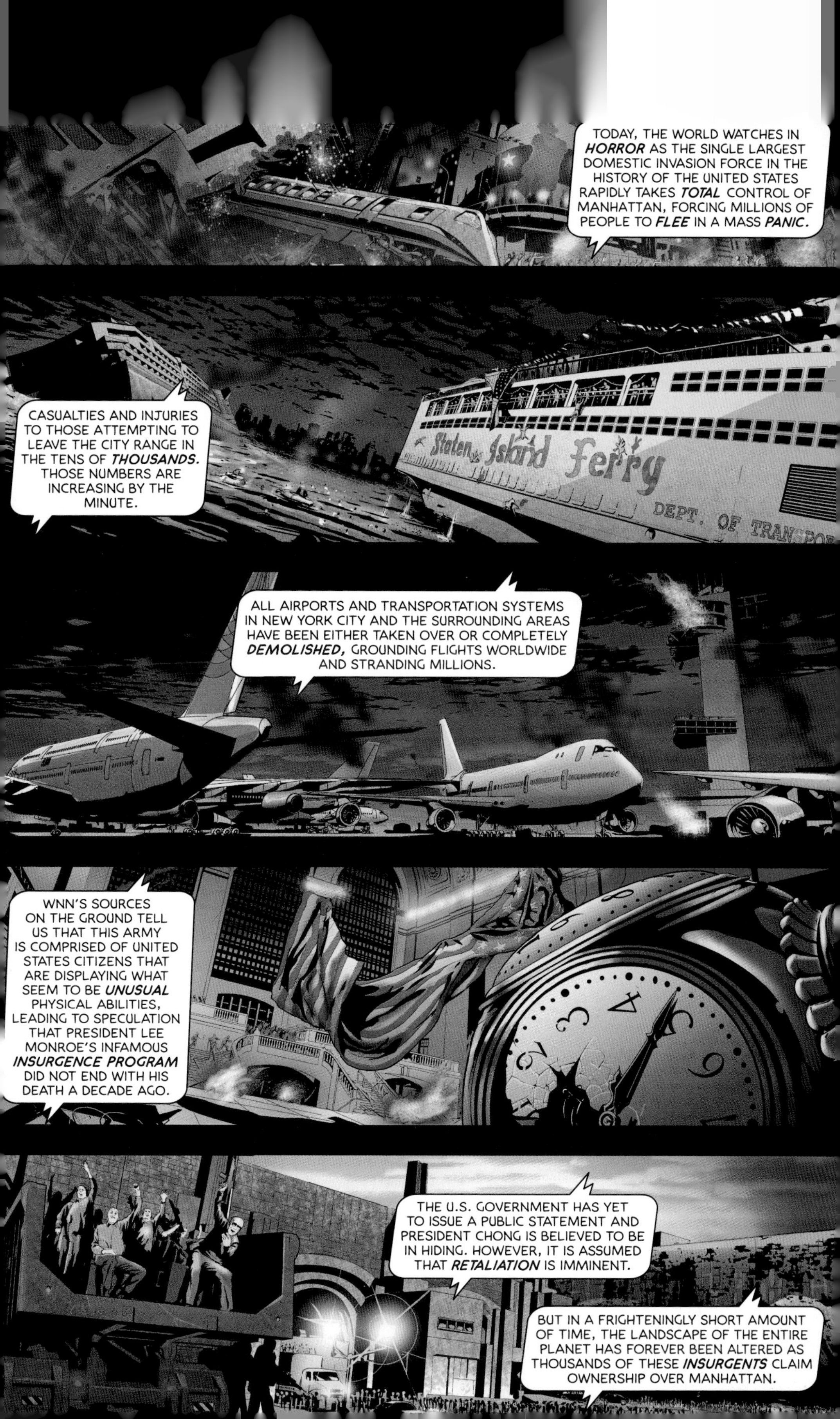
TODAY, THE WORLD WATCHES IN HORROR AS THE SINGLE LARGEST DOMESTIC INVASION FORCE IN THE HISTORY OF THE UNITED STATES RAPIDLY TAKES TOTAL CONTROL OF MANHATTAN, FORCING MILLIONS OF PEOPLE TO FLEE IN A MASS PANIC.
CASUALTIES AND INJURIES TO THOSE ATTEMPTING TO LEAVE THE CITY RANGE IN THE TENS OF THOUSANDS. THOSE NUMBERS ARE INCREASING BY THE MINUTE.
Staten Island Ferry
DEPT. OF TRANSPOR
ALL AIRPORTS AND TRANSPORTATION SYSTEMS IN NEW YORK CITY AND THE SURROUNDING AREAS HAVE BEEN EITHER TAKEN OVER OR COMPLETELY DEMOLISHED, GROUNDING FLIGHTS WORLDWIDE AND STRANDING MILLIONS.
WNN'S SOURCES ON THE GROUND TELL US THAT THIS ARMY IS COMPRISED OF UNITED STATES CITIZENS THAT ARE DISPLAYING WHAT SEEM TO BE UNUSUAL PHYSICAL ABILITIES, LEADING TO SPECULATION THAT PRESIDENT LEE MONROE'S INFAMOUS INSURGENCE PROGRAM DID NOT END WITH HIS DEATH A DECADE AGO.
THE U.S. GOVERNMENT HAS YET TO ISSUE A PUBLIC STATEMENT AND PRESIDENT CHONG IS BELIEVED TO BE IN HIDING. HOWEVER, IT IS ASSUMED THAT RETALIATION IS IMMINENT.
BUT IN A FRIGHTENINGLY SHORT AMOUNT OF TIME, THE LANDSCAPE OF THE ENTIRE PLANET HAS FOREVER BEEN ALTERED AS THOUSANDS OF THESE INSURGENTS CLAIM OWNERSHIP OVER MANHATTAN.

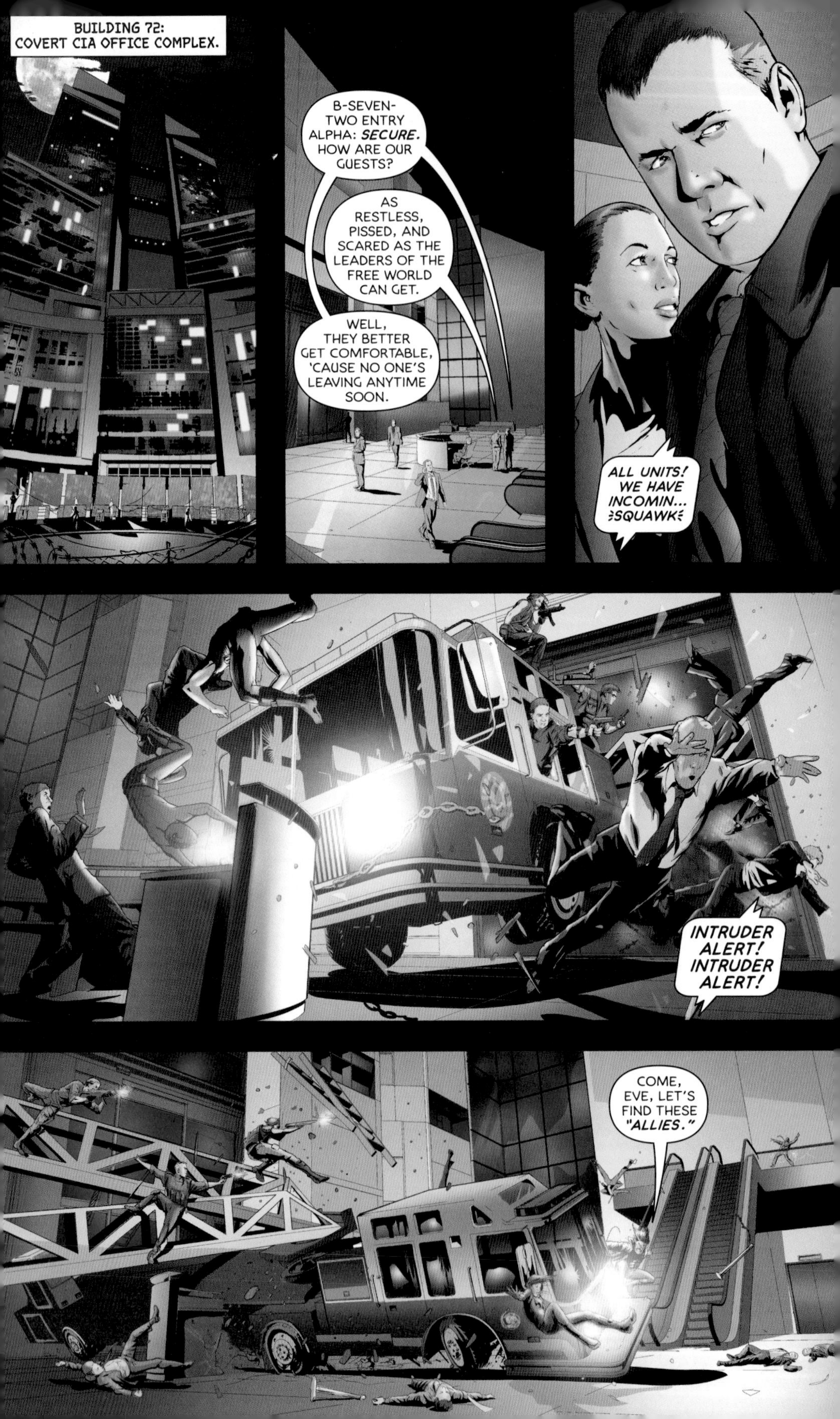
BUILDING 72:
COVERT CIA OFFICE COMPLEX.
B-SEVEN-TWO ENTRY ALPHA: SECURE. HOW ARE OUR GUESTS?
AS RESTLESS, PISSED, AND SCARED AS THE LEADERS OF THE FREE WORLD CAN GET.
WELL, THEY BETTER GET COMFORTABLE, 'CAUSE NO ONE'S LEAVING ANYTIME SOON.
ALL UNITS! WE HAVE INCOMIN... SQUAWK
INTRUDER ALERT! INTRUDER ALERT!
COME, EVE, LET'S FIND THESE "ALLIES."

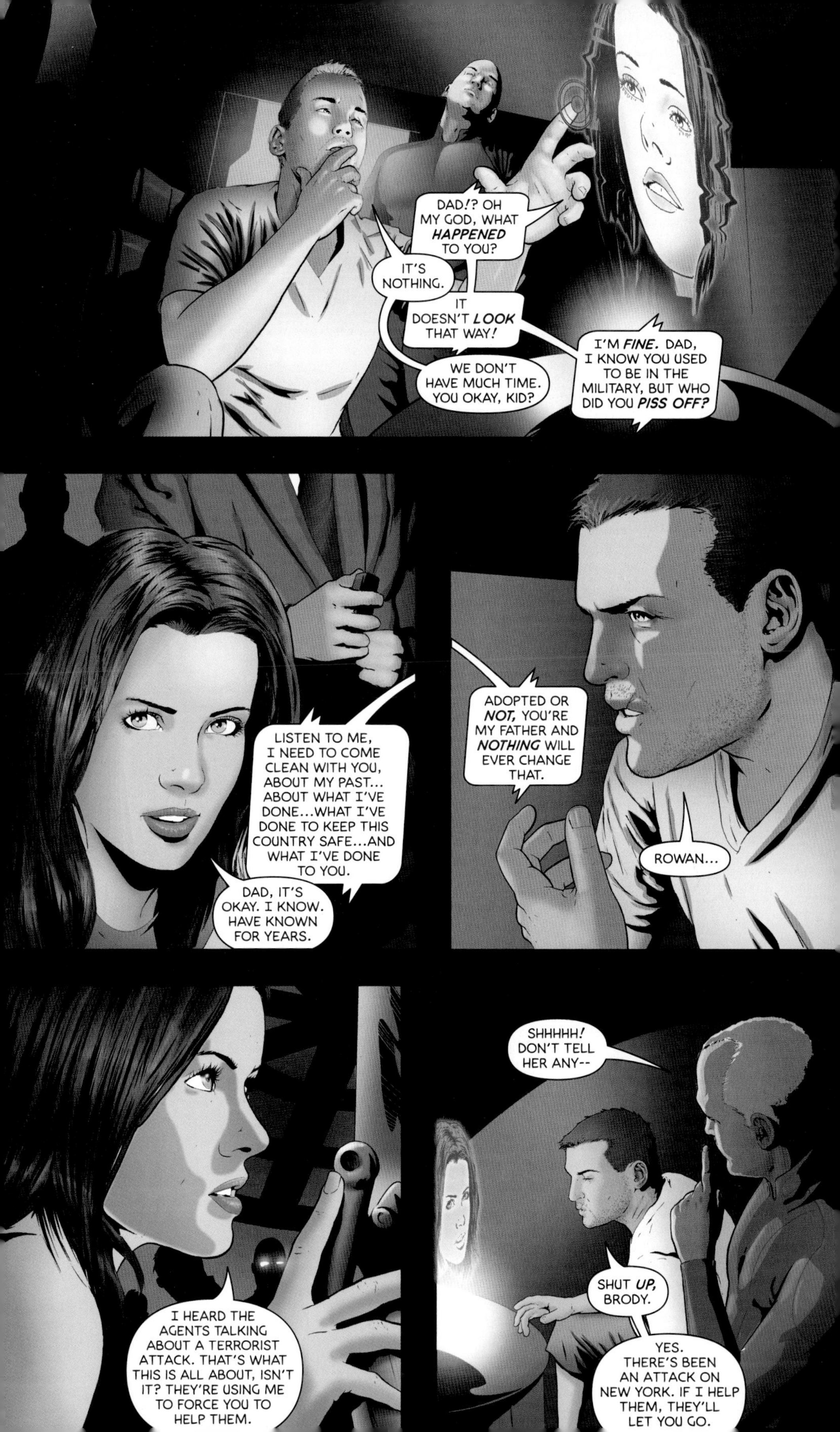
DAD!? OH MY GOD, WHAT HAPPENED TO YOU?
IT'S NOTHING.
IT DOESN'T LOOK THAT WAY!
WE DON'T HAVE MUCH TIME. YOU OKAY, KID?
I'M FINE. DAD, I KNOW YOU USED TO BE IN THE MILITARY, BUT WHO DID YOU PISS OFF?
LISTEN TO ME, I NEED TO COME CLEAN WITH YOU, ABOUT MY PAST... ABOUT WHAT I'VE DONE...WHAT I'VE DONE TO KEEP THIS COUNTRY SAFE...AND WHAT I'VE DONE TO YOU.
DAD, IT'S OKAY. I KNOW. HAVE KNOWN FOR YEARS.
ADOPTED OR NOT, YOU'RE MY FATHER AND NOTHING WILL EVER CHANGE THAT.
ROWAN...
I HEARD THE AGENTS TALKING ABOUT A TERRORIST ATTACK. THAT'S WHAT THIS IS ALL ABOUT, ISN'T IT? THEY'RE USING ME TO FORCE YOU TO HELP THEM.
SHHHHH! DON'T TELL HER ANY--
SHUT UP, BRODY.
YES. THERE'S BEEN AN ATTACK ON NEW YORK. IF I HELP THEM, THEY'LL LET YOU GO.

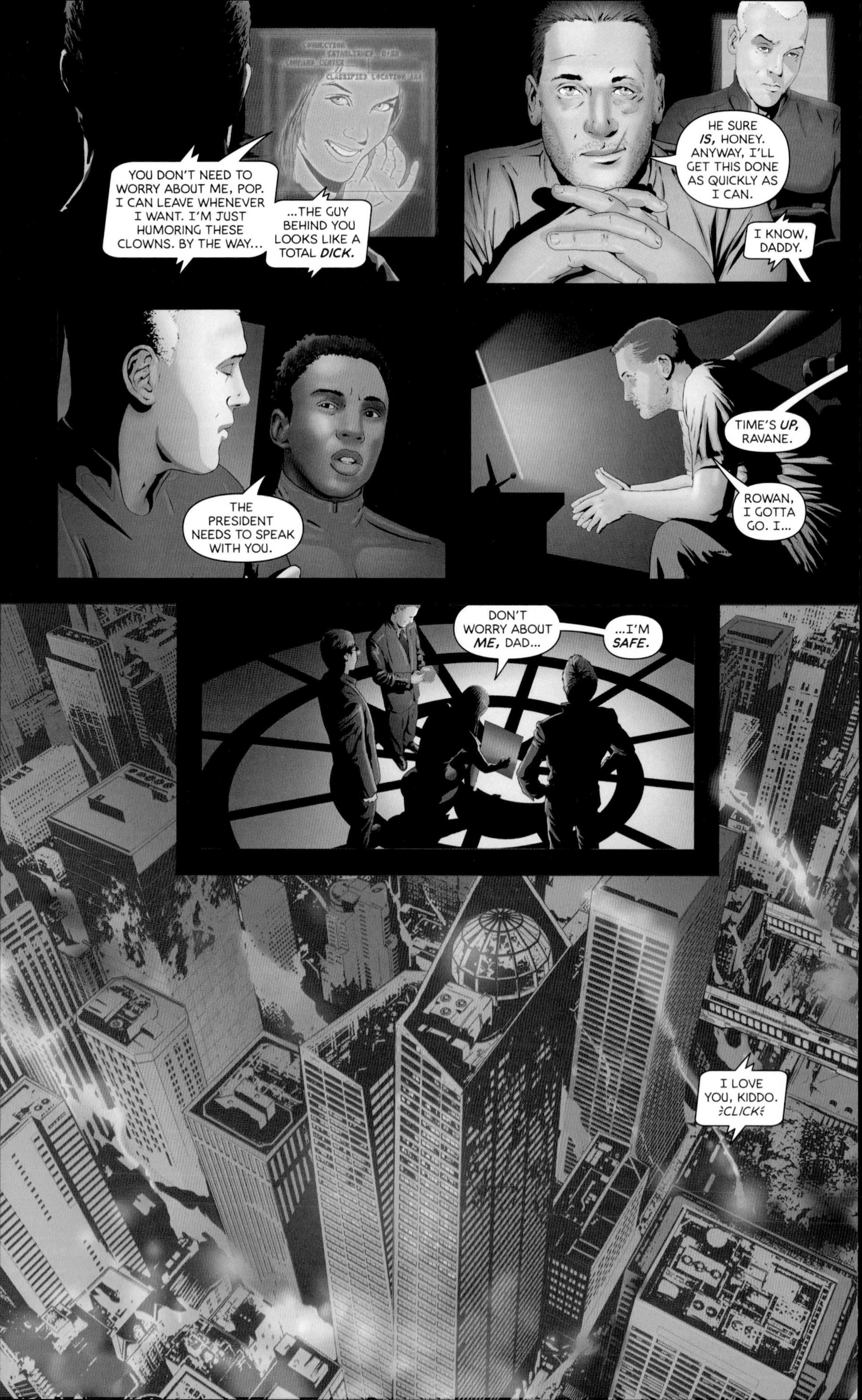
YOU DON'T NEED TO WORRY ABOUT ME, POP. I CAN LEAVE WHENEVER I WANT. I'M JUST HUMORING THESE CLOWNS. BY THE WAY...
...THE GUY BEHIND YOU LOOKS LIKE A TOTAL *DICK.*
HE SURE *IS,* HONEY. ANYWAY, I'LL GET THIS DONE AS QUICKLY AS I CAN.
I KNOW, DADDY.
THE PRESIDENT NEEDS TO SPEAK WITH YOU.
TIME'S *UP,* RAVANE.
ROWAN, I GOTTA GO. I...
DON'T WORRY ABOUT *ME,* DAD...
...I'M *SAFE.*
I LOVE YOU, KIDDO.
CLICK

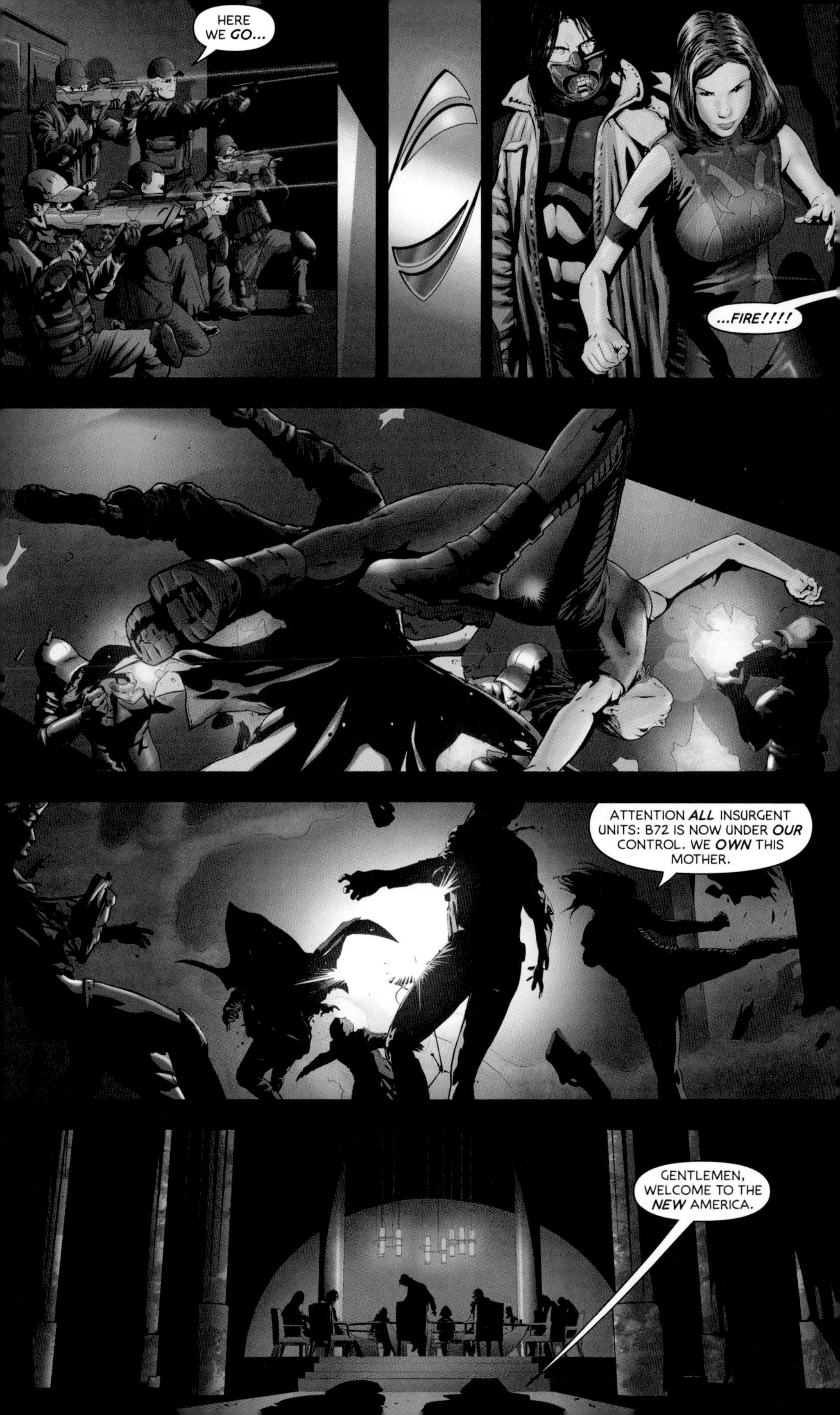
HERE WE GO...
...FIRE!!!!
ATTENTION ALL INSURGENT UNITS: B72 IS NOW UNDER OUR CONTROL. WE OWN THIS MOTHER.
GENTLEMEN, WELCOME TO THE NEW AMERICA.

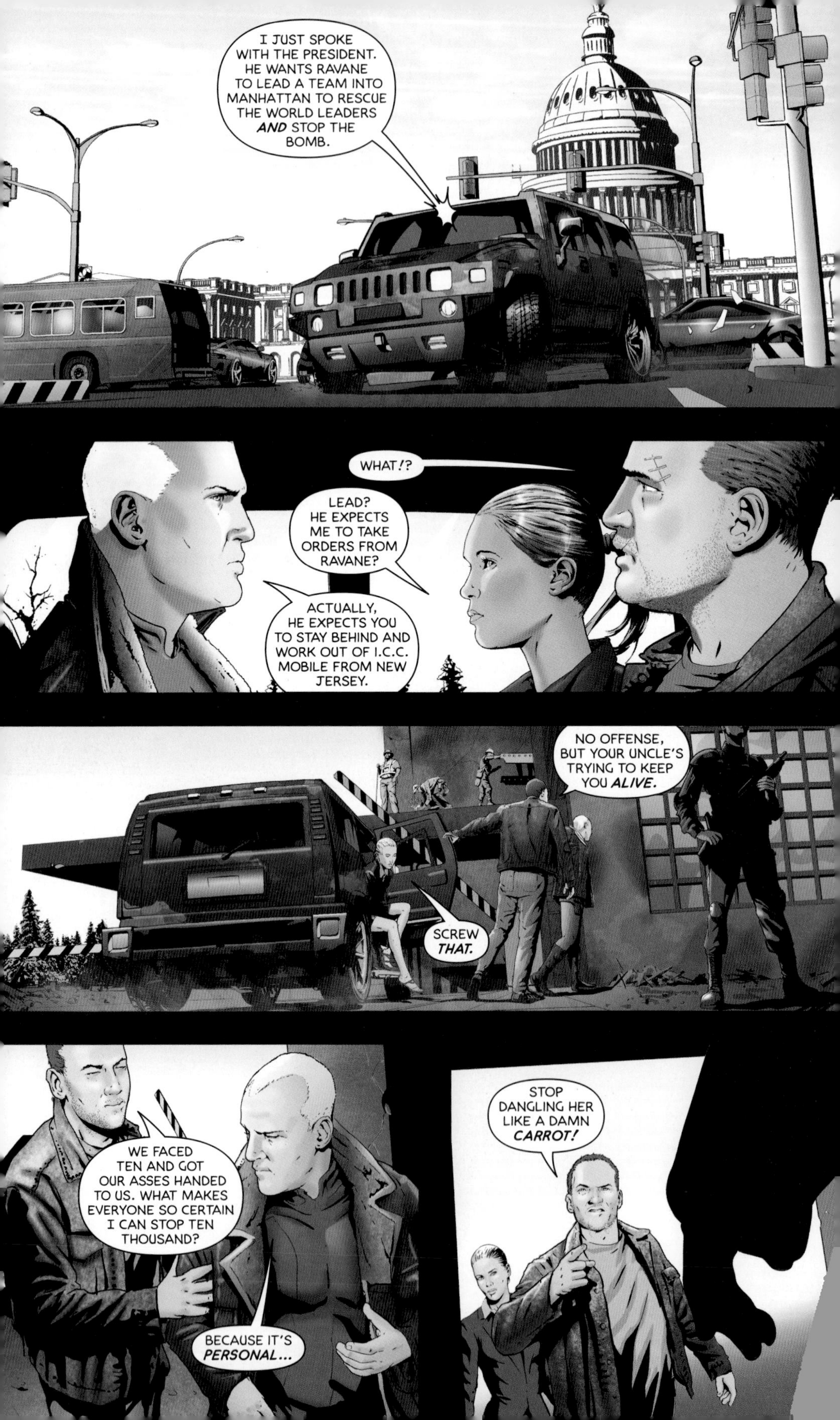
I JUST SPOKE WITH THE PRESIDENT. HE WANTS RAVANE TO LEAD A TEAM INTO MANHATTAN TO RESCUE THE WORLD LEADERS AND STOP THE BOMB.
WHAT!?
LEAD? HE EXPECTS ME TO TAKE ORDERS FROM RAVANE?
ACTUALLY, HE EXPECTS YOU TO STAY BEHIND AND WORK OUT OF I.C.C. MOBILE FROM NEW JERSEY.
NO OFFENSE, BUT YOUR UNCLE'S TRYING TO KEEP YOU ALIVE.
SCREW THAT.
WE FACED TEN AND GOT OUR ASSES HANDED TO US. WHAT MAKES EVERYONE SO CERTAIN I CAN STOP TEN THOUSAND?
BECAUSE IT'S PERSONAL...
STOP DANGLING HER LIKE A DAMN CARROT!

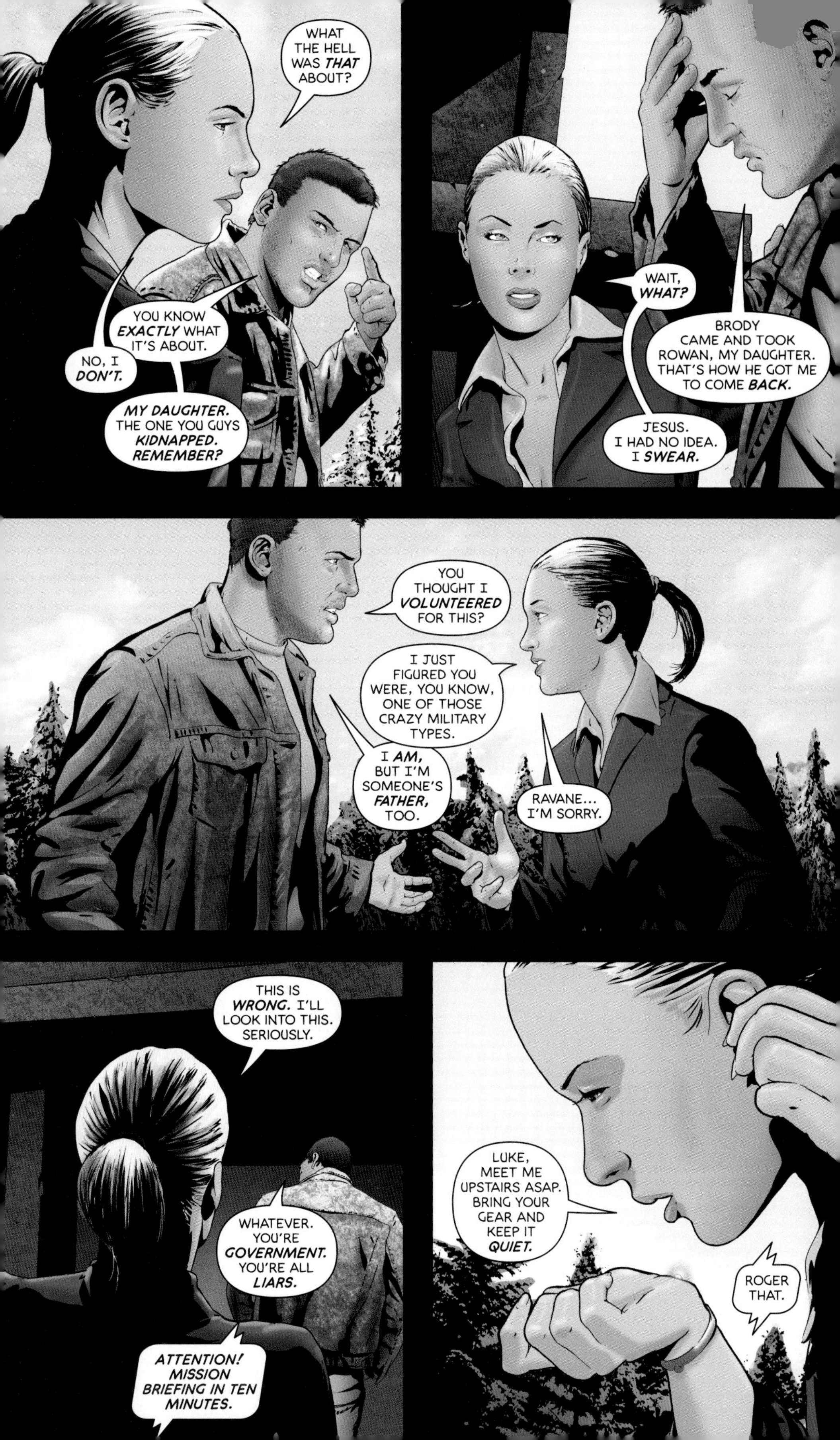
WHAT THE HELL WAS THAT ABOUT?
YOU KNOW EXACTLY WHAT IT'S ABOUT.
NO, I DON'T.
MY DAUGHTER. THE ONE YOU GUYS KIDNAPPED. REMEMBER?
WAIT, WHAT?
BRODY CAME AND TOOK ROWAN, MY DAUGHTER. THAT'S HOW HE GOT ME TO COME BACK.
JESUS. I HAD NO IDEA. I SWEAR.
YOU THOUGHT I VOLUNTEERED FOR THIS?
I JUST FIGURED YOU WERE, YOU KNOW, ONE OF THOSE CRAZY MILITARY TYPES.
I AM, BUT I'M SOMEONE'S FATHER, TOO.
RAVANE... I'M SORRY.
THIS IS WRONG. I'LL LOOK INTO THIS. SERIOUSLY.
WHATEVER. YOU'RE GOVERNMENT. YOU'RE ALL LIARS.
ATTENTION! MISSION BRIEFING IN TEN MINUTES.
LUKE, MEET ME UPSTAIRS ASAP. BRING YOUR GEAR AND KEEP IT QUIET.
ROGER THAT.

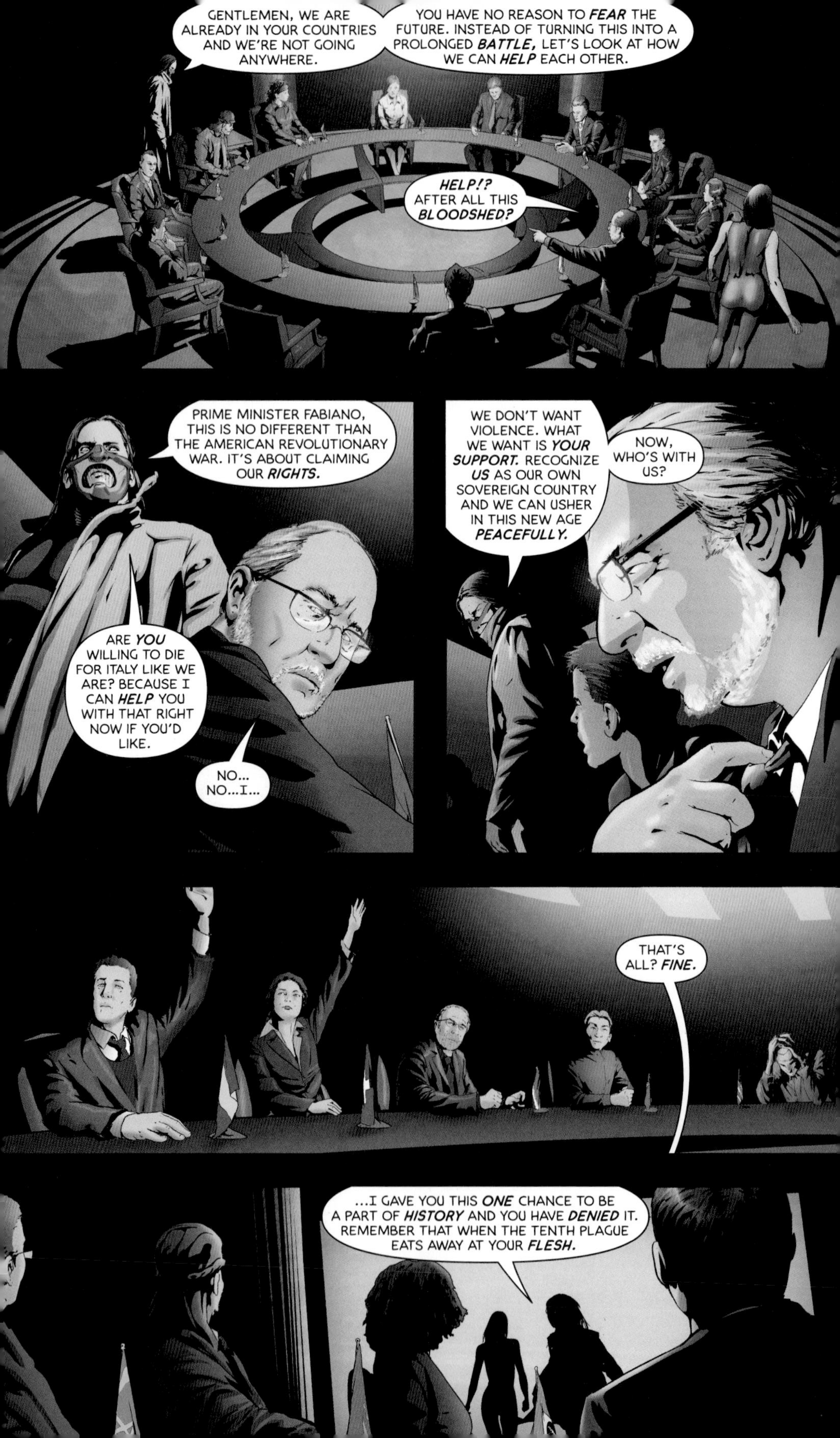

GENTLEMEN, WE ARE ALREADY IN YOUR COUNTRIES AND WE'RE NOT GOING ANYWHERE.
YOU HAVE NO REASON TO *FEAR* THE FUTURE. INSTEAD OF TURNING THIS INTO A PROLONGED *BATTLE,* LET'S LOOK AT HOW WE CAN *HELP* EACH OTHER.
HELP!? AFTER ALL THIS *BLOODSHED?*
PRIME MINISTER FABIANO, THIS IS NO DIFFERENT THAN THE AMERICAN REVOLUTIONARY WAR. IT'S ABOUT CLAIMING OUR *RIGHTS.*
ARE *YOU* WILLING TO DIE FOR ITALY LIKE WE ARE? BECAUSE I CAN *HELP* YOU WITH THAT RIGHT NOW IF YOU'D LIKE.
NO... NO...I...
WE DON'T WANT VIOLENCE. WHAT WE WANT IS *YOUR SUPPORT.* RECOGNIZE *US* AS OUR OWN SOVEREIGN COUNTRY AND WE CAN USHER IN THIS NEW AGE *PEACEFULLY.*
NOW, WHO'S WITH US?
THAT'S ALL? *FINE.*
...I GAVE YOU THIS *ONE* CHANCE TO BE A PART OF *HISTORY* AND YOU HAVE *DENIED* IT. REMEMBER THAT WHEN THE TENTH PLAGUE EATS AWAY AT YOUR *FLESH.*

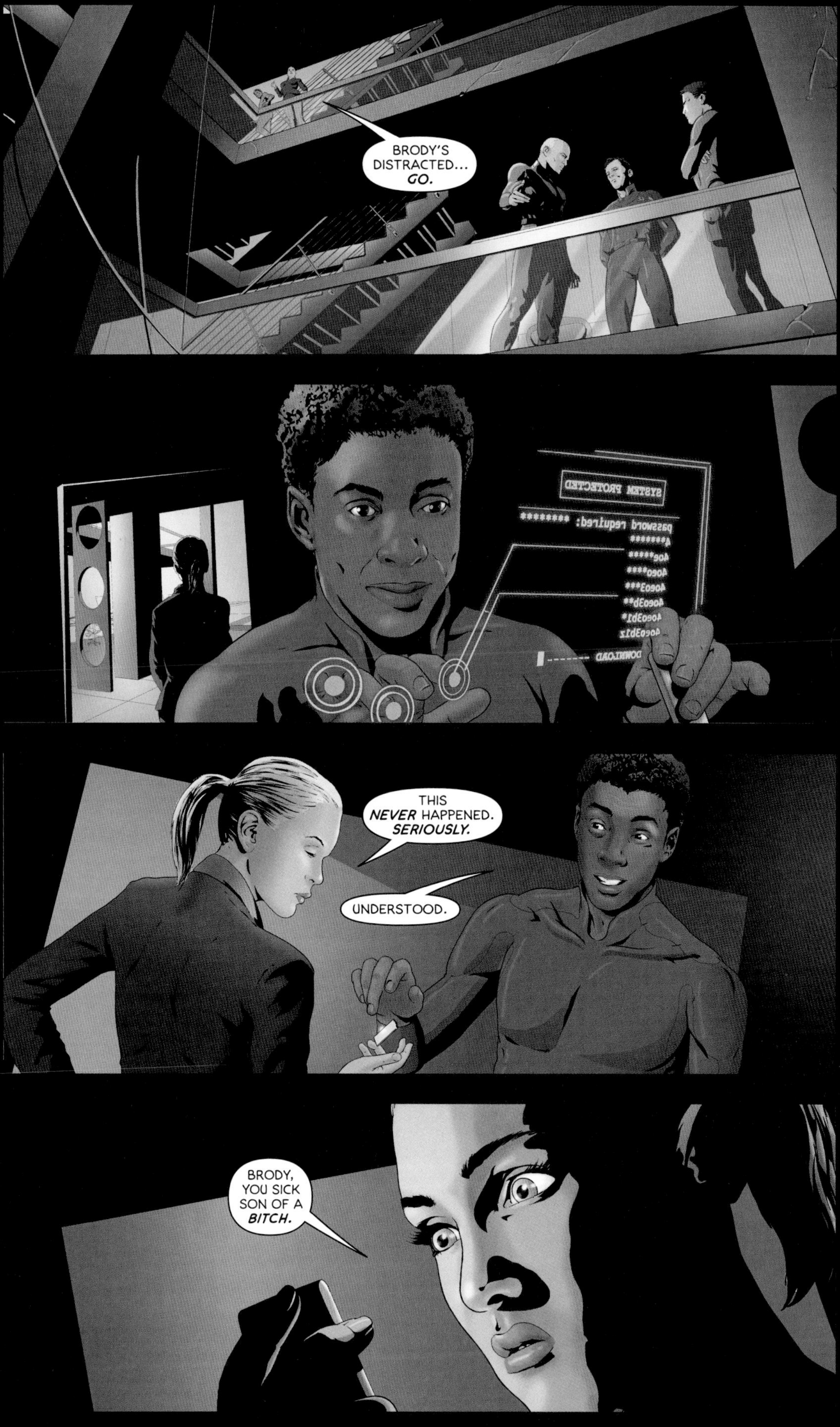
BRODY'S DISTRACTED... GO.
THIS NEVER HAPPENED. SERIOUSLY.
UNDERSTOOD.
BRODY, YOU SICK SON OF A BITCH.

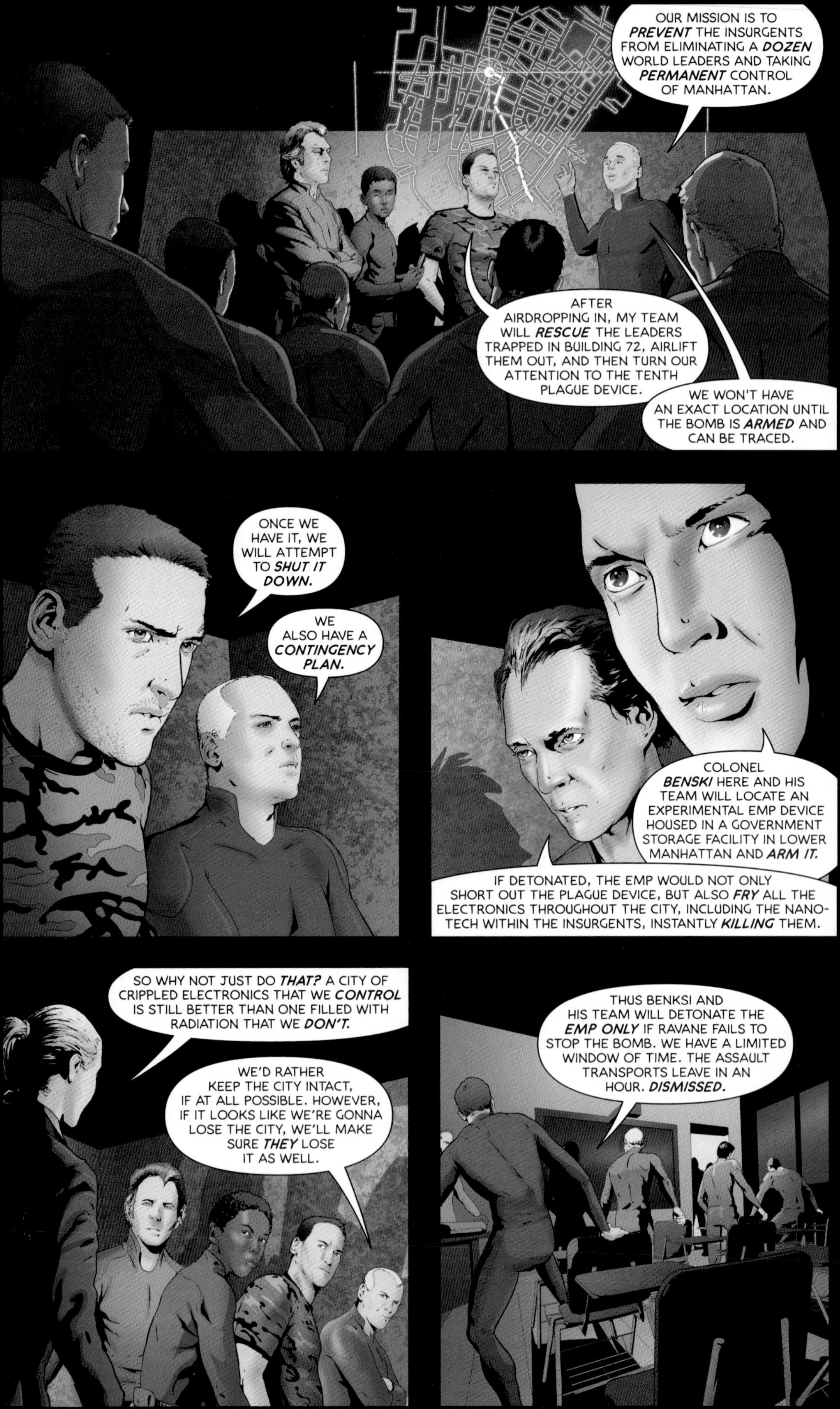
OUR MISSION IS TO PREVENT THE INSURGENTS FROM ELIMINATING A DOZEN WORLD LEADERS AND TAKING PERMANENT CONTROL OF MANHATTAN.
AFTER AIRDROPPING IN, MY TEAM WILL RESCUE THE LEADERS TRAPPED IN BUILDING 72, AIRLIFT THEM OUT, AND THEN TURN OUR ATTENTION TO THE TENTH PLAGUE DEVICE.
WE WON'T HAVE AN EXACT LOCATION UNTIL THE BOMB IS ARMED AND CAN BE TRACED.
ONCE WE HAVE IT, WE WILL ATTEMPT TO SHUT IT DOWN.
WE ALSO HAVE A CONTINGENCY PLAN.
COLONEL BENSKI HERE AND HIS TEAM WILL LOCATE AN EXPERIMENTAL EMP DEVICE HOUSED IN A GOVERNMENT STORAGE FACILITY IN LOWER MANHATTAN AND ARM IT.
IF DETONATED, THE EMP WOULD NOT ONLY SHORT OUT THE PLAGUE DEVICE, BUT ALSO FRY ALL THE ELECTRONICS THROUGHOUT THE CITY, INCLUDING THE NANO-TECH WITHIN THE INSURGENTS, INSTANTLY KILLING THEM.
SO WHY NOT JUST DO THAT? A CITY OF CRIPPLED ELECTRONICS THAT WE CONTROL IS STILL BETTER THAN ONE FILLED WITH RADIATION THAT WE DON'T.
WE'D RATHER KEEP THE CITY INTACT, IF AT ALL POSSIBLE. HOWEVER, IF IT LOOKS LIKE WE'RE GONNA LOSE THE CITY, WE'LL MAKE SURE THEY LOSE IT AS WELL.
THUS BENKSI AND HIS TEAM WILL DETONATE THE EMP ONLY IF RAVANE FAILS TO STOP THE BOMB. WE HAVE A LIMITED WINDOW OF TIME. THE ASSAULT TRANSPORTS LEAVE IN AN HOUR. DISMISSED.

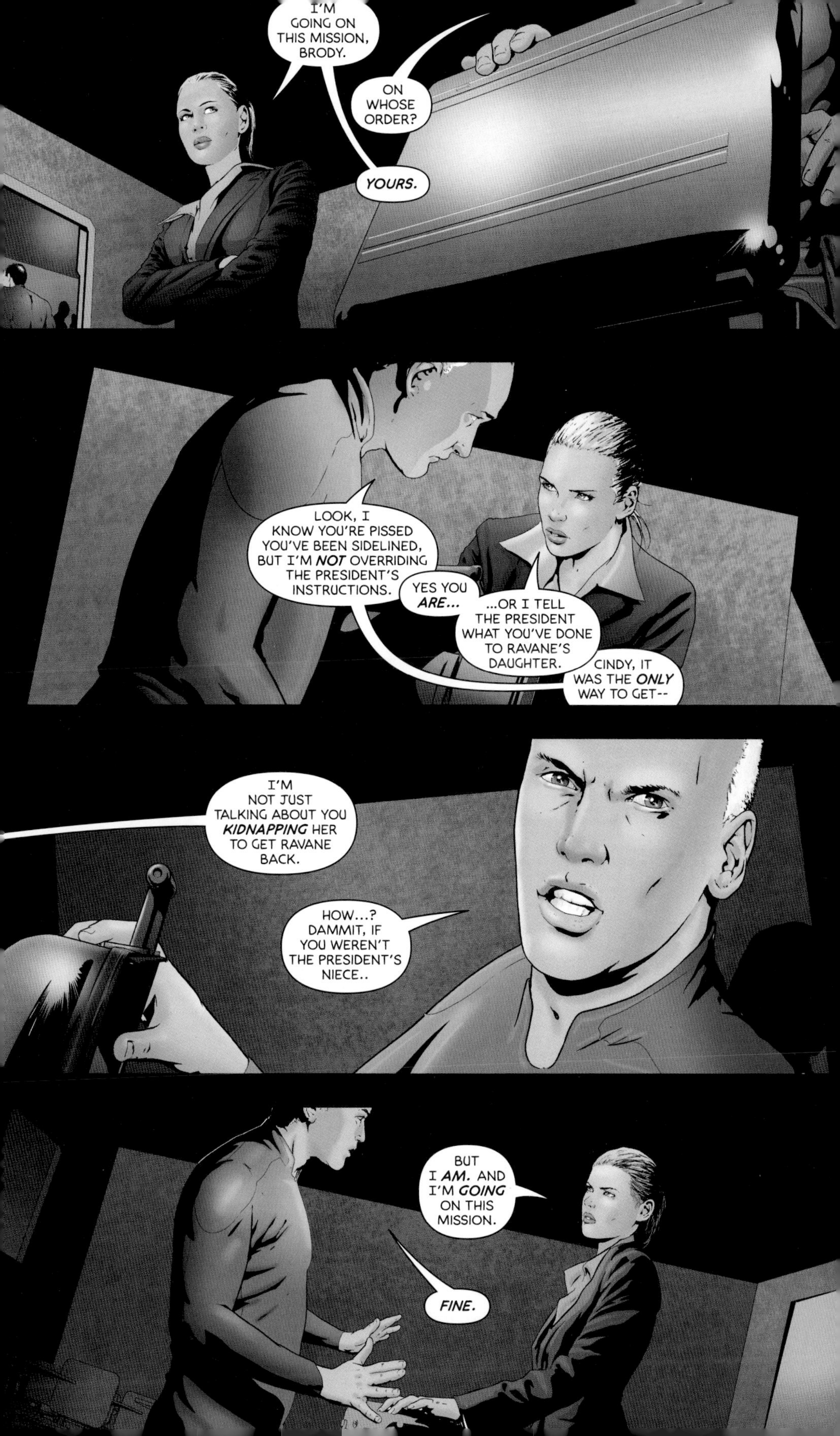
I'M GOING ON THIS MISSION, BRODY.
ON WHOSE ORDER?
YOURS.
LOOK, I KNOW YOU'RE PISSED YOU'VE BEEN SIDELINED, BUT I'M NOT OVERRIDING THE PRESIDENT'S INSTRUCTIONS.
YES YOU ARE...
...OR I TELL THE PRESIDENT WHAT YOU'VE DONE TO RAVANE'S DAUGHTER.
CINDY, IT WAS THE ONLY WAY TO GET--
I'M NOT JUST TALKING ABOUT YOU KIDNAPPING HER TO GET RAVANE BACK.
HOW...? DAMMIT, IF YOU WEREN'T THE PRESIDENT'S NIECE..
BUT I AM. AND I'M GOING ON THIS MISSION.
FINE.

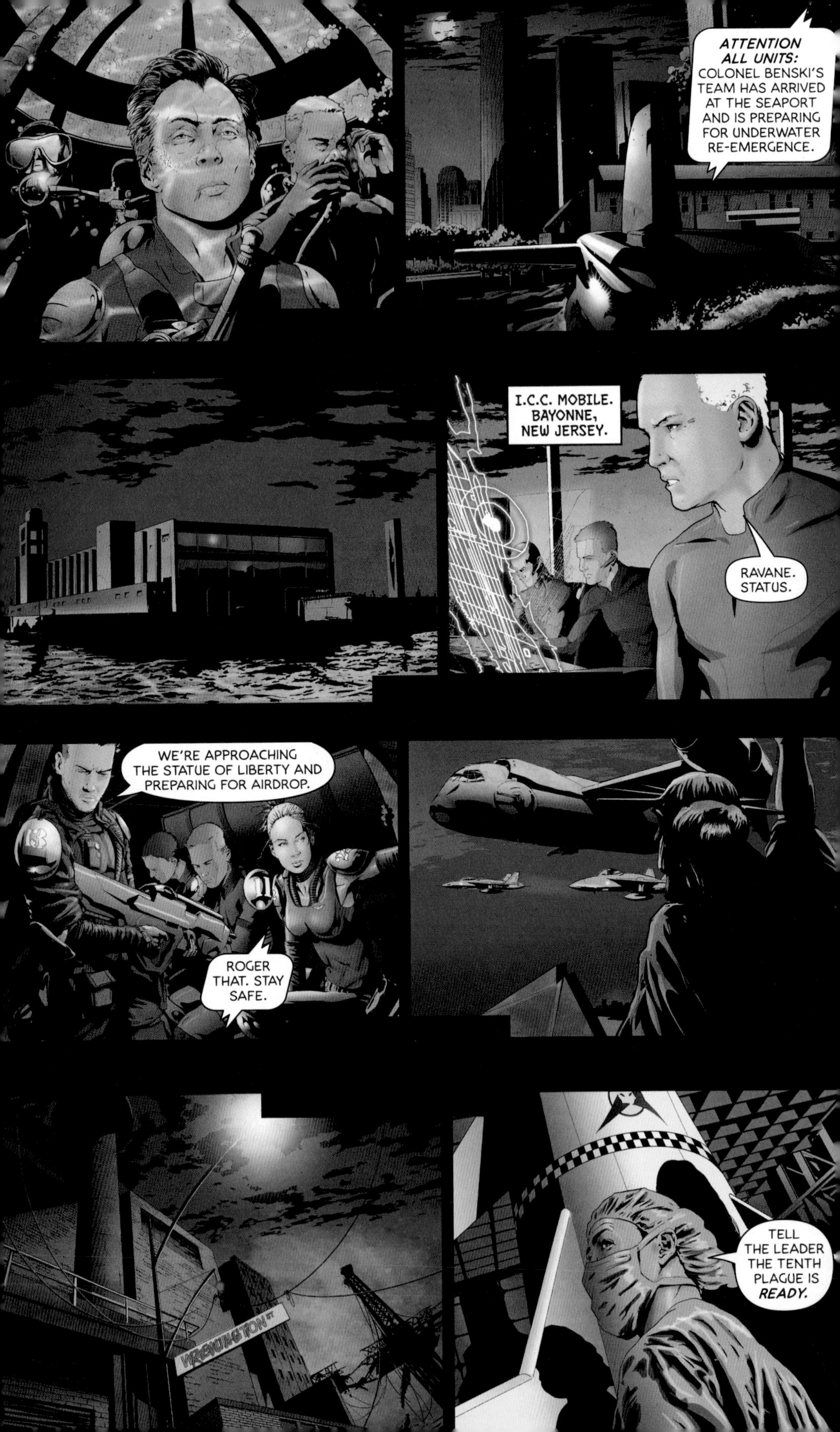
ATTENTION ALL UNITS: COLONEL BENSKI'S TEAM HAS ARRIVED AT THE SEAPORT AND IS PREPARING FOR UNDERWATER RE-EMERGENCE.
I.C.C. MOBILE. BAYONNE, NEW JERSEY.
RAVANE. STATUS.
WE'RE APPROACHING THE STATUE OF LIBERTY AND PREPARING FOR AIRDROP.
ROGER THAT. STAY SAFE.
TELL THE LEADER THE TENTH PLAGUE IS READY.

CHAPTER 4

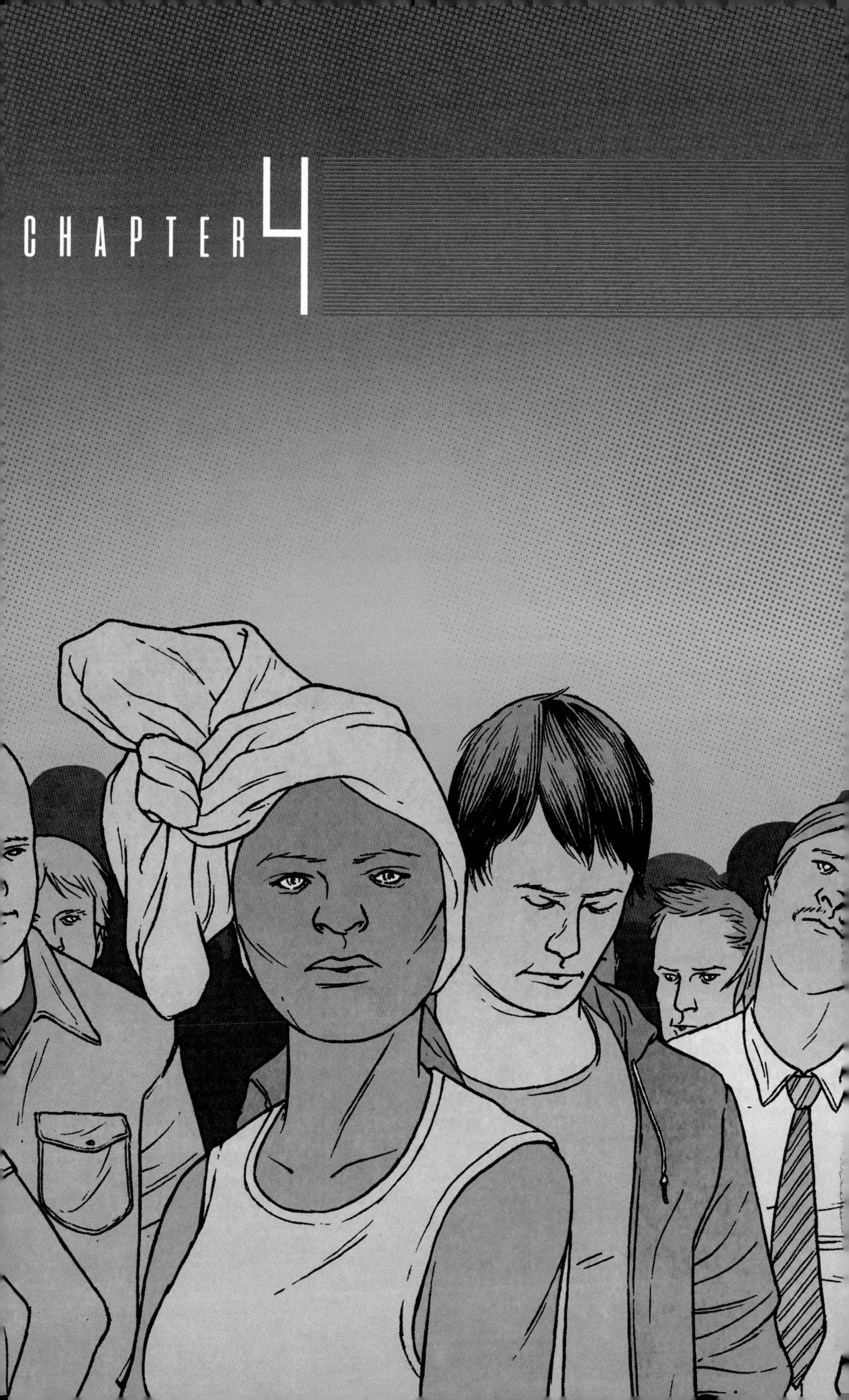

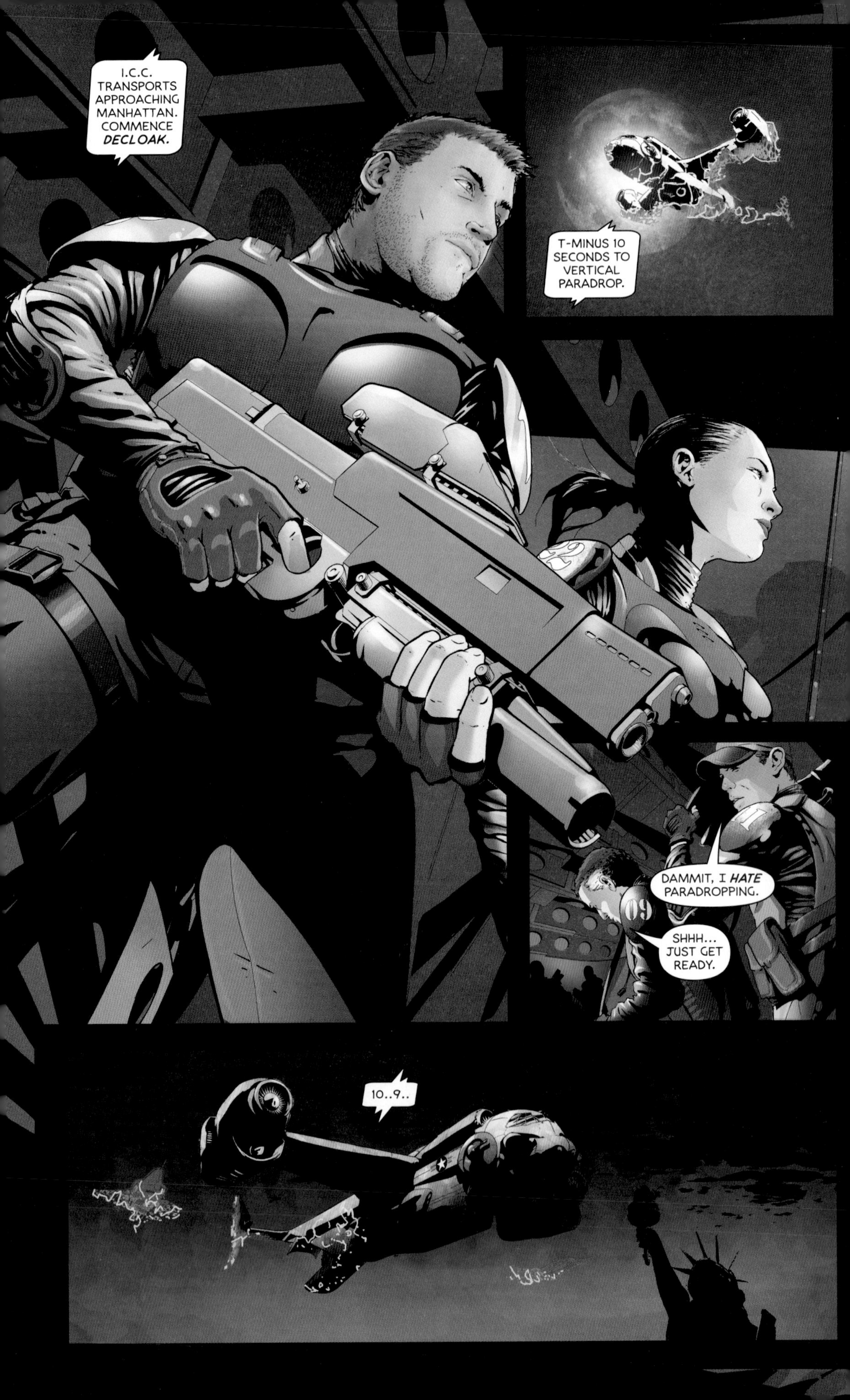
I.C.C. TRANSPORTS APPROACHING MANHATTAN. COMMENCE DECLOAK.
T-MINUS 10 SECONDS TO VERTICAL PARADROP.
DAMMIT, I HATE PARADROPPING.
SHHH... JUST GET READY.
10..9..

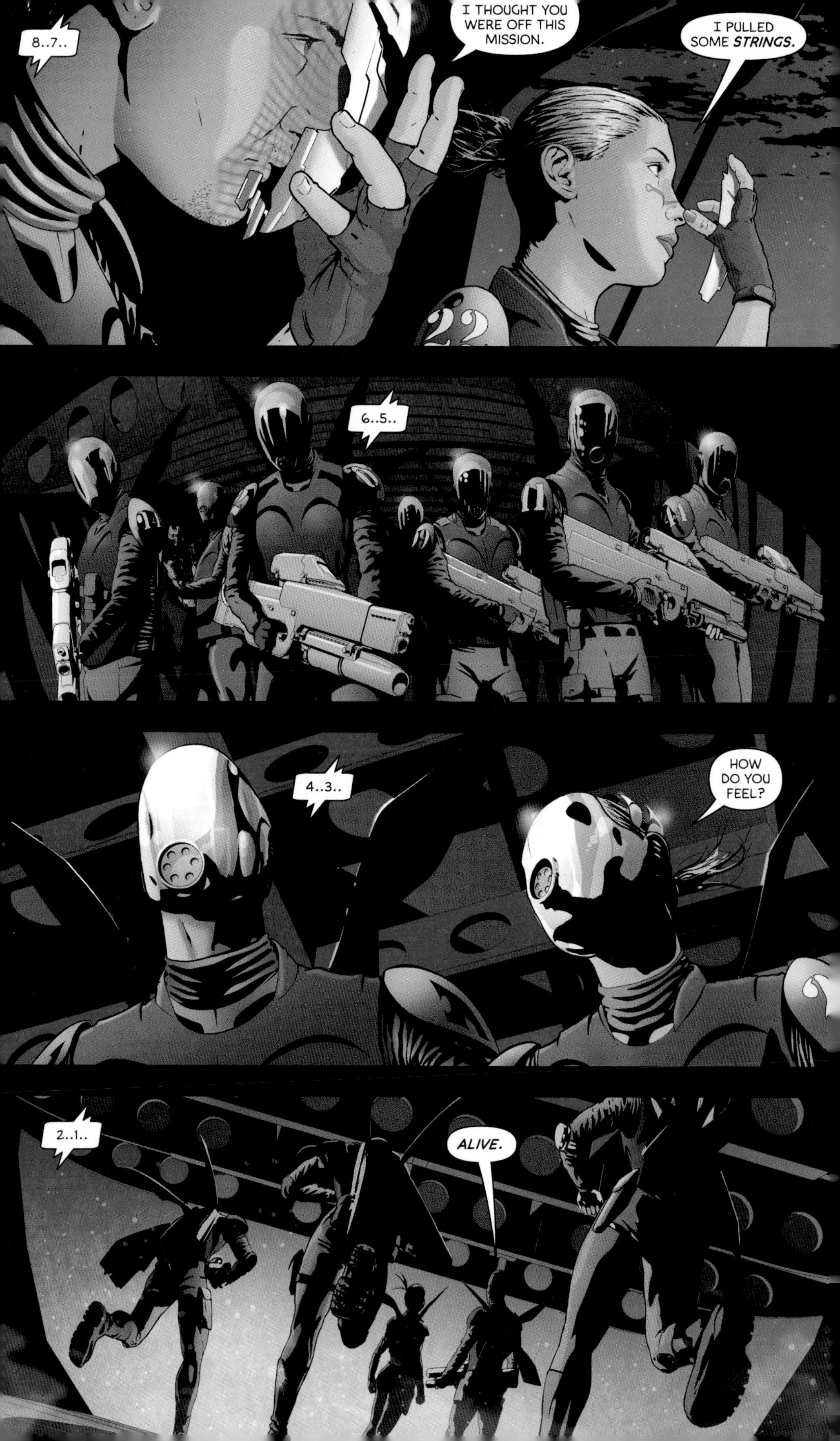
8..7..
I THOUGHT YOU WERE OFF THIS MISSION.
I PULLED SOME STRINGS.
6..5..
4..3..
HOW DO YOU FEEL?
2..1..
ALIVE.

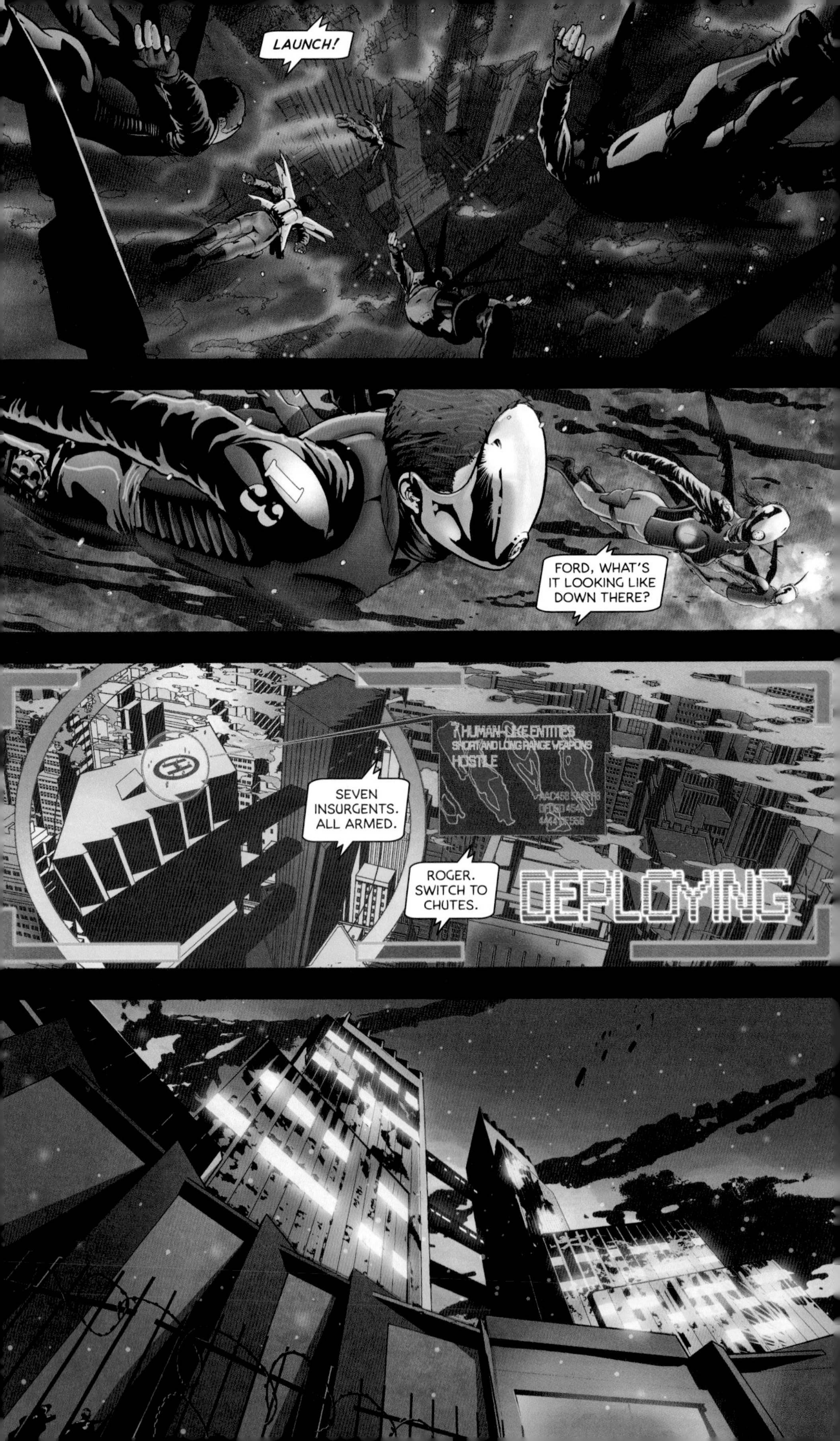
LAUNCH!
FORD, WHAT'S IT LOOKING LIKE DOWN THERE?
7 HUMAN-LIKE ENTITIES
SHORT AND LONG RANGE WEAPONS
HOSTILE
SEVEN INSURGENTS. ALL ARMED.
ROGER. SWITCH TO CHUTES.
DEPLOYING

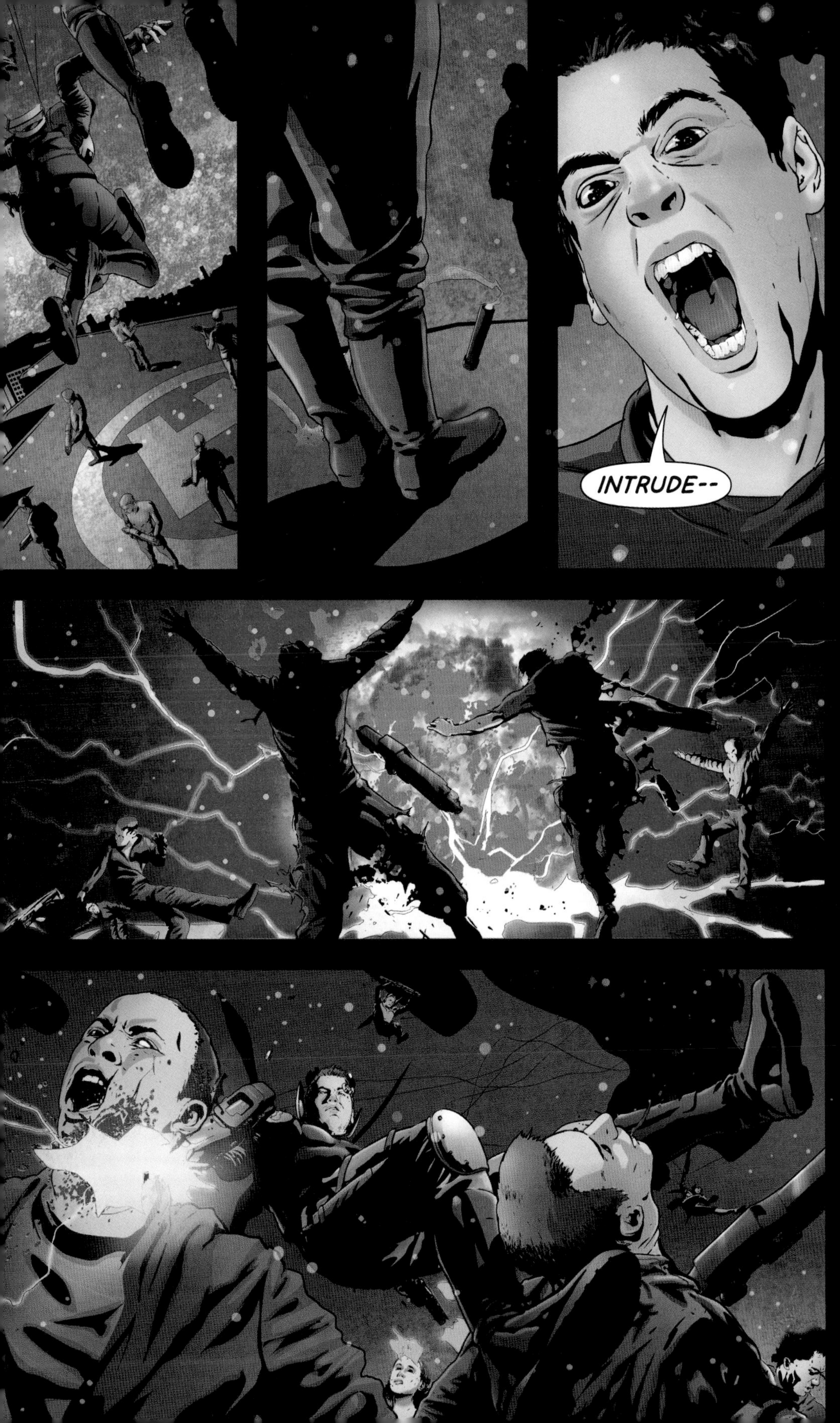
INTRUDE--

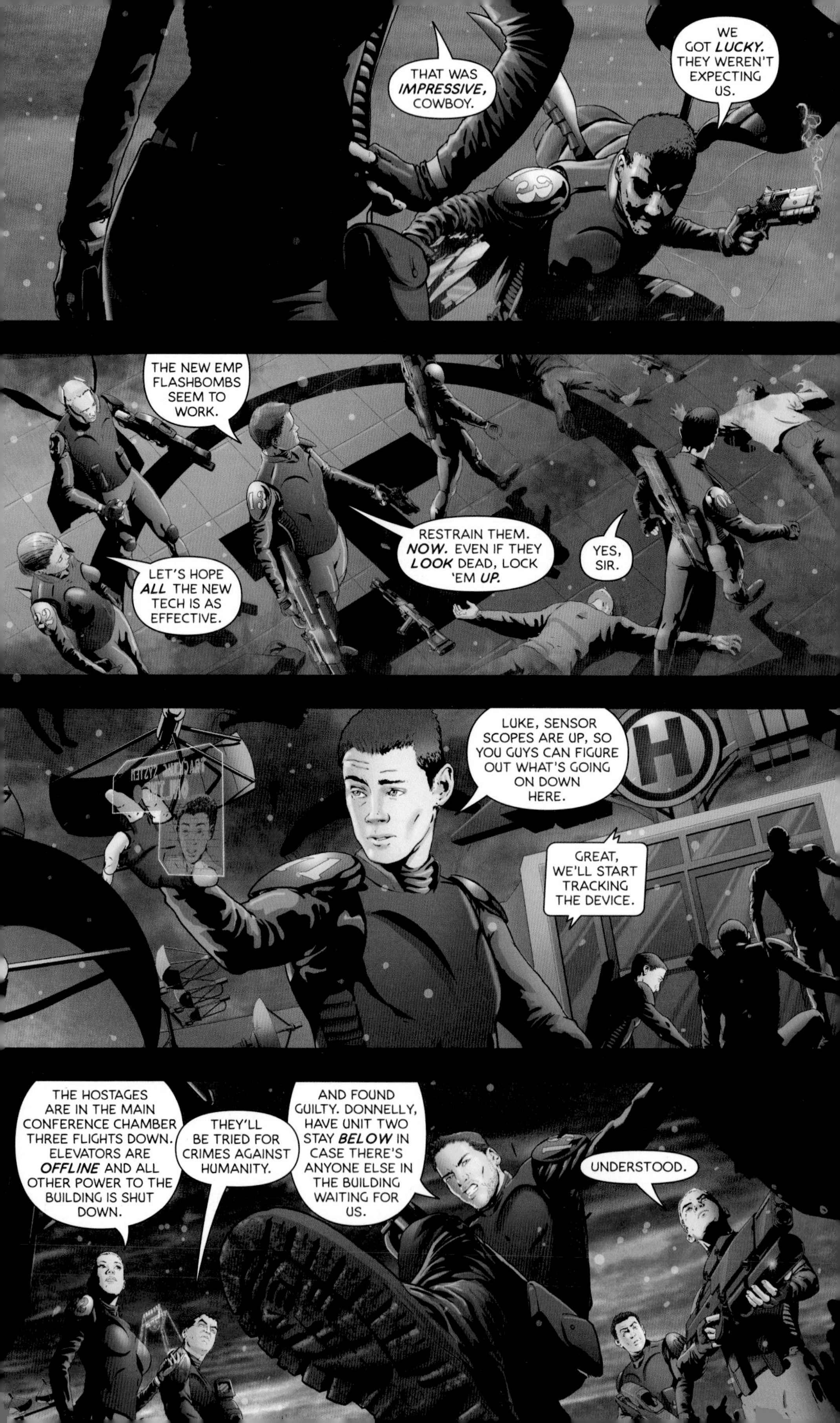
THAT WAS *IMPRESSIVE,* COWBOY.
WE GOT *LUCKY.* THEY WEREN'T EXPECTING US.
THE NEW EMP FLASHBOMBS SEEM TO WORK.
LET'S HOPE *ALL* THE NEW TECH IS AS EFFECTIVE.
RESTRAIN THEM. *NOW.* EVEN IF THEY *LOOK* DEAD, LOCK 'EM *UP.*
YES, SIR.
LUKE, SENSOR SCOPES ARE UP, SO YOU GUYS CAN FIGURE OUT WHAT'S GOING ON DOWN HERE.
GREAT, WE'LL START TRACKING THE DEVICE.
THE HOSTAGES ARE IN THE MAIN CONFERENCE CHAMBER THREE FLIGHTS DOWN. ELEVATORS ARE *OFFLINE* AND ALL OTHER POWER TO THE BUILDING IS SHUT DOWN.
THEY'LL BE TRIED FOR CRIMES AGAINST HUMANITY.
AND FOUND GUILTY. DONNELLY, HAVE UNIT TWO STAY *BELOW* IN CASE THERE'S ANYONE ELSE IN THE BUILDING WAITING FOR US.
UNDERSTOOD.

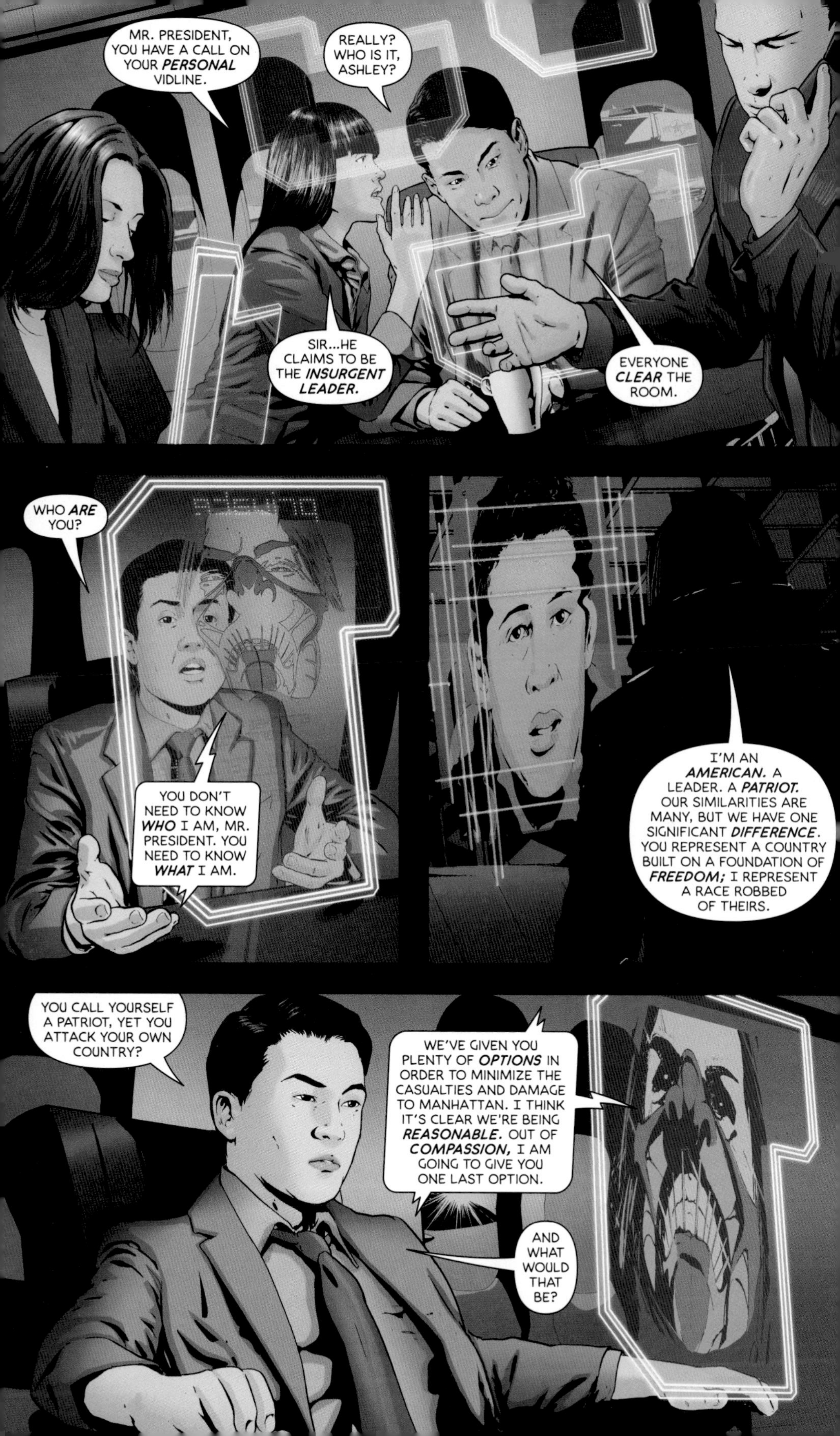
MR. PRESIDENT, YOU HAVE A CALL ON YOUR *PERSONAL* VIDLINE.
REALLY? WHO IS IT, ASHLEY?
SIR...HE CLAIMS TO BE THE *INSURGENT LEADER.*
EVERYONE *CLEAR* THE ROOM.
WHO *ARE* YOU?
YOU DON'T NEED TO KNOW *WHO* I AM, MR. PRESIDENT. YOU NEED TO KNOW *WHAT* I AM.
I'M AN *AMERICAN.* A LEADER. A *PATRIOT.* OUR SIMILARITIES ARE MANY, BUT WE HAVE ONE SIGNIFICANT *DIFFERENCE*. YOU REPRESENT A COUNTRY BUILT ON A FOUNDATION OF *FREEDOM;* I REPRESENT A RACE ROBBED OF THEIRS.
YOU CALL YOURSELF A PATRIOT, YET YOU ATTACK YOUR OWN COUNTRY?
WE'VE GIVEN YOU PLENTY OF *OPTIONS* IN ORDER TO MINIMIZE THE CASUALTIES AND DAMAGE TO MANHATTAN. I THINK IT'S CLEAR WE'RE BEING *REASONABLE.* OUT OF *COMPASSION,* I AM GOING TO GIVE YOU ONE LAST OPTION.
AND WHAT WOULD THAT BE?

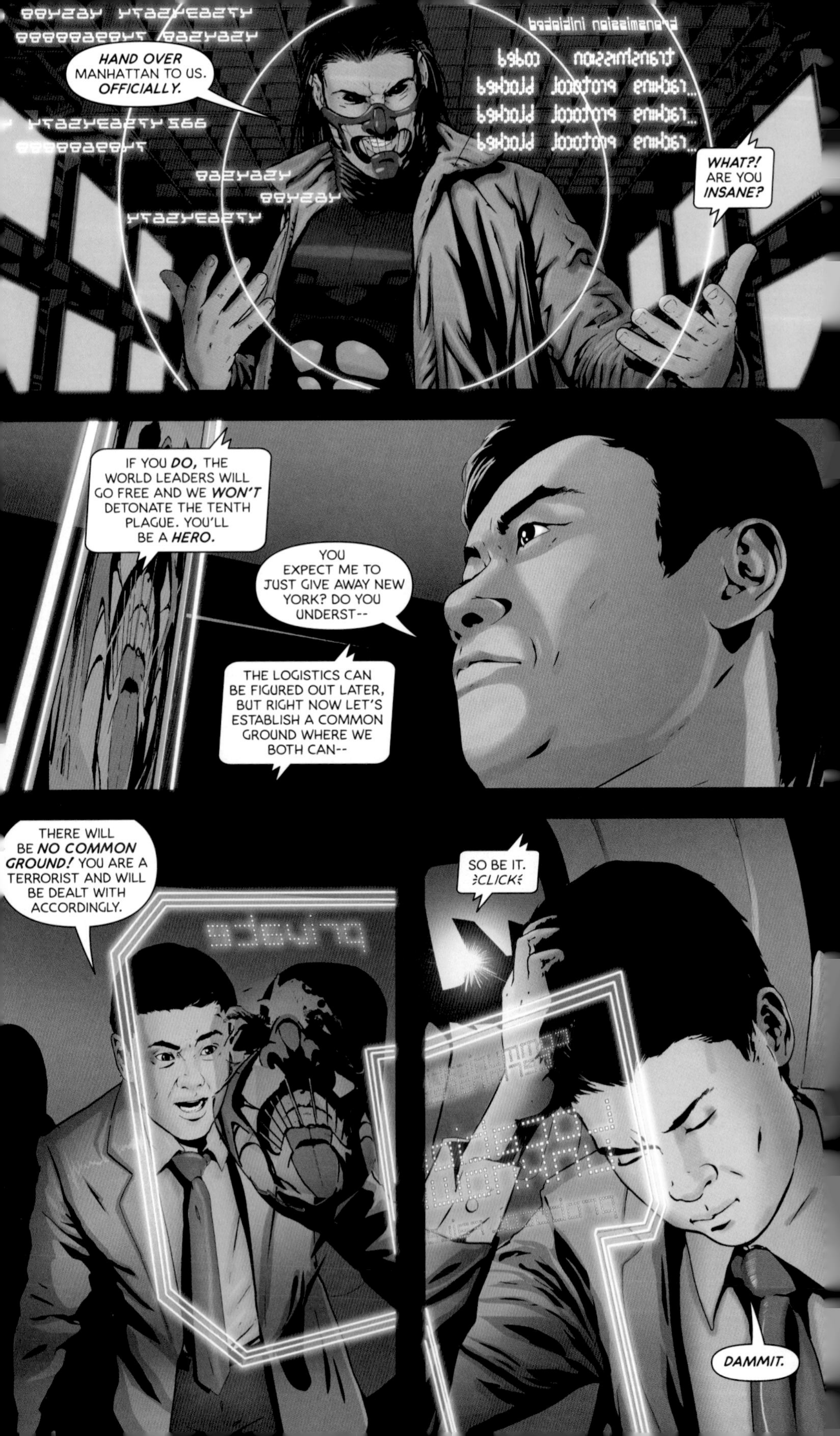
HAND OVER MANHATTAN TO US. OFFICIALLY.
WHAT?! ARE YOU INSANE?
IF YOU DO, THE WORLD LEADERS WILL GO FREE AND WE WON'T DETONATE THE TENTH PLAGUE. YOU'LL BE A HERO.
YOU EXPECT ME TO JUST GIVE AWAY NEW YORK? DO YOU UNDERST--
THE LOGISTICS CAN BE FIGURED OUT LATER, BUT RIGHT NOW LET'S ESTABLISH A COMMON GROUND WHERE WE BOTH CAN--
THERE WILL BE NO COMMON GROUND! YOU ARE A TERRORIST AND WILL BE DEALT WITH ACCORDINGLY.
SO BE IT.
CLICK
DAMMIT.

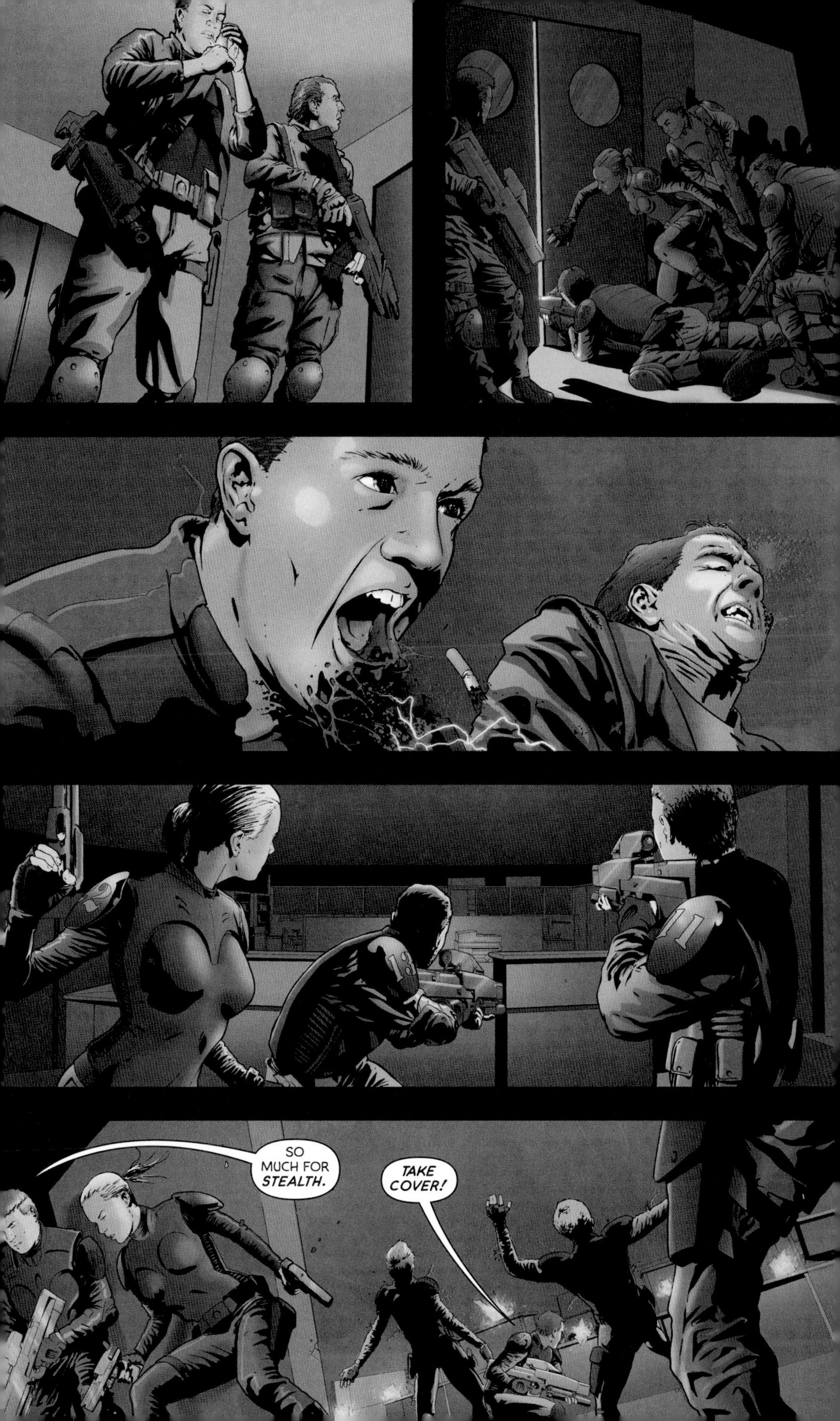
SO MUCH FOR STEALTH.
TAKE COVER!

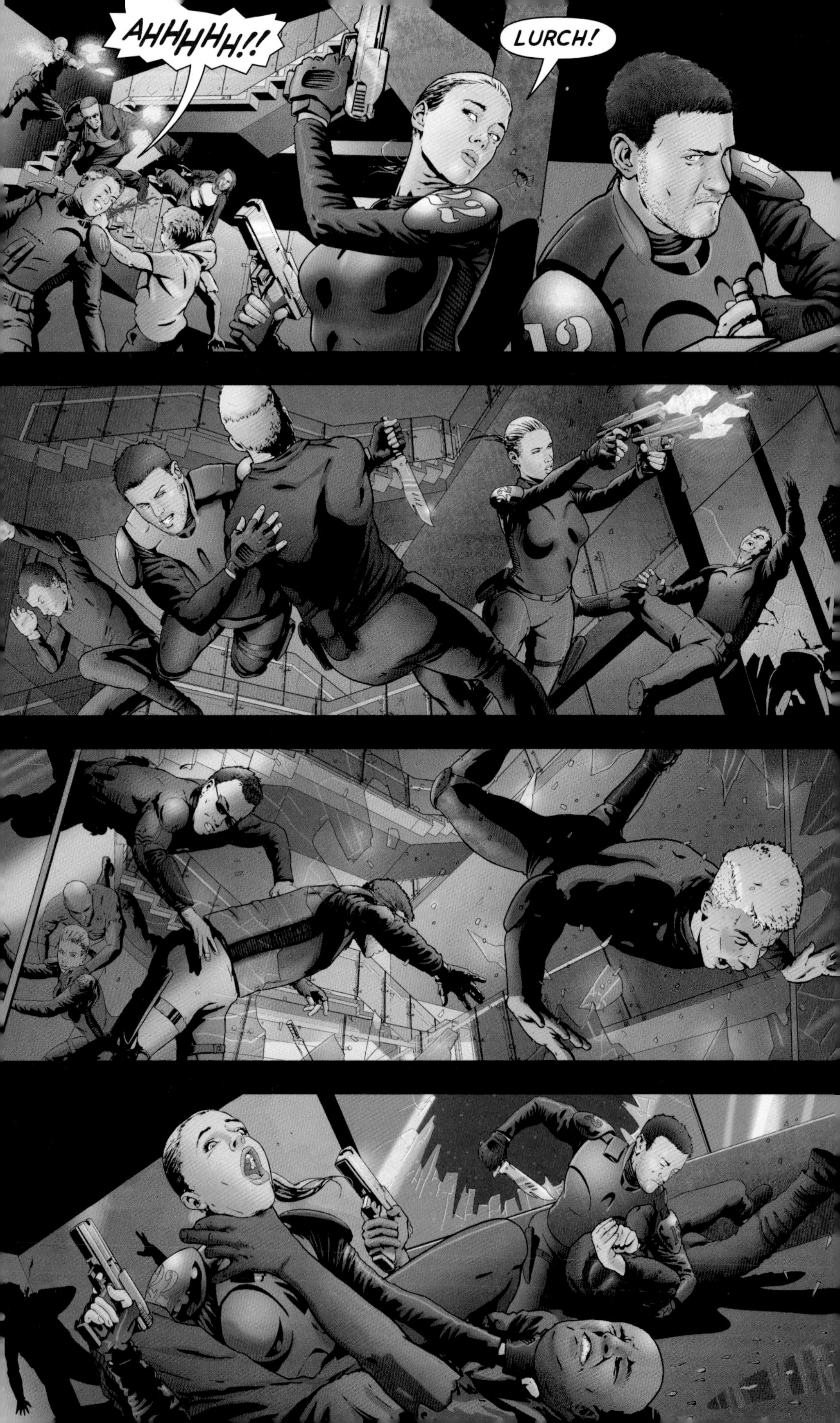
AHHHHH!!
LURCH!

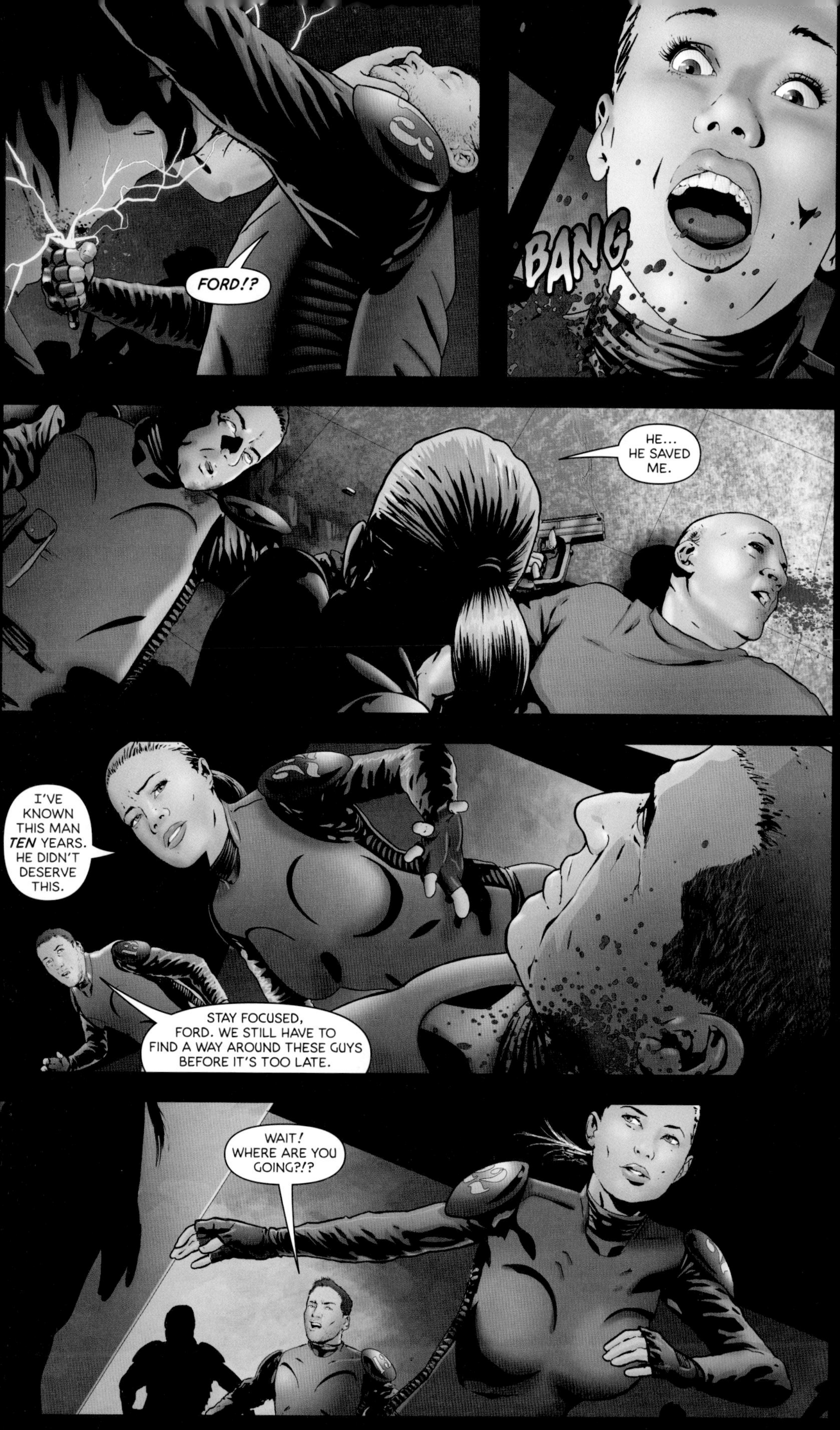
FORD!?
BANG
HE... HE SAVED ME.
I'VE KNOWN THIS MAN TEN YEARS. HE DIDN'T DESERVE THIS.
STAY FOCUSED, FORD. WE STILL HAVE TO FIND A WAY AROUND THESE GUYS BEFORE IT'S TOO LATE.
WAIT! WHERE ARE YOU GOING?!?

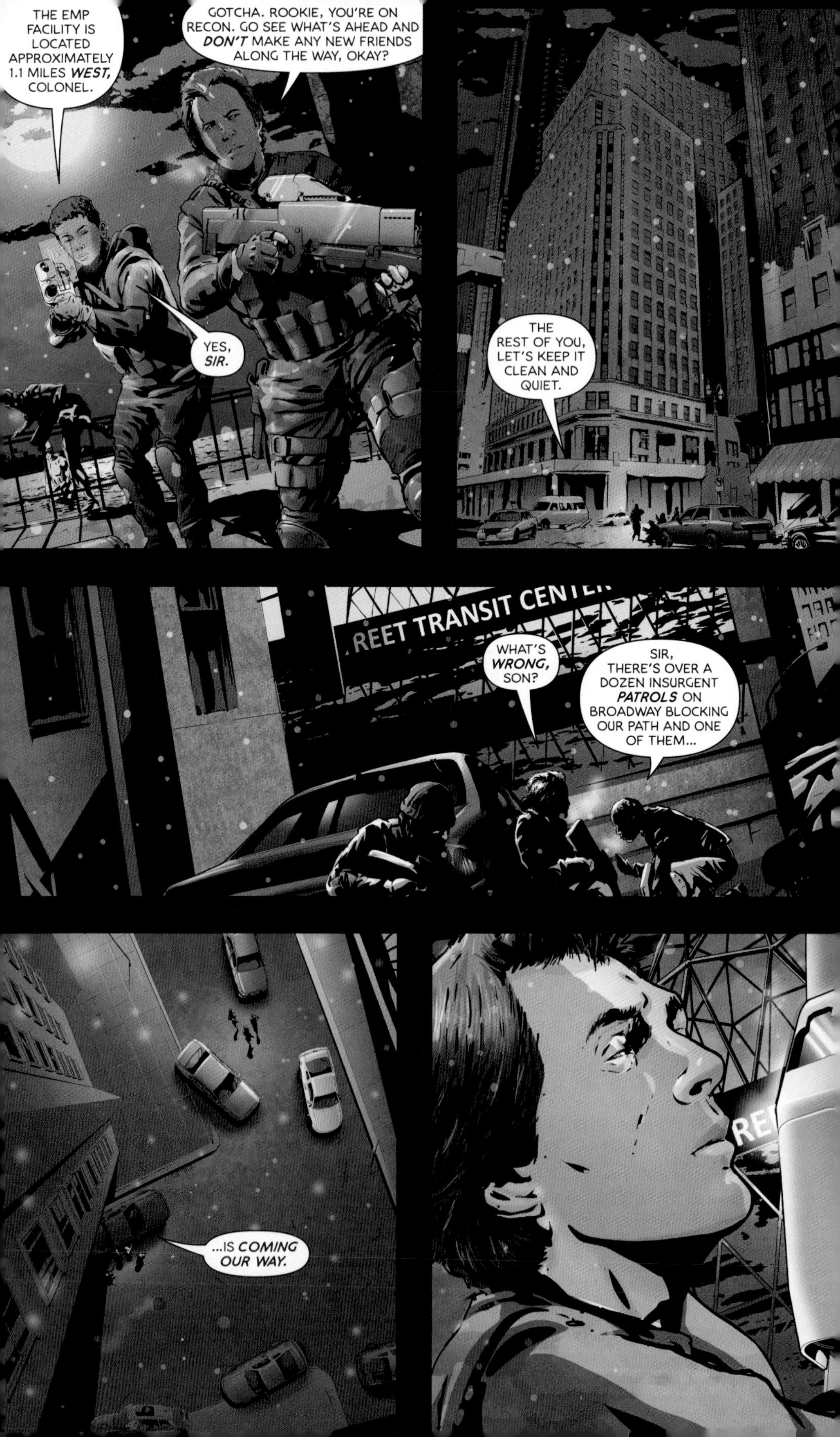
THE EMP FACILITY IS LOCATED APPROXIMATELY 1.1 MILES *WEST,* COLONEL.
GOTCHA. ROOKIE, YOU'RE ON RECON. GO SEE WHAT'S AHEAD AND ***DON'T*** MAKE ANY NEW FRIENDS ALONG THE WAY, OKAY?
YES, ***SIR.***
THE REST OF YOU, LET'S KEEP IT CLEAN AND QUIET.
REET TRANSIT CENTE
WHAT'S ***WRONG,*** SON?
SIR, THERE'S OVER A DOZEN INSURGENT ***PATROLS*** ON BROADWAY BLOCKING OUR PATH AND ONE OF THEM...
...IS ***COMING OUR WAY.***

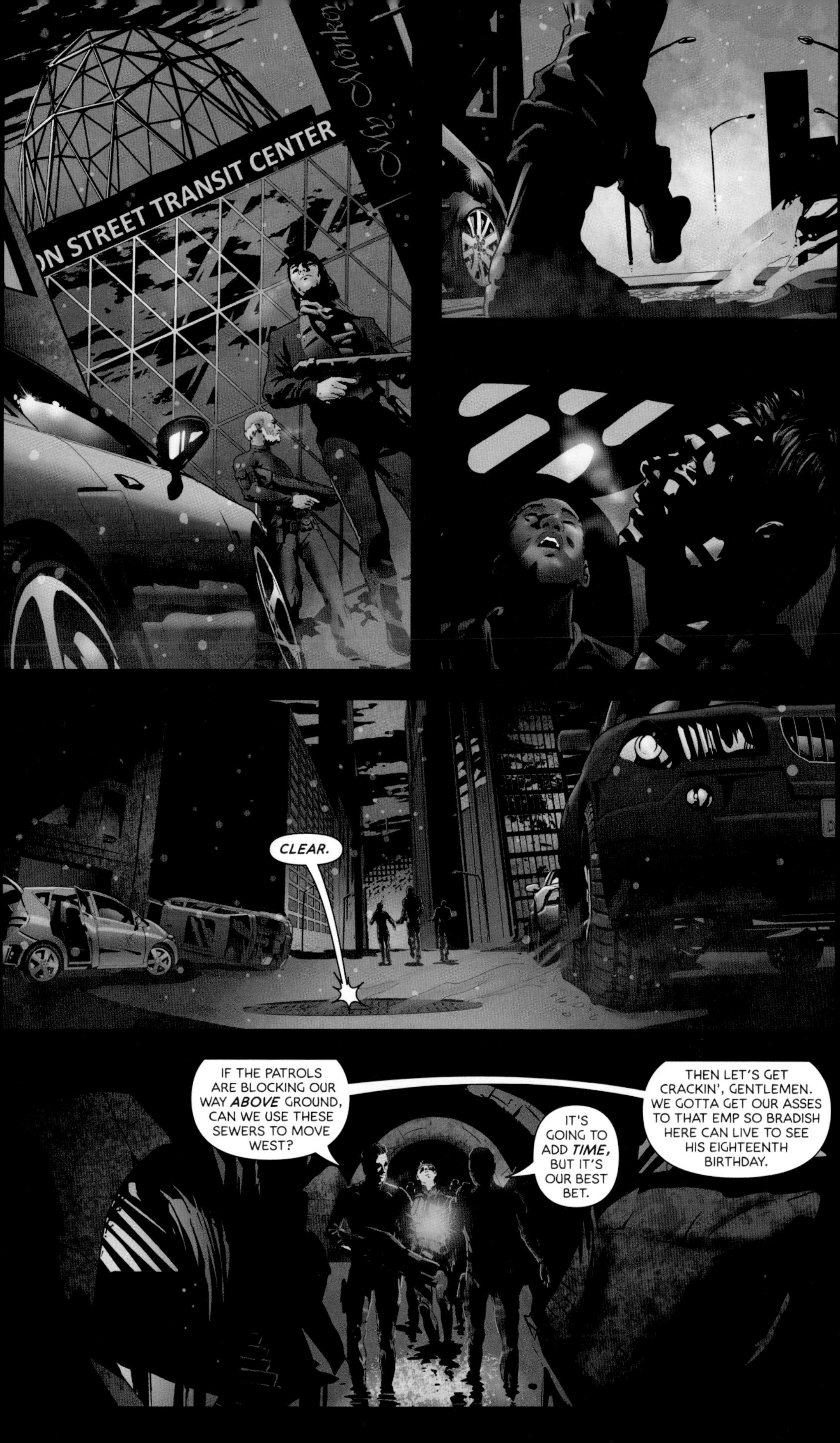
ON STREET TRANSIT CENTER
CLEAR.
IF THE PATROLS ARE BLOCKING OUR WAY *ABOVE* GROUND, CAN WE USE THESE SEWERS TO MOVE WEST?
IT'S GOING TO ADD *TIME,* BUT IT'S OUR BEST BET.
THEN LET'S GET CRACKIN', GENTLEMEN. WE GOTTA GET OUR ASSES TO THAT EMP SO BRADISH HERE CAN LIVE TO SEE HIS EIGHTEENTH BIRTHDAY.

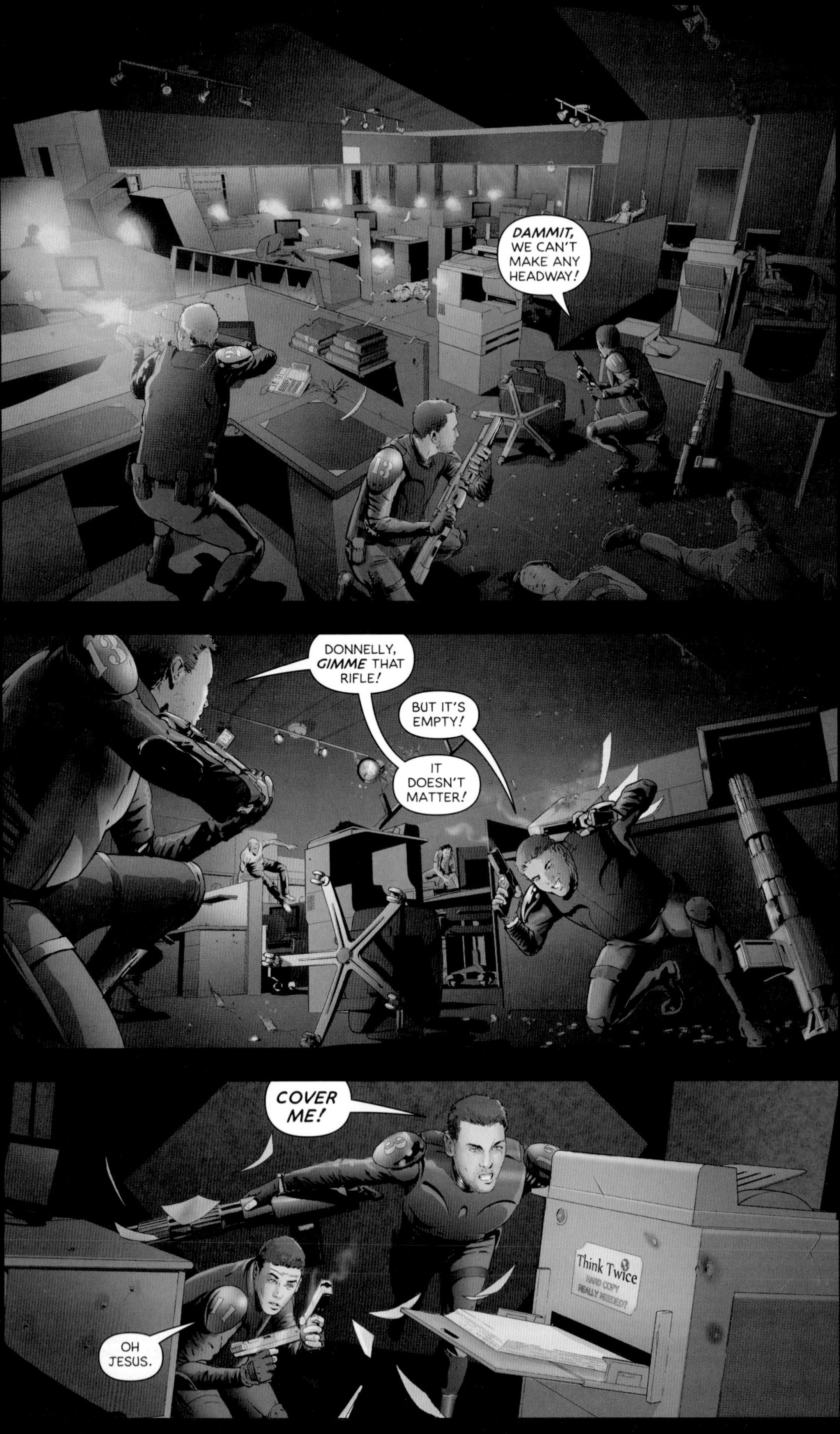

DAMMIT, WE CAN'T MAKE ANY HEADWAY!
DONNELLY, GIMME THAT RIFLE!
BUT IT'S EMPTY!
IT DOESN'T MATTER!
COVER ME!
Think Twice
HARD COPY REALLY NEEDED?
OH JESUS.

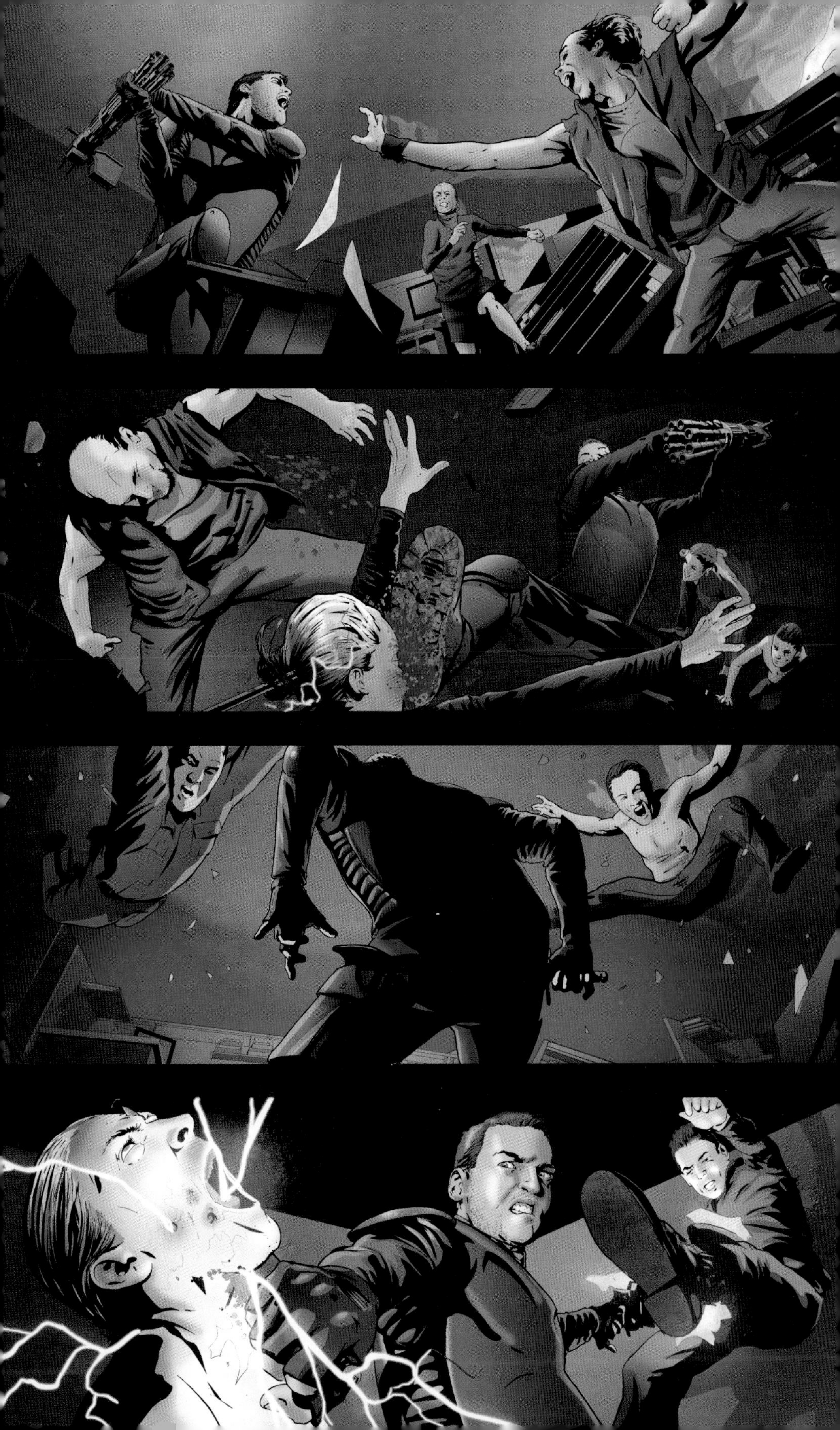

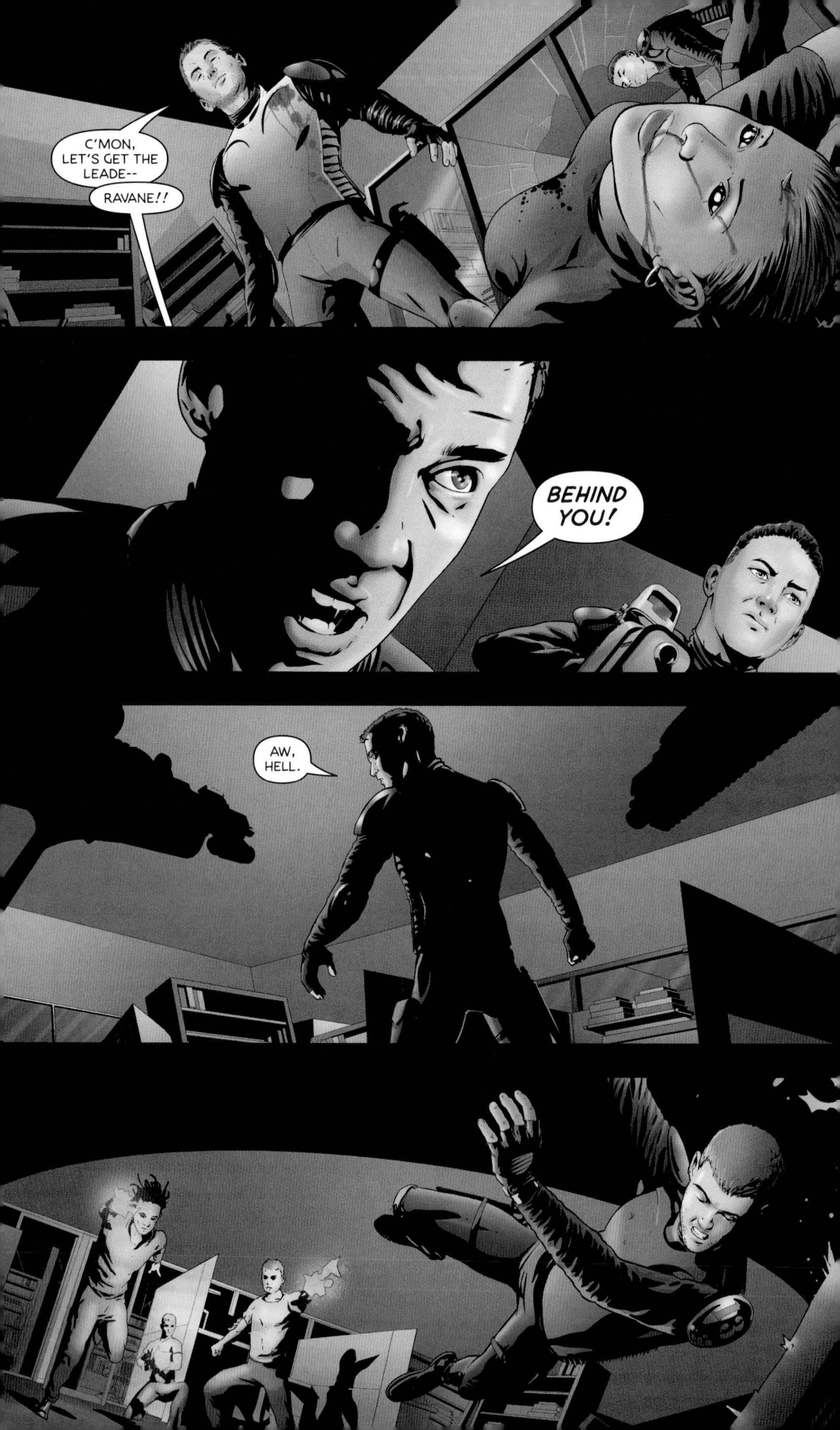
C'MON, LET'S GET THE LEADE--
RAVANE!!
BEHIND YOU!
AW, HELL.

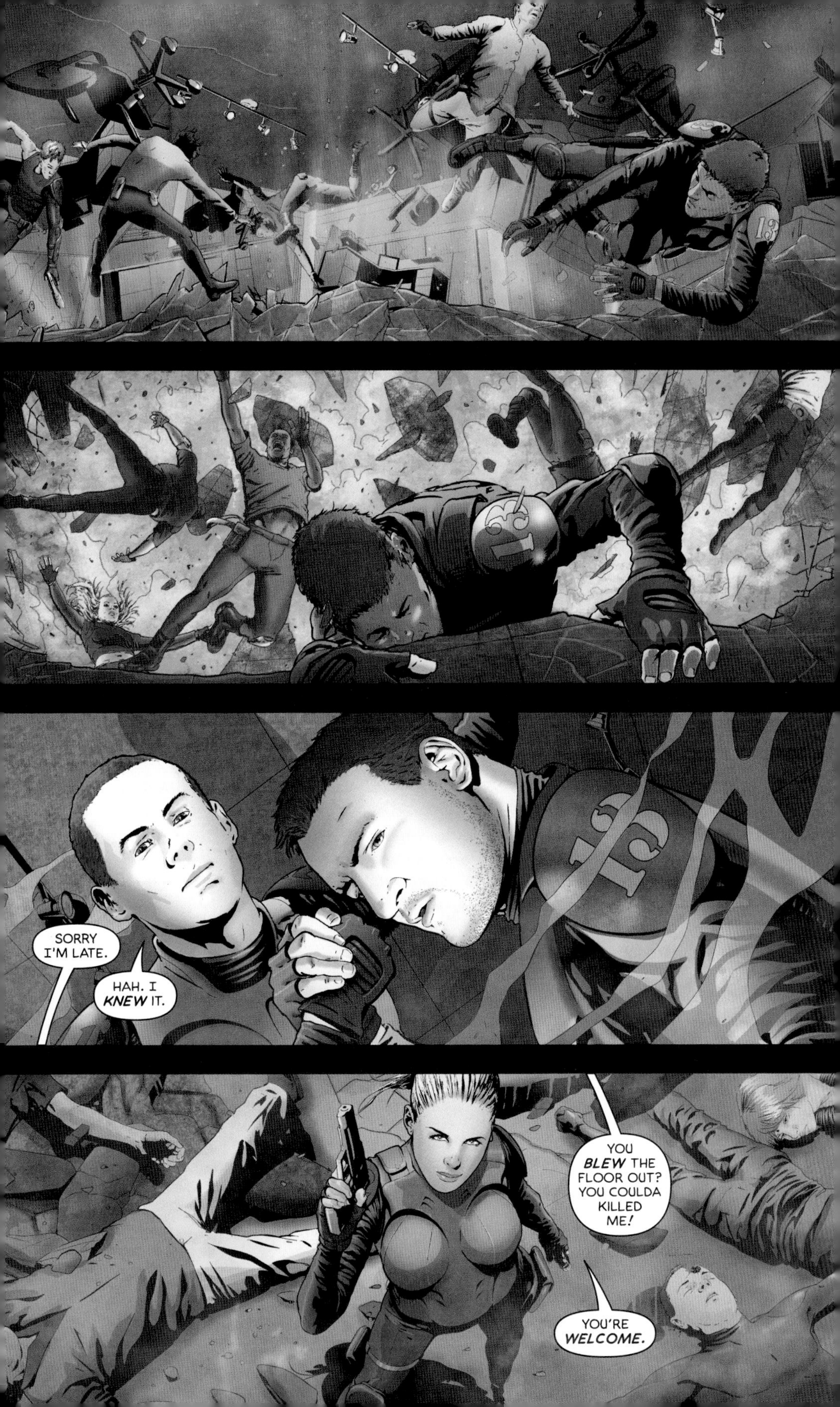
SORRY I'M LATE.
HAH. I **KNEW** IT.
YOU **BLEW** THE FLOOR OUT? YOU COULDA KILLED ME!
YOU'RE **WELCOME.**

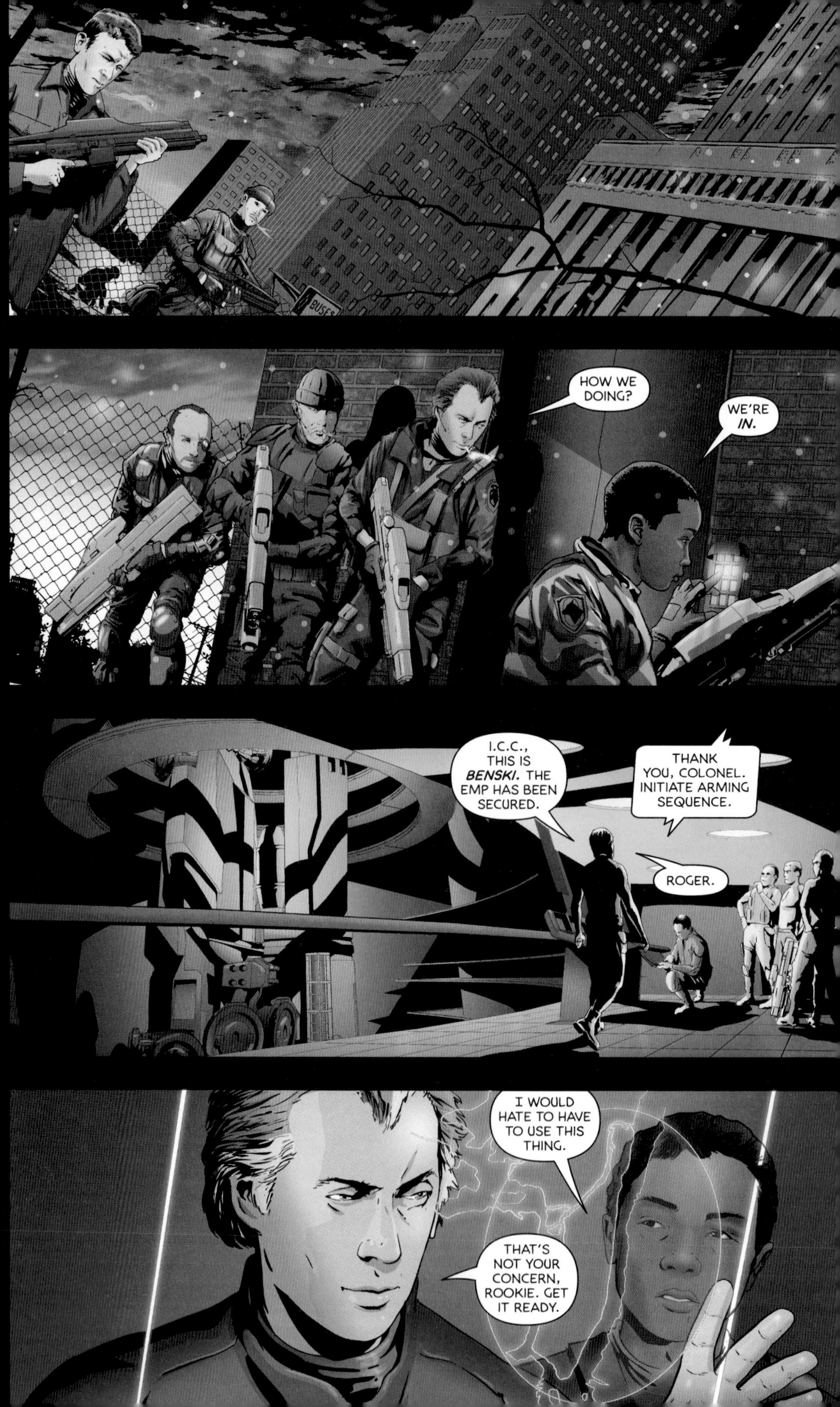
BUSES
HOW WE DOING?
WE'RE *IN.*
I.C.C., THIS IS ***BENSKI.*** THE EMP HAS BEEN SECURED.
THANK YOU, COLONEL. INITIATE ARMING SEQUENCE.
ROGER.
I WOULD HATE TO HAVE TO USE THIS THING.
THAT'S NOT YOUR CONCERN, ROOKIE. GET IT READY.

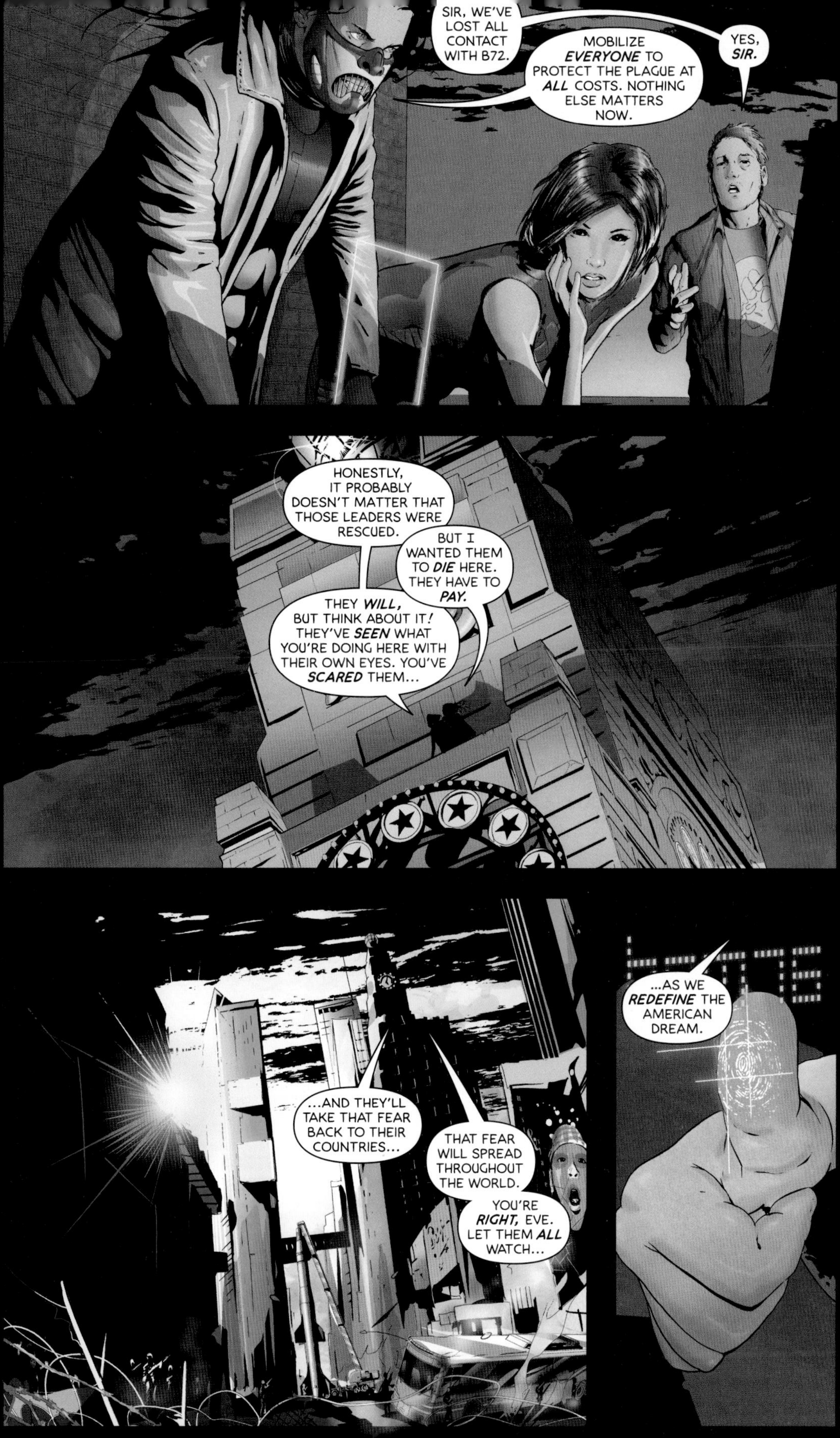
SIR, WE'VE LOST ALL CONTACT WITH B72.
MOBILIZE *EVERYONE* TO PROTECT THE PLAGUE AT *ALL* COSTS. NOTHING ELSE MATTERS NOW.
YES, *SIR.*
HONESTLY, IT PROBABLY DOESN'T MATTER THAT THOSE LEADERS WERE RESCUED.
BUT I WANTED THEM TO *DIE* HERE. THEY HAVE TO *PAY.*
THEY *WILL,* BUT THINK ABOUT IT! THEY'VE *SEEN* WHAT YOU'RE DOING HERE WITH THEIR OWN EYES. YOU'VE *SCARED* THEM...
...AND THEY'LL TAKE THAT FEAR BACK TO THEIR COUNTRIES...
THAT FEAR WILL SPREAD THROUGHOUT THE WORLD.
YOU'RE *RIGHT,* EVE. LET THEM *ALL* WATCH...
...AS WE *REDEFINE* THE AMERICAN DREAM.

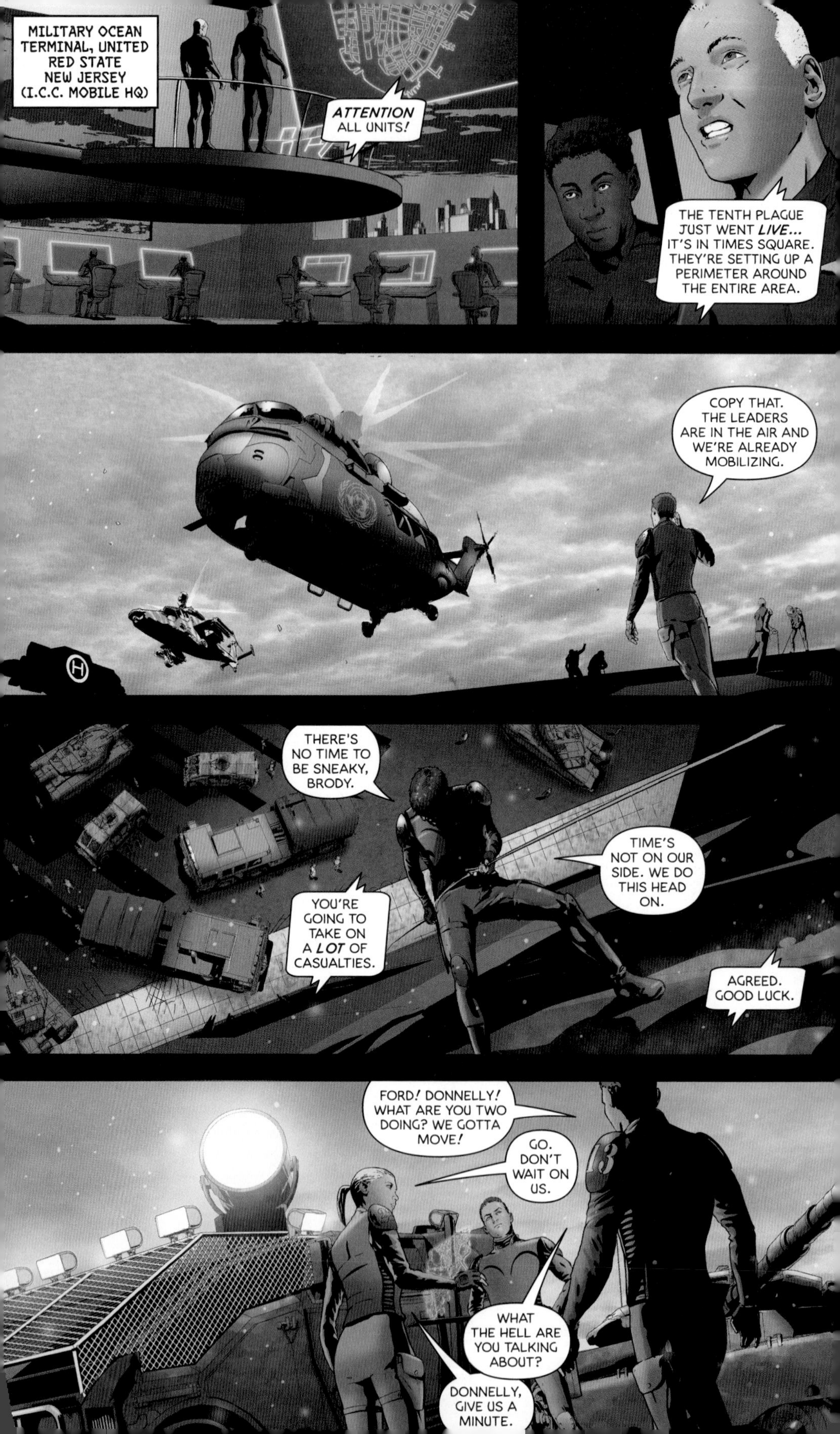
MILITARY OCEAN TERMINAL, UNITED RED STATE NEW JERSEY (I.C.C. MOBILE HQ)
ATTENTION ALL UNITS!
THE TENTH PLAGUE JUST WENT LIVE... IT'S IN TIMES SQUARE. THEY'RE SETTING UP A PERIMETER AROUND THE ENTIRE AREA.
COPY THAT. THE LEADERS ARE IN THE AIR AND WE'RE ALREADY MOBILIZING.
THERE'S NO TIME TO BE SNEAKY, BRODY.
YOU'RE GOING TO TAKE ON A LOT OF CASUALTIES.
TIME'S NOT ON OUR SIDE. WE DO THIS HEAD ON.
AGREED. GOOD LUCK.
FORD! DONNELLY! WHAT ARE YOU TWO DOING? WE GOTTA MOVE!
GO. DON'T WAIT ON US.
WHAT THE HELL ARE YOU TALKING ABOUT?
DONNELLY, GIVE US A MINUTE.

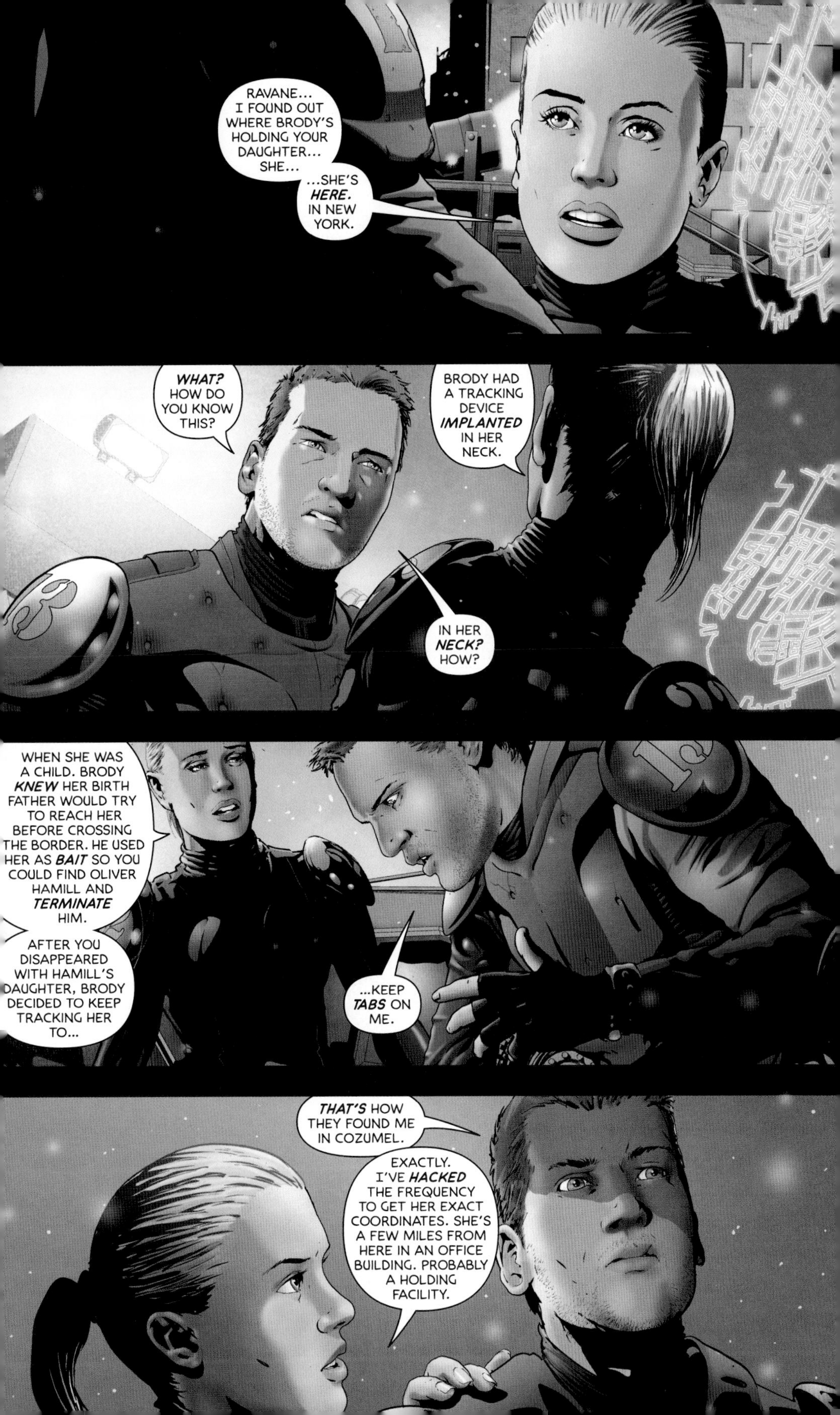
RAVANE... I FOUND OUT WHERE BRODY'S HOLDING YOUR DAUGHTER... SHE...
...SHE'S *HERE.* IN NEW YORK.
WHAT? HOW DO YOU KNOW THIS?
BRODY HAD A TRACKING DEVICE *IMPLANTED* IN HER NECK.
IN HER *NECK?* HOW?
WHEN SHE WAS A CHILD. BRODY *KNEW* HER BIRTH FATHER WOULD TRY TO REACH HER BEFORE CROSSING THE BORDER. HE USED HER AS *BAIT* SO YOU COULD FIND OLIVER HAMILL AND *TERMINATE* HIM.
AFTER YOU DISAPPEARED WITH HAMILL'S DAUGHTER, BRODY DECIDED TO KEEP TRACKING HER TO...
...KEEP *TABS* ON ME.
THAT'S HOW THEY FOUND ME IN COZUMEL.
EXACTLY. I'VE *HACKED* THE FREQUENCY TO GET HER EXACT COORDINATES. SHE'S A FEW MILES FROM HERE IN AN OFFICE BUILDING. PROBABLY A HOLDING FACILITY.

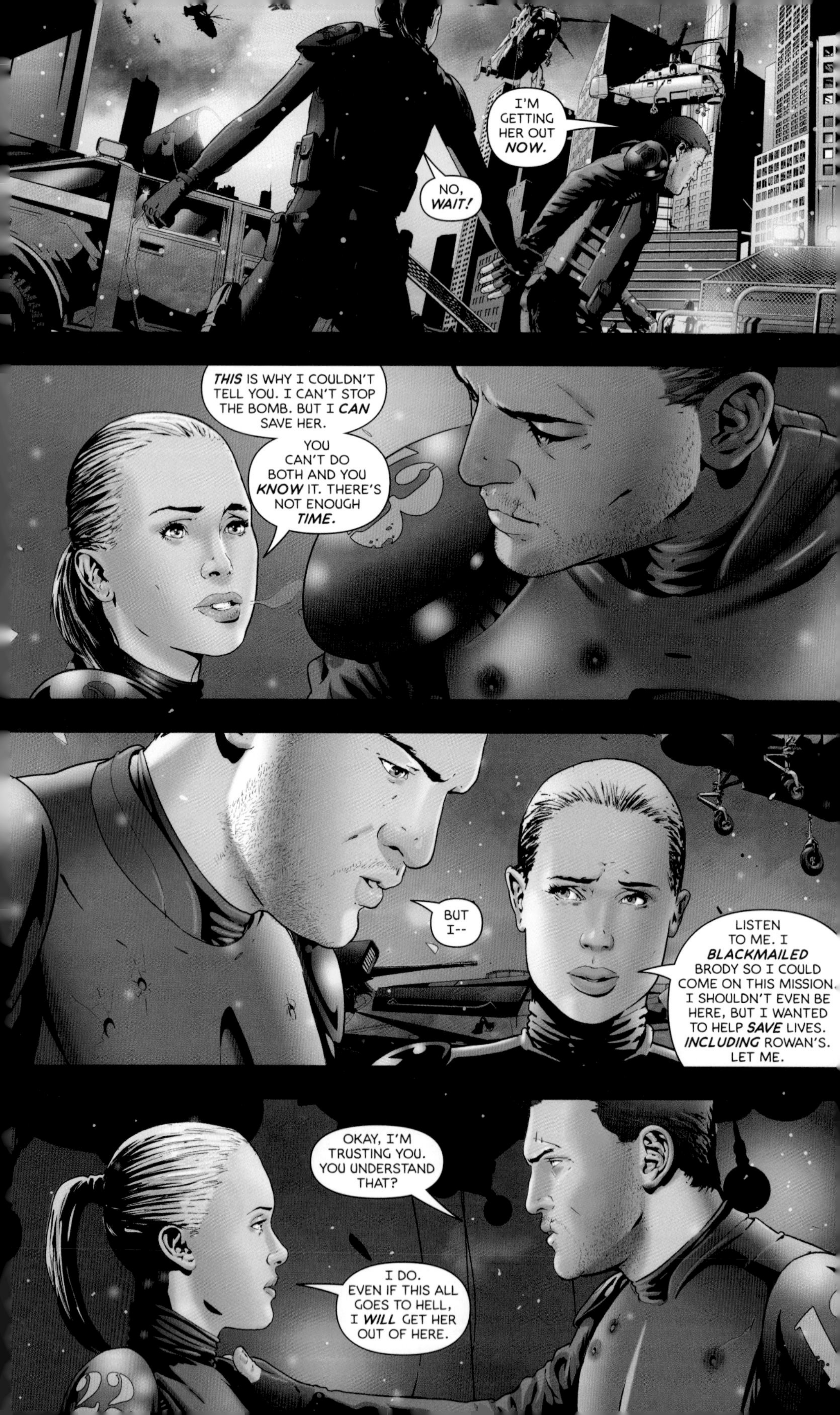

I'M GETTING HER OUT NOW.
NO, WAIT!
THIS IS WHY I COULDN'T TELL YOU. I CAN'T STOP THE BOMB. BUT I CAN SAVE HER.
YOU CAN'T DO BOTH AND YOU KNOW IT. THERE'S NOT ENOUGH TIME.
BUT I--
LISTEN TO ME. I BLACKMAILED BRODY SO I COULD COME ON THIS MISSION. I SHOULDN'T EVEN BE HERE, BUT I WANTED TO HELP SAVE LIVES. INCLUDING ROWAN'S. LET ME.
OKAY, I'M TRUSTING YOU. YOU UNDERSTAND THAT?
I DO. EVEN IF THIS ALL GOES TO HELL, I WILL GET HER OUT OF HERE.

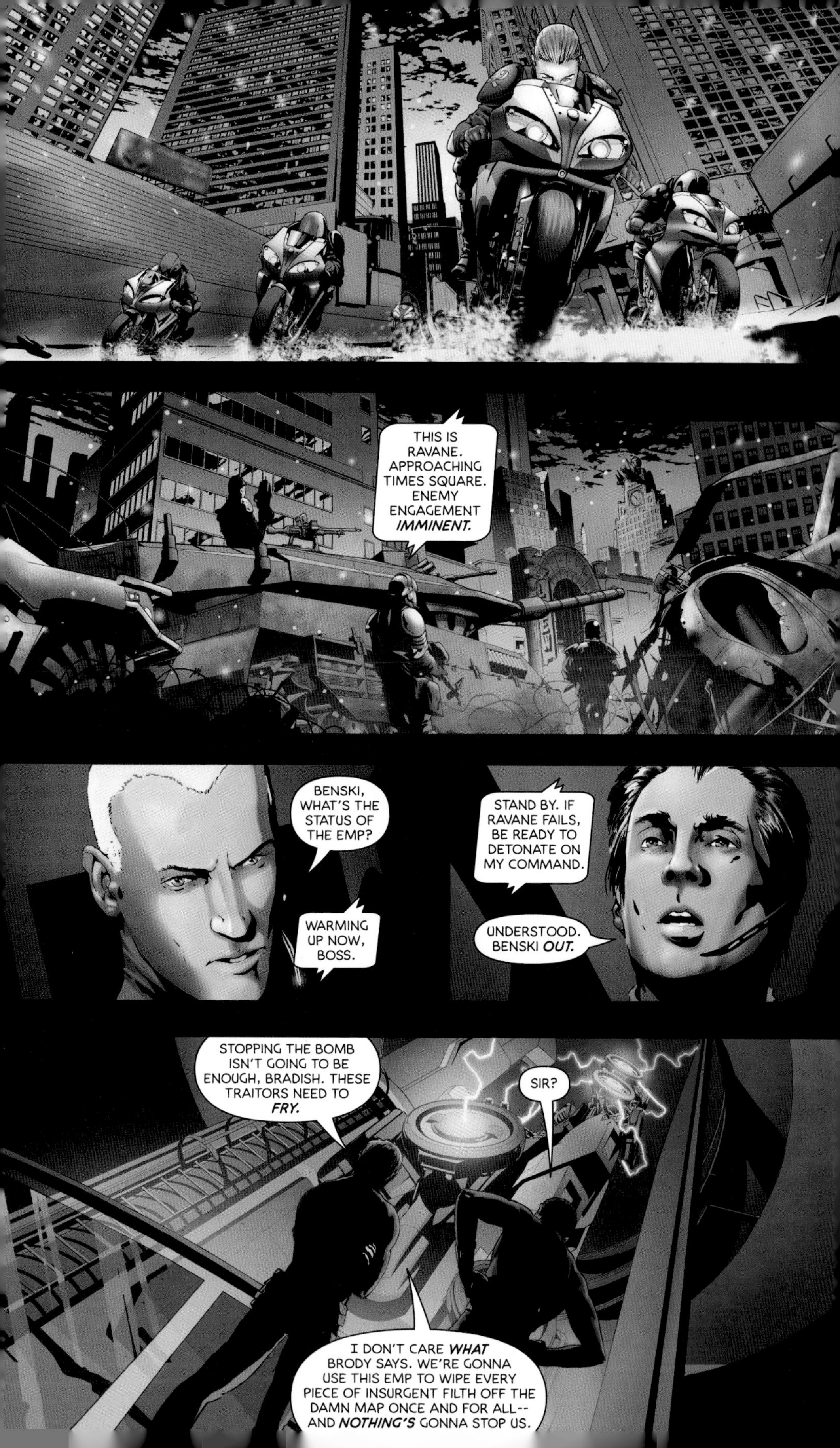

THIS IS RAVANE. APPROACHING TIMES SQUARE. ENEMY ENGAGEMENT *IMMINENT.*
BENSKI, WHAT'S THE STATUS OF THE EMP?
WARMING UP NOW, BOSS.
STAND BY. IF RAVANE FAILS, BE READY TO DETONATE ON MY COMMAND.
UNDERSTOOD. BENSKI *OUT.*
STOPPING THE BOMB ISN'T GOING TO BE ENOUGH, BRADISH. THESE TRAITORS NEED TO *FRY.*
SIR?
I DON'T CARE *WHAT* BRODY SAYS. WE'RE GONNA USE THIS EMP TO WIPE EVERY PIECE OF INSURGENT FILTH OFF THE DAMN MAP ONCE AND FOR ALL-- AND *NOTHING'S* GONNA STOP US.

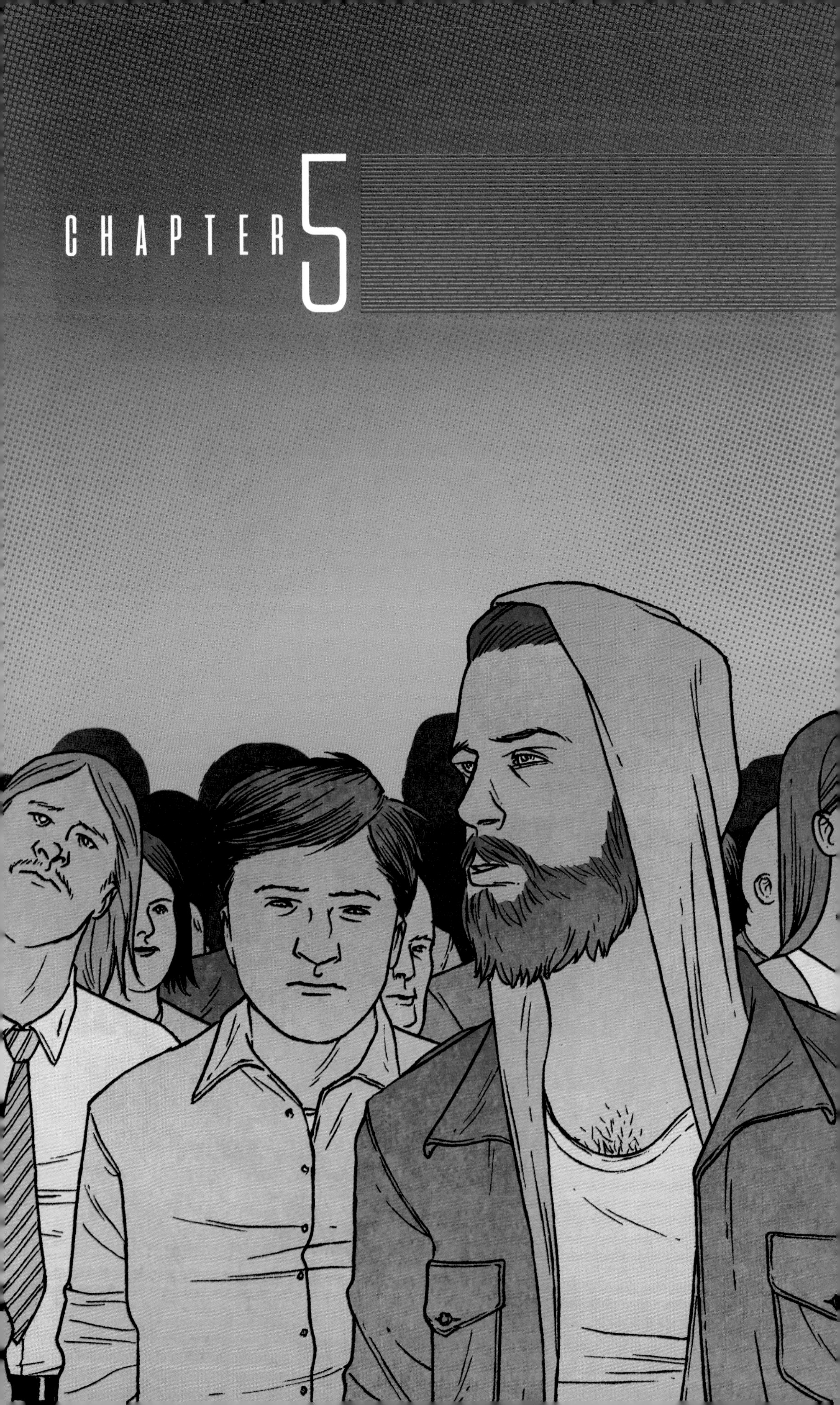
CHAPTER 5

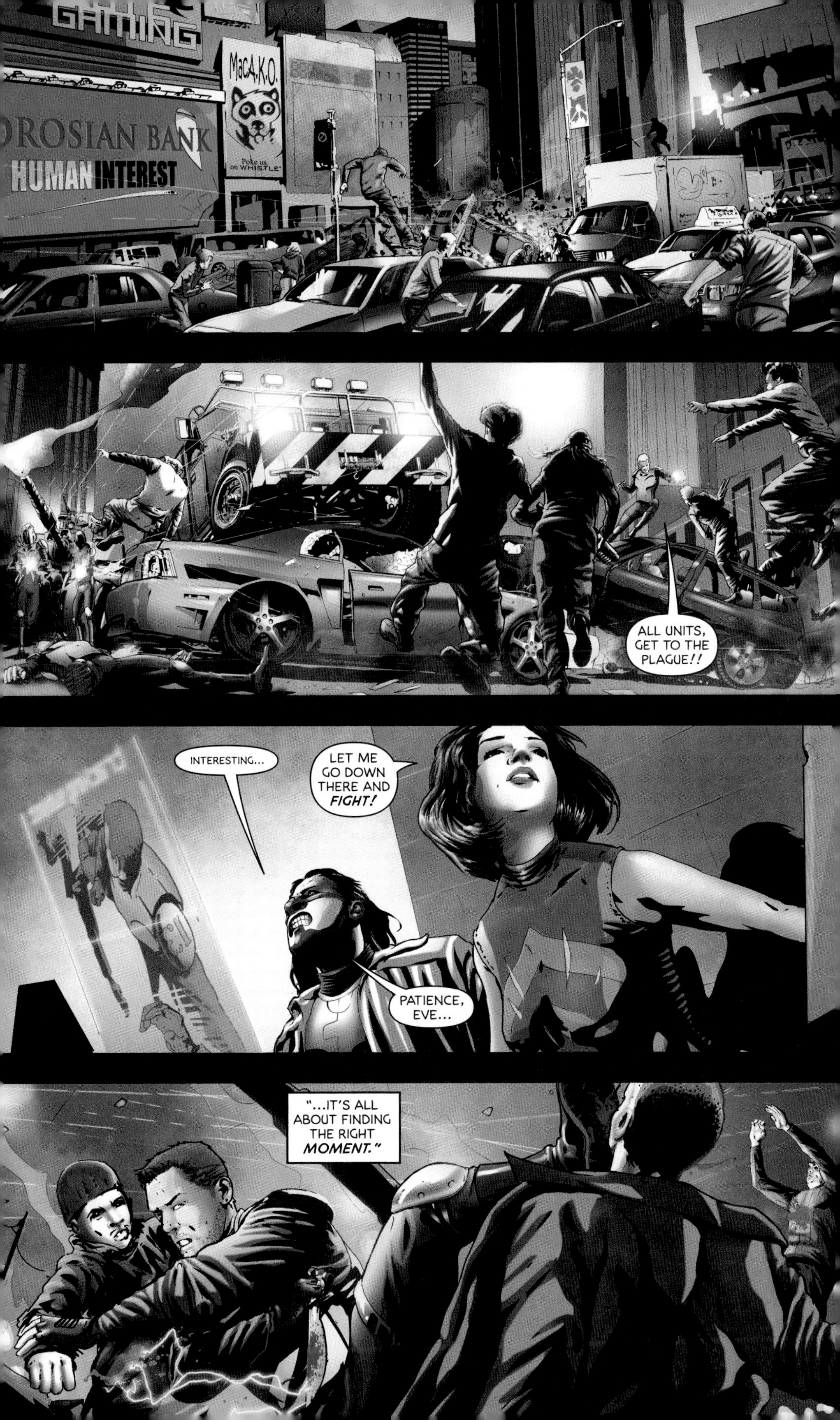
GAMING
MacA.K.O.
Poke us on WHISTLE
OROSIAN BANK
HUMAN INTEREST
ALL UNITS, GET TO THE PLAGUE!!
INTERESTING...
LET ME GO DOWN THERE AND *FIGHT!*
PATIENCE, EVE...
"...IT'S ALL ABOUT FINDING THE RIGHT *MOMENT.*"

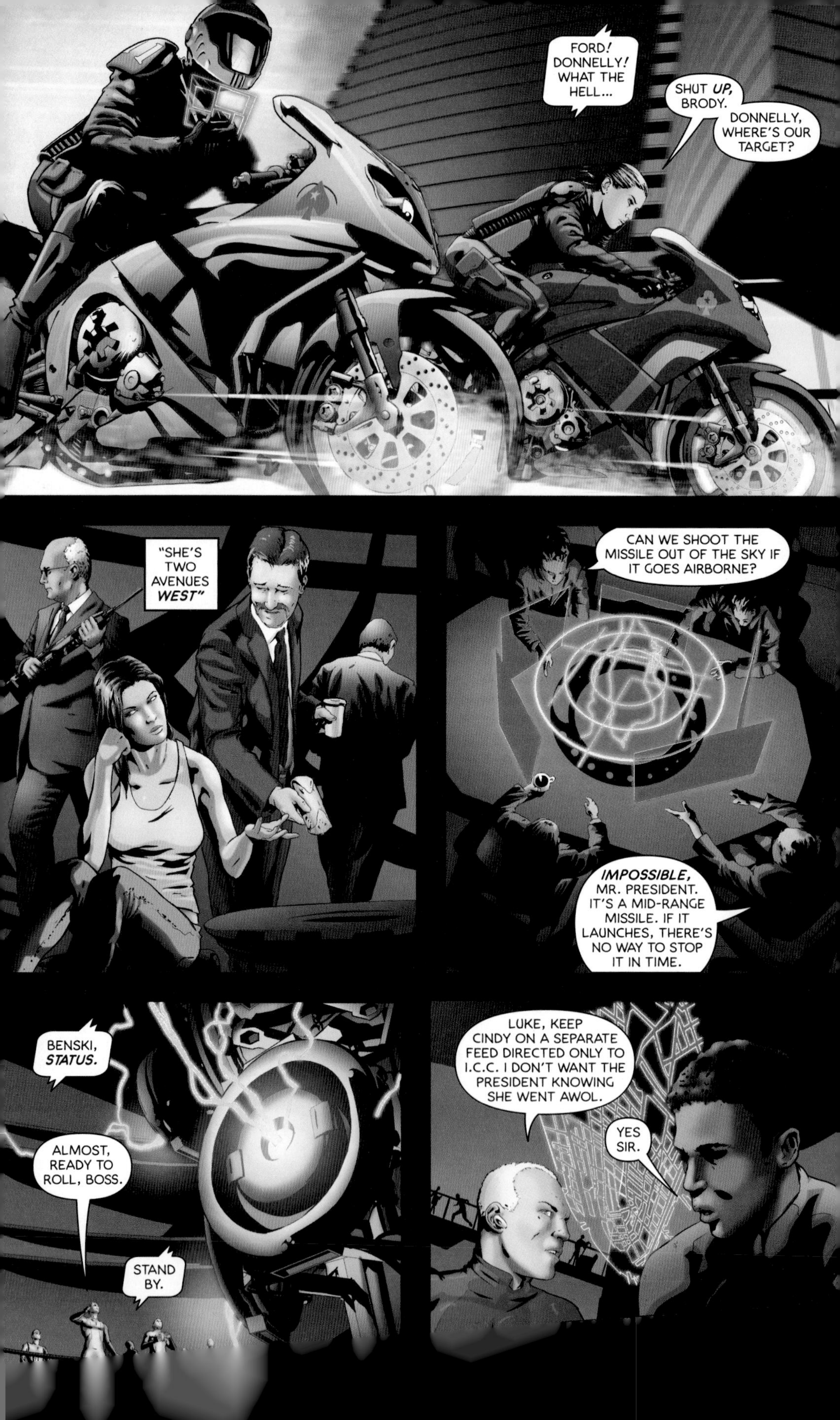
FORD! DONNELLY! WHAT THE HELL...
SHUT UP, BRODY.
DONNELLY, WHERE'S OUR TARGET?
"SHE'S TWO AVENUES WEST"
CAN WE SHOOT THE MISSILE OUT OF THE SKY IF IT GOES AIRBORNE?
IMPOSSIBLE, MR. PRESIDENT. IT'S A MID-RANGE MISSILE. IF IT LAUNCHES, THERE'S NO WAY TO STOP IT IN TIME.
BENSKI, STATUS.
ALMOST, READY TO ROLL, BOSS.
STAND BY.
LUKE, KEEP CINDY ON A SEPARATE FEED DIRECTED ONLY TO I.C.C. I DON'T WANT THE PRESIDENT KNOWING SHE WENT AWOL.
YES SIR.

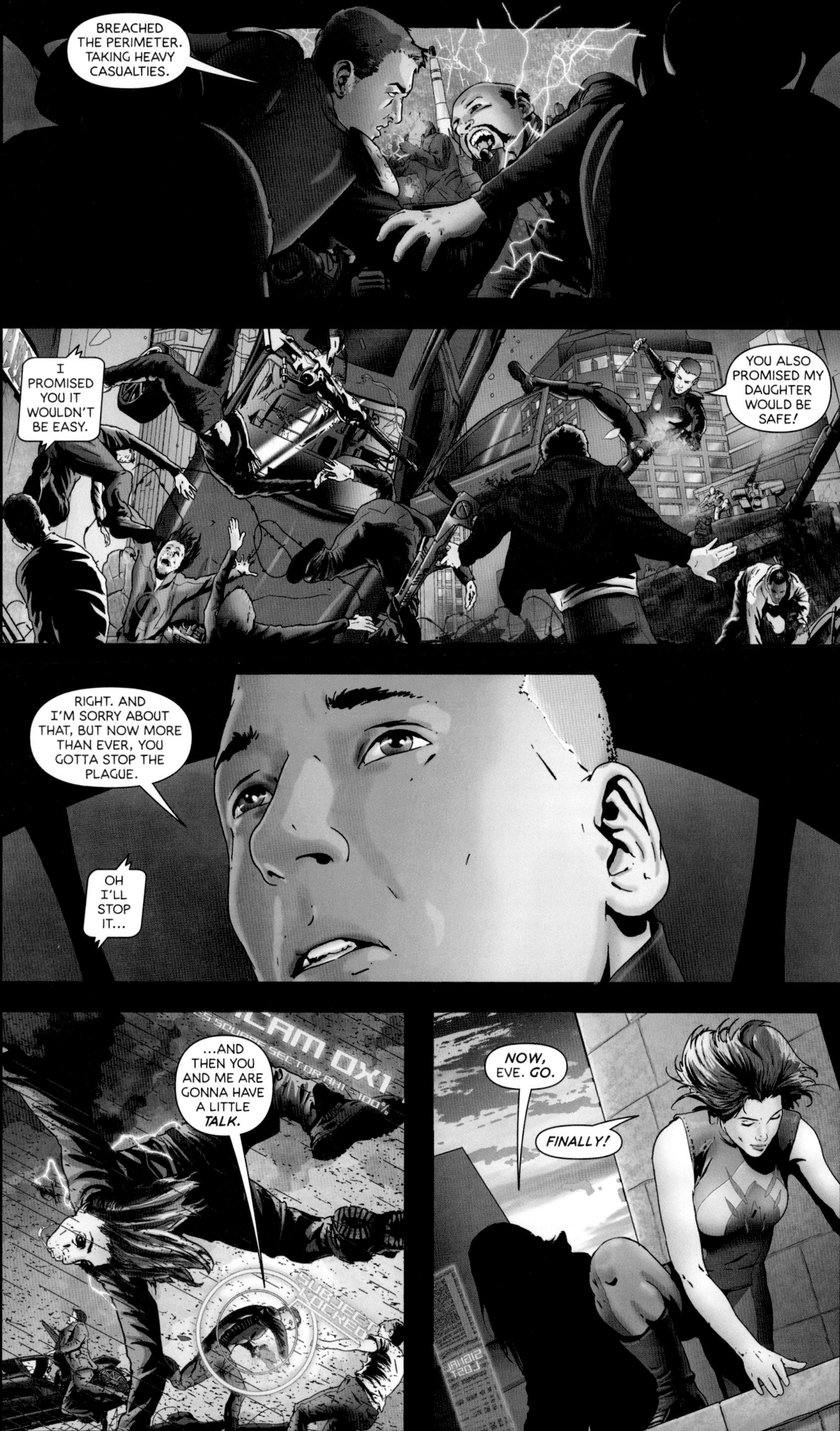
BREACHED THE PERIMETER. TAKING HEAVY CASUALTIES.
I PROMISED YOU IT WOULDN'T BE EASY.
YOU ALSO PROMISED MY DAUGHTER WOULD BE SAFE!
RIGHT. AND I'M SORRY ABOUT THAT, BUT NOW MORE THAN EVER, YOU GOTTA STOP THE PLAGUE.
OH I'LL STOP IT...
...AND THEN YOU AND ME ARE GONNA HAVE A LITTLE *TALK.*
NOW, EVE. GO.
FINALLY!

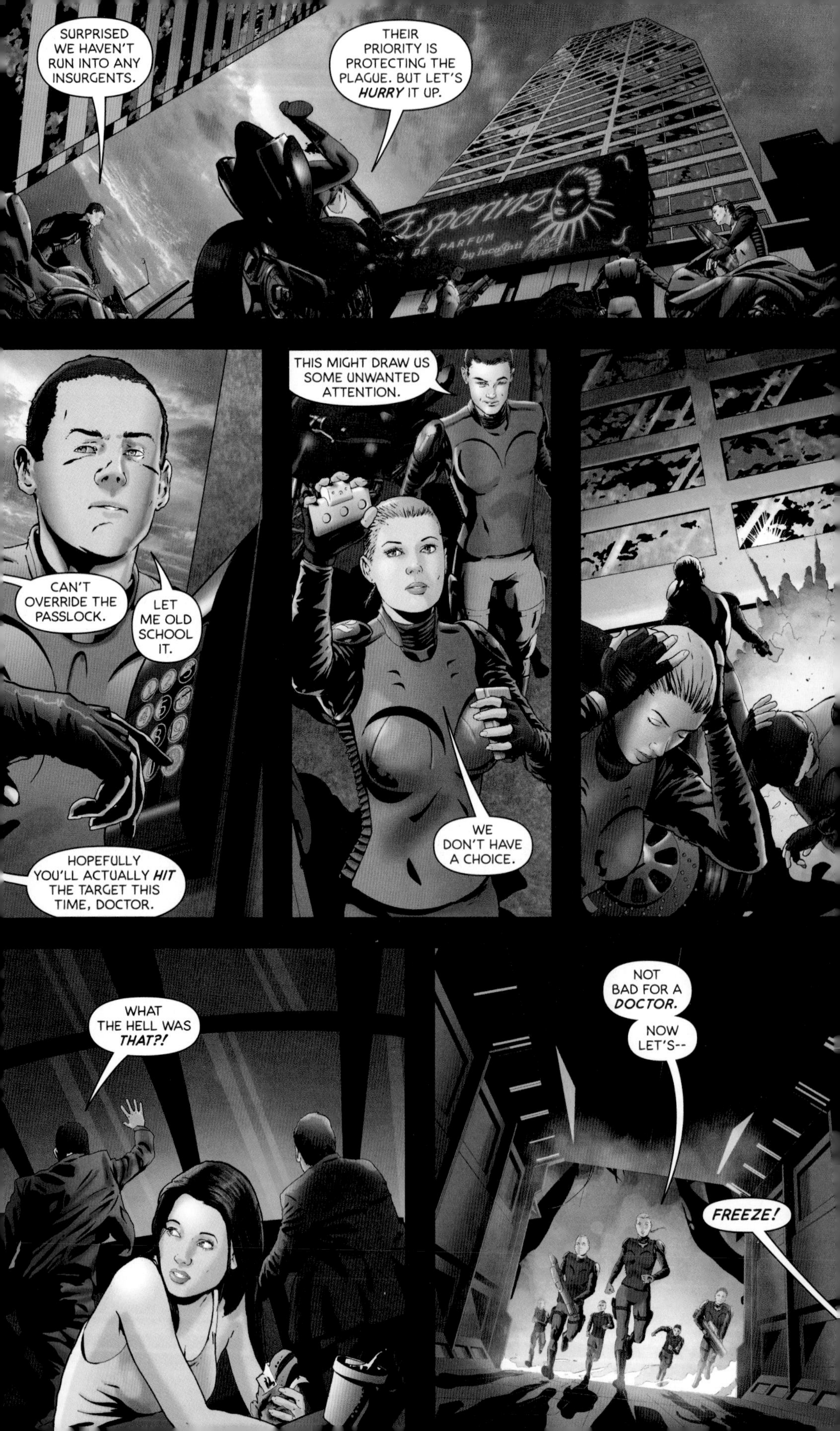
SURPRISED WE HAVEN'T RUN INTO ANY INSURGENTS.
THEIR PRIORITY IS PROTECTING THE PLAGUE. BUT LET'S *HURRY* IT UP.
CAN'T OVERRIDE THE PASSLOCK.
LET ME OLD SCHOOL IT.
HOPEFULLY YOU'LL ACTUALLY *HIT* THE TARGET THIS TIME, DOCTOR.
THIS MIGHT DRAW US SOME UNWANTED ATTENTION.
WE DON'T HAVE A CHOICE.
WHAT THE HELL WAS *THAT?!*
NOT BAD FOR A *DOCTOR.*
NOW LET'S--
FREEZE!

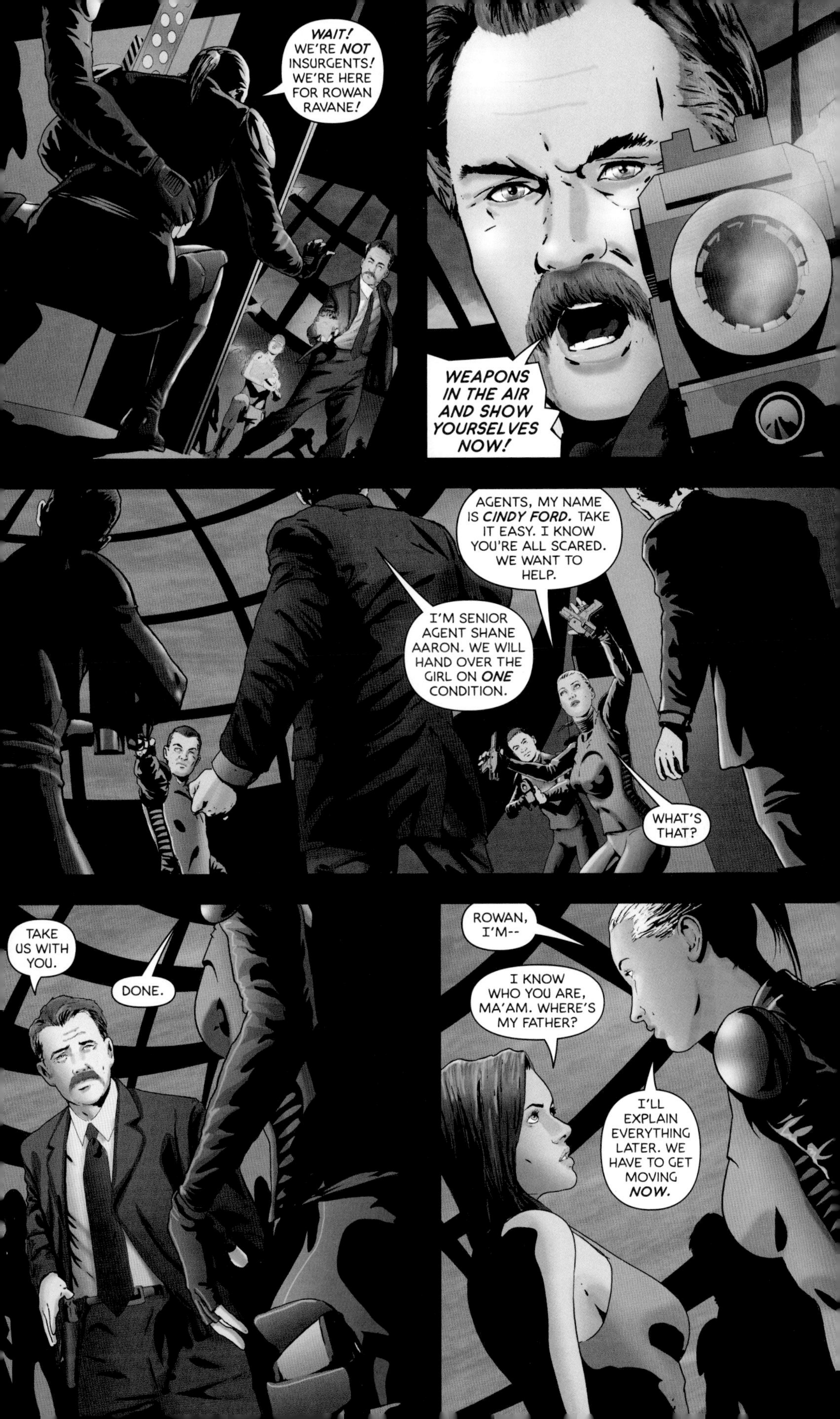
WAIT! WE'RE NOT INSURGENTS! WE'RE HERE FOR ROWAN RAVANE!
WEAPONS IN THE AIR AND SHOW YOURSELVES NOW!
AGENTS, MY NAME IS CINDY FORD. TAKE IT EASY. I KNOW YOU'RE ALL SCARED. WE WANT TO HELP.
I'M SENIOR AGENT SHANE AARON. WE WILL HAND OVER THE GIRL ON ONE CONDITION.
WHAT'S THAT?
TAKE US WITH YOU.
DONE.
ROWAN, I'M--
I KNOW WHO YOU ARE, MA'AM. WHERE'S MY FATHER?
I'LL EXPLAIN EVERYTHING LATER. WE HAVE TO GET MOVING NOW.

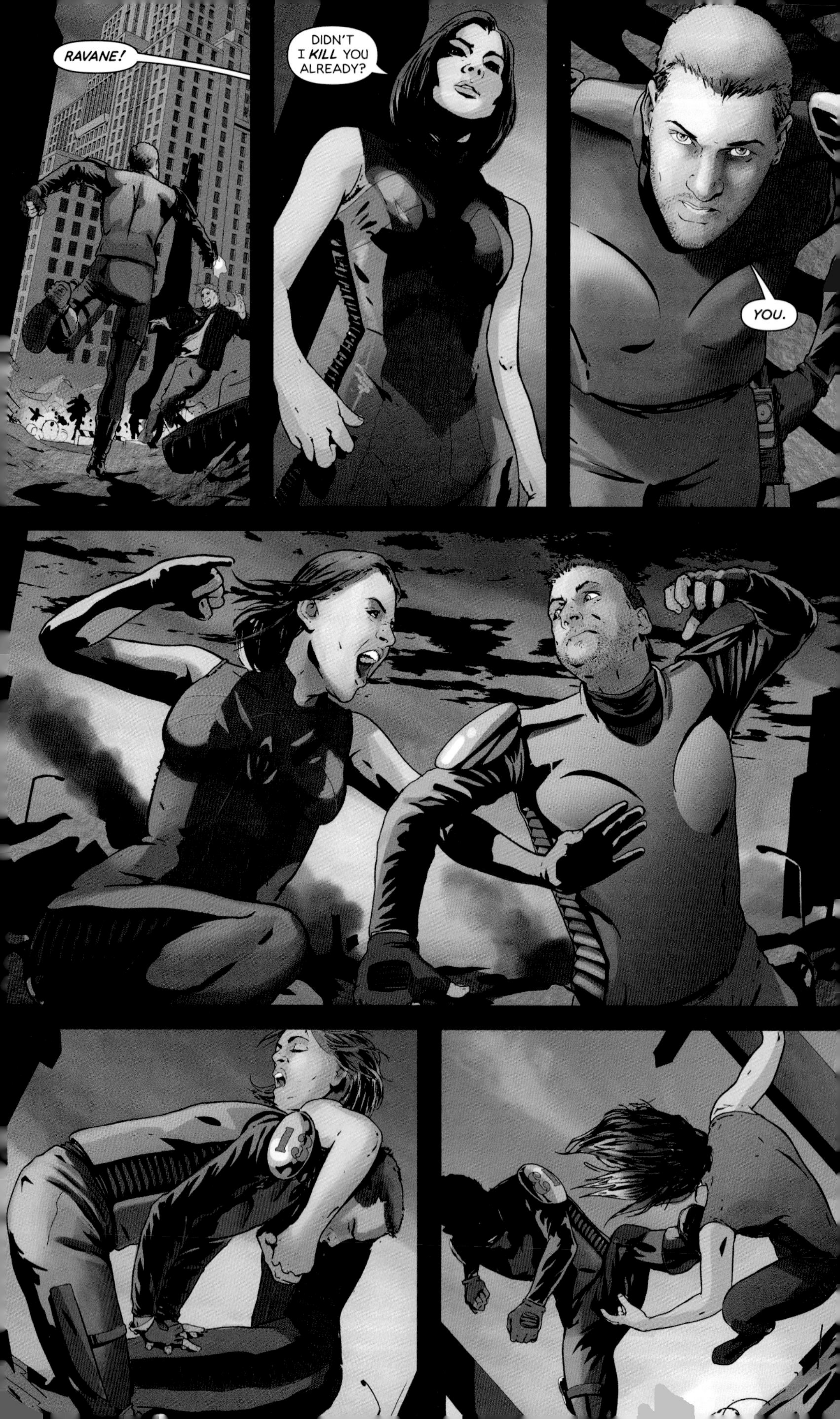
RAVANE!
DIDN'T I KILL YOU ALREADY?
YOU.

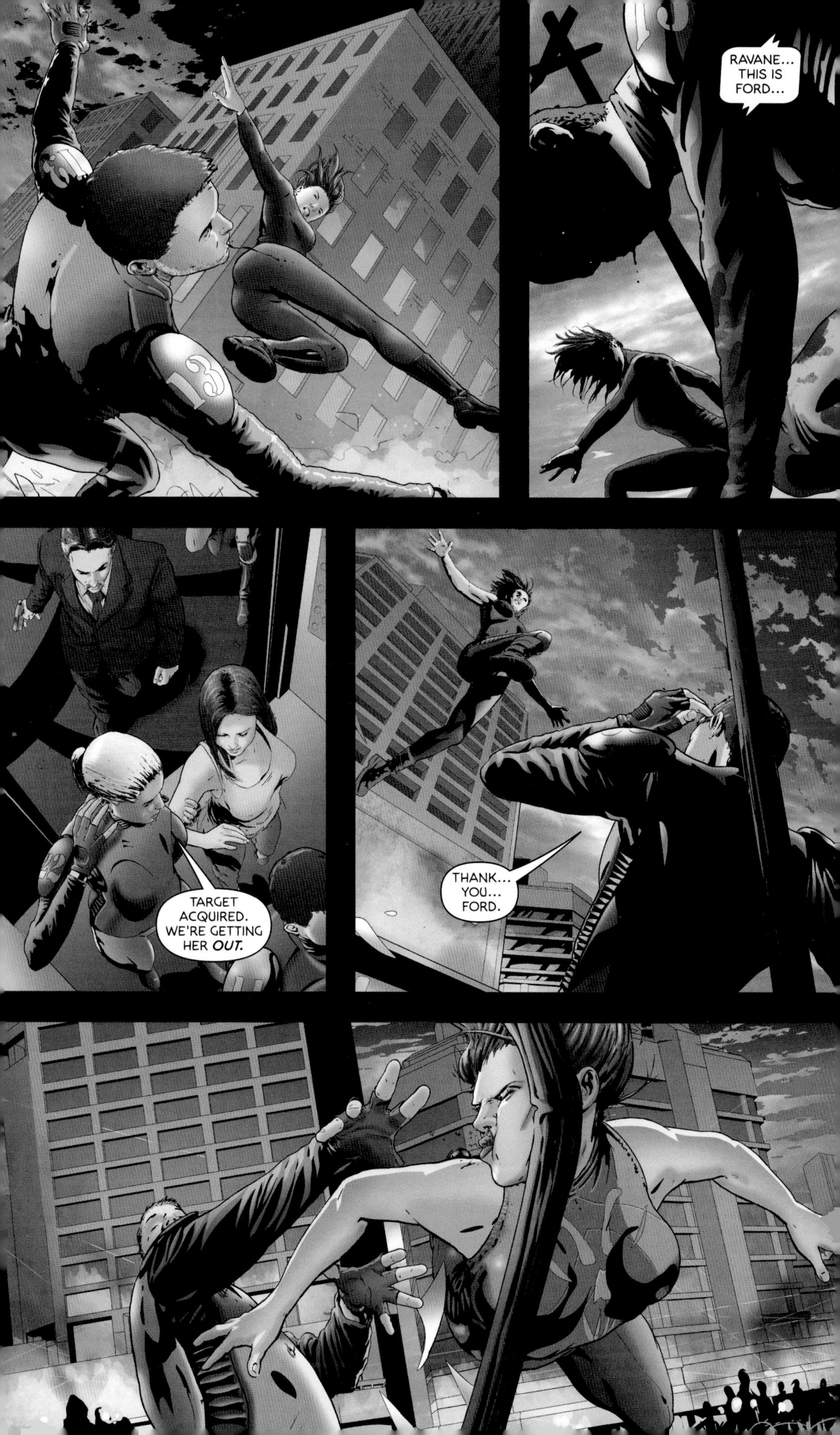
RAVANE... THIS IS FORD...
TARGET ACQUIRED. WE'RE GETTING HER *OUT.*
THANK... YOU... FORD.

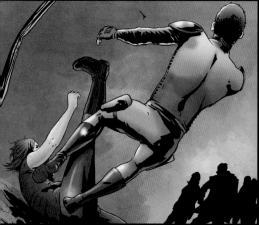

ARRRRRRRR...

...ACK!

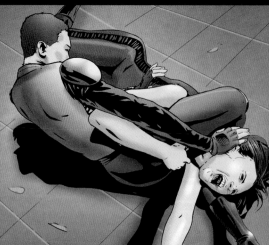

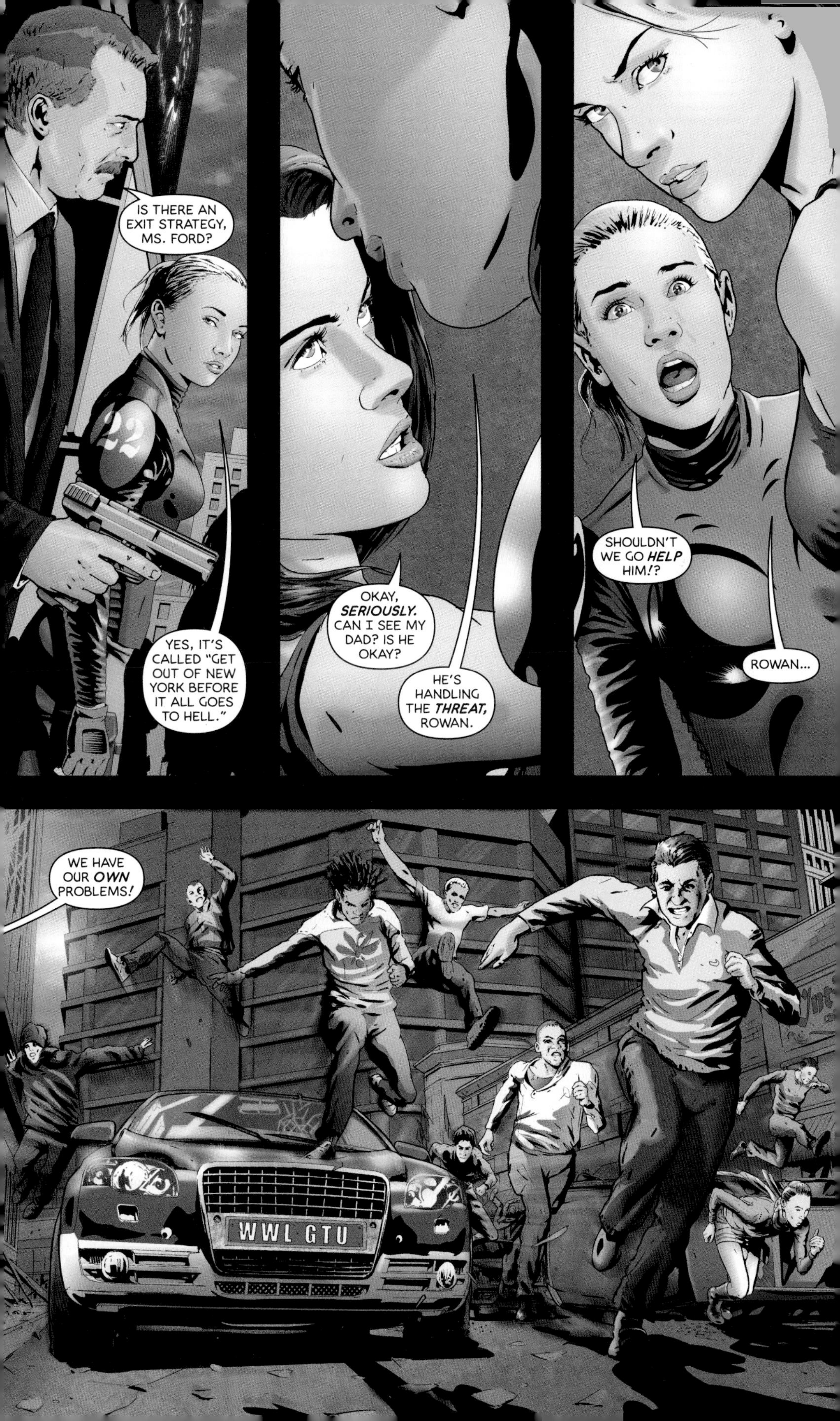
IS THERE AN EXIT STRATEGY, MS. FORD?
YES, IT'S CALLED "GET OUT OF NEW YORK BEFORE IT ALL GOES TO HELL."
OKAY, *SERIOUSLY.* CAN I SEE MY DAD? IS HE OKAY?
HE'S HANDLING THE *THREAT,* ROWAN.
SHOULDN'T WE GO *HELP* HIM*!*?
ROWAN...
WE HAVE OUR *OWN* PROBLEMS*!*
WWL GTU

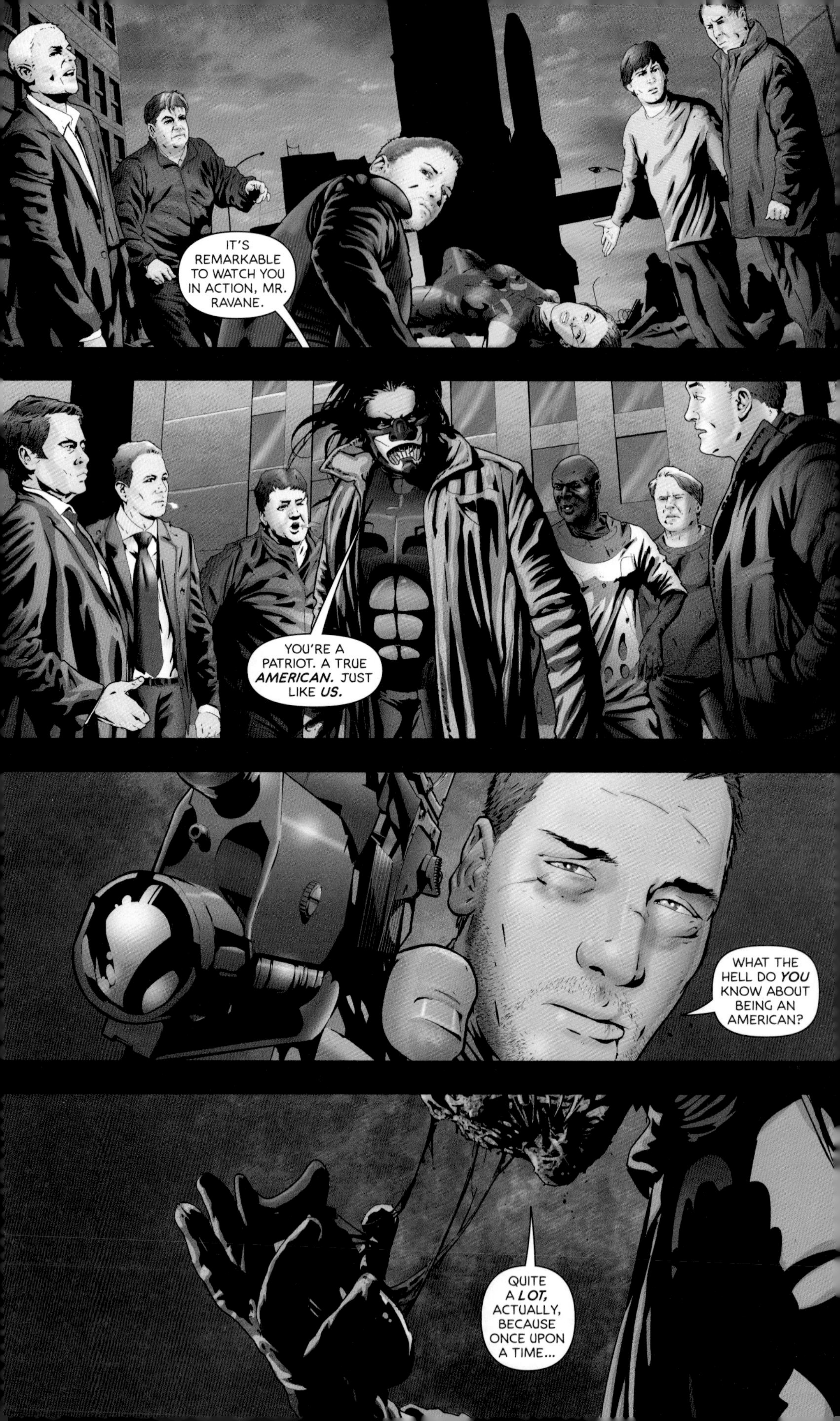
IT'S REMARKABLE TO WATCH YOU IN ACTION, MR. RAVANE.
YOU'RE A PATRIOT. A TRUE *AMERICAN.* JUST LIKE *US.*
WHAT THE HELL DO *YOU* KNOW ABOUT BEING AN AMERICAN?
QUITE A *LOT,* ACTUALLY, BECAUSE ONCE UPON A TIME...

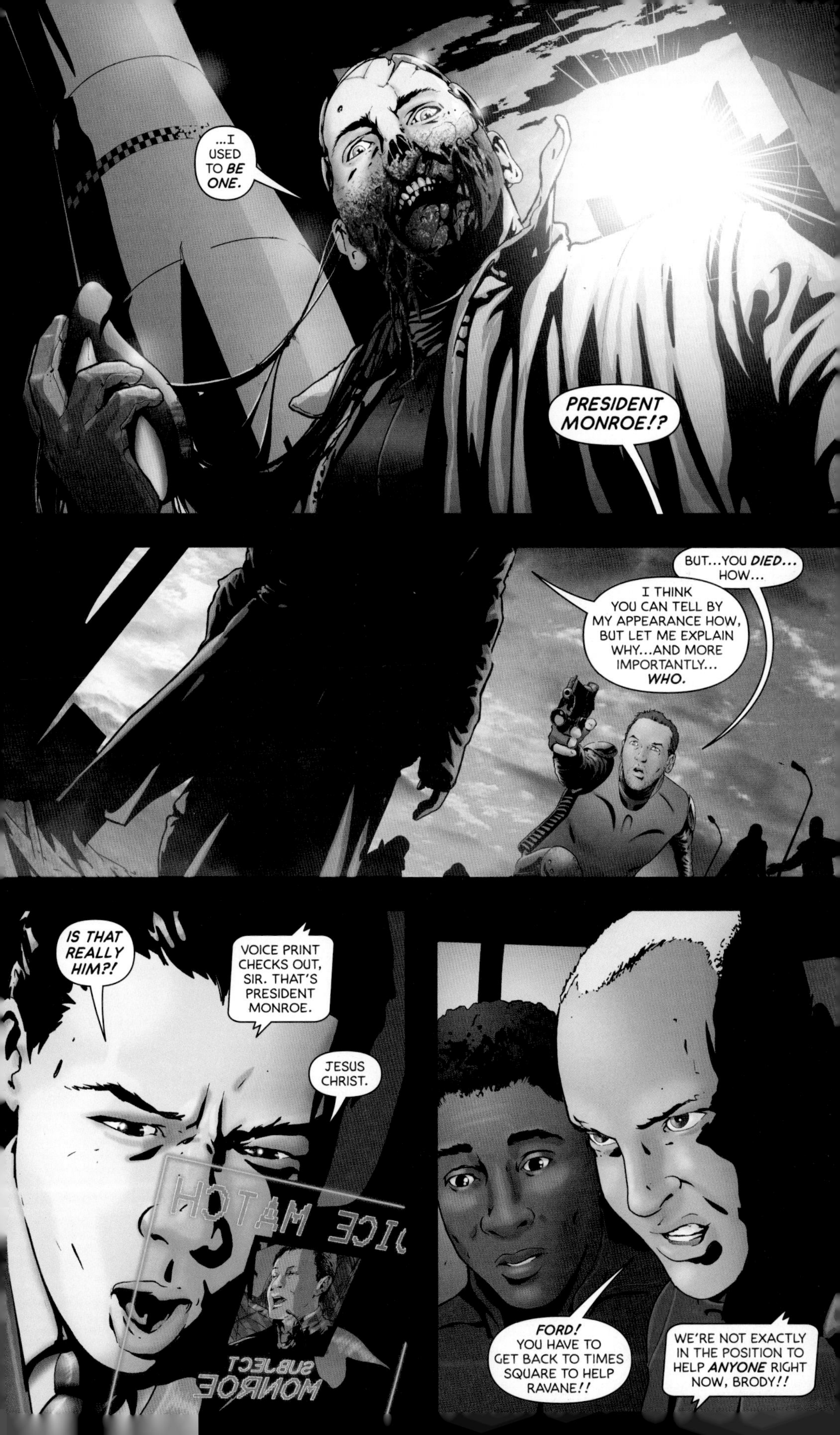

...I USED TO *BE ONE.*
PRESIDENT MONROE!?
BUT...YOU *DIED...* HOW...
I THINK YOU CAN TELL BY MY APPEARANCE HOW, BUT LET ME EXPLAIN WHY...AND MORE IMPORTANTLY... *WHO.*
IS THAT REALLY HIM?!
VOICE PRINT CHECKS OUT, SIR. THAT'S PRESIDENT MONROE.
JESUS CHRIST.
FORD! YOU HAVE TO GET BACK TO TIMES SQUARE TO HELP RAVANE!!
WE'RE NOT EXACTLY IN THE POSITION TO HELP *ANYONE* RIGHT NOW, BRODY!!

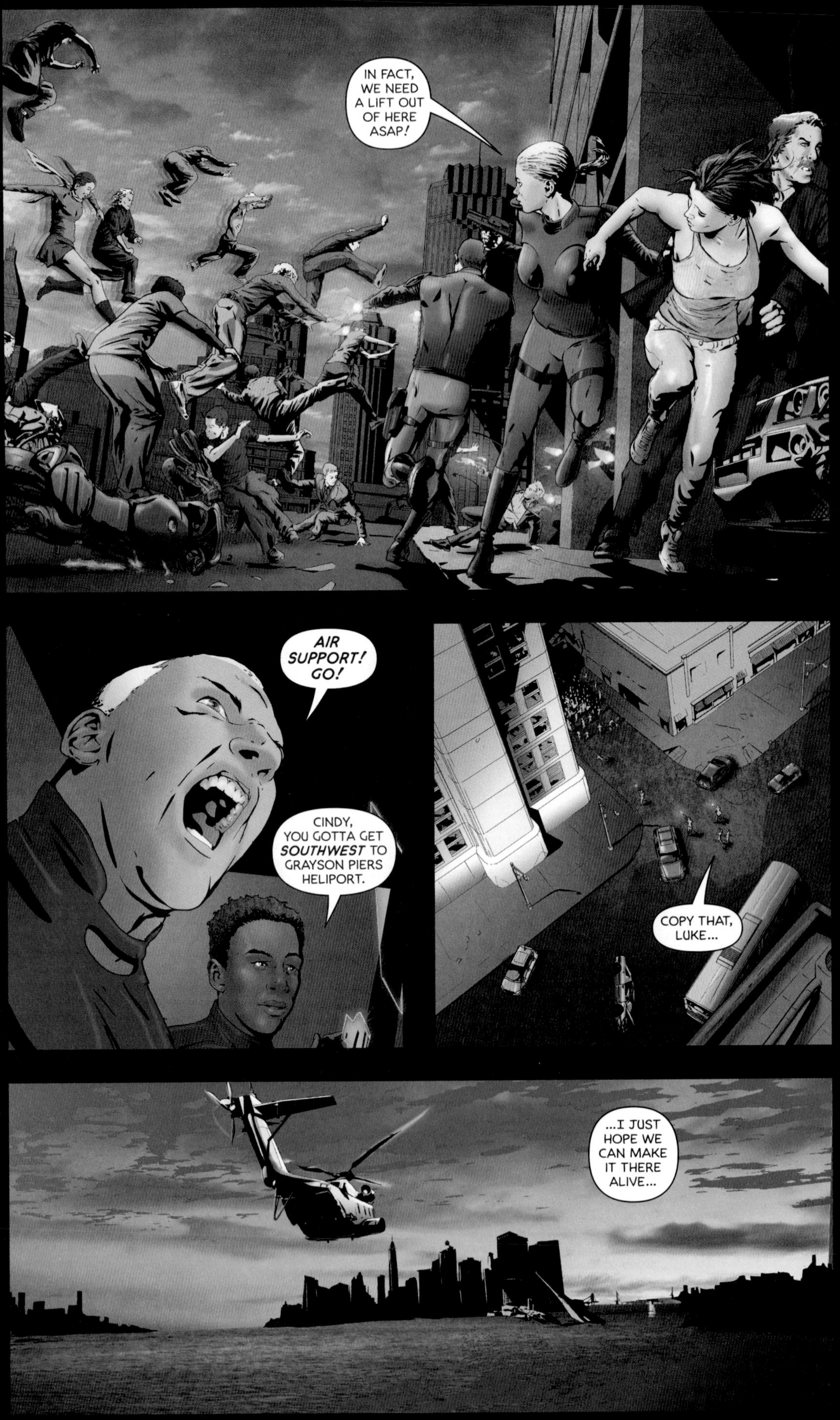
IN FACT, WE NEED A LIFT OUT OF HERE ASAP!
AIR SUPPORT! GO!
CINDY, YOU GOTTA GET SOUTHWEST TO GRAYSON PIERS HELIPORT.
COPY THAT, LUKE...
...I JUST HOPE WE CAN MAKE IT THERE ALIVE...

WHY HAVE YOU DONE THIS?

LOOK AROUND YOU! EVERYONE YOU SEE HERE HAS HAD THEIR LIVES TAKEN AWAY FROM THEM!

BY YOU! IT WAS YOUR PROGRAM!!

MY INSURGENCE PROGRAM WAS ABOUT AUGMENTING INJURED SOLDIERS WHO VOLUNTEERED, NOT PLACING NANOTECH INSIDE INNOCENT PEOPLE. THAT WAS CHONG'S "VISION". HE'S RESPONSIBLE FOR ALL OF THIS. I'M RESCUING THE VICTIMS OF HIS CRIMES!

"ONCE I DISCOVERED THAT HE WAS PLANNING TO USE THE NANOTECH, I SHUT THE ENTIRE PROGRAM DOWN. I THOUGHT THAT WAS THE END OF IT, BUT HIS MASTERPLAN WAS ALREADY IN MOTION..."

"OLIVER HAMILL, THE LAST ORIGINAL INSURGENT, WAS ENLISTED TO LEAK THE EXISTENCE OF THE PROGRAM TO THE PRESS. CHONG MADE SURE THAT THE INFORMATION GIVEN TO HAMILL WAS ALTERED TO FRAME ONLY ME FOR EVERYTHING THAT HAD HAPPENED."

"HAMILL FOOLISHLY THOUGHT HE HAD CUT A DEAL THAT WOULD ALLOW HIM AND HIS DAUGHTER TO LEAVE THE COUNTRY IN PEACE. CHONG DIDN'T WANT ANY LOOSE ENDS, SO HE ORDERED THE COUNTRY'S BEST INSURGENT HUNTER, YOU, TO INTERCEPT AND ELIMINATE HAMILL."

"THEN ONE OF CHONG'S ASSASSINS MADE SURE I WOULD NEVER GET THE CHANCE TO EXPLAIN, ALLOWING HIM TO TAKE CONTROL OF THE COUNTRY.

"HOWEVER, I ANTICIPATED THAT AND HAD MY OWN CONTINGENCY PLAN IN PLACE."

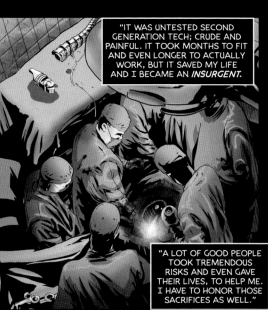

"IT WAS UNTESTED SECOND GENERATION TECH; CRUDE AND PAINFUL. IT TOOK MONTHS TO FIT AND EVEN LONGER TO ACTUALLY WORK, BUT IT SAVED MY LIFE AND I BECAME AN INSURGENT.

"A LOT OF GOOD PEOPLE TOOK TREMENDOUS RISKS AND EVEN GAVE THEIR LIVES, TO HELP ME. I HAVE TO HONOR THOSE SACRIFICES AS WELL."

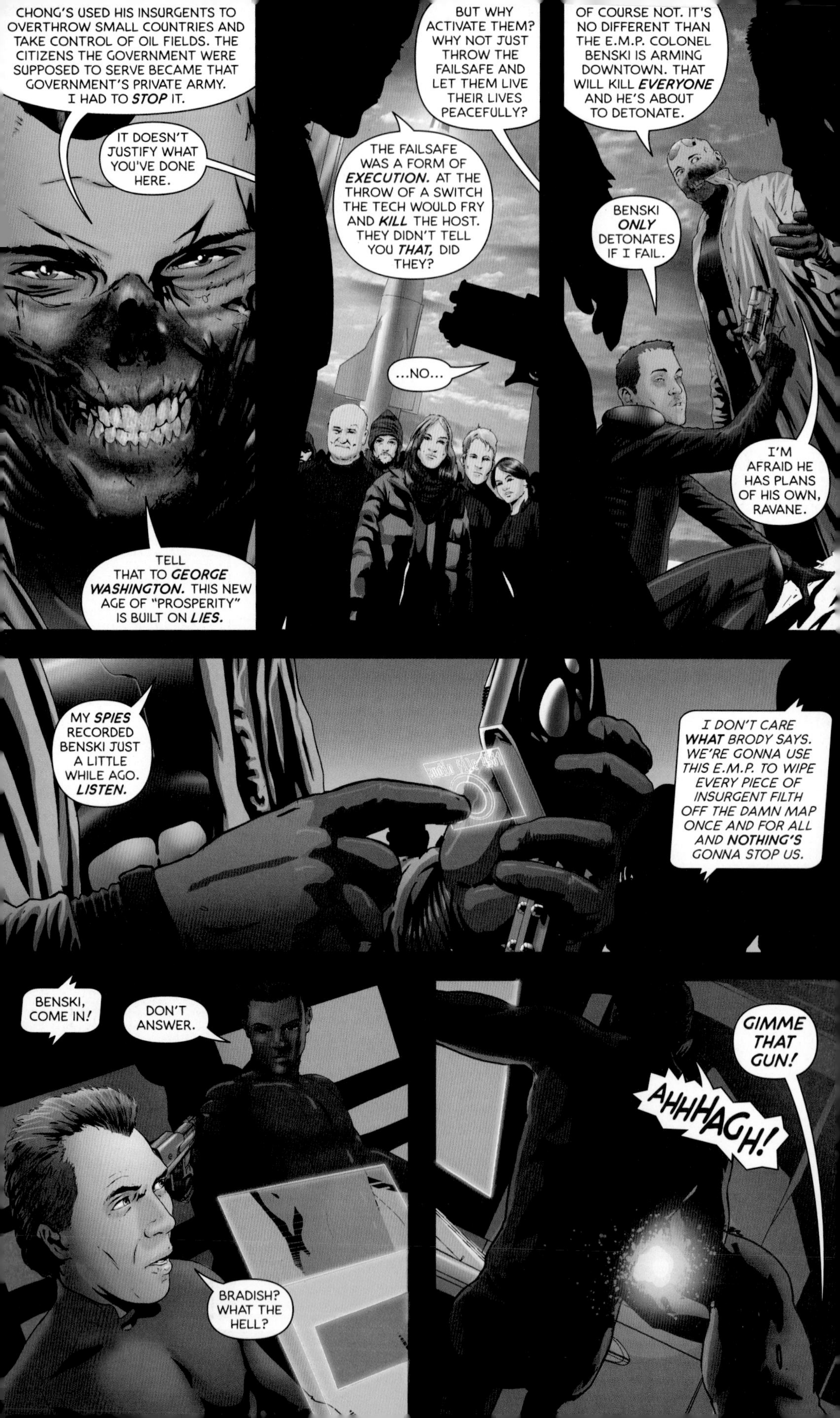
CHONG'S USED HIS INSURGENTS TO OVERTHROW SMALL COUNTRIES AND TAKE CONTROL OF OIL FIELDS. THE CITIZENS THE GOVERNMENT WERE SUPPOSED TO SERVE BECAME THAT GOVERNMENT'S PRIVATE ARMY. I HAD TO STOP IT.
IT DOESN'T JUSTIFY WHAT YOU'VE DONE HERE.
TELL THAT TO GEORGE WASHINGTON. THIS NEW AGE OF "PROSPERITY" IS BUILT ON LIES.
BUT WHY ACTIVATE THEM? WHY NOT JUST THROW THE FAILSAFE AND LET THEM LIVE THEIR LIVES PEACEFULLY?
THE FAILSAFE WAS A FORM OF EXECUTION. AT THE THROW OF A SWITCH THE TECH WOULD FRY AND KILL THE HOST. THEY DIDN'T TELL YOU THAT, DID THEY?
...NO...
OF COURSE NOT. IT'S NO DIFFERENT THAN THE E.M.P. COLONEL BENSKI IS ARMING DOWNTOWN. THAT WILL KILL EVERYONE AND HE'S ABOUT TO DETONATE.
BENSKI ONLY DETONATES IF I FAIL.
I'M AFRAID HE HAS PLANS OF HIS OWN, RAVANE.
MY SPIES RECORDED BENSKI JUST A LITTLE WHILE AGO. LISTEN.
I DON'T CARE WHAT BRODY SAYS. WE'RE GONNA USE THIS E.M.P. TO WIPE EVERY PIECE OF INSURGENT FILTH OFF THE DAMN MAP ONCE AND FOR ALL AND NOTHING'S GONNA STOP US.
BENSKI, COME IN!
DON'T ANSWER.
BRADISH? WHAT THE HELL?
GIMME THAT GUN!
AHHHAGH!

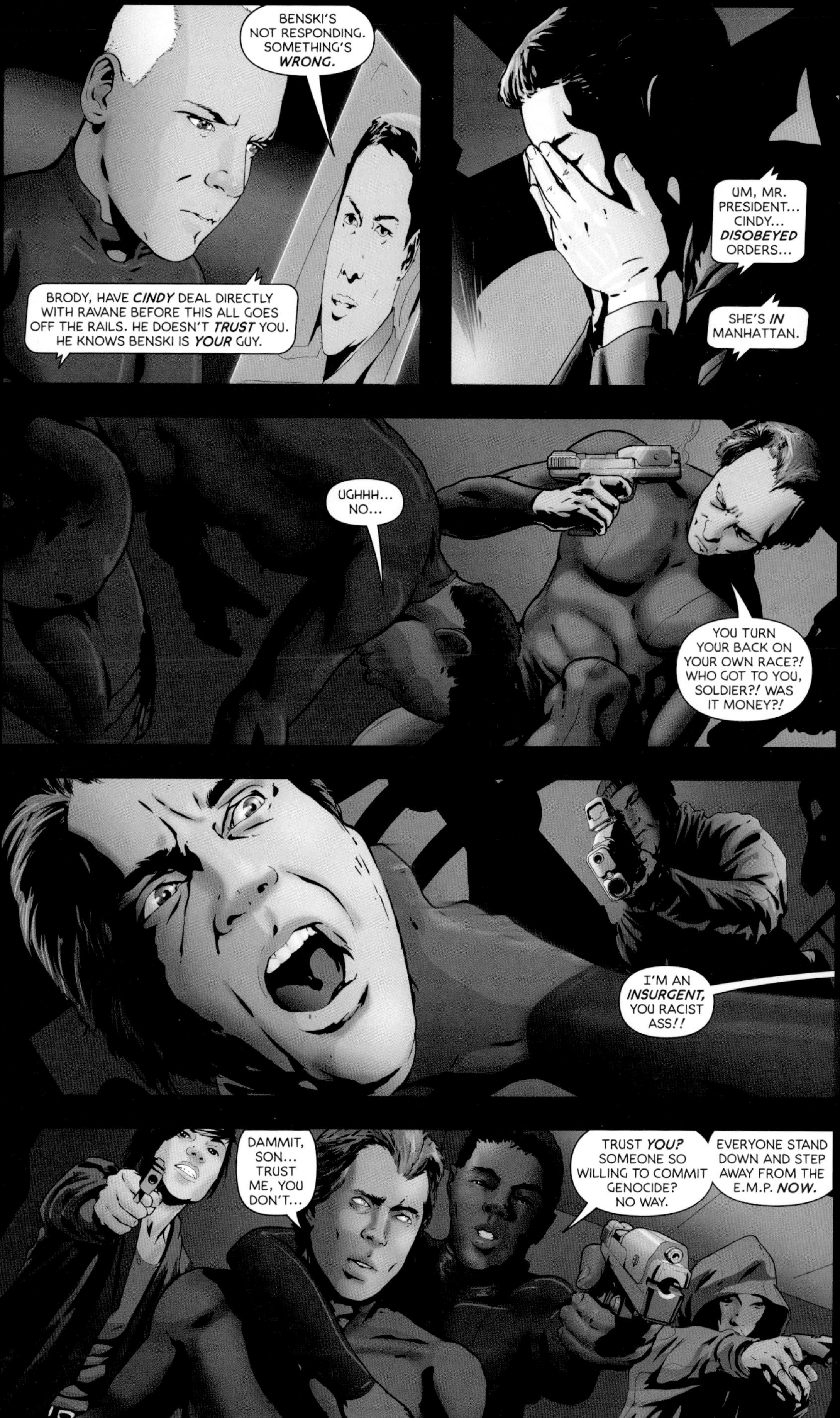
BENSKI'S NOT RESPONDING. SOMETHING'S *WRONG.*
BRODY, HAVE *CINDY* DEAL DIRECTLY WITH RAVANE BEFORE THIS ALL GOES OFF THE RAILS. HE DOESN'T *TRUST* YOU. HE KNOWS BENSKI IS *YOUR* GUY.
UM, MR. PRESIDENT... CINDY... *DISOBEYED* ORDERS...
SHE'S *IN* MANHATTAN.
UGHHH... NO...
YOU TURN YOUR BACK ON YOUR OWN RACE?! WHO GOT TO YOU, SOLDIER?! WAS IT MONEY?!
I'M AN *INSURGENT,* YOU RACIST ASS!!
DAMMIT, SON... TRUST ME, YOU DON'T...
TRUST *YOU?* SOMEONE SO WILLING TO COMMIT GENOCIDE? NO WAY.
EVERYONE STAND DOWN AND STEP AWAY FROM THE E.M.P. *NOW.*

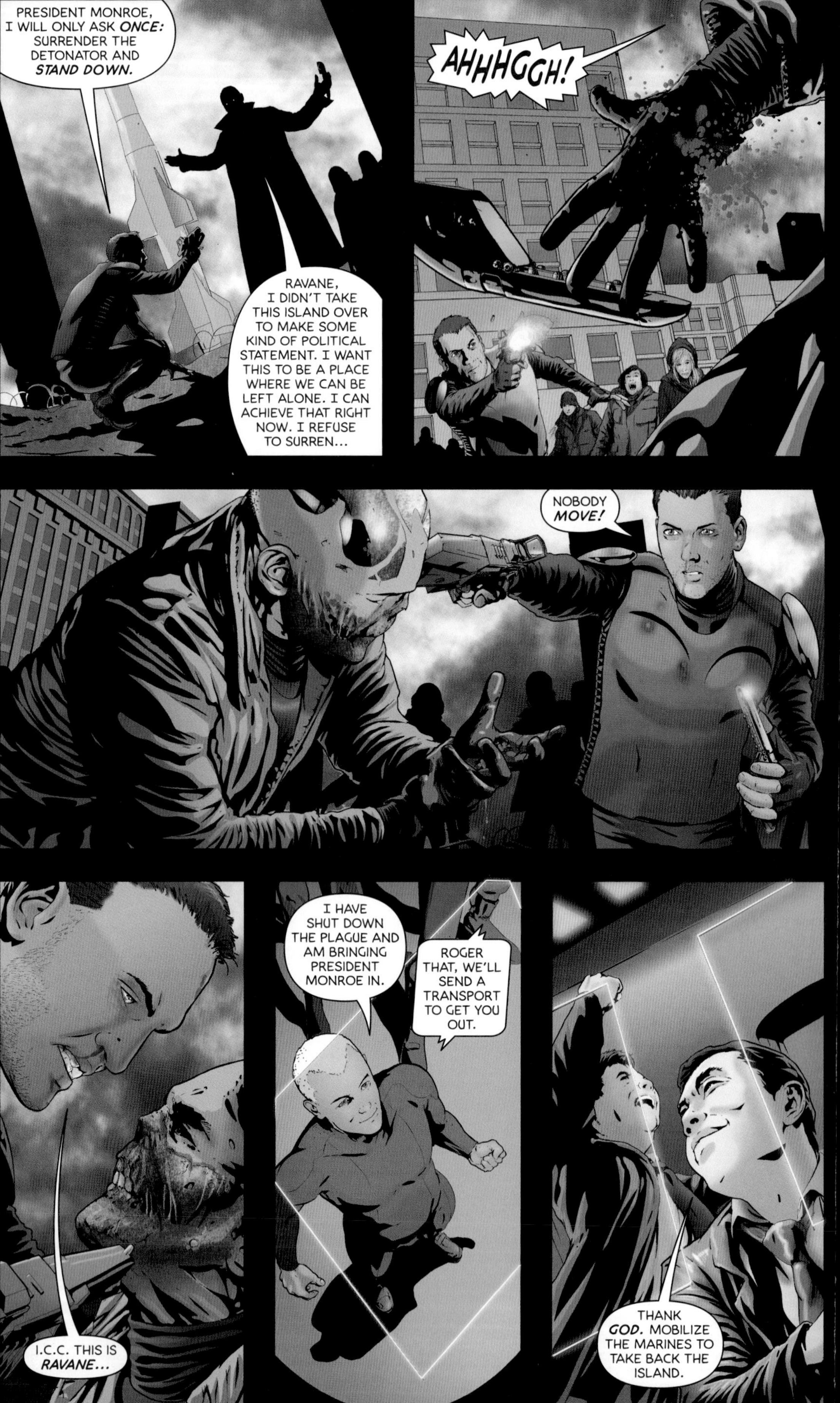
PRESIDENT MONROE, I WILL ONLY ASK *ONCE:* SURRENDER THE DETONATOR AND *STAND DOWN.*
RAVANE, I DIDN'T TAKE THIS ISLAND OVER TO MAKE SOME KIND OF POLITICAL STATEMENT. I WANT THIS TO BE A PLACE WHERE WE CAN BE LEFT ALONE. I CAN ACHIEVE THAT RIGHT NOW. I REFUSE TO SURREN...
AHHHGGH!
NOBODY *MOVE!*
I.C.C. THIS IS *RAVANE...*
I HAVE SHUT DOWN THE PLAGUE AND AM BRINGING PRESIDENT MONROE IN.
ROGER THAT, WE'LL SEND A TRANSPORT TO GET YOU OUT.
THANK *GOD.* MOBILIZE THE MARINES TO TAKE BACK THE ISLAND.

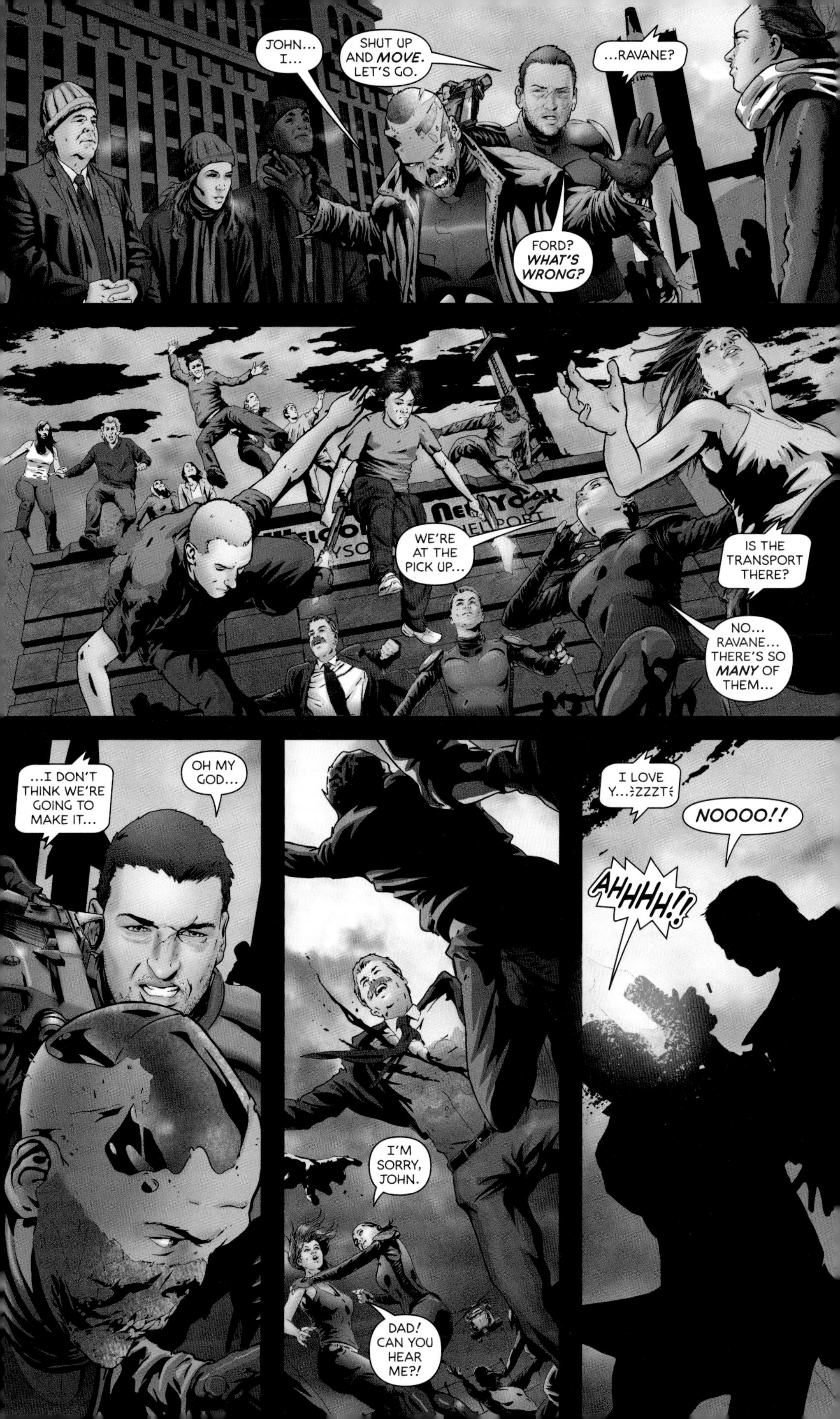
JOHN... I...
SHUT UP AND *MOVE.* LET'S GO.
...RAVANE?
FORD? *WHAT'S WRONG?*
WE'RE AT THE PICK UP...
IS THE TRANSPORT THERE?
NO... RAVANE... THERE'S SO *MANY* OF THEM...
...I DON'T THINK WE'RE GOING TO MAKE IT...
OH MY GOD...
I'M SORRY, JOHN.
DAD! CAN YOU HEAR ME?!
I LOVE Y...ZZZT
NOOOO!!
AHHHH!!

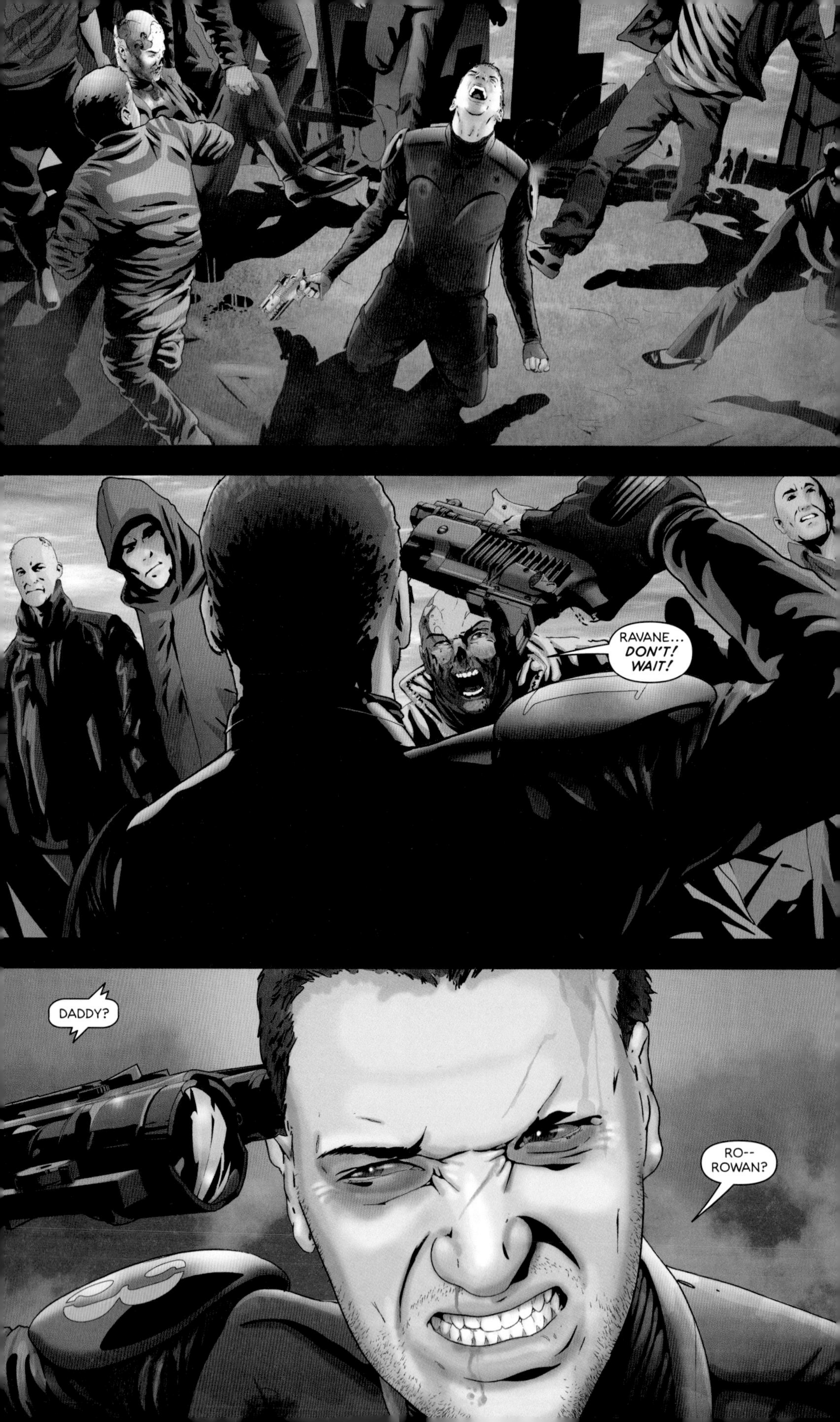
RAVANE... DON'T! WAIT!
DADDY?
RO-- ROWAN?

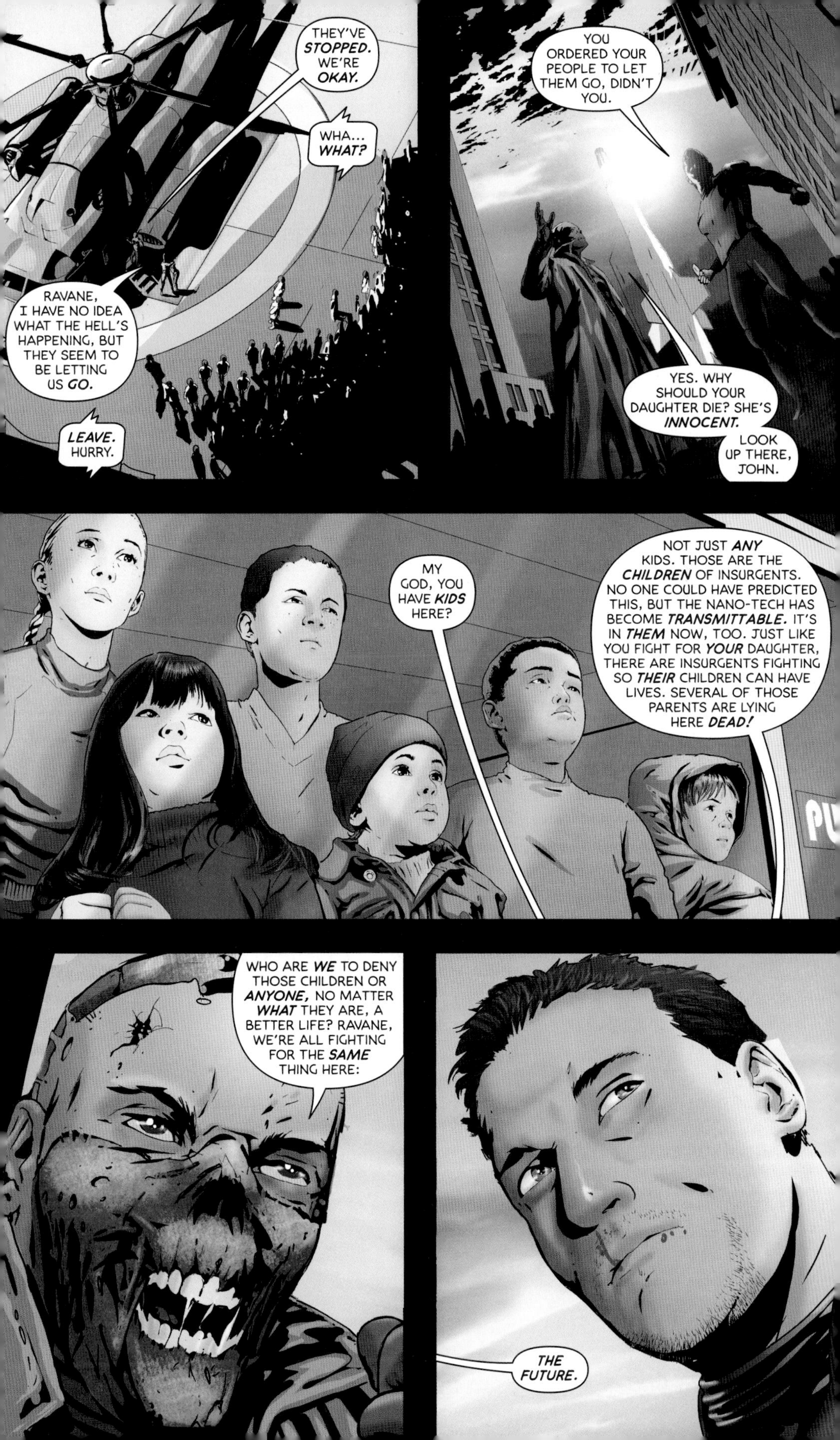
THEY'VE STOPPED. WE'RE OKAY.
WHA... WHAT?
RAVANE, I HAVE NO IDEA WHAT THE HELL'S HAPPENING, BUT THEY SEEM TO BE LETTING US GO.
LEAVE. HURRY.
YOU ORDERED YOUR PEOPLE TO LET THEM GO, DIDN'T YOU.
YES. WHY SHOULD YOUR DAUGHTER DIE? SHE'S INNOCENT.
LOOK UP THERE, JOHN.
MY GOD, YOU HAVE KIDS HERE?
NOT JUST ANY KIDS. THOSE ARE THE CHILDREN OF INSURGENTS. NO ONE COULD HAVE PREDICTED THIS, BUT THE NANO-TECH HAS BECOME TRANSMITTABLE. IT'S IN THEM NOW, TOO. JUST LIKE YOU FIGHT FOR YOUR DAUGHTER, THERE ARE INSURGENTS FIGHTING SO THEIR CHILDREN CAN HAVE LIVES. SEVERAL OF THOSE PARENTS ARE LYING HERE DEAD!
WHO ARE WE TO DENY THOSE CHILDREN OR ANYONE, NO MATTER WHAT THEY ARE, A BETTER LIFE? RAVANE, WE'RE ALL FIGHTING FOR THE SAME THING HERE:
THE FUTURE.

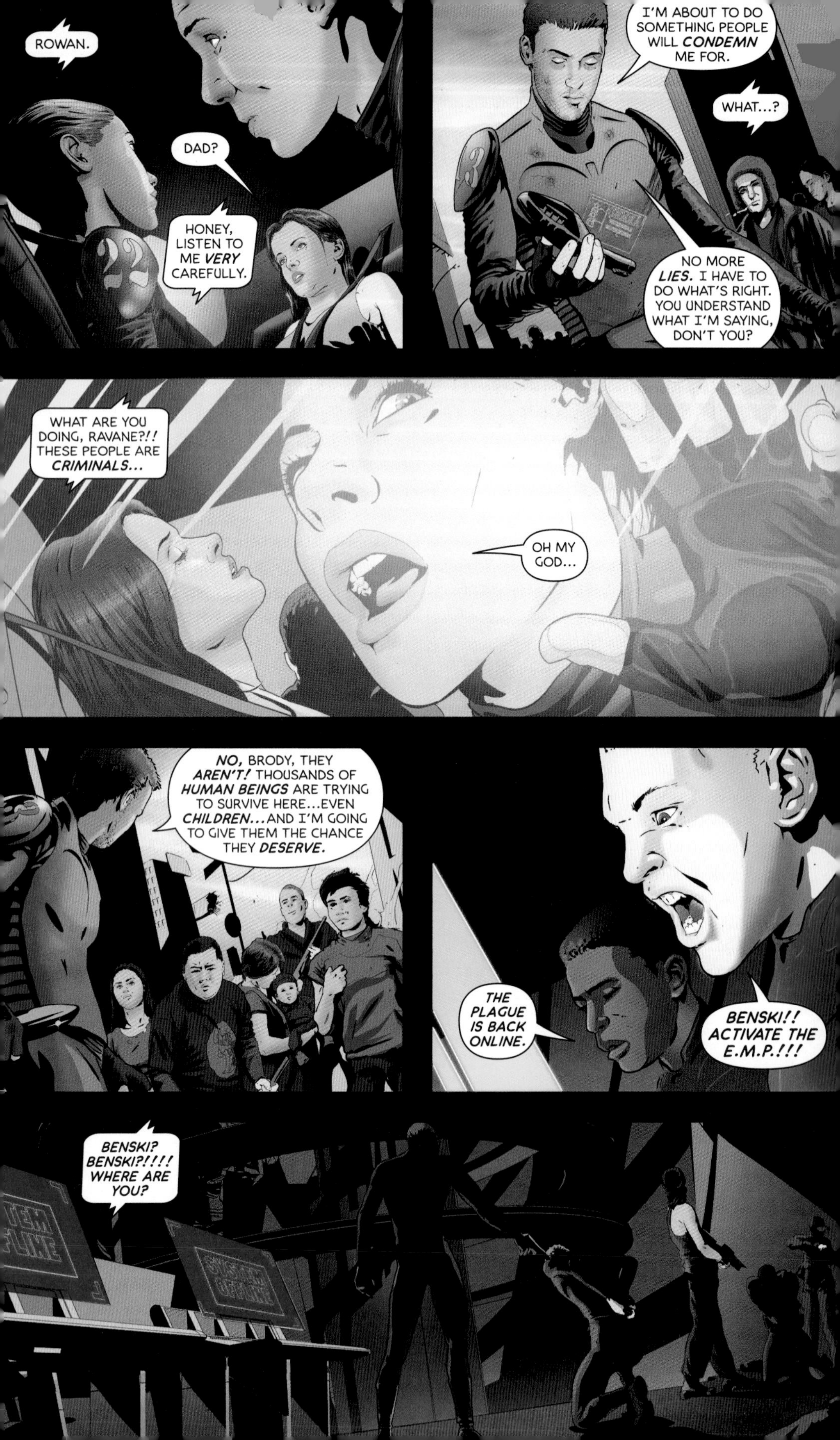
ROWAN.
DAD?
HONEY, LISTEN TO ME VERY CAREFULLY.
I'M ABOUT TO DO SOMETHING PEOPLE WILL CONDEMN ME FOR.
WHAT...?
NO MORE LIES. I HAVE TO DO WHAT'S RIGHT. YOU UNDERSTAND WHAT I'M SAYING, DON'T YOU?
WHAT ARE YOU DOING, RAVANE?!! THESE PEOPLE ARE CRIMINALS...
OH MY GOD...
NO, BRODY, THEY AREN'T! THOUSANDS OF HUMAN BEINGS ARE TRYING TO SURVIVE HERE...EVEN CHILDREN...AND I'M GOING TO GIVE THEM THE CHANCE THEY DESERVE.
THE PLAGUE IS BACK ONLINE.
BENSKI!! ACTIVATE THE E.M.P.!!!
BENSKI? BENSKI?!!!! WHERE ARE YOU?

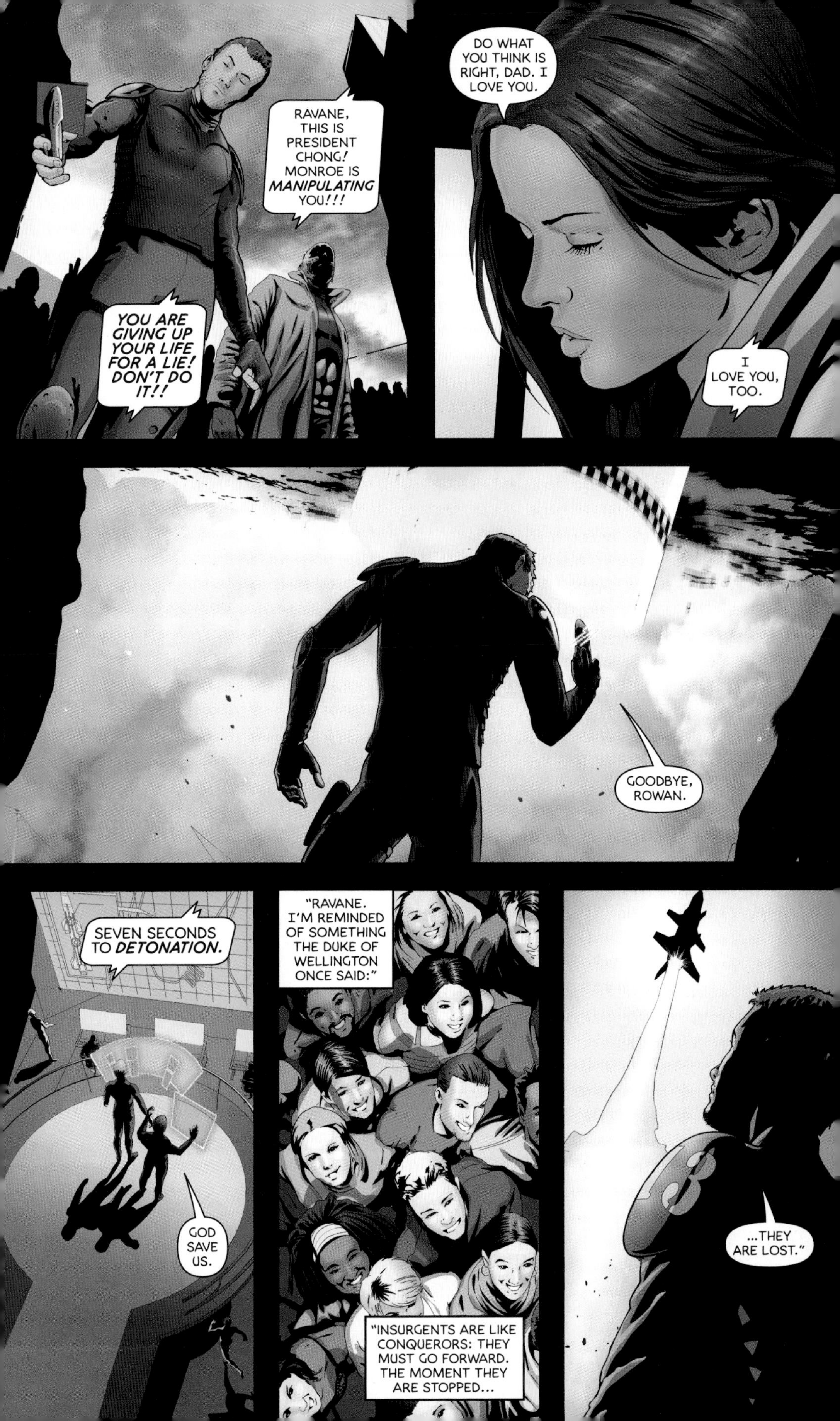
RAVANE, THIS IS PRESIDENT CHONG! MONROE IS MANIPULATING YOU!!!
YOU ARE GIVING UP YOUR LIFE FOR A LIE! DON'T DO IT!!
DO WHAT YOU THINK IS RIGHT, DAD. I LOVE YOU.
I LOVE YOU, TOO.
GOODBYE, ROWAN.
SEVEN SECONDS TO DETONATION.
GOD SAVE US.
"RAVANE. I'M REMINDED OF SOMETHING THE DUKE OF WELLINGTON ONCE SAID:"
"INSURGENTS ARE LIKE CONQUERORS: THEY MUST GO FORWARD. THE MOMENT THEY ARE STOPPED...
...THEY ARE LOST."

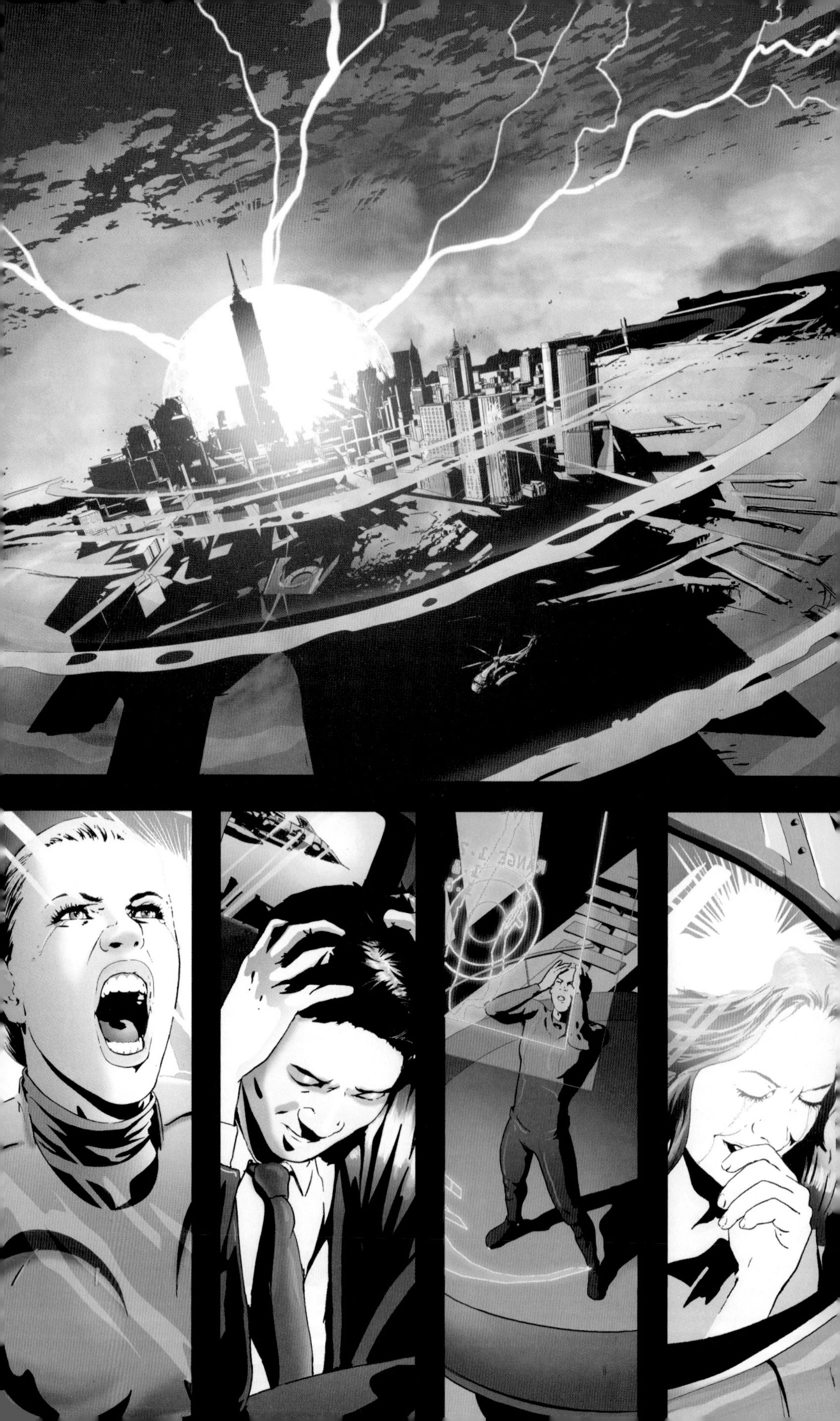

CHAPTER 6

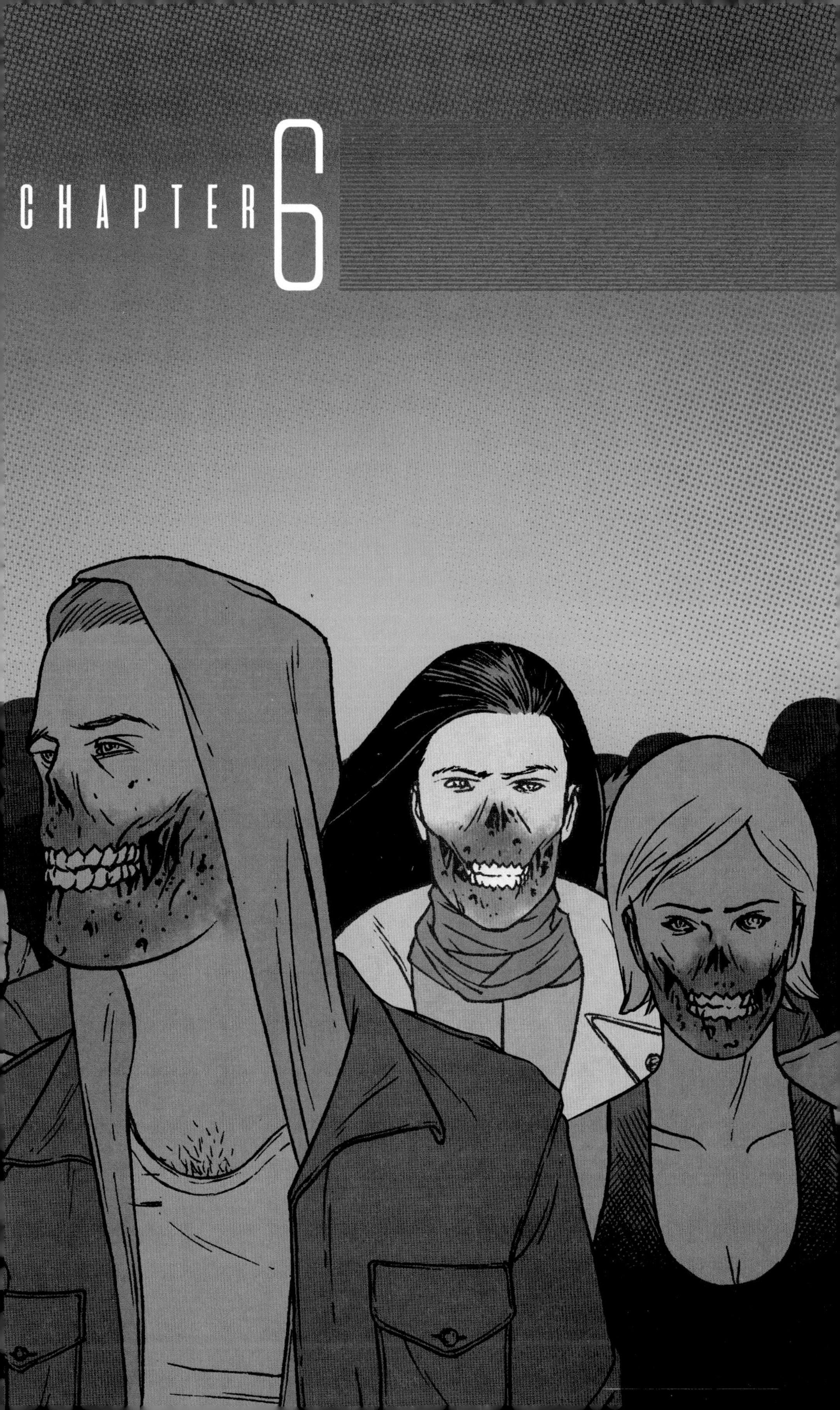

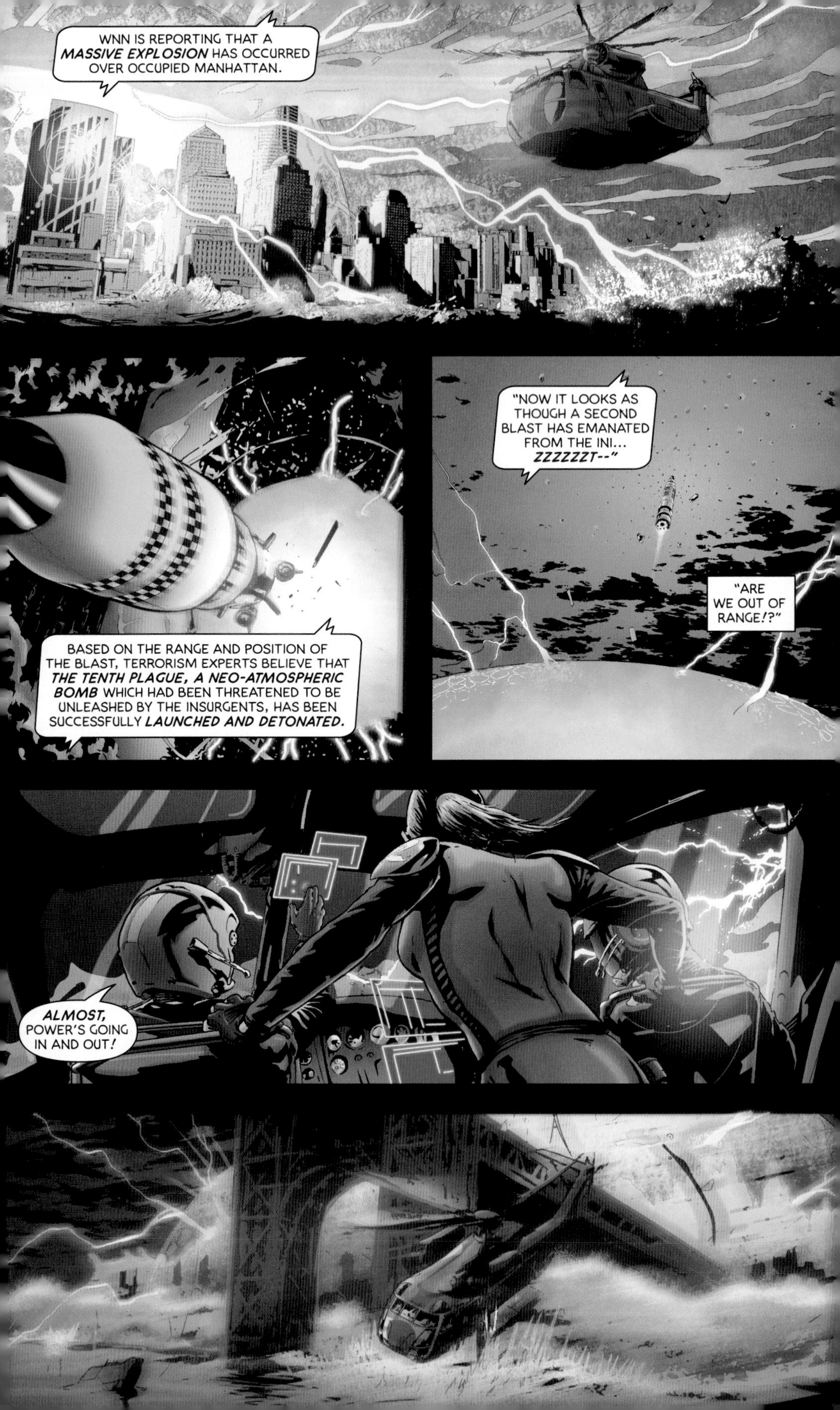
WNN IS REPORTING THAT A MASSIVE EXPLOSION HAS OCCURRED OVER OCCUPIED MANHATTAN.
BASED ON THE RANGE AND POSITION OF THE BLAST, TERRORISM EXPERTS BELIEVE THAT THE TENTH PLAGUE, A NEO-ATMOSPHERIC BOMB WHICH HAD BEEN THREATENED TO BE UNLEASHED BY THE INSURGENTS, HAS BEEN SUCCESSFULLY LAUNCHED AND DETONATED.
"NOW IT LOOKS AS THOUGH A SECOND BLAST HAS EMANATED FROM THE INI... ZZZZZZT--"
"ARE WE OUT OF RANGE!?"
ALMOST, POWER'S GOING IN AND OUT!

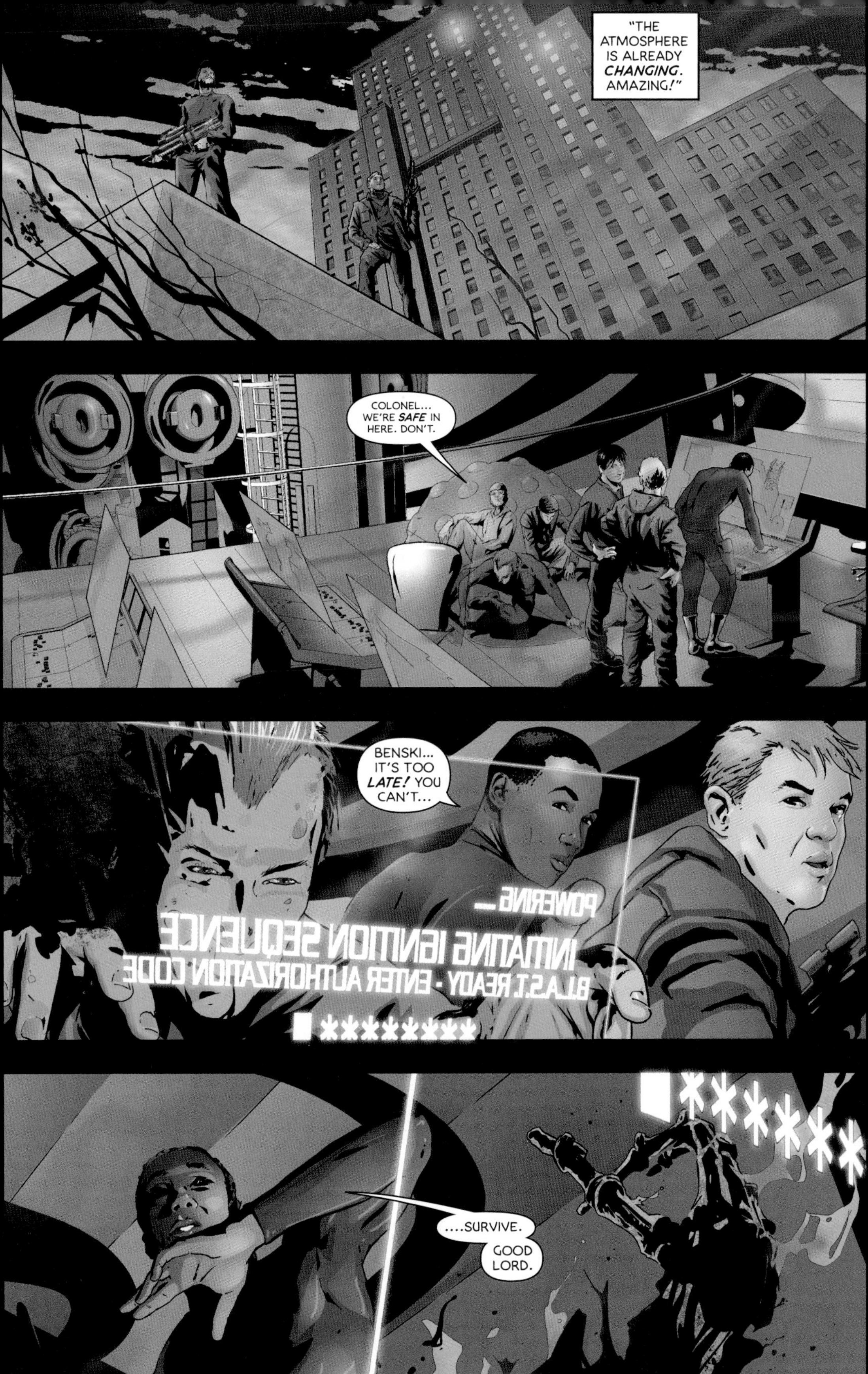
"THE ATMOSPHERE IS ALREADY CHANGING. AMAZING!"
COLONEL... WE'RE SAFE IN HERE. DON'T.
BENSKI... IT'S TOO LATE! YOU CAN'T...
POWERING...
INITIATING IGNITION SEQUENCE
B.L.A.S.T. READY - ENTER AUTHORIZATION CODE
....SURVIVE.
GOOD LORD.

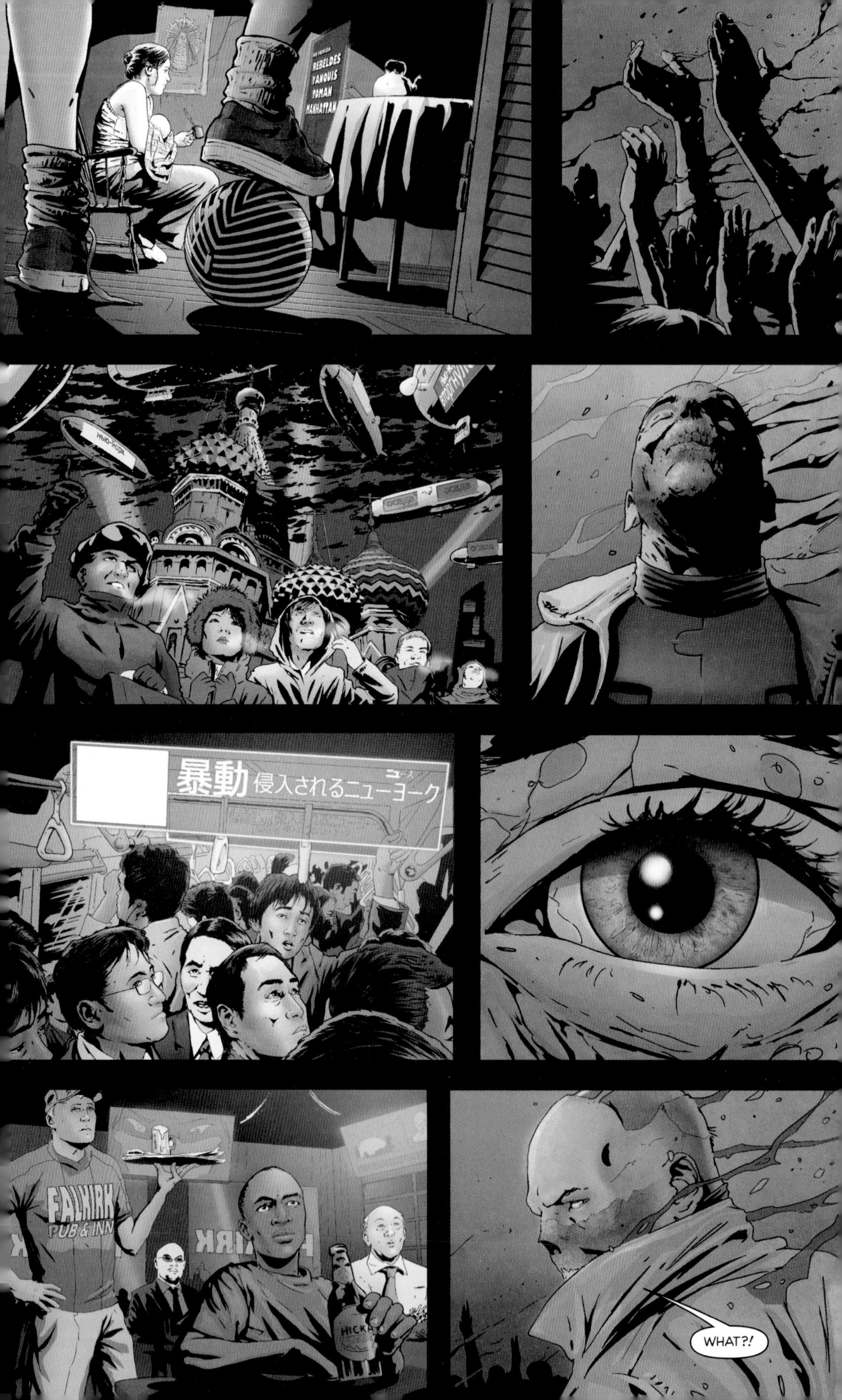

REBELDES
YANQUIS
TOMAN
MANHATTAN
НЬЮ-ЙОРК
暴動 侵入されるニューヨーク
FALKIRK
PUB & INN
WHAT?!

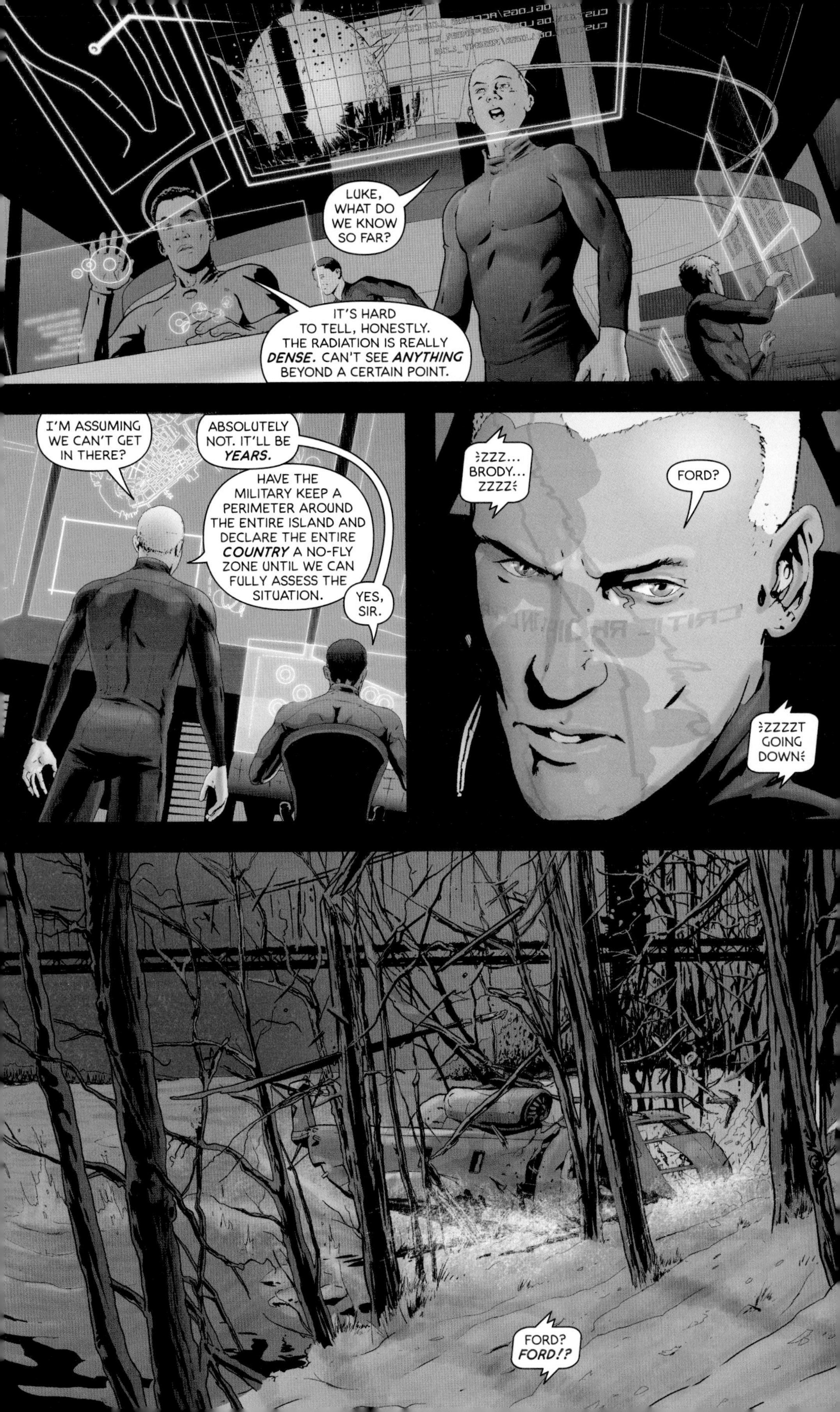
LUKE, WHAT DO WE KNOW SO FAR?
IT'S HARD TO TELL, HONESTLY. THE RADIATION IS REALLY *DENSE.* CAN'T SEE *ANYTHING* BEYOND A CERTAIN POINT.
I'M ASSUMING WE CAN'T GET IN THERE?
ABSOLUTELY NOT. IT'LL BE *YEARS.*
HAVE THE MILITARY KEEP A PERIMETER AROUND THE ENTIRE ISLAND AND DECLARE THE ENTIRE *COUNTRY* A NO-FLY ZONE UNTIL WE CAN FULLY ASSESS THE SITUATION.
YES, SIR.
ZZZ... BRODY... ZZZZ
FORD?
ZZZZT GOING DOWN
FORD? *FORD!?*

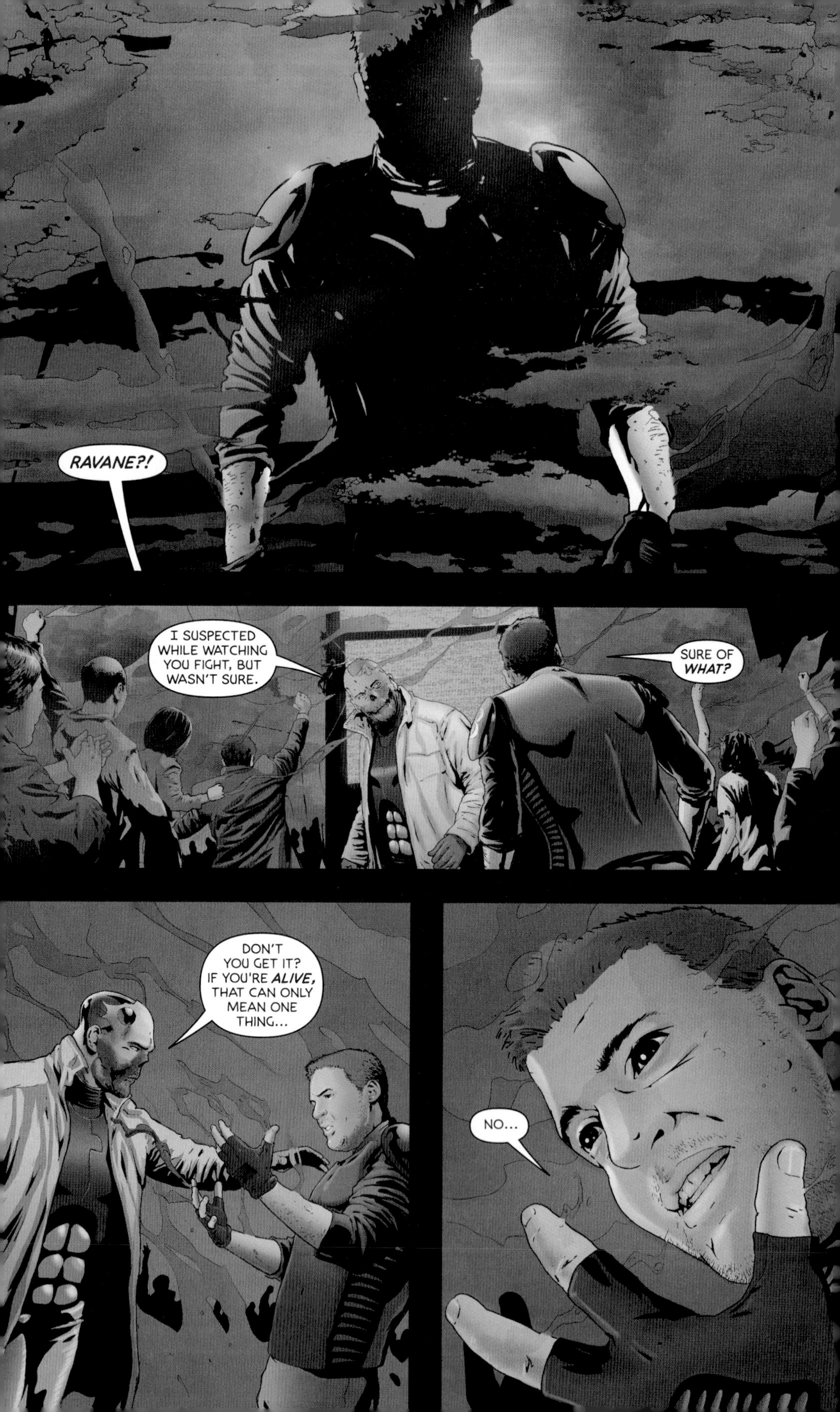
RAVANE?!
I SUSPECTED WHILE WATCHING YOU FIGHT, BUT WASN'T SURE.
SURE OF *WHAT?*
DON'T YOU GET IT? IF YOU'RE *ALIVE,* THAT CAN ONLY MEAN ONE THING...
NO...

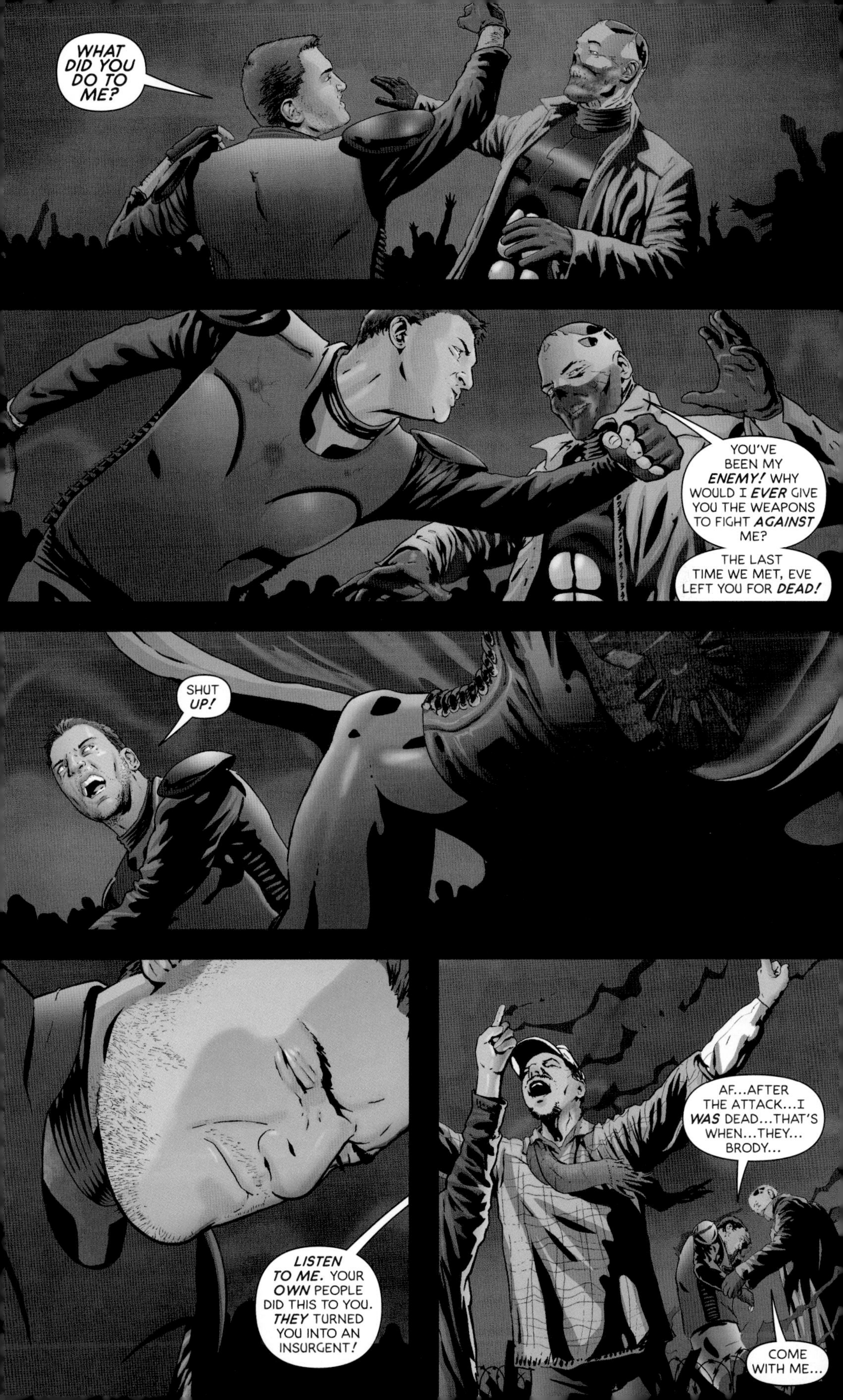
WHAT DID YOU DO TO ME?
YOU'VE BEEN MY *ENEMY!* WHY WOULD I *EVER* GIVE YOU THE WEAPONS TO FIGHT *AGAINST* ME?
THE LAST TIME WE MET, EVE LEFT YOU FOR *DEAD!*
SHUT *UP!*
LISTEN TO ME. YOUR *OWN* PEOPLE DID THIS TO YOU. *THEY* TURNED YOU INTO AN INSURGENT*!*
AF...AFTER THE ATTACK...I *WAS* DEAD...THAT'S WHEN...THEY... BRODY...
COME WITH ME...

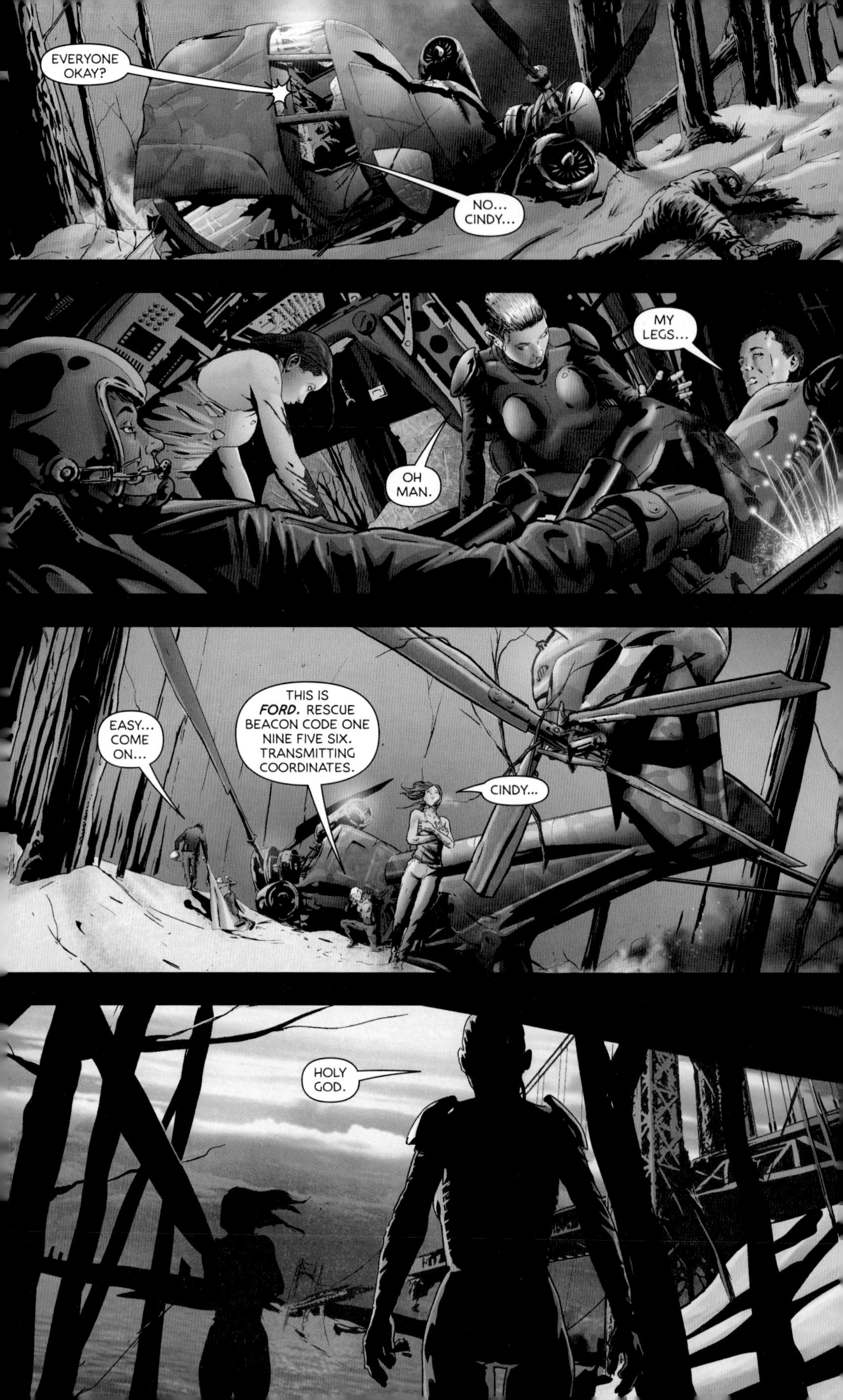
EVERYONE OKAY?
NO... CINDY...
MY LEGS...
OH MAN.
EASY... COME ON...
THIS IS *FORD.* RESCUE BEACON CODE ONE NINE FIVE SIX. TRANSMITTING COORDINATES.
CINDY...
HOLY GOD.

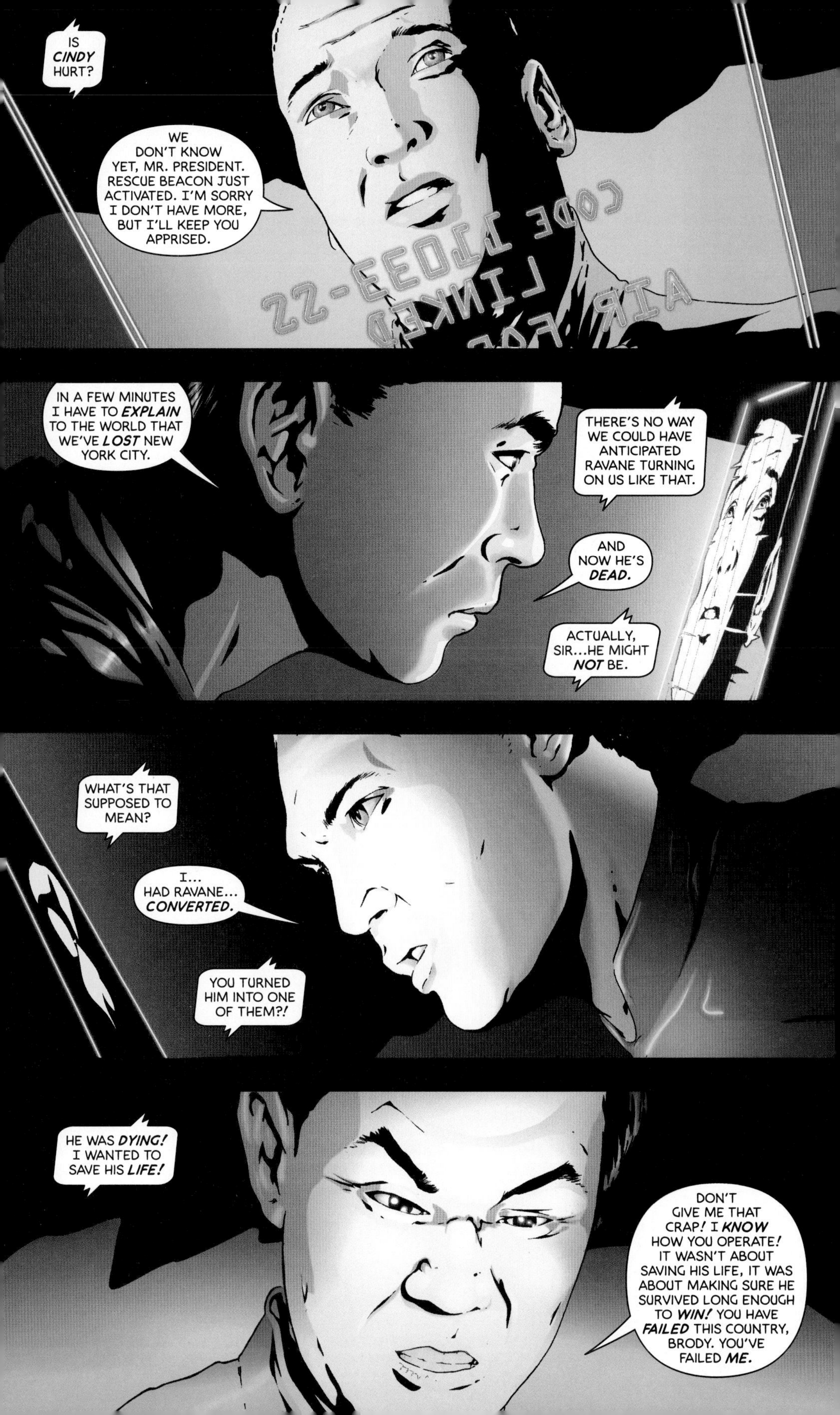
IS *CINDY* HURT?
WE DON'T KNOW YET, MR. PRESIDENT. RESCUE BEACON JUST ACTIVATED. I'M SORRY I DON'T HAVE MORE, BUT I'LL KEEP YOU APPRISED.
IN A FEW MINUTES I HAVE TO ***EXPLAIN*** TO THE WORLD THAT WE'VE ***LOST*** NEW YORK CITY.
THERE'S NO WAY WE COULD HAVE ANTICIPATED RAVANE TURNING ON US LIKE THAT.
AND NOW HE'S ***DEAD.***
ACTUALLY, SIR...HE MIGHT ***NOT*** BE.
WHAT'S THAT SUPPOSED TO MEAN?
I... HAD RAVANE... ***CONVERTED.***
YOU TURNED HIM INTO ONE OF THEM?!
HE WAS ***DYING!*** I WANTED TO SAVE HIS ***LIFE!***
DON'T GIVE ME THAT CRAP! I ***KNOW*** HOW YOU OPERATE! IT WASN'T ABOUT SAVING HIS LIFE, IT WAS ABOUT MAKING SURE HE SURVIVED LONG ENOUGH TO ***WIN!*** YOU HAVE ***FAILED*** THIS COUNTRY, BRODY. YOU'VE FAILED ***ME.***

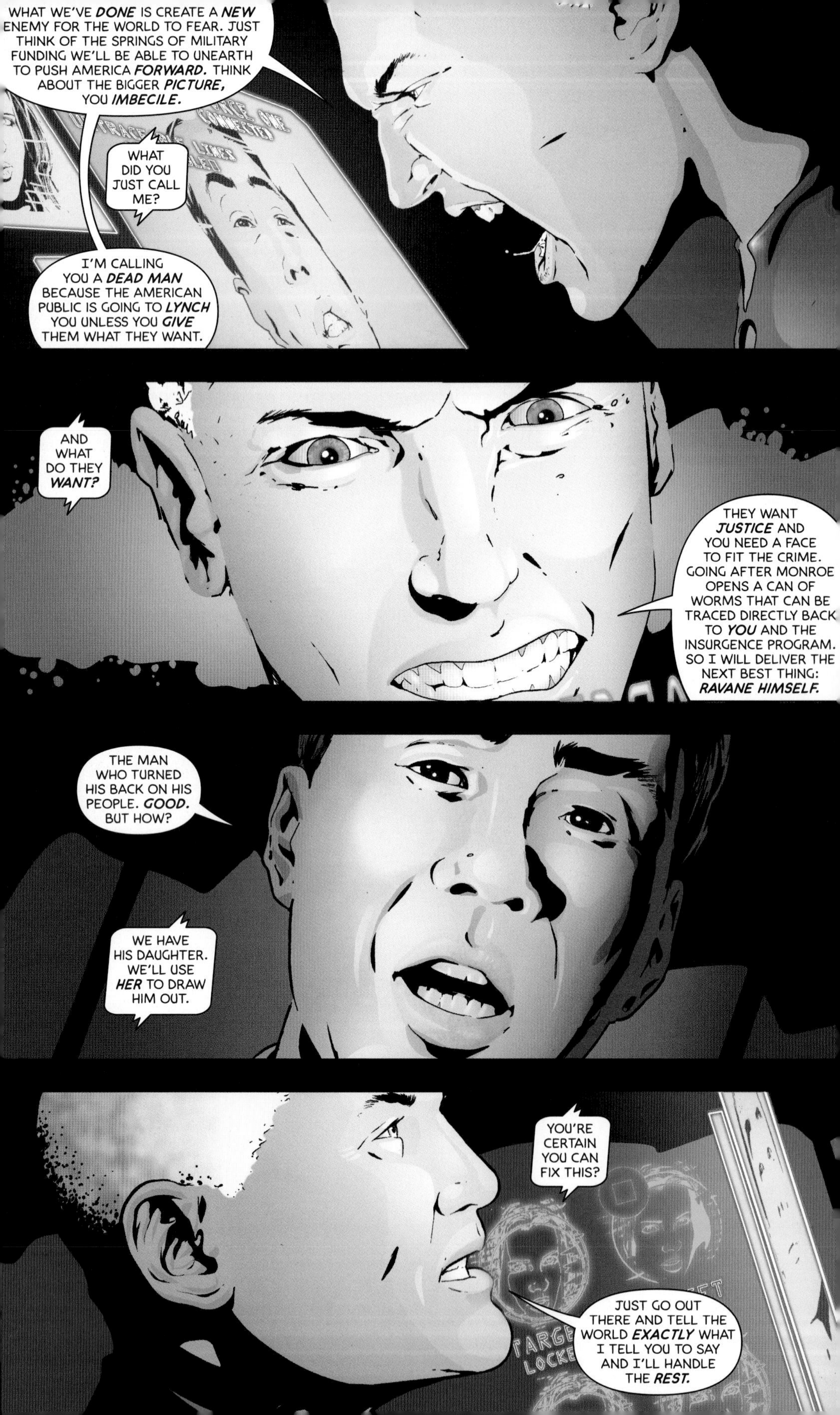
WHAT WE'VE DONE IS CREATE A NEW ENEMY FOR THE WORLD TO FEAR. JUST THINK OF THE SPRINGS OF MILITARY FUNDING WE'LL BE ABLE TO UNEARTH TO PUSH AMERICA FORWARD. THINK ABOUT THE BIGGER PICTURE, YOU IMBECILE.
WHAT DID YOU JUST CALL ME?
I'M CALLING YOU A DEAD MAN BECAUSE THE AMERICAN PUBLIC IS GOING TO LYNCH YOU UNLESS YOU GIVE THEM WHAT THEY WANT.
AND WHAT DO THEY WANT?
THEY WANT JUSTICE AND YOU NEED A FACE TO FIT THE CRIME. GOING AFTER MONROE OPENS A CAN OF WORMS THAT CAN BE TRACED DIRECTLY BACK TO YOU AND THE INSURGENCE PROGRAM. SO I WILL DELIVER THE NEXT BEST THING: RAVANE HIMSELF.
THE MAN WHO TURNED HIS BACK ON HIS PEOPLE. GOOD. BUT HOW?
WE HAVE HIS DAUGHTER. WE'LL USE HER TO DRAW HIM OUT.
YOU'RE CERTAIN YOU CAN FIX THIS?
JUST GO OUT THERE AND TELL THE WORLD EXACTLY WHAT I TELL YOU TO SAY AND I'LL HANDLE THE REST.

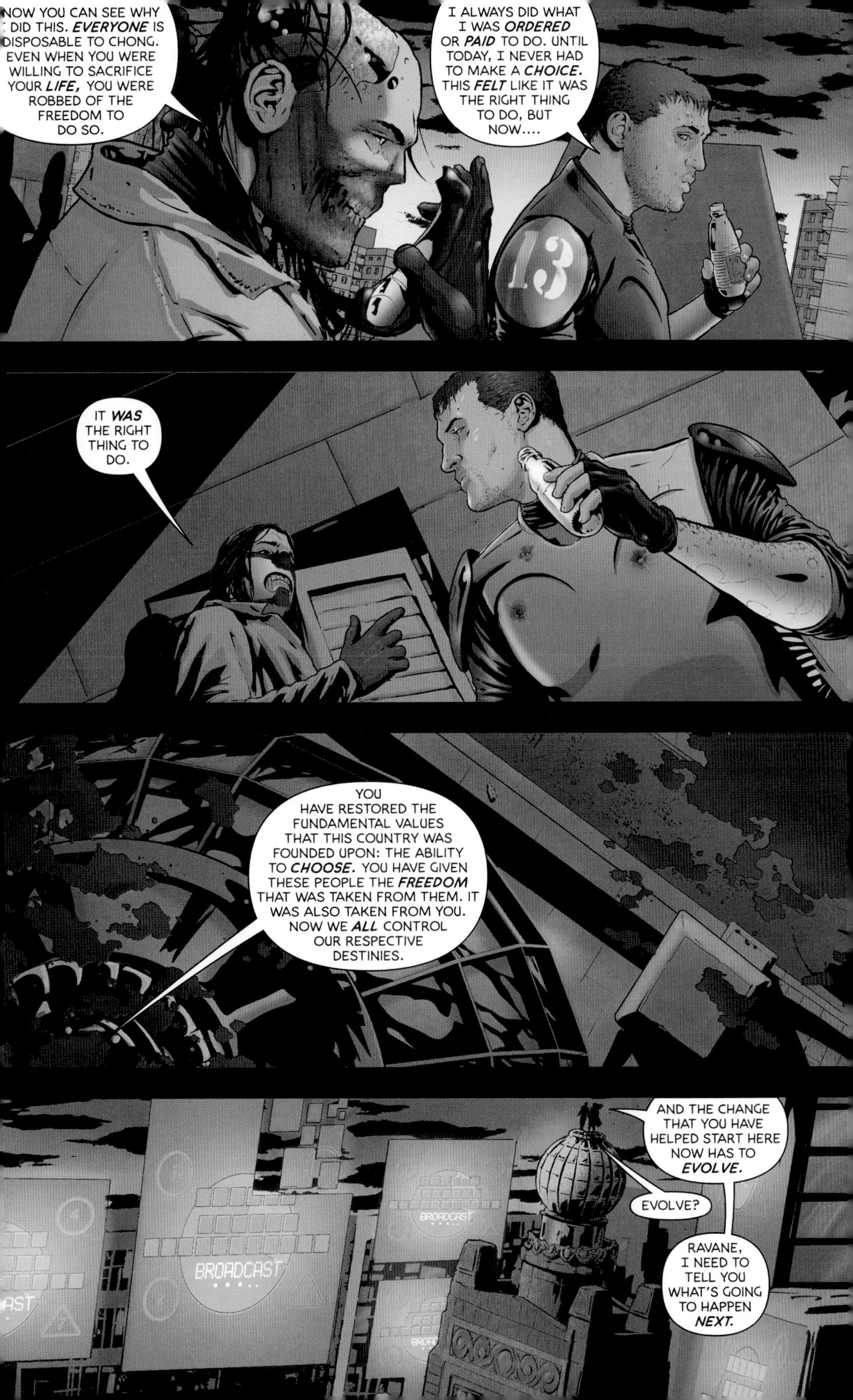
NOW YOU CAN SEE WHY I DID THIS. EVERYONE IS DISPOSABLE TO CHONG. EVEN WHEN YOU WERE WILLING TO SACRIFICE YOUR LIFE, YOU WERE ROBBED OF THE FREEDOM TO DO SO.
I ALWAYS DID WHAT I WAS ORDERED OR PAID TO DO. UNTIL TODAY, I NEVER HAD TO MAKE A CHOICE. THIS FELT LIKE IT WAS THE RIGHT THING TO DO, BUT NOW....
13
IT WAS THE RIGHT THING TO DO.
YOU HAVE RESTORED THE FUNDAMENTAL VALUES THAT THIS COUNTRY WAS FOUNDED UPON: THE ABILITY TO CHOOSE. YOU HAVE GIVEN THESE PEOPLE THE FREEDOM THAT WAS TAKEN FROM THEM. IT WAS ALSO TAKEN FROM YOU. NOW WE ALL CONTROL OUR RESPECTIVE DESTINIES.
AND THE CHANGE THAT YOU HAVE HELPED START HERE NOW HAS TO EVOLVE.
EVOLVE?
RAVANE, I NEED TO TELL YOU WHAT'S GOING TO HAPPEN NEXT.
BROADCAST
BROADCAST

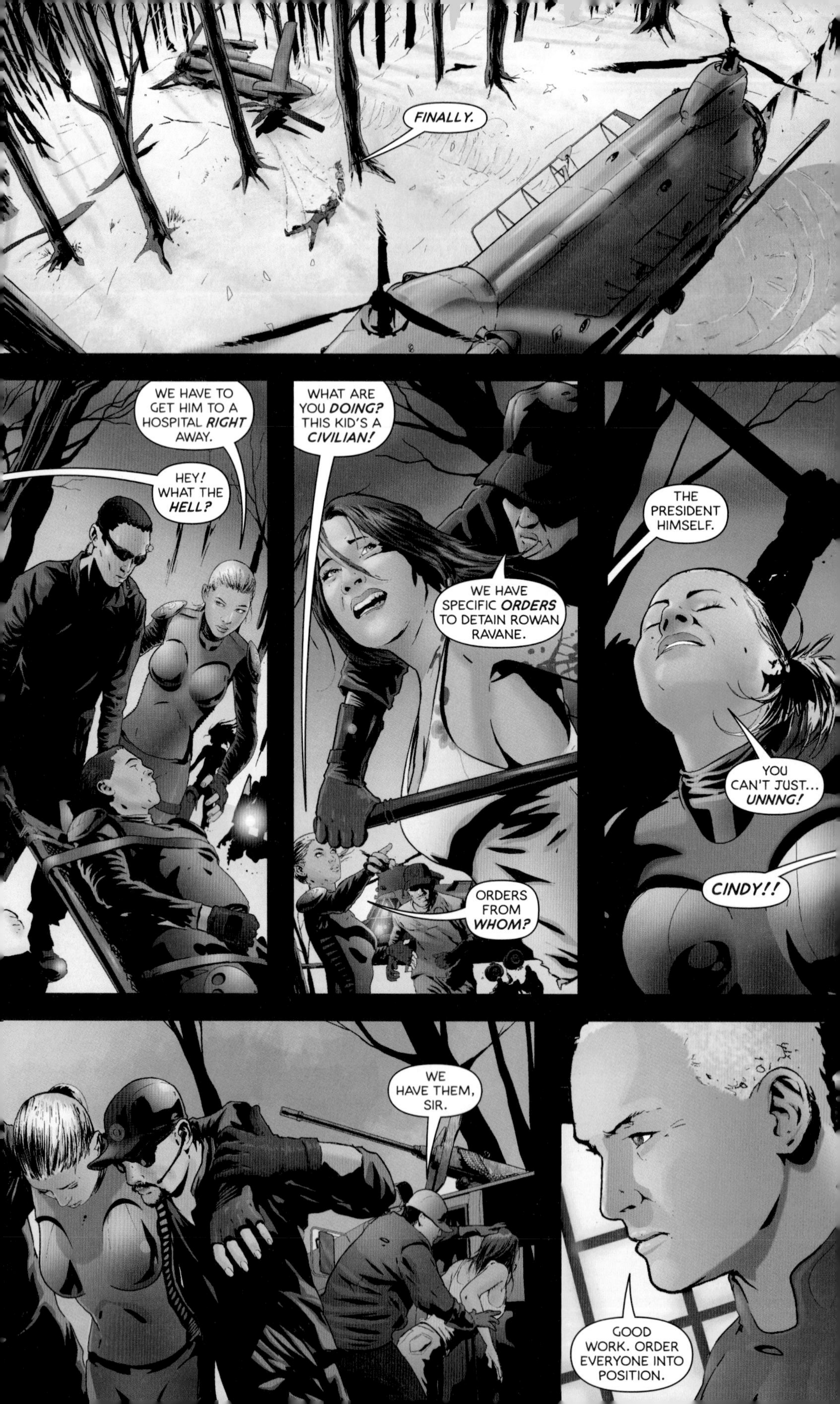

FINALLY.
WE HAVE TO GET HIM TO A HOSPITAL RIGHT AWAY.
HEY! WHAT THE HELL?
WHAT ARE YOU DOING? THIS KID'S A CIVILIAN!
WE HAVE SPECIFIC ORDERS TO DETAIN ROWAN RAVANE.
ORDERS FROM WHOM?
THE PRESIDENT HIMSELF.
YOU CAN'T JUST... UNNNG!
CINDY!!
WE HAVE THEM, SIR.
GOOD WORK. ORDER EVERYONE INTO POSITION.

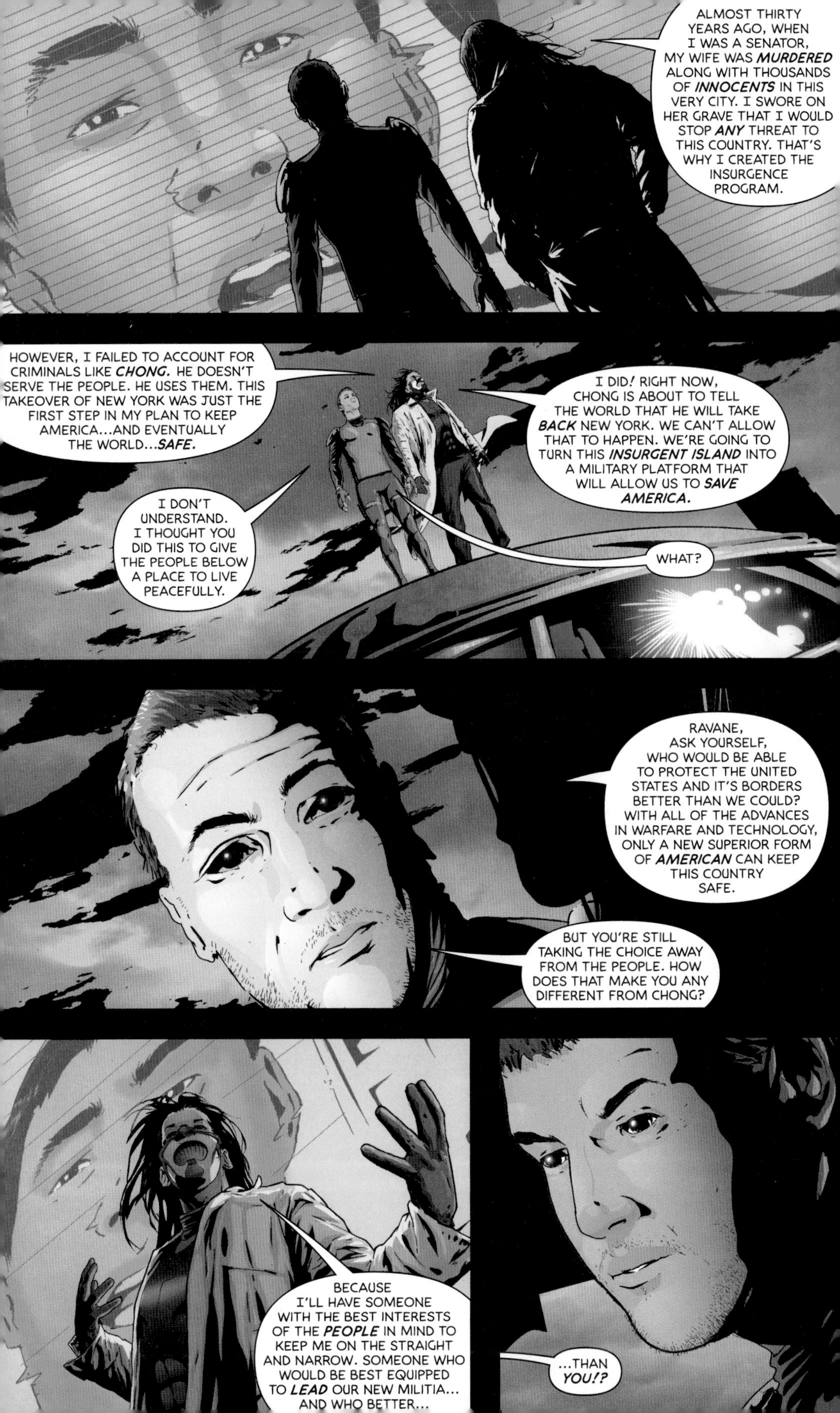
ALMOST THIRTY YEARS AGO, WHEN I WAS A SENATOR, MY WIFE WAS *MURDERED* ALONG WITH THOUSANDS OF *INNOCENTS* IN THIS VERY CITY. I SWORE ON HER GRAVE THAT I WOULD STOP *ANY* THREAT TO THIS COUNTRY. THAT'S WHY I CREATED THE INSURGENCE PROGRAM.
HOWEVER, I FAILED TO ACCOUNT FOR CRIMINALS LIKE *CHONG.* HE DOESN'T SERVE THE PEOPLE. HE USES THEM. THIS TAKEOVER OF NEW YORK WAS JUST THE FIRST STEP IN MY PLAN TO KEEP AMERICA...AND EVENTUALLY THE WORLD...*SAFE.*
I DON'T UNDERSTAND. I THOUGHT YOU DID THIS TO GIVE THE PEOPLE BELOW A PLACE TO LIVE PEACEFULLY.
I DID! RIGHT NOW, CHONG IS ABOUT TO TELL THE WORLD THAT HE WILL TAKE *BACK* NEW YORK. WE CAN'T ALLOW THAT TO HAPPEN. WE'RE GOING TO TURN THIS *INSURGENT ISLAND* INTO A MILITARY PLATFORM THAT WILL ALLOW US TO *SAVE AMERICA.*
WHAT?
RAVANE, ASK YOURSELF, WHO WOULD BE ABLE TO PROTECT THE UNITED STATES AND IT'S BORDERS BETTER THAN WE COULD? WITH ALL OF THE ADVANCES IN WARFARE AND TECHNOLOGY, ONLY A NEW SUPERIOR FORM OF *AMERICAN* CAN KEEP THIS COUNTRY SAFE.
BUT YOU'RE STILL TAKING THE CHOICE AWAY FROM THE PEOPLE. HOW DOES THAT MAKE YOU ANY DIFFERENT FROM CHONG?
BECAUSE I'LL HAVE SOMEONE WITH THE BEST INTERESTS OF THE *PEOPLE* IN MIND TO KEEP ME ON THE STRAIGHT AND NARROW. SOMEONE WHO WOULD BE BEST EQUIPPED TO *LEAD* OUR NEW MILITIA... AND WHO BETTER...
...THAN *YOU!?*

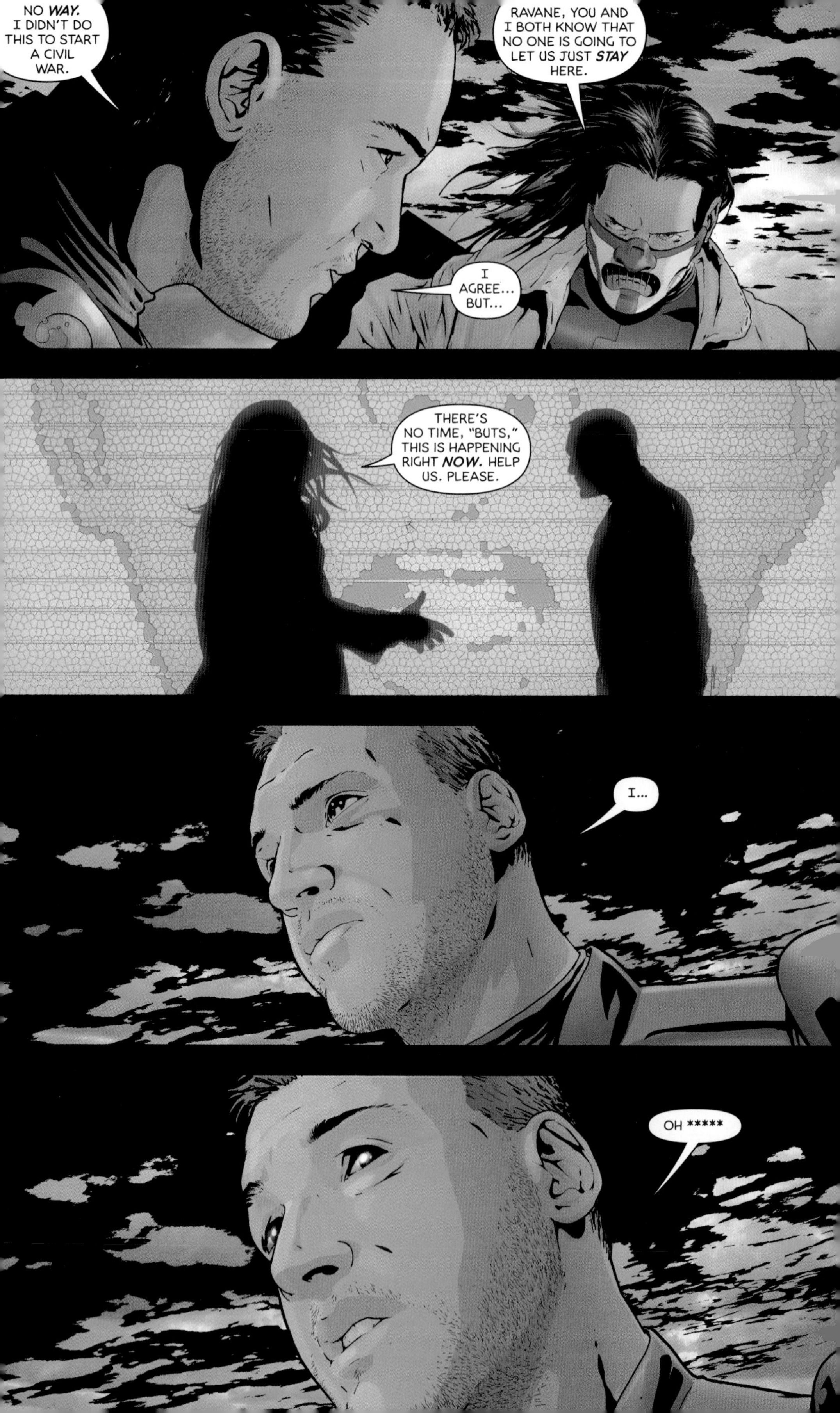
NO WAY. I DIDN'T DO THIS TO START A CIVIL WAR.
RAVANE, YOU AND I BOTH KNOW THAT NO ONE IS GOING TO LET US JUST STAY HERE.
I AGREE... BUT...
THERE'S NO TIME, "BUTS," THIS IS HAPPENING RIGHT NOW. HELP US. PLEASE.
I...
OH *****

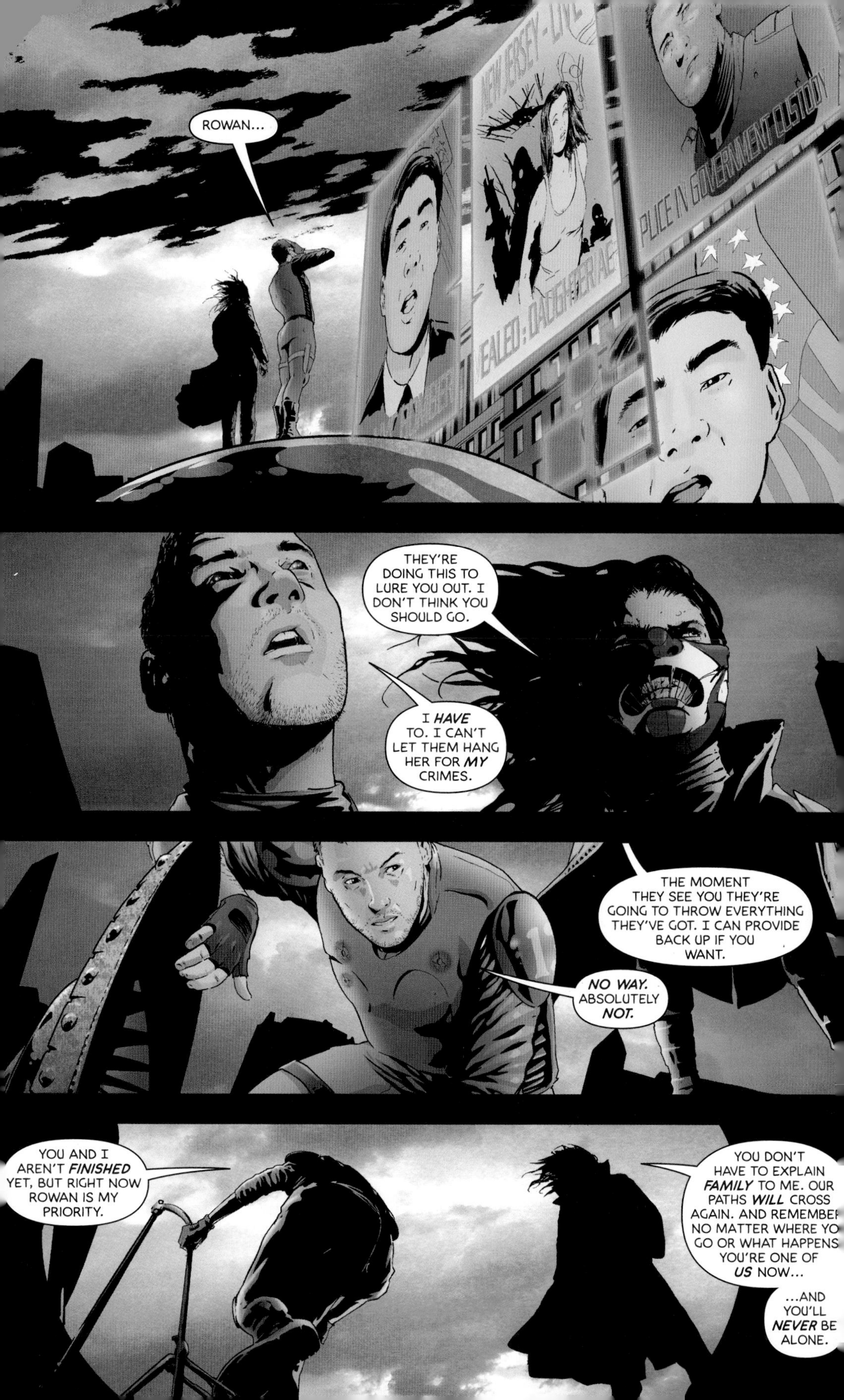

ROWAN...
THEY'RE DOING THIS TO LURE YOU OUT. I DON'T THINK YOU SHOULD GO.
I *HAVE* TO. I CAN'T LET THEM HANG HER FOR *MY* CRIMES.
THE MOMENT THEY SEE YOU THEY'RE GOING TO THROW EVERYTHING THEY'VE GOT. I CAN PROVIDE BACK UP IF YOU WANT.
NO WAY. ABSOLUTELY *NOT.*
YOU AND I AREN'T *FINISHED* YET, BUT RIGHT NOW ROWAN IS MY PRIORITY.
YOU DON'T HAVE TO EXPLAIN *FAMILY* TO ME. OUR PATHS *WILL* CROSS AGAIN. AND REMEMBEF NO MATTER WHERE YO GO OR WHAT HAPPENS YOU'RE ONE OF *US* NOW...
...AND YOU'LL *NEVER* BE ALONE.

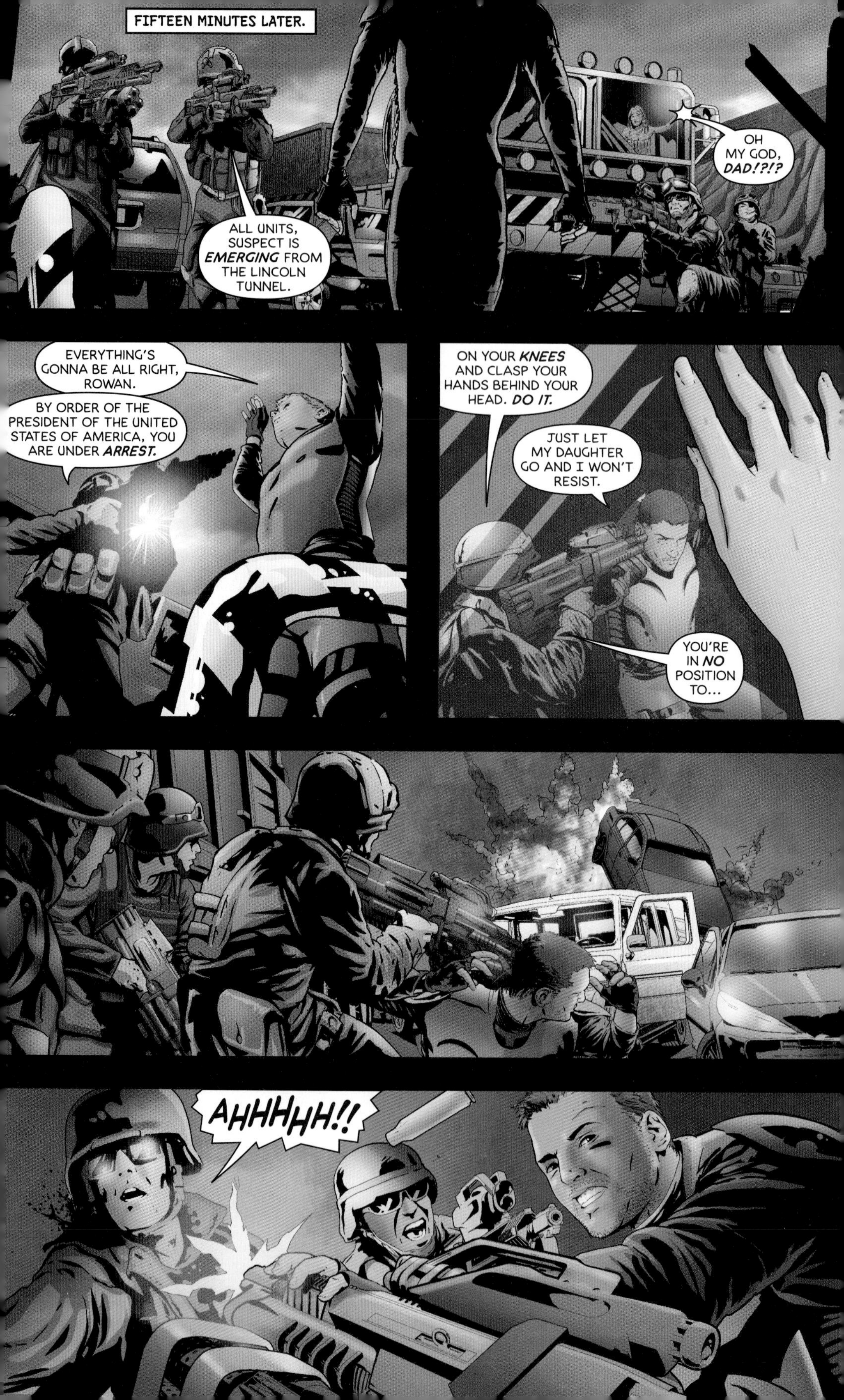
FIFTEEN MINUTES LATER.
OH MY GOD, DAD!?!?
ALL UNITS, SUSPECT IS EMERGING FROM THE LINCOLN TUNNEL.
EVERYTHING'S GONNA BE ALL RIGHT, ROWAN.
BY ORDER OF THE PRESIDENT OF THE UNITED STATES OF AMERICA, YOU ARE UNDER ARREST.
ON YOUR KNEES AND CLASP YOUR HANDS BEHIND YOUR HEAD. DO IT.
JUST LET MY DAUGHTER GO AND I WON'T RESIST.
YOU'RE IN NO POSITION TO...
AHHHHH!!

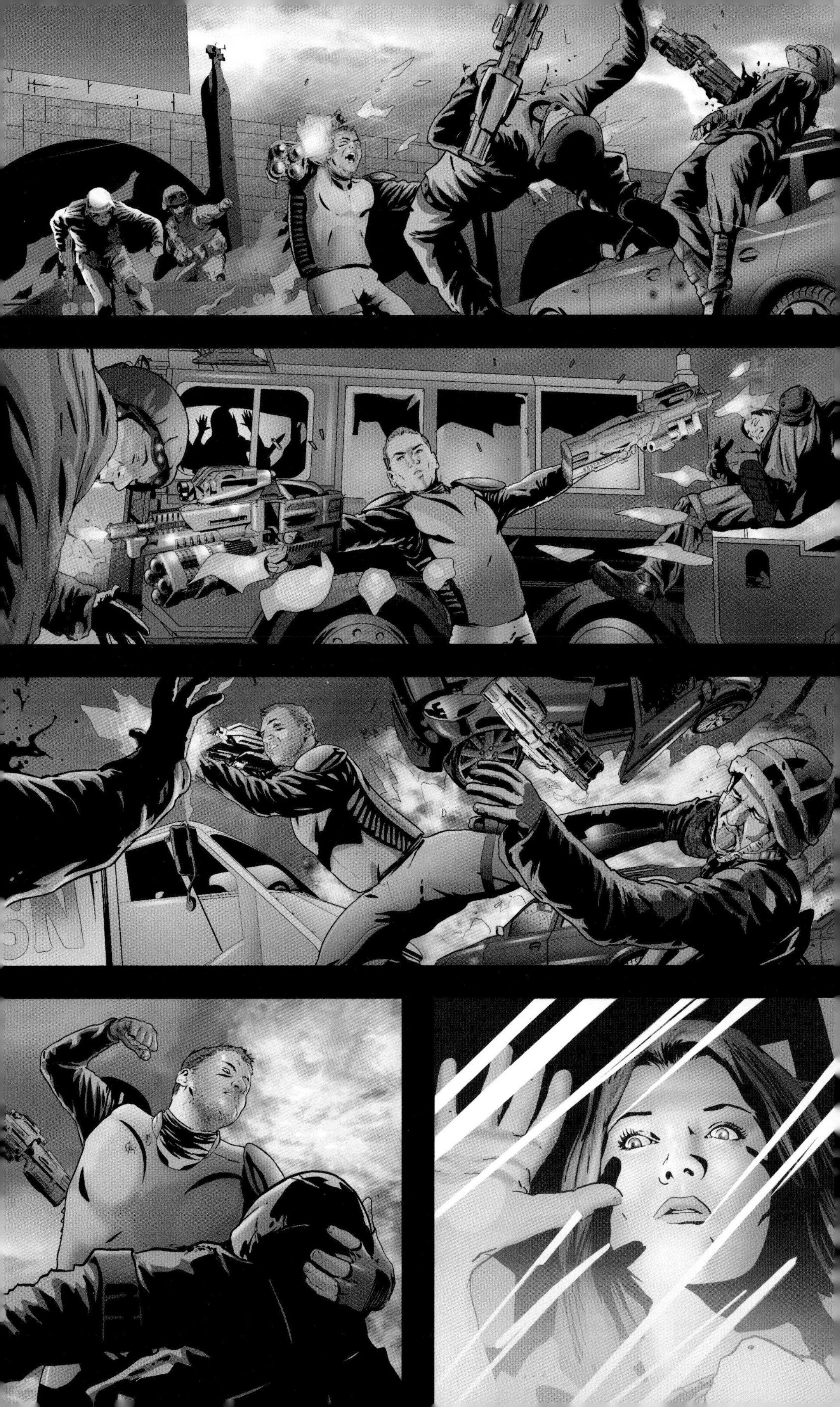

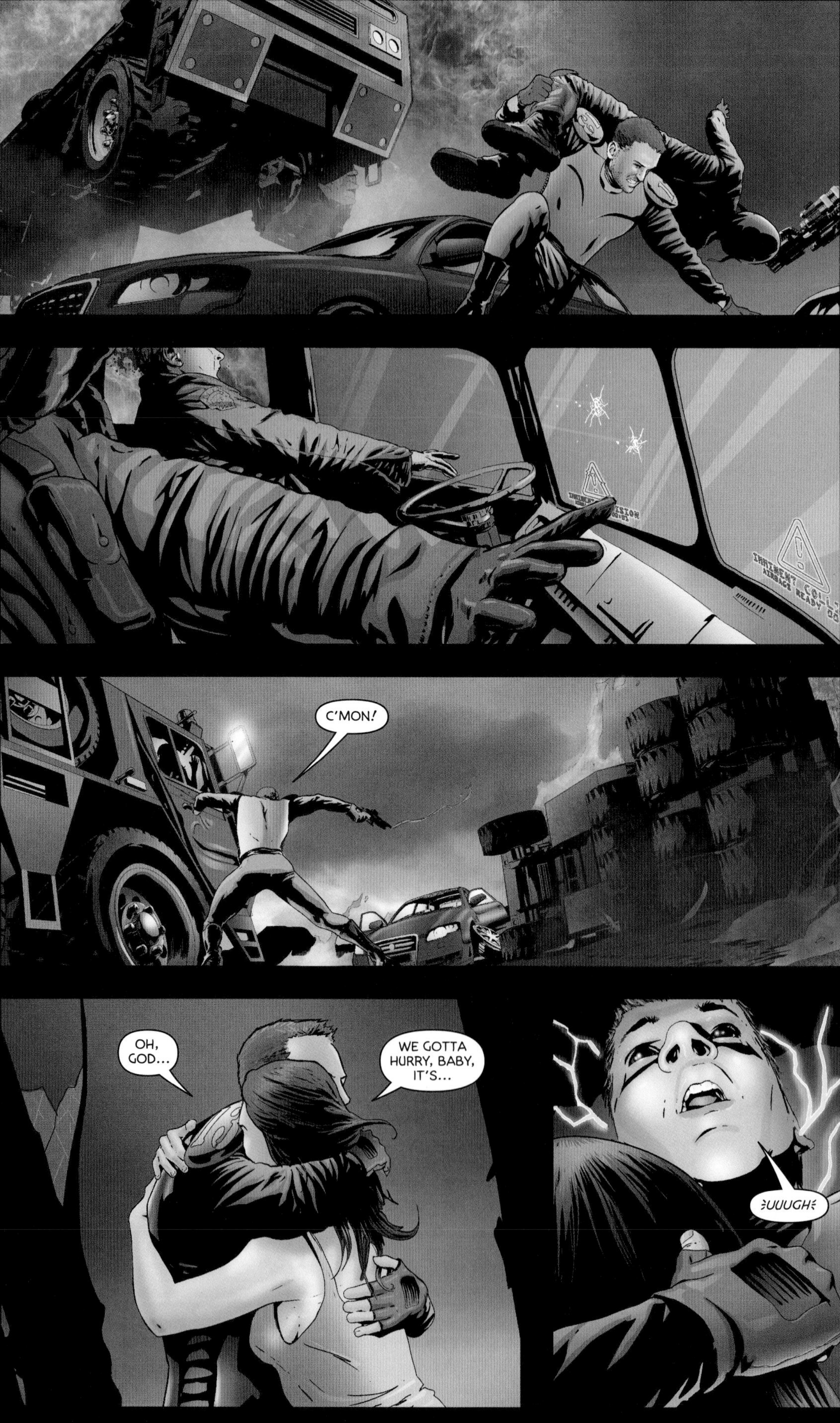
C'MON!
OH, GOD...
WE GOTTA HURRY, BABY, IT'S...
UUUGH

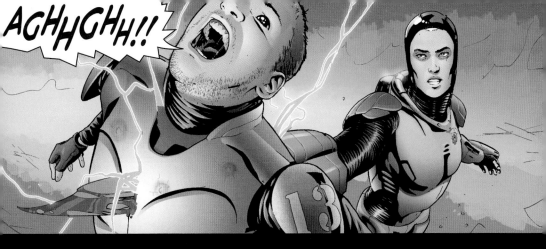

AGHHGHH!!

YOU COULD HAVE BEEN EVERYTHING WE TALKED ABOUT WHEN WE WERE CADETS. A *HERO*. ALL YOU HAD TO DO WAS *LISTEN* TO ME!

BRO...DY...

INSTEAD, HISTORY IS GOING TO REMEMBER YOU AS THE SINGLE GREATEST DOMESTIC *TERRORIST* THIS COUNTRY HAS EVER KNOWN. AND THE WORLD WILL KNOW ME AS THE MAN THAT STOPPED...

...YOUUUUUUUU...

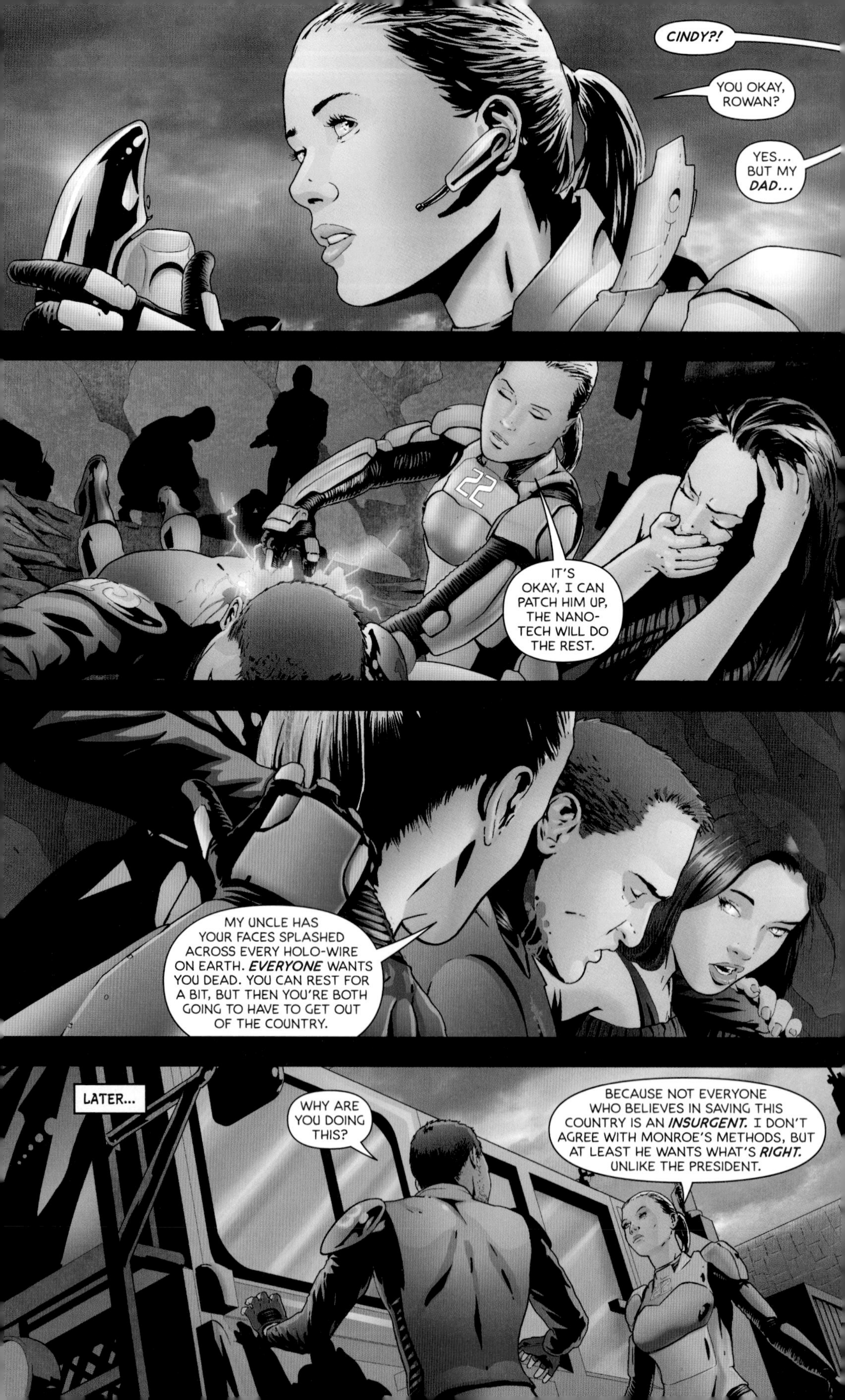
CINDY?!
YOU OKAY, ROWAN?
YES... BUT MY DAD...
IT'S OKAY, I CAN PATCH HIM UP, THE NANO-TECH WILL DO THE REST.
MY UNCLE HAS YOUR FACES SPLASHED ACROSS EVERY HOLO-WIRE ON EARTH. EVERYONE WANTS YOU DEAD. YOU CAN REST FOR A BIT, BUT THEN YOU'RE BOTH GOING TO HAVE TO GET OUT OF THE COUNTRY.
LATER...
WHY ARE YOU DOING THIS?
BECAUSE NOT EVERYONE WHO BELIEVES IN SAVING THIS COUNTRY IS AN INSURGENT. I DON'T AGREE WITH MONROE'S METHODS, BUT AT LEAST HE WANTS WHAT'S RIGHT. UNLIKE THE PRESIDENT.

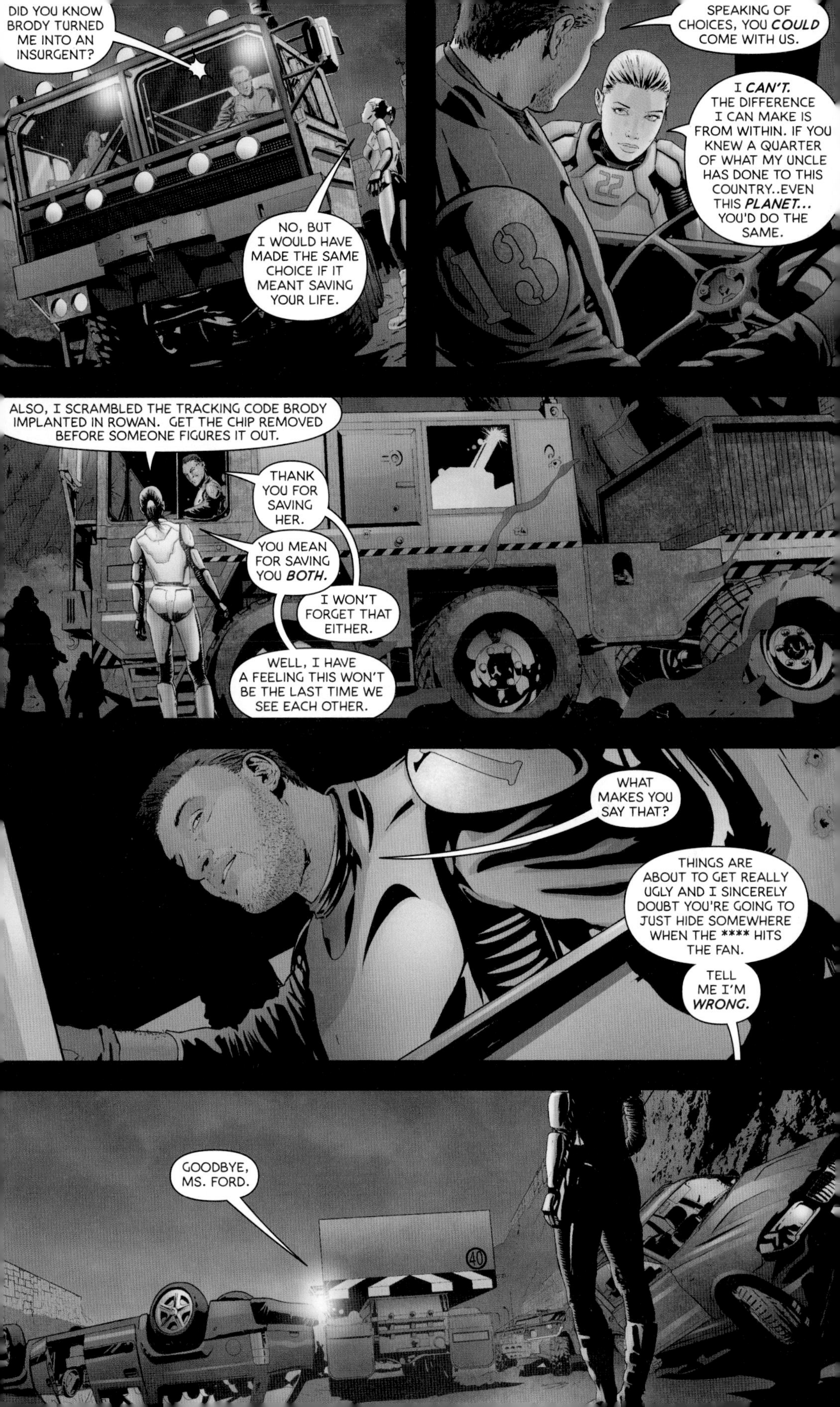

DID YOU KNOW BRODY TURNED ME INTO AN INSURGENT?
NO, BUT I WOULD HAVE MADE THE SAME CHOICE IF IT MEANT SAVING YOUR LIFE.
SPEAKING OF CHOICES, YOU *COULD* COME WITH US.
I *CAN'T.* THE DIFFERENCE I CAN MAKE IS FROM WITHIN. IF YOU KNEW A QUARTER OF WHAT MY UNCLE HAS DONE TO THIS COUNTRY..EVEN THIS *PLANET...* YOU'D DO THE SAME.
ALSO, I SCRAMBLED THE TRACKING CODE BRODY IMPLANTED IN ROWAN. GET THE CHIP REMOVED BEFORE SOMEONE FIGURES IT OUT.
THANK YOU FOR SAVING HER.
YOU MEAN FOR SAVING YOU *BOTH.*
I WON'T FORGET THAT EITHER.
WELL, I HAVE A FEELING THIS WON'T BE THE LAST TIME WE SEE EACH OTHER.
WHAT MAKES YOU SAY THAT?
THINGS ARE ABOUT TO GET REALLY UGLY AND I SINCERELY DOUBT YOU'RE GOING TO JUST HIDE SOMEWHERE WHEN THE **** HITS THE FAN.
TELL ME I'M *WRONG.*
GOODBYE, MS. FORD.

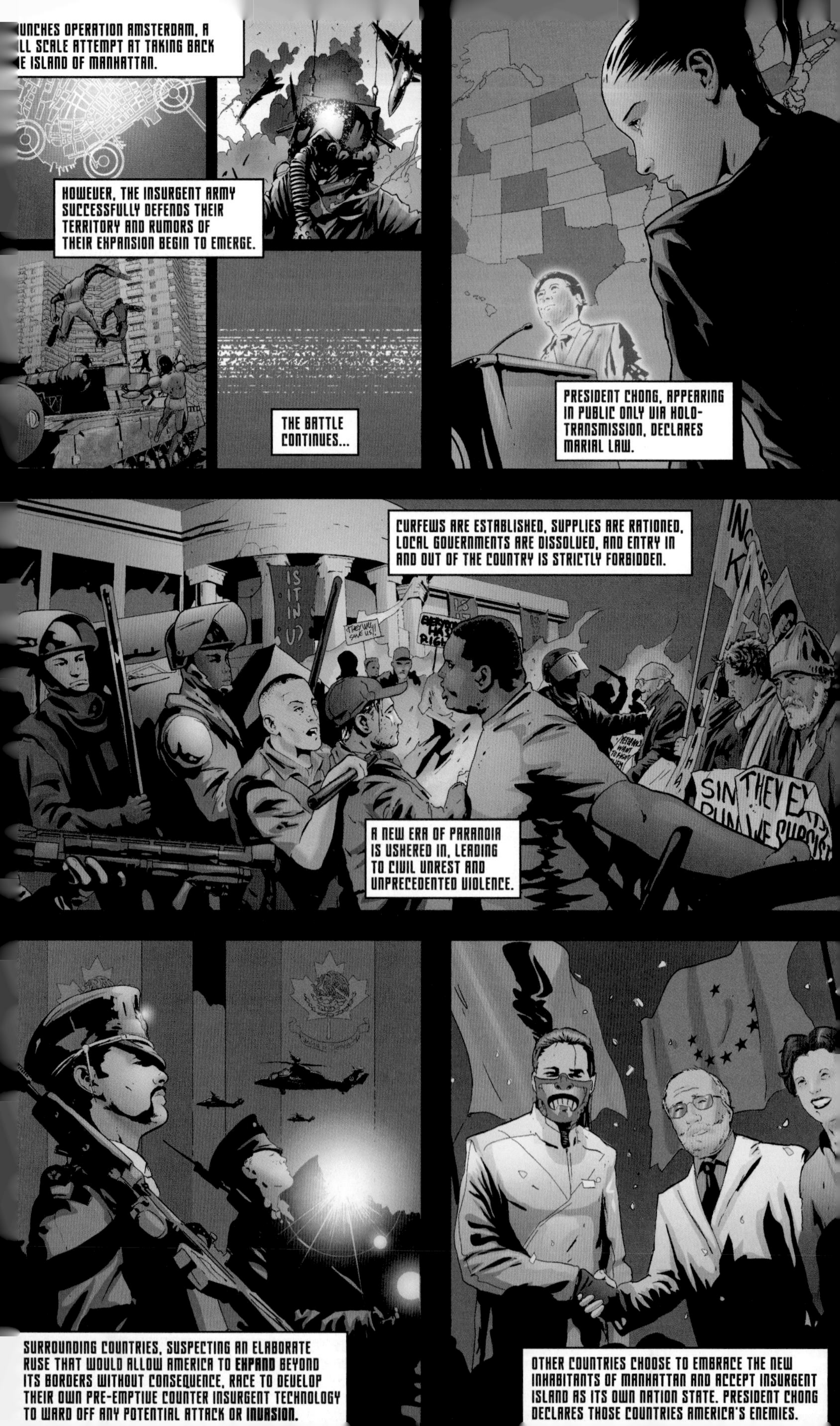
UNCHES OPERATION AMSTERDAM, A
LL SCALE ATTEMPT AT TAKING BACK
E ISLAND OF MANHATTAN.
HOWEVER, THE INSURGENT ARMY SUCCESSFULLY DEFENDS THEIR TERRITORY AND RUMORS OF THEIR EXPANSION BEGIN TO EMERGE.
THE BATTLE CONTINUES...
PRESIDENT CHONG, APPEARING IN PUBLIC ONLY VIA HOLO-TRANSMISSION, DECLARES MARIAL LAW.
CURFEWS ARE ESTABLISHED, SUPPLIES ARE RATIONED, LOCAL GOVERNMENTS ARE DISSOLVED, AND ENTRY IN AND OUT OF THE COUNTRY IS STRICTLY FORBIDDEN.
IS IT IN U?
A NEW ERA OF PARANOIA IS USHERED IN, LEADING TO CIVIL UNREST AND UNPRECEDENTED VIOLENCE.
SURROUNDING COUNTRIES, SUSPECTING AN ELABORATE RUSE THAT WOULD ALLOW AMERICA TO EXPAND BEYOND ITS BORDERS WITHOUT CONSEQUENCE, RACE TO DEVELOP THEIR OWN PRE-EMPTIVE COUNTER INSURGENT TECHNOLOGY TO WARD OFF ANY POTENTIAL ATTACK OR INVASION.
OTHER COUNTRIES CHOOSE TO EMBRACE THE NEW INHABITANTS OF MANHATTAN AND ACCEPT INSURGENT ISLAND AS ITS OWN NATION STATE. PRESIDENT CHONG DECLARES THOSE COUNTRIES AMERICA'S ENEMIES.

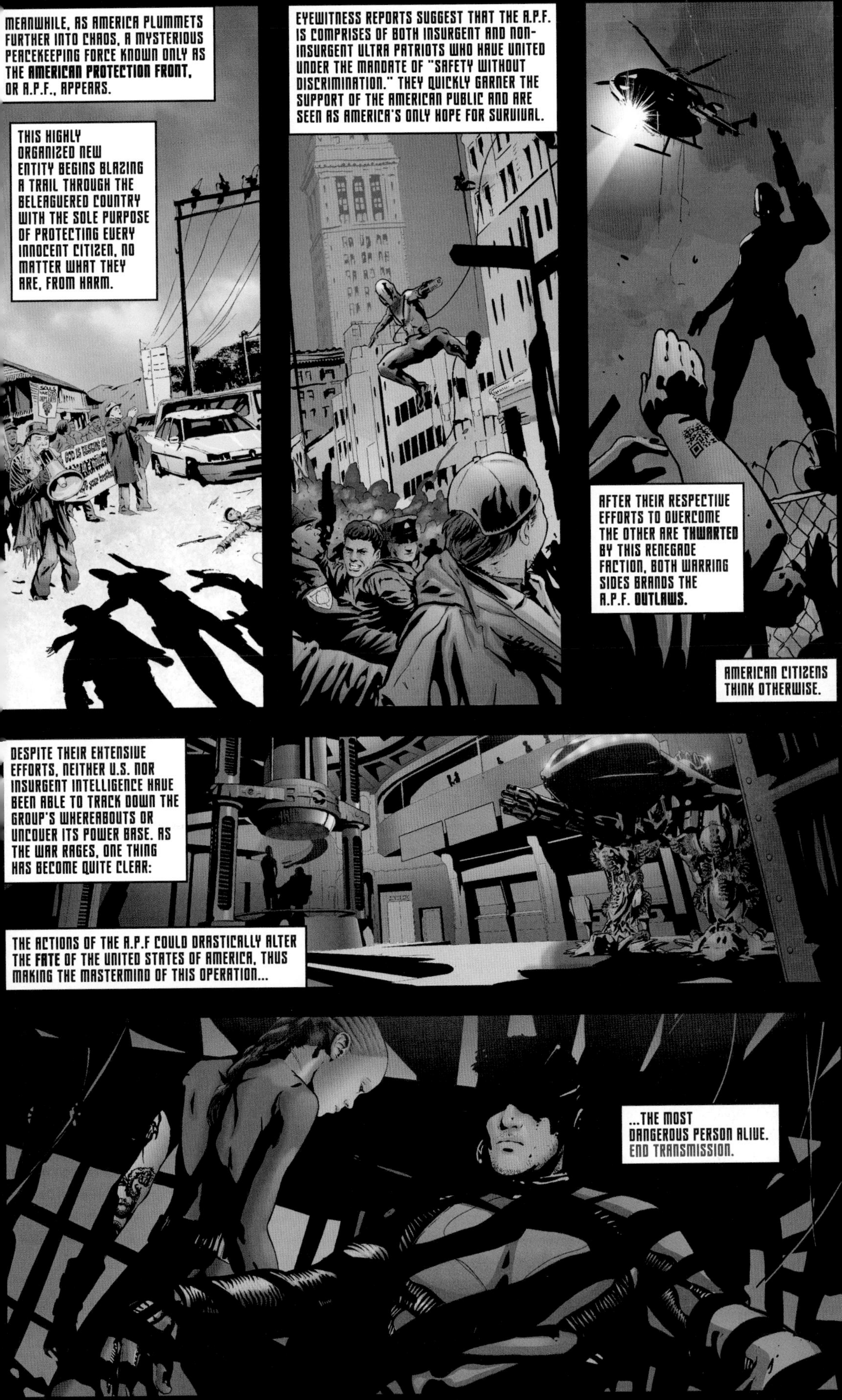
MEANWHILE, AS AMERICA PLUMMETS FURTHER INTO CHAOS, A MYSTERIOUS PEACEKEEPING FORCE KNOWN ONLY AS THE AMERICAN PROTECTION FRONT, OR A.P.F., APPEARS.
THIS HIGHLY ORGANIZED NEW ENTITY BEGINS BLAZING A TRAIL THROUGH THE BELEAGUERED COUNTRY WITH THE SOLE PURPOSE OF PROTECTING EVERY INNOCENT CITIZEN, NO MATTER WHAT THEY ARE, FROM HARM.
EYEWITNESS REPORTS SUGGEST THAT THE A.P.F. IS COMPRISES OF BOTH INSURGENT AND NON-INSURGENT ULTRA PATRIOTS WHO HAVE UNITED UNDER THE MANDATE OF "SAFETY WITHOUT DISCRIMINATION." THEY QUICKLY GARNER THE SUPPORT OF THE AMERICAN PUBLIC AND ARE SEEN AS AMERICA'S ONLY HOPE FOR SURVIVAL.
AFTER THEIR RESPECTIVE EFFORTS TO OVERCOME THE OTHER ARE THWARTED BY THIS RENEGADE FACTION, BOTH WARRING SIDES BRANDS THE A.P.F. OUTLAWS.
AMERICAN CITIZENS THINK OTHERWISE.
DESPITE THEIR EXTENSIVE EFFORTS, NEITHER U.S. NOR INSURGENT INTELLIGENCE HAVE BEEN ABLE TO TRACK DOWN THE GROUP'S WHEREABOUTS OR UNCOVER ITS POWER BASE. AS THE WAR RAGES, ONE THING HAS BECOME QUITE CLEAR:
THE ACTIONS OF THE A.P.F COULD DRASTICALLY ALTER THE FATE OF THE UNITED STATES OF AMERICA, THUS MAKING THE MASTERMIND OF THIS OPERATION...
...THE MOST DANGEROUS PERSON ALIVE. END TRANSMISSION.

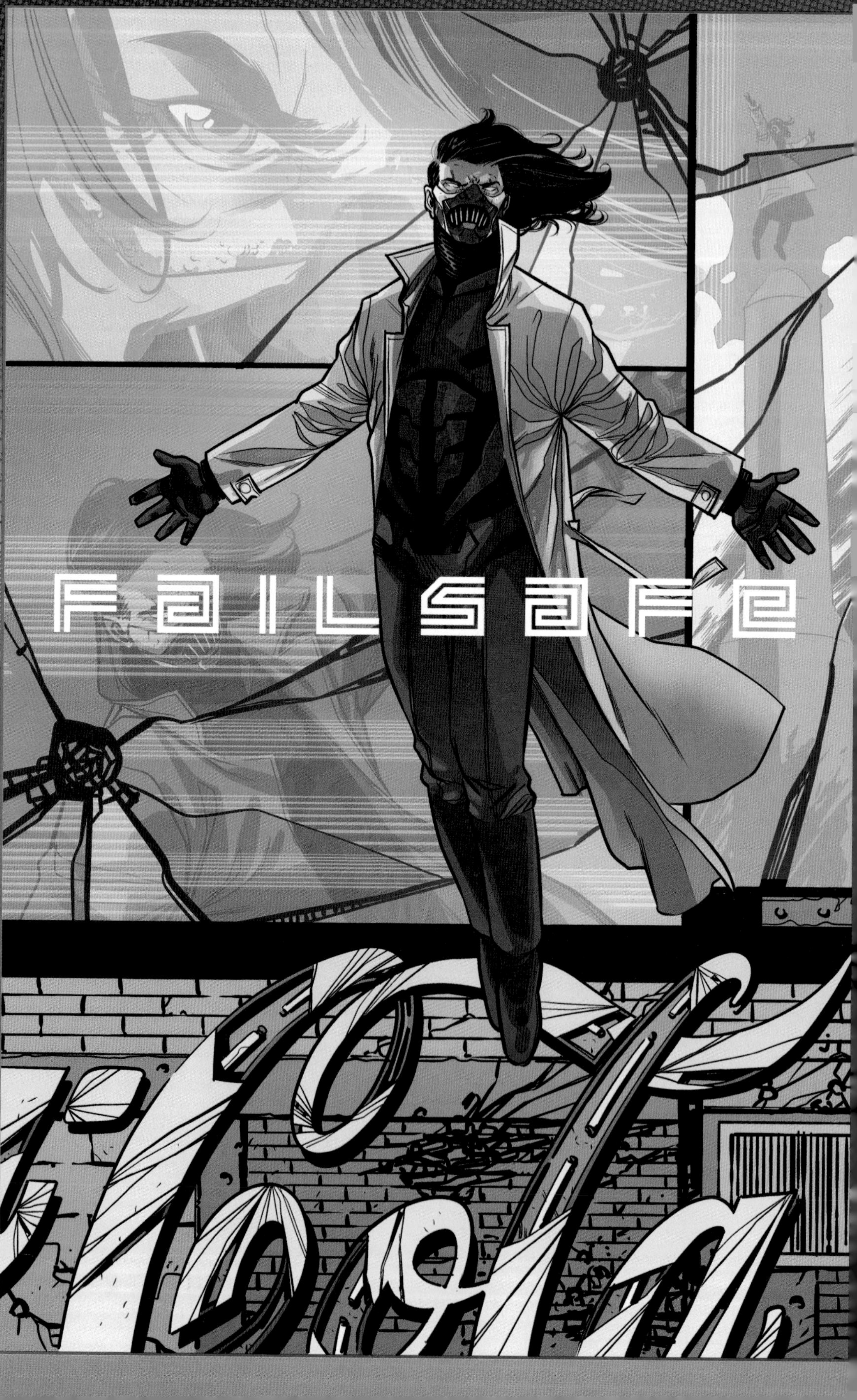
FAILSAFE